WALK
DON'T WALK

GORDON WILLIAMS

WALK DON'T WALK

When shit turns to gold
the poor will be born without arseholes.
Old Brazilian saying.

ST. MARTIN'S PRESS
NEW YORK

98302

For information, write: St. Martin's Press, Inc., 175 Fifth Avenue, New York, N.Y. 10010.

The characters in this book are entirely imaginary and bear no relation to any living person. Copyright © 1972 by Gordon Williams. All rights reserved.

Printed in Great Britain.

Library of Congress Catalog Card Number: 72-78179. First published in the United States of America 1972.

AFFILIATED PUBLISHERS: Macmillan & Company, Limited, London—also at Bombay, Calcutta, Madras and Melbourne—The Macmillan Company of Canada, Limited, Toronto.

Dedicated to
NELSON ALGREN

A Scots Burgh Boy's Dream of America

Nobody was rich in the jungle
of Ferguslie Park Avenue but in our house
we had shoes and a complete set of the Waverley Novels
of Sir Walter Scott
and food parcels from our Auntie in Texas,
bubble gum and spam and white sugar cubes,
Superman comics.
Oh aye, America was our bigtime dream place
in the years of gas masks and shrapnel.
A G.I. showed us how to throw a ball baseball-fashion
and signed our autograph books
Babe Ruth.
He told our class at the John Neilson Institution
that he lunched last week with Marlene Dietrich
and often played golf with Bing.
Lots of Yanks came to our town and walked hand in hand
down the High Street with the kind of girls
our parents called cheap. Nobody had ever seen
couples hand in hand before.
It was fair scandalous, so it was.
Our father met a black Yank who said
he was more at home in Glasgow
than he was at home.
Glasgow neds took white Yanks up alleys and
put the leather in something chronic.
Wee boys didn't understand what they meant when
they said big-mouthed, fat-bellied
G.I.s were riding our women while our lads were
dying in the desert.
We boys knew more about Flash Gordon going to Mars

and the rock round which Johnny Mack Brown
galloped every Saturday at the West End,
a bug-hut cinema very popular in summer
when there was no football.
Gene Autry never sent me his signed photo
from Burbank, so I gave him up.

Then the G.I. war brides sailed from Greenock,
the town men thought this was a big joke,
they said they were cheap hoors
who were in for a big shock when they found
their rich Yanks lived in wooden shacks
with no shoes. Most of the kids in Feegie Park
had shoes by then, thanks to Hitler.

One day we were going to be Alan Ladd in
Chicago Deadline,
or Kirk Douglas in *Champion*, or Sterling Hayden
in *The Asphalt Jungle*.
Rhonda Fleming and Virginia Mayo were
our big hubba-hubba women. We would marry them
when we learned the trumpet and took over
from Harry James.

Andra Carnegie was a wee Scots laddie who did weel
for himself in America; that's what we were all going to do,
probably in Canada where we would play ice-hockey and
come home in peg-topped trousers and sky-blue raincoats
and stand about looking dead gallus at Paisley Cross.

America was the bigtime place.
What was there bigtime at home?
Bottle-heaving at Ibrox Park and
drunks on Young's buses
and Wilson's Zoo?

We knew our country was a smalltime dump
where nothing ever happened and
there was nothing to do.
And nobody had a name like Jelly Roll Morton.

Chapter One

FAME CALLS. I AM READY. I ALWAYS KNEW I WAS SPECIAL.

To fly to New York *is* to be a celebrity, thinks jaunty, side-breezered Graham Cameron, apprentice literary nobody from the wrong side of the tracks Britannica, sliding into his seat on the mighty jet. Flying is so boring, dahling, they are always writing in the smart columns, but not for a fantasy-ridden fool who has, until now, been nowhere more glamorous than Palma, Majorca, on a cut-price, ten-day, package-holiday cattle flight from Southend airport. This loon even got a thrill from using the suave lavatory in the B.O.A.C. terminal at Victoria. He knows he has come home at last. *He is a jet-setter!* People look at him and he looks at people. He keeps an enigmatic face and pretends to be many different things. A Mafia supervisor fresh from carving out a new territory in the London bingo hall wars? A rough-hewn, devil-may-care, huge-earning wildcatter who'll fly anywhere in the world at thirty minutes' notice to put out an oil-well inferno? A hardened pro hired by the U.S. syndicate to bring the magic into American soccer?

As for Cameron himself, the actual person behind the Mister Mystery Man behind the passport unlikeness? Ah ... by tomorrow he will be famous and a satisfactory identity finally conferred.

These and other irridescent lunacies sizzled through the commuter-like brain of the unknown celebrity as he eased between an elderly Polish-American lady returning to Chicago after re-visiting the Communistic hell of her native land and an elderly Irish lady going to live in New Jersey with a sister she had not seen in forty-one years. This was the fateful morning when he zoomed off from, or out of, London Airport en route for fame and fortune in the United States of America. It was a Boeing 707 of an American line, B.O.A.C. being overbooked so heavily that scoundrelly patriotism had been impracticable. In front of Our Hero were rows of box-angled scalps barbered to the bone, the new Roman legions going home on furlough. The dominant sound in the cabin was the tuning-up drone of American bagpipe voices. Not having roughed it in the dear dead days of Luftwaffe blitzes and companionable queues, Americans do not travel lightly, nor with humility—they had paid good money, goddamit, and they wanted service here and now, with none of the cosy grin-and-bear-it mien that characterises those who have grown up with filthy British trains and cold British trains and late British trains. Behind the Steve Cochran exterior, Cameron felt vaguely furtive, being a shifty Celt and sober. The Steve Cochran exterior? Navy blue shirt; brand new electric-blue suit; dark, smooth hair. Died on a yacht crewed by teenage nymphos. The tenement answer to Franchot Tone. Alan Ladd's doppelgangster. Anyway, the old ladies knew him for a side-burned young subversive and excluded him from their conversations, a mean feat considering they took place under his nose and across his chest. His three-year-old, thirty-shilling, empire-produce, heel-listing shoes might have supplied a little shabby British integrity but they were out of sight. With a couple of whiskies in him Our Man would have been telling them the story of his life but he kept quiet. In any case, did you ever hear of a world-star in the making who thought to fly the Atlantic in possession of exactly one pound note? Thinking of that precious sheet his hand shot to his hip-pocket. For an uncharacteristic moment he felt unfit for the glory ahead. Then they were airborne over all the secret lakes west of Hounslow. The Great Adventure had begun. Six hours to New York, without enough money to buy cigarettes, paperbacks, magazines, drinks. I thought all American jets had film shows. Let us become the first passenger in air history to read the emergency instructions—in all languages to boot.

"I don't want to go—I couldn't stand being away from home," he says to Sheina the wife, without nearly enough sincerity. The telegram had just come, Tannenbaum Publishing Inc.'s invitation to tour America coast to coast promoting his book. He already saw himself standing at a lectern wowing the blue-rinse set.

"You must go, it's what you've always wanted," says the wife, adding with cruelly accurate prescience, "if you don't go you'll blame me for the rest of your life. It's a wonderful opportunity—for someone like you."

"I suppose so," he says reluctantly, already seeing himself paying three months' advance rent on Burt Lancaster's former Bel Air mansion, with swimming pool. "Mind you, it will be an ordeal. Why don't you come too?"

"The babies couldn't take the travelling."

"Hire a nanny and leave the little buggers here. Princess Margaret does it, why not us?"

"Leave the babies for two months? You must be mad."

"Get a flat in New York then—a coldwater walkup under the El— a duplex, whatever that may be."

"We'd all be murdered."

"You don't mind me being murdered on my own, is that it, you selfish bitch?"

"When you're rich and famous I wonder how long you'll put up with your dreary wife and children."

"If that's what you think I definitely won't go."

"You might as well get it out of your system. You'd better wear clean underpants over there or no self-respecting starlet slut will have you."

"Lay me, you mean. Over there they nail each other down like carpets."

"And for God's sake don't drink too much."

"Who—me?"

The Reluctant Celebrity became so hysterical rushing round London getting a new passport and a visa and forgetting where he'd hidden the air ticket for safety that he failed to present himself at the bank. On the Friday morning they had three pound notes and four shillings' worth of sixpences in the oft-pilfered whisky-bottle piggy bank. Sheina had a fever and could not get out of bed. He had to make the breakfasts and change both sets of nappies. He left two pounds to see them over the weekend. It was not until he was on the plane, reaching for the life-saving instructions, that he saw on his wrist a dried smear of light brown baby shit. Good God, it isn't exactly like being Paul Newman, is it?

Gosh by Jove, isn't the Atlantic Ocean big? Do the engines sound healthy? How long could a poor dog-paddler keep himself afloat? If tomorrow is the day you are due to be famous, today becomes a million dangerous seconds. Somebody should have said that. Just shows you, all them famous buggers didn't know everything. Would it now be theoretically wiser to swim westwards? Ah, we true artists, we are all Hemingways haunted by Death. This is why we must live Life to The Hilt. Starlets here I come! Tragic accidents are newspaper stories about people you never heard of. Flying is statistically safer than crossing Old Compton Street at night with a skinful. Even if we do develop a fuel leak and the crew gets ptomaine poisoning from the fish lunch and the mad Cuban runs amok with his Luger, death is by no means guaranteed. There are weather ships anchored all along the route. (Extremely long chains is the secret.) Massive air-sea rescue networks are poised on both sides, U.S. coastguard cutters, R.A.F. Shackletons, not to mention whole traffic jams of solo heroes rowing with one hand and writing drama-packed diaries for worldwide syndication with the other. This plane is groaning under the weight of sophisticated emergency gear, inflatable life-rafts, flares, yellow staining fluids, shark-repellent fluids, miniature radio-beacons, compact pack-rations, hand-operated sea-water convertors, plain men's guides to practical cannibalism. So the pilot and co-pilot both flake out—that shear-cropped, thick-necked yank across the gangway flew Sabres in Korea, ten years dollar-raping Europe have fattened him but left his personal heroism unimpaired. He'll be given miraculously simple instructions by radio from Gandar. He'll keep us up here above that Saltwater Sahara while we raffle the crew parachutes.

Most of the passengers, being Americans with no tradition of bands on deck playing 'Abide With Me' till the waves lap into their trombones, will panic, but not Carruthers Cameron, who carries his old dears to the escape hatch and jumps with one under each arm. The delicate pattern of white horses turns out, on closer inspection, to comprise of forty-foot breakers. On the two-man life-raft Cameron The Quiet Hero Of Giant Jet's Ocean Bale Out Drama thinks fast. It is below zero so to beat the pitiless cold we must flap our arms and sing 'Rock of Ages'. In the days that follow he fashions a rain-water trap from his shirt and makes a crude fishing-hook from a kirby-grip, or bobby-pin if it comes from the blue-rinsed head of the Chicago lady. We drift into the pitiless tropics. A black fin follows us, day by relentless day. We are miles away from all shipping lanes. Cameron weakens physically but draws on miraculous reserves of sheer British guts. He shows the old ladies how to ease their blackened tongues by sucking on small metal objects ripped from their corsets. They come to the last square of dark concentrated chocolate. This is the end of the road. Cameron prepares to give his companions a slim chance for life by slipping noiselessly into the unfathomable depths, proving the Welfare State can also sow its Captain Oates. Drowning is the sweetest form of death, reliable eye-witnesses always maintain. But—wait—what's that? A bird! A red-shanked oriole, unique to the Everglades! Swollen, parched lips croak agonisingly from cracked, blackened faces. We peer into the pitiless, blinding sun. Breakers on a white strand. We have just enough strength to head the raft for a narrow break in the deadly, jagged edges of the coral reef. The raft capsizes. Cameron has just enough strength to

12

drag his two companions on to the dry sand. Three bundles of emaciated rags have just enough strength to awaken at the knobbly feet of a party of evil-countenanced Seminal Indians. Thank God, they are urbanised. They rush us to hospital in station wagons. We look black, we have neither cash nor Blue Cross cover. We are refused admittance. Who the hell do you think I am—Bessie Smith— he snarls, just as *Time Life*'s Florida bureau staffer holds out pen and six-figure contract for exclusive world rights. Tony Curtis auditions for the Cameron role. Rhonda Fleming, lovelier than ever, is hauled out of retirement to play the Irish lady, a minor adjustment of age-bracket vital for box-office success. The Polish-American lady becomes a worldly, wise-cracking nun, played by Thelma Ritter in drag. Tony Curtis insists on doing the underwater shark fight scene with a double.

The grey skirt of a cool, lipsticked American stewardess pulled tautly across her hips as she passed along the plastic lunch trays. Six other American serving wenches hurried past the economy-class rabble to tend the curtained-off wants of first-class passenger Elkan J. Rhumboid III, fun-loving privacy fetishist and little-photographed czar of the petro-chemical and ghetto fire insurance conglomerate. Don't worry, Elkan, I'll soon be in there with you, junketing.

You do intend to make the return journey then?

So there's you and this svelte, busty starlet clawing and gouging each other in a penthouse sexfest and the Hilton goes on fire and you have to jump ninety floors down, hand in hand, into the safety net. That's going to get a whirl on the T.V. news. Howja think ya'll get outa this one, explanation-wise, wife-wise? As we are falling in the nude down the side of the skyscraper I shall just keep shouting, "I have never seen this woman before in my life." Limey Scribe in Penthouse Love Nest Death Blaze Nude Rescue Dive Drama.

What the hell would you actually do with a hundred thousand dollars? Well—if one was carrying a pen like a proper author to note flashing insights into the human condition, one would divide it by the current dollar rate to convert it into real money. Say thirty thousand pounds? Is that enough to join the other patriots in Swiss canton tax havens? P. & O. cruises to Tenerife? Two pairs of shoes? Not more Bob Dylan records for God's sake. I'm bored to bloody agony. These old dolls don't want to talk—in the movies they would have been hot-eyed nubiles. Life isn't like the movies, you know that? That's why the movies are so important. As the all-knowing wife often says, I am not a man with inner resources. Without a typewriter in front of me my brain doesn't seem capable of prolonged attention to anything. Pelmanism cures the butterfly brain. Close your eyes and think. This is an exciting experience, for God's sake. I have nothing to declare but my genius. There's an idea! Come on, man, you're supposed to be a wordsmith. One uniquely brilliant phrase and you join the pantheon of immortal wits.

CUSTOMS OFFICER: Have you anything to declare?

SON OF OSCAR: Hmm ... Well now. I have nothing to declare but my jeans. But my genes. But my genie. But my Gene Autry fan club badge. But my infinite capacity for taking pints.

He awoke in the general shuffle caused by the first sight of the New World, fire-brown island bleaknesses and then the silent, unchanging forests of Canada, green and vast, millions and millions of tree-hidden acres waiting through a millennium of misty sunlight for the coming of man. All this from a quick peek over the shoulder of the old biddy in the window seat? Ah yes, I can already feel this trip making me blossom forth into global significance as a writer, oracle and close friend of many of the world's leading beauties.

New York came towards them from a purple-brown haze, dream city of the world, Babel defying impotent Jehovah, man's own monument to Man the Giant, true ruler of the earth and the skies.

"It's a little-known fact that New York is on the same latitude as Madrid," he said pleasantly to Kathleen ni Houlihan, both of them craning towards the porthole.

"I don't know about that," she said dismissively, stuck-up old sow.

The plane, with its precious cargo of immortality material, went over the airport and then over some sandy beaches and then over a green sea and then back again to the airport and then back again to sea, each turn involving a sideways lurch during which the mighty jet stood on one wing. They call it stacking, but surely if God had meant us to fly he'd have given us more airports? The weather changed. The sun disappeared. The rain came on. The sea changed from darkish green to foam-flecked black. The Boeing ploughed back and forth. Millions of Chinese were born and died. The rain bucketed down. Among the bodies washed ashore was that of Graham Cameron, 33, an unknown hack from London taken cruelly within hours of being acclaimed the John Updike of literature.

Then the rain-washed reds and blues of John F. Kennedy sliced by the sluiced perspex. The plane hit the runway and ran away to the left in a shuddering skid, righting itself only a few yards short of tarmac touchdown mass death horror.

14

Coldly inspected but, strangely, not questioned by a flintily blue-eyed Immigration Vigilante with a sheriff's badge pinned to a blue shirt, Cameron passed through to the large Customs Hall, an affluent shambles of well-heeled refugees. He collected his suitcase and joined what might have been, infinitesimally, the shortest queue. The word declare pounded about his brain. Home-coming Americans got in line with haughty Brazilians and chattering Puerto Ricans and West Indians in Sunday best, little girls with white-ribboned pigtails, here and there a long-haired, buckskin-jacketed hippy toting a guitar case in total rejection of society's values. The right remark would make him famous overnight. Book sales would rocket. Original manuscripts would be sold for taxfree fortunes to American universities, cultural dustbins of the western world. *Time* magazine would make him the season's fifteenth new Mark Twain. Definitive biographies would be commissioned, coupled with anthologies of previous witticisms. The baggage train moved slowly towards a knee-high ramp at the other end of which was a blue-uniformed Customs Official destined unknowingly to become one of posterity's bit players. Small wonder these gentry are supposed to be the rudest oafs in America—anyone would be testy waiting all these years for the new Oscar.

Half an hour passed just as tediously as it would have in the Old World. Fresh planeloads joined the queues. From large observation windows high round the hall the newcomers were anxiously surveyed by relatives who had already wormed their way into America. The line moved like grass growing, only when not watched. By nightfall the Tannenbaum Corporation would have handouts on city desks and news desks, trans-Atlantic and cisatlantic. Talent-hungry T.V. producers would bark orders to get this Cameron guy under contract. Gore Vidal would demolish him with urbane acidity in *Esquire*. Agencies would clamour to offer him lecture tours at fifteen hundred bucks a throw and all the sophomores he could despoil.

At last—only two passengers between Cameron and immortality. The stealing of shirts belonging to culture-mad hosts would become a lovable foible. John Malcolm Brinnin would ask him out for a booze-up.

Now.

The Customs Officer had one stoutly-shod foot on the ramp, one elbow on the blunt knee of the raised leg, fine quality barathea straining on a sturdy American steak-fed calf. He was chewing, looking anywhere but at the young Voltaire, who cleared his throat. The Customs man held out a cardboard rectangle on which was pasted some typographical officialese. Cameron poised, braining singing. Give me the cue, man, *the cue*! The Customs man frowned impatiently, shoving the cardboard nearer to Cameron's expectant face. When he spoke it was a guttural rasp:

"Yareddanotiz?"

"What?"

The Customs Officer tapped the board with a blunt but well-manicured finger. Cameron saw something about foodstuffs and plants. Chewing gum poised on curled tongue, the Customs man barked again:

"YAREDDANOTIZMAC?"

A bored nod finally gave next week's new literary sensation permission to scurry through the barrier into God's own country.

Chapter Two

GIRL FANS. ALGONQUIN DRINKS. FUNNY ENOUGH DOROTHY
PARKER DIED YESTERDAY.

Fame only momentarily postponed, it was as an out-of-town killer
brought in by Lepke on a contract to hit Augie Minelli, defecting
northside numbers racket bagman, that he wended his way incognito
through the crowded but disappointingly petty ramifications of the
terminal to the currency window, where he came behind an Indian,
Sikh not Sioux, changing a hefty wad of illegally-exported sterling
into greenbacks. Cameron's pound note was worth two dollars and
some loose, American change, small coins of dubious texture, as is all
foreign money. Cameron fished out his stout British change and held
it towards the man.

"You handle this stuff?" he asked, sounding sickeningly British
for the Cincinnati ice-pick artist.

"That's no good, sir," said the American gentleman cheerfully,
"unless you happen on a blind beggar looking the other way."

Cameron took his dollar fortune up an escalator in search of
cigarettes. In an open-fronted, all-purpose, airport souvenir type of
shop a little man with a cigar and other resemblances to Edward G.
Robinson gave him twenty Disque Bleu, which all London progressives were smoking that year, and chucked three book matches on to
a pile of New York *Post*s, the whole front page of which was given
to a dramatically grainy picture of a cab-driver shot dead behind the
wheel after a traffic light tiff.

"No, I want a box of matches," Cameron said.

"So yawan a metch," the little man said, pushing the three book
matches across the windscreen of the victim's vehicle. Of course!
Americans don't have boxes of matches, you dumb hick.

"How much are they?" he asked, quite coldly.

"Ya gett'm f'r nuttin ya buy somptn, who buys a metch?"

Phoning the Tannenbaum Corporation offices in Manhattan was
also great fun, considering he knew nothing of area codes and kept
interrupting his perusal of the dialling instructions to make sure
nobody had whipped his suitcase, which would not fit into the little
booth. Eventually a lady from the Bell company desk had to come

and show him what to do. Milton wasted no time on pleasantries. They were all waiting for him to descend by helicopter on to the roof of the Pan Am building. Better hustle, Graham.

The helicopter taking him to instant fame and the kind of private life a Turkish pasha might find disgustingly voluptuous chug-chugged over the backyards of what he presumed was Queens, where Don Murray lived in *Bachelor Party*. In every backyard was a round blue disc—possibly the tops of personalised gasometers?

Swimming pools! That bloody yareddanotiz had disorientated him, for this was not a foreign country with strange foreign customs, this was America and he had lived around here for the better part of his life, climbed the skyscraper with King Kong, hauled the piano up by rope in *A Tree Grows in Brooklyn*, tramped the tenement streets with Don Taylor in *The Naked City*, bought and sold the Brooklyn Bridge, struck out for the Yankees with Gary Cooper, dodged hails of lead with Dutch Schultz, thrown the old lady down the stairs in the bathchair with Tommy Udo, grinning insanely, fished stiffs with cement slippers from the Hudson, lifted apples from stalls with Leo Gorcey and the Gang.

And now he was actually here and not just as a bum immigrant but as a star-in-the-making, with the whole works waiting for him on the Pan Am roof. The eagle shits tonight, baby! On your door they'll pin a star, preferably Rita Hayworth, you gerontophiliac swine.

The helicopter crossed the East River and here were the Himalayas of Manhattan, exactly as in the movies, exactly. The rain had cleared symbolically and weak sun touched the dark green rectangle of Central Park and tonight he would be slipping it home to some brittle lovely in an uptown luxury apartment and nothing could be finer in the state of semolina. There were steam geysers on the shabby summits of the skyscrapers, curiously domestic little plateaux where he half expected to see lines of washing. The helicopter chugged up and down Manhattan waiting for the landing clearance. There was the Empire State and U.N.O. and the overlapping gold leaves of the Chrysler Building. The stewardess was a plump-armed doll, a tough babe who said toime for time. He imagined her in Brooklyn dancehalls and wondered if his range of romantic patter encompassed the open sesame for slick cookies like her. He peered down at the ant streams of traffic, feeling more and more powerfully the sensation that he was coming home. Down there men chivvied and lied and mugged and hustled for the dollar, some with a gun and some with a routing lien, but it was all energy, wasn't it, the same energy that had pushed

18

these spires into the sky, the energy of American Man who had seen the vastness of Nature and had not been awed; a thunderous upward avalanche of power, Man freed from the chains of superstition and tyranny, not pygmy European Man crouching timorously on the blood-drenched midden of his own history but get-up-and-go American Man. Who was it who said that as soon as men reach the shores of America over them comes a feeling that nothing is impossible? Cameron Kayos Clay In 5th, Wins Pulitzer Prize, Denies Jackie Romance Rumour.

"The heliport is 808 feet above sea level and this should mean wind," said the New York Airways card. "*No*. Specially-designed vanes greet the wind at the edge—regardless of direction or velocity ... this heliport is almost as big as three baseball diamonds ..."

As instructed by Milton he was the last passenger to step out of the helicopter. At this point he had only vague ideas of what happened to incandescent new luminaries in the literary firmament, amorphous manifestations of the culture vulture crowd, granting interviews to the better class of columnist, cosy dinner parties with elegant widows concealing perfumed lusts under Guggenheim Foundation garments, that sort of thing. In London the book responsible for this hoo-ha had been received, as they say, with diluted enthusiasm thanks to the moronic swinishness and imbecilic snobbery of semi-literate clowns masquerading as critics, but over here it was going to be justifiably big, movies, book clubs, huge paperback deals, networked T.V. shows, honorary membership of the Rat Pack, my friends the stars, the Bigtime.

Non-existent, vane-deflected wind lashed hair across his eyes. He stopped on the top step, feeling a cheerful impulse to throw out his arms and bawl greetings to the whole of New York City. From a small glass hut on the mighty plateau came Milton Tannenbaum and a photographer, followed by two girls in orange-stripped mini-dresses fighting the non-wind to carry giant, hand-lettered placards to the helicopter steps, the Hilary and Tensing Everest Show in Drag.

Welcome to Graham Cameron
THE NEW
LADIES'
MAN

Jesus wept!
That was meant to be a book title, not a boast!

"Hullo there, Graham," Milton shouts up against the engine rattle. "We only have but two minutes. Get a girl on each arm—stay right up there." Their faces are heavy with orange make-up. The wind flaps my overlong British hair in the wrong directions. Two other men grin up at me. "You gonna be a big rich author, is that right?" says one girl. "So they say. Is that why you came along?" I screech back. "Fifteen bucks an hour is why we came along, honey," she simpers at the top of her voice. "The boss man wants you should smile some more, Graham doll," yells the other hired model. My fans, my public. They sign-direct me to put my arms round their waists and hug them close to my chest. I am to be cheesecake, not Emile but Gorgon. Handshakes. Thank God that shit is over, I begin to say wryly, but it is not. We go into the little glass hut and down an escalator into a restaurant bar where, horror upon horror, Milton wants more pictures, me and the orange-striped book connoisseurs in intimate groupings, people staring, smile again, honey, look as though you're laughing, Graham, pretend to be showing the girls something real funny from the book, all the people staring, smile and smile again until the very teeth ache.

A big man in a blue blazer, just like Paul in Perry Mason, comes up to examine the placards, the lapel buttons (I'm the New Ladies' Man) and finally my face.

"The noo ladies' man, huh?" he snorts with entirely justified derision. "Howja do it, boy, ya stranglem with your hairnet fust, huh?" He laughs heartily in the direction of his much-amused friends. I die each dawn.

"Okay that just about wraps it up I guess," says Milton. "Graham, this is Chuck Brown of Two-World motion pictures, he'll see you to your hotel, tomorrow Saturday you're coming to my place, Chuck will give you the directions, I have to catch my train at Grand Central in seven minutes, tomorrow we can talk. Welcome to America."

I mumble something. Maybe that's why celebrities get such a bad name for haughtiness, they're scared out of their wits. This Chuck Brown is bigger than me, which doesn't help, thirtyish, black hair, reddish cheeks. He grins a lot. Me, I'm finished smiling for keeps.

"You look like you could use a snort, fella."

"I'll have a beer, please, I'm parched."

"Didn't you have a belt or two on the flight?"

"I didn't have any money. Maybe it's just as well—I had this mental picture of myself reeling pissed off the helicopter and tottering off the edge of the landing roof."

"One way of hitting the front pages."

"Might have been easier than posing with these models. Christ, I feel ill."

"That's the name of the game, fella. You'll get to like it—by the end of this little bitty tour you'll dig it so much you'll have gotten yourself a personal flack."

"Flack?"

"Press agent."

"No, I'm the modest type, I've just discovered."

"That's what they all say."

New York, Friday afternoon, temperature around ninety, shirt wet before they crossed the Park Avenue West Ramp, Cameron carrying his own case, no cabs available in the mid-afternoon rush-hour, scurries of tight-faced, tight-buttoned business execs hurrying to grab places in club bars of commuter trains to Bridgeport or New Haven, so that's Grand Central Station, a narrow-brimmed army of grim-faced Jack Lemmons, steam heat, yellow cabs, cops with guns, neck strain from looking up at skyscrapers, if God had meant us to live so high up he wouldn't have put the streets so near the ground, a blind negro beggar with a smart transistor radio hanging from a leather strap round his neck, tin cup in hand, music while you beg, shuffling his flat-footed way against the mechanical flow of tight-assed white men in time to 'Baby Love' by the Supremes.

"That jig panhandler makes more'n a hundred a week and goes home in a Caddy," says Chuck. At every corner the crowds step out in hesitant unison when the red DON'T WALK changes to the green WALK, obedient walking dolls, hardly the pushy, live-wire New Yorkers of popular myth. By the time we reach Fifth Avenue it's obvious Nabokov knew an erogenous zone when he saw one—the droves of young teenage girls, hundreds of them, ripe and lush, bare brown legs and downy arms, English Hack Draws 5 to 10 On Minors Morals Rap.

"Jay-walking is legal in New York," says Chuck. "It's fatal but legal."

The skyscrapers are glass and concrete Eigers, the traffic comes in never-ending torrents, not the distant rumble of London but all around you, whamming and roaring into your brain. We turn into 52nd Street. The main avenues, running approximately north to south, are thundering canyons, the narrower connecting streets are cool chasms. Two suntanned policemen, dark glasses, shoulder flashes,

21

nasty guns on rolling hips, one smoking, the uniform a subtly rich, almost voluptuous blue, I've got it now, attitude and latitude shared with Madrid, the cool awnings of the shaded side streets, the loading bays and the open shop doorways where swarthy men in shirt sleeves honk adenoidal witticisms from cigar-juggling mouths and pat sausage-folded necks with bunched handkerchiefs. The Spanish tinge, that's what it is, even to the dark aroma, not the stale piss pong of London but the hot sweet reek of wine-drinker's shit.

"Is that *the* Algonquin?"

"The only one I know, fella."

"H. L. Mencken and Dorothy Parker and Alexander Woolcott and Groucho Marx? Can *anybody* just go in there and listen to the wit?"

"It's changed. Funny enough Dorothy Parker died yesterday."

We walk on to my hotel, near the corner of Sixth Avenue, otherwise known as the Avenue of Americas. A sombre place. The desk staff look like recently dried-out alcoholics. A heavy-breathing negro porter, my case in hand, taken almost by force, leads up to a room almost as gloomy as himself, fine view of the dirty glazed brick of an inside well, not an obvious touch of America in the place, dark and big and shabby. T.V., of course—and a coin-box by the bed. It's a bed-shaker, put a quarter in the slot and your mattress will vibrate for ten minutes, thereby inducing deep, relaxed sleep.

"Milton thought you'd like this place, the English atmosphere and all," says Chuck, looking at his watch as he tips the wheezing negro with the other hand, neither of the two Americans looking directly at each other.

"I'd have preferred a bit of good old American razzamatazz myself. My wife says I have the worst taste she knows."

"You'll see plenty enough bad taste on the tour. Wait till you hit Dallas. Now—you want to wash up? We can hoist a couple in the Algonquin if that grabs you."

Why does he keep looking at his watch? The most bored Englishman will still give little nods and half-smiles and say mmm, or, is that so? A disinterested American just pulls the curtains in complete withdrawal. Never mind, I can be jolly enough for two. Where's the action? Let's live a little!

The Algonquin was busy with smart, tense, active people newly released from high-pressured offices, the Friday afternoon crowd unwinding after a hard week keeping in the good books of genial but treacherous Fred MacMurray. There was only a touch of diffused lighting, hardly enough to determine the ethnic classification of the barman. Had the lights fused—or was New York having one of those ridiculous air raid alerts? The visiting drinking man might profitably hire a guide-dog. If it was always this dark the Algonquin set probably used torches to discover who had just said what *bon mot*. They sat on stools at the end of the bar. On Chuck's right was a man in a three-button suit and button-down shirt collar, visible when he used his gold Zippo flame-thrower, his back against the end wall, his foot on the rail. He did not allow their intervention to interrupt a harshly monotone conversation with the man sitting on Cameron's left.

"Anyways that's what I said to him, what's wrong, you nuts?" said the standing man.

"I told him that already," said the sitting man. "Bucking *that* guy for the job!"

"Cheers," said Cameron, lifting his glass, which held a good quarter pint of whisky and as much ice as the average British fridge can make in a day.

"It's the only way to fly," said Chuck mechanically.

"*You* told him," the standing man was saying. "I told him a hundred times for Chrissake. Buck for the job, yeah, I told him, but you don't buck the chairman's son! Sweet Christ!"

"I told him," said the sitting man. "You're entitled to buck for the job but you buck the chairman's son where in hell does that leave you? Huh? Nobody bucks the chairman's son, shit!"

"Ah sweet Christ I told him that twenty times."

"You think you were the only one? I told him. Roober told him. Every goddam friend he has told him. Would he be told? Phhh!"

"Funny guy!"

"Funny guy? What the fuck's the matter with you, boy, I said, you *want* them to drive a great big shaft right up your ass, huh?"

"Fucking stoopid asshole."

"So this is Fun City," Cameron murmured at Chuck's faintly luminous profile.

"The very same," said Chuck. "Look, Graham, I have this problem ..."

"You think they'll can Harold now?" the standing man said.

Chuck swivelled on his stool and spoke to the standing man, wearily but with menace.

"Listen, fella, I'm getting kinda pissed off listening to your goddam voice, you know that?"

Cameron prepared for action, London Novelist in Algonquin Set-To Brawl Fracas.

"Come on," the standing man said to his friend, pretending not to have heard Chuck, "we can have a coupla shots in the Oyster Bar at Grand Central, whaddya say?"

They left. Cameron felt excited. The manly glories of a two-fisted rampage through Fun City's throbbing night seemed imminent. Chuck, now more animated, produced an envelope with a hundred dollars in twenties, a little spending money from Milton. On the back of the envelope he wrote instructions for catching a train to Milton's place the next morning. Cameron did not realise for some seconds that his new buddy was not taking him off on a rumbustious night of brawls and broads. Chuck had sort of promised Milton to take care of Cameron on his first night but he also had this cousin flying in from Detroit on his way to a Peace Corps assignment in Africa?

"You oughta be hitting the sack early anyways, Graham, otherwise the time difference soon catches up with you."

"I suppose so." They walked to Fifth Avenue, looking for a taxi.

"You going to your hotel?"

"I might take a stroll round town, soak up atmosphere, hoist a few in friendly neighbourhood bars."

"Take it easy now, fella. It ain't all love and kisses in this man's city, And a friendly word—you find you're drifting into West 42nd Street you just turn right on round and make tracks."

"Why?"

"After dark that's the human jungle down there—junkies, faggots, psychopaths, perverts, muggers, hustlers, hookers with a coupla strong-arm men up an alley—there's animals down there will kick your head off for a quarter."

Chuck waved and bawled at various cabs, saying he still felt kinda lousy at leaving Cameron alone like this. A yellow cab shot diagonally across two crowded lanes and zoomed into the kerb, then rocketed Chuck off into the teeming New York night. For a moment Cameron stood there, caught in his pose as laconic British chap to whom public emotion is anathema. It didn't last. All right, you bastards, let's find this West 42nd Street human jungle and see how tough you all think you are. When I become truly rich and famous I'm going to travel with a fawning entourage that will make the Sugar Ray Robinson circus seem like a decimated Brownie troop. Of course I know what folly I may be heading for. It's like women and childbirth, Nature

24

makes all women forget the pain of the first, otherwise they would never willingly have a second.

In the Times Square-Broadway area every other shop sold pornography or old coins or trendy lapel buttons, the new wise-cracking subversion, *Draft George Hamilton, Yetta Bronstein for President, Pot is God, Irish Power,*

LBJ, LBJ,
How many kids did you kill today?

It was half past nine but trade was roaring. Arab-Israeli war-crisis headlines scudded round the giant news-flasher. A group of negro queers fluttered girlishly by a subway entrance, one of them with bright ginger hair, all of them ignored by two policemen who, in turn, had fingers splayed on hip-bones, bare fore-arms making isosceles triangles against their bodies, the flagrant effeminacy of the boogie faggots mocking the more controlled narcissism of the lounging harness bulls. The sky was dark but the pavement was garishly bright, the general impression being of a flood-lit rubbish dump.

He noticed several old ladies of the Spring Byington type, in pairs and alone. Were they all fiendish gang-leaders using the old Grandma Moses disguise trick? Middle-classes always have these fantasies about one area of every city, Soho in London, Gorbals in Glasgow, Tiger Bay in Cardiff, Scotland Road in Liverpool—these are the places they tell you the cops have to walk in pairs, the essential component of the myth, police in pairs, dicks in doubles, cops in couples, tecs in tandem, filth in fusion, old Bill bifid. That man and wife are obvious tourists, nervously alert, him with the tartan shirt and string-tie hanging from china neck-plaque, snap-happy innocents from Humansville, Missouri, or Dunkirk, Indiana, or Versailles, Missouri. Funny, a big strapping guy like Chuck having these old maid's notions, it's more like the human carnival, roll up folks, patronise your friendly jungle fleapit, catch the all-family show, *Kangro, Terror Fungus From Outer Space*, with *Blood Fiends of the Virgin Tomb*. The pornography shops have the same lines as their London branches, a bit more bloodthirsty this alien porn but pain is still the staff of life. Let us patronise this neighbourhood hostelry, bigger than I visualised the Tug and Maul, brightly lit, no cocktail bar shennanigans in here, the bartender is older and uglier than Jack Dempsey, big and battered, bulging beer belly, bet he isn't hired to chat sympathetically to tired businessmen. Beer. Okay, mac, thirty cents. Perched on the next stool is a grey-faced man in a shabby American suit, than which there is none shabbier, telling sad story of life to wearily knowledge-

25

able woman whose hips cascade over the circumference of stool. The great mystery of other countries lies in not being able to imagine the homes of the people you see in bars. The barman has a face to conjecture with, every dent and dunt is a possible chapter in this nation's lumpen history, from the starving ditches of Connemara, railroad gangs and lumber camps and shanty towns and boxing booths and Pinkerton's strike-breakers and panhandles and pick handles and ridden rods and Okies and pokies and that's what it's all about. A flaunty homosexual faggot nancy boy pervert stands on the sidewalk by the big glass window waiting for rough trade; grotesque, it seems, in American styling, the crew-cut and the college-style sports coat in mock tartan and the white socks, not queer gear as we know it, back there, in the old country. Let us try another bar in search of life.

The great American night sky looks down on this seething human dustbin, the garbage can in the corner of the backyard of the continental United States. *Krak, Jelly Monster from Mars.* Guys beg here, the quick dart across the sidewalk, the ingratiating mumble, the limpet attachment, the mistaken belief that this suit means I'm middle-class and easily embarrassed. Fun City and the night street is full of lost sheep pretending to be human tigers. Here is another inn. Let us sip small beer with the ruddy-cheeked yokels.

"Yah gat nuthin smallernat?"

"Sorry?"

"Hats a twenny."

By mistake, a twenty instead of a one. Their banknotes are all the same colour and size—must be hard on the blind. Well, don't you remember how Frankie and Rabbit wanted to know who gave Blind Pig a fair count on the roll he lifted from the dead Louie? No, you didn't read the book, only saw the daft Kim Novak movie? Trust a man named Nelson to think of the blind.

"Ya've had enuff, son, bettah beat it outa heer, ya onna ship or somptn? Bettah beat it back dere, lotsa punks about heer giveya bad time f'r twenny bucks."

"It's all right," smiling, "I'm not used to your money yet, only arrived here this afternoon."

"Ya give twennies f'r ones ya won't have time ta git uset ta it. Scram backaya ship or what, ya don't git servet no more heer. Beat it."

Half past ten. How humiliating. Admit it, slight frisson of fear. Next time put single dollars in hip pocket, leave twenties under the mattress, wise up to this man's city, buy merchant navy money belt with anti-skull brass buckle, wear knuckle-dusters, don't shave, snarl first, zap guys with zoop gun or wham punks with rat gat. Beat it back to hotel. Become indignant at barman's unreasonable truculence. Complain waspishly to Mayor Leezie Lindsay, White Anglo-Scottish Provost. Sir, in my time I have been requested by the managements of many an olde-worlde hostelry to take my custom elsewhere but never, sir, so grossly and erroneously insulted as to be alleged intoxicated on the whim-wham of a few weak, over-priced, under-sized, ersatz beers.

Ten fifty in the gloom room of the English-style hotel. Cold shower. Head muzzy. Dry briskly. Fresh linen. Small nap. New sweat. Hark the awful sirens go. Banshee wails. Sense of danger. From now on stick to Stork and 21 and Toots Shors and other celebrity watering-holes. Fame will cure everything.

It was still dark when he awoke. As he had no watch he did not know how much of the night had passed. Down below in the hot, humid darkness the traffic rumbled and the sirens went on whooping. He switched on the T.V., hoping to dispel an almost electric sense of being alone. The muzzy picture was of a quality not seen in Britain since James Logie Baird used a foot-pedal to transmit to the next room. All active channels were showing old movies, John Payne with sword, John Payne with pistol. He thought about going out again, like a newly-crashed fighter pilot, another immediate dose being the nerve's only chance. He opened the door and listened cautiously for the sound of a whoopee ring-ding party being thrown by visiting firemen, but all he heard were the remote and often inexplicable noises common to all hotels, chairs being dragged across floors on marathon furniture rearrangements, moans and coughs, flat and relentless monologues from deep, vibratory male throats, the boom echo of T.V. speakers, the soft beep-beeping of an American phone. Lennie Bruce had watched spiders in many such situations, he had the best idea, a central information desk where lonely guy on fifth floor seeks unattached lady, aged 15 to 55, for dinner and com-pany, no strings, let's kill a lonely night together, huh, passing ships, coupla drinks, coupla laffs. He switched off the T.V., John Payne fresh back from the Civil War to find his best gal married to his best pal. He got another pint of metallic water down his throat. Outside, down there at sea level, garbage men banged ashcans. Night people shouted at each other. Then silence. Great stars are often lonely because everyone thinks they are drinking champagne out of warm slippers when, in fact, they are alone in hotel rooms wishing somebody would ask them to a party, only everybody is frightened to ask them because they think big stars have loads of glamorous friends and can go to much better parties. A man of character, like John Payne or Joel McCrea, would smoke a last, leisurely cigarette and vibrate himself to sleep, manually or mechanically. No doubt Sheina is back there at home in the basement imagining me frolicking with some predatory home-wrecker.

That first giddy night in famesville found the hungry, wide-awake Cameron reading his way through the melting-pot exotica of the Manhattan telephone directory, reassuring himself with the star-spangled prospect of scintillating debaucheries soon to come.

Saturday at the Tannenbaum residence, Scarsdale. They all have American accents! Wait eagerly for dinner party, knowing that it is considered normal practice to provide female escort for unaccompanied celebrity. Sit between pock-marked paperback exec and balding magazine writer who keeps saying, it has to be a great feeling, when you've got it made. I wonder if he's referring to some form of do-it-yourself carpentry but apparently to have made it means success. Like, you've got so much going for you. I am glad when the conversation turns to literature. The big sellers this season are Styron, Kaufman and Massie. *Who?*

Sunday morning Milton takes me down to the local carwash prior to our drive to Washington where I am to be displayed at the nation's book convention. A keen-faced neighbor lad comes along, about fourteen by the looks of him, not that you can tell with American kids, them all being so big, the well-fed ones anyway.

"Hi, sir," says the be-sneakered youth.

"Hi, Stanley," says Milton, his deep, heavy voice making this pleasantry sound like a sentence of death.

"Mr. Tannenbaum, sir, this true what Dad says—Fred Kromidas only got but a quarter million for the *Naked Supermarket* movie rights?"

"Half a million, Stanley."

"That's what I told Dad, sir. I bet you got him a healthy slice of the gross on top."

"Of course, Stanley."

"I was sure of that, Mr. Tannenbaum."

"Bye, Stanley."

"Bye, sir."

That's what the fourteen-year-olds were talking about that year, in America.

"Typical American smalltalk, eh?" I say satirically.

"You find it amusing?" says Milton, turning down my plea for clemency. I stammer inconclusively. Revolving brushes swish water and soapsuds over the body of the car. It is very hot. I wish I were inside the car.

And then we are setting out for Washington, Milton steering the big blue Fairlane shooting brake with the white-walled tyres and the electrically-operated windows, across the mighty, wind-battered bridge over the Hudson river into New Jersey, the scenery much more filmic than the films ever suggested, Milton driving with face set hard as if in hatred of every presumptuous yard that has to be flattened before we reach where the business is at, all of it so *American* as to make me feel part of a great montage of *their* history, Cox's army and Sam Ingersoll and Don Ameche ad-libbing 'Poor Old Joe' at the dying negro's bedside and Judy Garland skipping off down the yellow road with the scarecrow and Canon Coughlin and dustbowls and Dewey busting big city gangs and Dana Andrews coming back from the war and Truman thumping the music critic and nice old daddy Ike raising his head on the downward swing to warn against the military-industrial complex ... the kids in baseball uniforms on sandlots, the lawns without fences, the mailboxes, the slip-racing streams of cars jockeying like brisk submarines to fill empty slots in the zooming lanes, American cars that have left behind the two-toned, tail-finned Flash Gordon lightheartedness and followed American ties into grey, formal respectability, Milton the thin, as unfathomable to my cosy British eye as the aluminium coaches (Americans pronounce it aloominum) whose dark green windows and dusty skirts suggest heroic journeys across states, deserts, continents, the inverted onion shapes of the New Jersey water towers, a New Jersey whose grimy, Mafia-rotten industrial towns are only turnpike exit signs; the Garden State indeed, for it is green and fertile and the Sunday afternoon people sit on bright grass in front of white board houses, not at all the New Jersey of corrupt mayors and foetid negro ghettoes, all on a screen in hazy Technicolor, the fast-moving young guys on the heat-shimmered tarmac of the Howard Johnson petrol area, eighteen non-imperial gallons going into the long Ford, Milton paying by credit card; blessed relief from the heat inside the Walt Whitman restaurant where Sunday afternoon American fathers wear those ludicrous bermuda shorts and long white socks, only, like crew-cuts, they are no longer so ludicrous when you know how hot America is; the Technicolored menu, Deep Fried Butterfly Gulf Shrimp with Creamy Cole Slaw ... Roast Young Native Turkey ... *in the event of an air raid alarm remain in your seats and obey instructions of the management* ... Dad wears shorts and Junior wears miniature long trousers and a bow tie and Mom looks tight and displeased ... the body of the Ford too hot to touch after only half an hour in the carpark, Milton putting on big dark glasses and turning himself into sinister Fred MacMurray planning *Double Indemnity* with Barbara Stanwyck in the supermarket ... the misty blue reaches of the Susquehanna, mighty waters coming out of the mysterious heart of America and swelling majestically to the sea between tree-covered cliffs where Red Indians might still be enjoying pre-history; mewing buzzards wheeling over eight lanes of flying steel and glass on the highway through the pines; tough, solitary men driving with one hairy arm resting out of the window; a disappearing sports car driven by a red-haired girl who looks preoccupied, Janet Leigh creating the false plot for *Psycho*; a bunch of Coke-tilting teensters bashing along in a tiger-striped banger; the tyrewhishing rush of the darkness into the Baltimore underpass tunnel; all of it racing and jockeying, Milton a superior being whose fingers on the wheel are space-age organs in direct touch with the vast forces of the American cosmos; the very names have the dream quality, Rappahannock, Susquehanna, Delaware, Potomac, the eye blurs on the map and wanders through a never-ending, shimmering afternoon, yes, that's what it is, the magic afternoon of America; you know why they are different now for nobody else lives in the afternoon; Rome—a cold dawn; Europe—a long, savage night in a blood-stenched dungeon; the British Empire—a brisk, sunny morning with Union Jacks slapping in a military breeze as they hang Danny Deever; but America—it is a golden afternoon of a country, from the copper-bronzed hunters out of Asia, high-cheeked and burned by the sun they took their magic from, the heavy, buzzing afternoon of the early Spaniards and the French and then the grizzled gringo trappers who came into the berry-laden hinterland, the bee-humming, buffalo-thundering, turkeygobbling paradise where the deer and the antelope did play. No matter the crimes, the mistakes, the soul-cemeteries of the refuse cities, this was where Man, for a while, was free of chains, free to let his spirit grow, the true American dream, the—

"I ought to lay it on the line, Graham, you don't carry the same weight as Kromidas with the movie companies, your book won't com-

30

mand half a million dollars, although I am hopefully optimistic of pulling off a good deal on your behalf with Two-World Pictures."

"I'll settle for quarter of a million, Milton, I'm not greedy."

"If we get your book in the lists you can certainly say hullo to quarter a million. My aim in all this—to give you income tax problems."

Is he *serious*? Up till now I haven't been making enough income to pay tax. I hope the money doesn't ruin my essential simplicity. Howdy Doody, Mister Big!

Chapter Three

DISGRACED BUT NOT DEFEATED CAMERON COMES UP OFF
FLOOR, BEATS SHOWER RAP WITH TOWEL WRAP.

When Our Hero came round he was stretched fully dressed on the carpet of his sixteen-dollar-a-day hotel room in Washington, D.C. Above him a fluorescent tube burned palely in a flood of American sunshine. He tried to move but his back was painfully stiff. It seemed easier to go on lying there, numbly aware that he could not remember the final stages of the night before. Three days in the United States and perhaps he had already committed the dreadful insult to the brain. Perhaps he ought to just lie there until they brought the oxygen tent. Nobody is nasty to dying men. Why did the chicken cross the road? Cowards always run away.

A key turned in his door. Before he could move, a negro cleaning-lady advanced into the room, her bowed, roughly-hewn legs towering above his face. She saw him and the yellows of her eyes widened.

"Yew all right down theah?"

She had roughly slippered feet. The skin of her ankles was alligatorial.

"I have a spinal condition."

"How's that agay-en?"

"It's all right, I always sleep on the floor." He sat up, wincing, then rising manfully to his feet, where he swayed a little as blood rushed in or out of his head and black spots oozed before his eyes.

"Yew always sleeps on the flo-ah?"

"I don't like to dirty the sheets with my shoes."

"Yewah shoes? Yew takes off yewah shoes in bay-ed!"

"Oh? Is that so?" He smiled brilliantly, eyes staring into her for signs of womanhood stirring. "No wonder my feet are always so hot."

She stared back. He grimaced and held his palm to his forehead. She took a deep breath, then threw herself into a head-rolling, bosom-jerking guffaw, as though she had seen too many coloured mammies in too many films.

"Oh no," she gasped breathlessly, "yew a forrun gennulmun?"

"No, madam, I am British."

"Oh ... Bridishers! Ah'll be back an' doo yewah room shortlee."

32

She went off murmuring something that sounded remarkably like lawdy, lawdy. How many Britishers could she have known? Perhaps this was our new global image, no longer tight-lipped Carrutherses in bowler hats but crazy bastards who lay about on hotel floors, hairy harbingers of pop and permissiveness, intrepid drunks with stiff upper hips. In the adjoining bathroom the face in the mirror was the familiar lump of pale disorder. Each day the daft drunkard wakes in dread of fearful punishment for unremembered crimes. Nobody with a face like that is destined to make a hundred thousand dollars. It's the soiled face of a fish-and-chip eater, of a nicotine-fingered, beer-breathing waster, a backstreet basement face, ferrety and Celtic, shifty and cowardly.

He stepped naked into the shower cabinet, a glass and steel cubicle built over a pink-tiled bath. My God, he felt powerfully randy, how about the cleaning-lady naked under the shower, soaping her great thighs with his tongue ...

"AAAAOW!"

The first spurt of tepid water had changed instantly to a steaming, scalding jet.

He skinned his shin on a tiled edge. His foot slipped and he almost castrated himself on stainless steel. Cursing viciously he rubbed his burned thigh and barked shin and battered groin. Jesus H. Gentleman!

He tried to turn off the hot tap, shielding his body behind the sliding glass door but the shower unit was fiendishly well-designed against counter-attacks. He tried to poke at the tap with the lavatory brush but its plastic handle bent futilely under the boiling cascade. He fetched a wire coat-hanger from the bedroom wardrobe. It was too short. He stood back, helpless and naked, arms clasped across his chest, hands of an inky-fingered writing fool clutching on to quivering shoulders. He looked out of the window at the tree-tops of the unseen capital city. At the foot of the hotel's grimy concrete escarpments beautiful, confident people were already sunbathing by the blue water of the heart-shaped swimming-pool. Somebody yesterday had described the architecture of the convention hotel as neo-Leavenworth. Americans could be very amusing, when they cared to take the time. Generally they found it more profitable to pay Bob Hope to take care of the wit department. Why pick puns when you could be picking pockets? Even at this height he could imagine he heard them bawling out cheerful American smalltalk at each other.

He considered shoving his bare arm under the blast of hot water. He could then rush screaming into the corridor. Nobody is nasty to men with third-degree burns. Come on, Cameron, try to behave with grace under pressure, as Rainier said to the deepsea diver.

"Eureka, the man shouted," he exclaimed, the solution coming as a vision from on high. He wrapped one end of the long white bath towel round his right arm and held the other end as a shield over the valuable if export-reject love muscle. Under the now carefully-regulated shower he sang lustily, defiant in the accusing face of hostile America:

> There's many a man of the Cameron clan,
> Who has followed his chief to the field,
> Who has sworn to defend him or die by his side,
> For a Cameron never can yield ...

Flashy American tarts, the all-knowing clever-bitch wife had said. That was an illusion for a start. Three days in the sex midden of the United States and the nearest I've been to a thrill was a carpet-level close-up of a great big pair of gnarled negro feet. Cameron—the man who realised the great American wet dream.

The corridor was deserted. Closed doors knew nothing of the seedy British scribbler sliding home on cheap empire shoes.

The lifts in the convention hotel were operated by negro girls who wore white uniforms with short sleeves and white gloves, a visual combination he thought enough to make any normal man come in his drawers, yet he had already noted that the delegates (he doubted that the hotel had any room for any mere *guests*) and the black staff existed separately, both physically present in the same space but apparently invisible to each other. The girl driving the freedom train looked like a black Ava Gardner. He gave her a hearty good morning and a warm, personalised smile. After all, weren't they both failures of the great American rat-race? The lift already contained three or four delegates, each with a plastic lapel badge bearing the man's name and the company he worked for. Looking down, he saw that he, too, was wearing such a badge. He did not remember pinning it on. He took it off smartly and put the stupid bloody thing in his pocket. He eyed the lift girl and the white delegates, all of them carefully ignoring each other. His whole life had been spent building up romantic shit about America, from Natty Bumpo to Nick the Greek he'd believed it all. He could well imagine what prudish outrage would explode if he were to press five clams into this black beauty's pinkish palm and mutter his room number—

Jesus H. Gentleman! He'd forgotten all about Sheina's money!

The lift stopped. More delegates piled in. He felt sick. Look at them, great plastic oafs, manufactured men, identical squares with their stupid Germanic names on their lapels—and turn-ups on their trousers. And those shoes! He hadn't worn clod-hoppers like those since the Boy Scouts. None of the racist swine gave the black girl so much as a nod, let alone a wink. America was for fools, he was well out of it. Was it legal to send dollars by post? Would he get home quicker than a letter?

He watched a small, sick-looking man glancing round the other passengers. When his turn came to be inspected he was surprised to see the small man's sad eyes widen in recognition.

"Grahamy! Ya crazy son of a gun! How d'ya feel?"

Heads turned. His face went red. The little man pushed towards him.

"Jeez, Grahamy, we sure hadda belt or two last night, din't we? Yessir, we sure hoisted a few. I ain't hadda night like that since I left the army!"

Over the little man's head he could see them smiling knowingly at each other. He didn't even remember the little nit's face let alone his name. He saw it on the lapel badge, *Harry G. Flagstad, Paterson Book Emporium*, the man who made Adolf Hitler sound like Whispering Jack Smith. He could see the point of the badge now. You stuck your name on your chest so that nobody could hurt you by being allowed to forget it. You protected yourself from finding out how unimportant you were to other people. What depraved depths of insecurity did these clowns inhabit?

"When did we split up last night?" he murmured, hoping his low tone would prove contagious. The lift stopped. More delegates piled in. Harry G. Flagstad's eager face was so close they might have been dancing.

"I left you guys at the Doubleday party—ya don't remember? I quit after that asshole waiter wouldn't give ya the bottle?"

"The bottle?"

"Ya said it's too long a hike between parties, we needa bottla nourishment for the elevator journeys. Then that ratfink waiter saw ya stick that quarta Scotch in your belt."

"Jesus."

They never caught Henry James nicking bottles of scotch at publishers' parties, I'll bet. If only I wrote verse—poets are *expected* to carry on like infantile maniacs, the public knows how difficult it is to find new rhymes all the time. Harry G. drew himself real close.

"Yeah, we must have a real getagither, just us, Grahamy, ya really gave me some insights last night, ya know that? I've always related strongly to creative writers—but *you* are special, Grahamy, ya're a person ta admire." He gripped Cameron's arm, fingers pressing meaningfully, face emoting intense sincerity. If he'd been English he'd have been up for male importuning. "Ya're gonna be a big success, Grahamy, ya know that? I know this because we drankagither last night and I came ta relate ta ya very strongly, as a human being. Ya're alive, Grahamy, ya know that? Me, I'm just a nobody, ask anybody here they'll tell ya, they don't know Harry Flagstad but *you* drank with me, Grahamy, and in my book that makes *you* people. Yessir, my kinda people."

Harry G. disappeared towards the stairs to the basement. Cameron walked into the main concourse, a lofty acreage of glass and gloss, palms in pots, bells pinging for porters, muzak humming softly through the droning hubbub of unknown people talking about unknown things, the great red carpet eddying with the comings and goings of delegates, most of them middle-aged men in various shades of grey.

A negro porter in a grey uniform and red cap walked diagonally through the main drift. In each hand he held the handle of a soft-topped tartan suitcase and under each weighted arm clasped another equally large case against his sides. Behind him walked a man and a woman, the man wearing a narrow-brimmed grey hat and a severe black raincoat, unbuttoned, one hand in a trouser pocket, the other holding the woman's upper arm. She wore white court shoes, black gabardine raincoat and white hat. Cameron followed this trio towards the desk. The woman's legs were not quite satisfactory, calves large but floppy in the American manner, rest of the leg too thin. Her coat covered her knees. The man's geometrically straight back and narrow hat gave him the look of a walking thumb. His head was turned questioningly towards the woman, who walked straight ahead, confident, formal, allowing herself to be ushered through the mob. Her face was tanned and hardened, while his was waxy, suggesting years in the great indoors. He had ulcerated his life force away in air-conditioned offices while she lolled by pools or played afternoon golf at the country club. It was clear in every line of their bodies that he was her servant.

You're very deep, Cameron, that's what makes you a truly creative writer and person to admire.

The negro put down the cases. His thick body lacked spring. The man put something in the negro's outstretched palm. The negro gave a little salute, which the man did not return. The woman ignored them both. Her hard bitch face was agelessly voracious. America must be a masochist's heaven, the husband and the negro, men locked together in a tangle of servitude. Come to think of it, there must have been some masochistic slaves who found Simon Legree's plantation an erotic paradise. Of course there weren't you dope, masochism hadn't been invented then.

Cameron moved to an empty part of the counter. No matter what, he had to send the money to Sheina, then he could blame the U.S. postal service.

"Excuse me, I wonder if ..." he began to the first clerk, who walked on by towards a louder voice. This happened three times. There was no queuing system, no response to anything but the loudest voice. He thought of Tommy Handley and 'after you, Claude ... no, after *you*, Cecil'. It didn't apply here. This was push and shove country. Never again would he despise the cosiness of dear old England.

There was a tap on his shoulder.

"Good morning, Graham," said Milton Tannenbaum, the man with no shoulders. "We are over this way."

It's a command. The moment of truth in the corridas of power. Every time my American puppet-master speaks I imagine words as shells being fired by teams of tiny artillerymen. He is not of earthly stock, this man who has decided to make feeble me rich. His head is globally large and almost hairless. The body is a snake-thin appendage, an undulating tendril hanging from a Martian brain whose terrestially blue, unblinking eyes can read my puny mind, every tiny book and cranny of it. Gathered round Him as I approach are Howard Abercrombie, vice-president, sales division, and Linda Raskin, Howard's secretary, the three of us subservient earthlings poised to do the bidding of Zorak, Laser King of the Ninth Galaxy.

"Morning all," nodding jauntily. "I think I have trouble at home, Milton, I might have to go back straightaway."

"Trouble?" Milton's eyes probed Cameron's primitive nervous system.

"I couldn't turn the bloody shower off either." Cameron grinned monkey-fashion at Linda. Nobody is nasty to certifiable lunatics.

At that moment in time a tallish man with an English officer's moustache stepped aside from a passing group and put his hand where Milton's shoulder might have been.

"Hi, folks. I see your liquid author is back from orbit, Milt. How's the head, Graham?"

Cameron smiled weakly. The man's badge said he was *Larry Castleberry, Pres. Eberett Griffiths Inc.*

"You were with Graham last night?" Milton's face was impassive.

"With him? Caught up in the blast off you mean. This is one helluva boy you got yourself here, Milt. Would you believe dancing with Sally Weber—at the Ballantine party? Would you believe a conga chain right out the entrance there and round the cab line and back to the Saddle Room? Yessir, he tells us, they always have conga chains at conventions, it's in all the movies, so we gotta have a conga chain. Would you believe it's three a.m. and he wants to take us to a nightclub? In Washington? Three a.m. Monday? Bed, he yells, *bed*? You weak-bellied American conformist faggots, let's live a little! I tell you, Milton, he didn't want to go to bed, no sir. It took Ken Campbell and Ackerman and myself half an hour to get him to his room—and he fought us every inch of the way!"

"It'll go down big on the networks," said Howard Abercrombie, wincing.

"He'll be a riot." Castleberry squeezed Cameron's right shoulder. "You still holding that invite open, Graham, we're all to spend next summer's vacation at your place in London?"

"Of course. How many of you did I invite? There's only one bedroom."

"Isn't he the greatest?" Castleberry roared with delight, punching Milton playfully where most people had chests. "I tell you, Milt, I could use a writer like Graham on my list. I know he can write—he told us that last night—and he sure would liven up my conventions. These good people don't treat you right, Graham, you drop by and see me and I'll fix you up."

Castleberry left them in the breezy wake of his roaring laughter.

"Was that why you wanted to go home?" said Milton.

"I think he's exaggerating a bit ..."

"But you're not sure, is that it?" Milton smiled, or at least his cheeks bunched a little. "You seem to have a real talent there for making—shall I say, an impact? That's the first time Castleberry has spoken to me in three years, since we took Leon Irving away from him. You recall the lady you were dancing with?"

"I didn't even know I could dance."

Milton turned to Howard. "A happy coincidence, Howard?"

"Could be," said Howard. "Did she enjoy the experience, Graham?"

"How would I know?"

Milton shook his head. He seemed amused.

"Let's turn some of the magic charm on the lady bookbuyers of America, Graham. Right, everybody? Let's go downstairs and open up shop."

Cameron said he had to send money to Sheina. Linda Raskin volunteered to fetch a correctly stamped envelope from the desk, Howard and Milton went downstairs. For a brief moment Cameron remembered he was going home, but he quickly dismissed that as a typically pessimistic decision taken in the usual depression of a hang-over, he was no introspective cringer, not any more, he was a big tough two-fisted hard-swilling tearaway who led rampaging conga chains through the foyers of flash American hotels and danced with women called Sally Weber. This was the place for him, the land of real drinking men, of Jack Barleycorn London, of Thomas Wolfe and Errol Flynn, of John L. Sullivan thumping the bar, of Philip Marlowe killing a lonely pint of rye, of Frankie Machine and Owner Antek and Eddie Condon and Wild Bill Davison and Cannery Row and Jack Kerouac and Dean driving a thousand miles for a beer-up in Denver ... he had done a lot of time in dreary rooms typing the damned stuff and now he was going to blossom forth into the man he had always known he really was. God Bless America.

When Linda Raskin came back he took the roll of dollars from his money pocket.

"Now then, how much can I spare for the family?" he said, fanning the notes, money being only stuff to throw off the back platform of moving trains. "Let's see, forty for the wife and kids, sixty for me, a man needs his whisky money, doesn't he?"

"You want to drop your wife a note?"

"Good thinking. I don't have any paper."

"I can get a sheet of hotel note-paper."

"Very flash. No, I'll use the back of a Tannenbaum Inc. press hand-out, let the old woman read what a great guy I am."

Using his open passport for support, he scribbled:

Dear Sheina, hope this reaches you before starvation. Haven't had

39

a spare moment so far, all very hectic. Will phone you. No starlets yet, missing you all, love, Graham.

He felt virtuous, somehow, at the large number of crosses he scrawled round his signature. He followed Linda Raskin to the letter-box, a slim, glass-fronted channel set into a marble wall. He watched the letter disappear into the floor.

"Now, you want to go downstairs before Milt sends out men with tracker dogs?"

When Linda Raskin had written to him with various erudite queries about his earlier book—*you say cobblers means ballocks but what does ballocks mean?*—he'd seen her as a Doris Day type New York publishing lady, changing costumes three times a day and hailing yellow cabs to fabulous cocktail lounges, waiting for an earthier Rock Hudson to probe under the Fifth Avenue glitter and awaken the raw, sensuous, *loving* woman. These career queens are to be pitied—and helped. Linda Raskin in the actuality, however, looked less like Doris Day than William Demarest in drag.

"Why was it a coincidence, me dancing with that woman?"

"Sally Weber? She handles author promotion for Goldcrest Books —they want your reprint rights."

"Paperbacks?"

"Softcover that's right. She may do the tour with you, if the deal goes through. Howard doesn't care to travel too much, with his angina problem."

"What—she'd travel round America with me? By Jove! Wouldn't we need a chaperon?"

"Weber chaperons chaperons, buster. She's strictly the nun type, you know, none shall conquer?"

"Really? She can't be all that nunish if she was dancing with me last night. Maybe she's a Carnalite nun."

"Is that a British type pun?"

He struck Linda Raskin off the list, sarcastic bitch.

Two uniformed guards were inspecting delegates at the entrance to the convention floor. They refused to let one man go in because he had no lapel badge. Cameron found his badge and pinned it onto his lapel. They got through without incident, although it was obvious the guard didn't care for the length of his hair. He decided he must stop reading half-baked psychological slop into practical matters. The badge was your credential. It got you in. That was all. Americans were practical people. He would learn to become part of

40

this grown-up, serious world, cut out all the quirks and convolutions of his amateurish British brain. He'd had his little fling, now he would give America everything he had.

Tell me more about Sally Weber!

Chapter Four

I AM GOING TO BE RICH. WHEN DO I GET TO SCREW A MOVIE
STAR?

I am wandering behind Sarky Raskin in the warm, bright light of
the huge basement convention. America's annual book mart. I sweat
a little, not being used to all this humility. I mean, I see this veritable
avalanche of culture and think of the tiny part my own apprentice
effort might play, typed as it was on the kitchen table with smears of
butter ruining expensive sheets of carbon. For a moment or two
I feel unworthy. All human knowledge is here, Etruscan artifacts to
Californian redwoods, Elizabethan architecture to space technology,
the teachings of Japanese garden philosophers, plain men's guides to
laughter or salmon-fishing or judo or child-rearing; here, if a man
had ten lives, he could read books that would make him an expert on
the haemophilia of the czars or international maritime jurisprudence;
he could learn the secrets of successful selling by direct-shot mailing,
or how to master an inferiority complex in his spare time. Small
wonder men increasingly want to specialise—to see how much there
is to learn leads you into calculations which keep ending with your
own death.

"How do you react to our display?" Milton asked when they
reached the Tannenbaum Inc stand. Cameron stood back, shaken
at the sight of his own photograph, blown up many times, occupy-
ing the most prominent position in the Technicolor panoply of
autumn list book jackets.

"I wish I was better looking," says Cameron. "I think I'll get my
hair cut—people stare a lot over here at these side-burns."

"You cannot have your hair cut now, that's how you look in the
publicity pix so that's how you have to look in the flesh."

"Oh. I'm glad it's happening here and not back home."

"Now I'm anxious to give you the picture as to our party tonight."

"Will we have naked showgirls leaping out of cakes?"

"Such vulgarities went out with Stanley Steamers. The important thing is that Kromidas is coming."

"Great! He's one of the two people I most wanted to meet in
the U.S.A."

"Who is the other?"

"Rhonda Fleming."

"Who?"

"A very lovely red-haired lady who used to titillate the cinema masses of my earlier days. My very first girl-friend looked like Rhonda. I never know whether I fell for Barbara because she looked like Rhonda or vice versa, I ..."

"Kromidas can be a lot of help to you, Graham, he's done the tour, he's faced the problems you'll have to face—the important thing is for you and he to hit it off together."

"Wasn't it strange—him making all those classic westerns and then coming up with a best-selling novel about high passion in a New England small town?"

"He got involved in that scene through his mistress—Stella Nelson?"

"What—*the* Stella Nelson?"

"My interest is to have you establish a helpful relationship with Kromidas—and to let the important book trade people see you in the Kromidas context. Some of the charisma must wash on to you."

"Will I look hellish naïve if I ask for their autographs?"

"It's just the kind of folksy schmaltz Kromidas loves. He's not the simplest of men, beneath it all. But if he takes a shine to you he can help a lot—he draws a lot of water with the big talkshow producers."

"Stella Nelson! You remember that film where she played the society heiress who took to stripping in low burlesque joints for kicks—and fell in love with the young taxi-driver who thought he was rescuing her from degradation, only ..."

"I don't get to see as many movies as you."

"Imagine me meeting Stella Nelson! Drink her bathwater? By the bucket!"

"Your verbal imagery is liable to turn the American stomach. I heard you use the expression lavatory. That is not acceptable—you think you can learn to call it the men's room—or the john?"

"It took me some years to learn not to call it the shithouse."

Milton winced. "I'm now going into conference with Goldcrest. I hope to finalise your reprint negotiations this morning. You want to meet me by the pool around two and I can tell you how rich my vulgar commercial methods have made you?"

Off he went. Cameron stared at his own ferrety face in the

blown-up display. Fame felt very dangerous. Every word had to be watched.

"Hi there, I'm Howard Abercrombie—how are *you*?"

A middle-aged woman in a draggy suit had half-stopped in front of the Tannenbaum stand.

"I'm sure you'd like to meet Graham Cameron—our English author? This is his book we're putting all our muscle behind."

Cameron stood well back, decently reticent. Howard pounced around with the glee of a ballgame cheer-leader.

"Graham, come and say hullo to Mary Graebner—we know her bookshop very well, one of the best on the coast—Graham's making a big promotional tour August through October? We're confident he's going to be very big."

"I'm six foot one already," Cameron said, grinning hopefully, sure the woman didn't give a fart for him or his wretched novel.

"We went to Paris two years back—we didn't stop over in London," said Mary Graebner. "What's your book, a novel?"

"Yes, or at least that's what they're ..."

"Is it a best-seller over in England?"

"It did quite well—it's not the kind you'd expect to sell a million, more the ..."

"The movies bought it?"

"I believe Two-World are negotiating, nothing is signed yet but ..."

"If it's a movie it'll go well. I saw that *Alfie*, you see that? With Michael Caine? He's very big. It was about London."

"I haven't actually seen it yet, I ..."

"You have a lotta that sex in your novel?"

"Well, actually, I tried to do it slightly differently, as if ..."

"I don't appreciate all that sex in novels. I guess it sells well, though."

When she had gone he turned to Howard: "Not exactly enthusiastic, was she?"

"Hit 'em with your natural charm, Graham baby."

"Is charm what they really want from an author?"

"We Americans are simple folks." Howard beamed, patting Cameron on the back. "We like our great men to be lovable."

Howard had fair, receding hair and a pink, boyish face, his age given away only by a suggestion of lined parchment under the eyes. He was very energetic, his headlong style of movement making the tails of his unbuttoned jacket whirl like mini-cloaks. As soon as people slowed down even momentarily he was out in the gangway

44

nabbing them for a lovable moment with the charm-packed author from swinging London. Most shook Cameron's hand with great enthusiasm, simply, it seemed, because he was a living author, albeit one they had never heard of.

"It's a good title," said a short cheery man. "Is it true you can get to hump just about any broad in London, for the asking?"

"Who told you that?"

"I have a friend, he was over there in London, last fall? He says he got to hump a few. Besta luck with the book, Graham, hope it makes you a lotta money."

Misconceptions died. There were shy Americans, quiet Americans, Americans with painful acnes, Americans with bad teeth, Americans who mumbled inarticulately. Yet all his life he had day-dreamed of the America of the films and here, actually in America, it was hard to remember he was not taking part in a film. A short, wide man in white sports coat and brown slacks showing two inches of white sock had the same smooth, blond quiff and sweep as Alan Ladd. A big-gutted man walked exactly like Robert Mitchum, shoulders back, belly out. The women, too, suggested some film star or another. But which of you proud beauties is Sally Weber? Jesus H. Gentleman—imagine going all round the Yewnited States with a woman! Incredible.

Yes, that's what Sheina would say, incredible, pass me the bread-knife.

"What say we knock off for lunch?" said Howard.

It was twelve-thirty. They went to a first-floor restaurant, the Marquee Room, joining a queue behind a white rope. On the way Cameron detected a foul odour. He must brush his teeth before meeting Milton by the pool. Purify all orifices!

"I've always wanted to line up behind a white rope." He was careful not to breathe on Howard. "It was always in films with Robert Taylor, he was always taking classy dames to packed night-clubs and they never had a reservation but Robert Taylor slipped the floor captain a bill and the floor captain always unhooked the white rope and there was always a dull-looking couple just sitting down at a ringside table and the waiter always snatched away their chairs and said there was a mistake and they had to move to a table at the back, behind a pillar, and Robert Taylor and his dame got the ringside table and then he always lit two cigarettes at once without looking at the match, staring into the dame's eyes without burning his nose. It always bothered me, Howard, why didn't the other people object to them jumping the queue?"

"I guess you've seen a lotta movies."

It took them another fifteen minutes to get a table. Howard was too tense for chat. He had been extremely relaxed and affable while pitching sales talk but now they had nothing to do but stand and talk he had become impatiently preoccupied. Business is their relaxation, Cameron deduced, Americans are interested only in action, minds continually pushing ahead towards unknown frontiers. The past is old stuff and the present is merely an obstacle to be battered down in the rush for the future. Why the hell don't you get a notebook and collect these profundities, make like a regular author? Look, buster, if I make a hundred thousand bucks you think I'm going on with this writing crap? In a pig's ear, baby.

He ordered a charcoal-broiled steak while Howard checked calory counts before ordering a tuna salad. The steak was a disappointment.

"Why isn't it hanging over both ends of a very large platter?"

"I guess you gotta funny idea of America from the movies."

We both do the four-minute lunch. I can't help liking Howard, he's older than me by far but he makes me feel old and devious. That's the strange thing about Americans, they make *me* feel like the foreigner. I can sense my own unhygienic, long-haired shiftiness as soon as I'm within ten yards of a yank. Howard is genuinely interested in England, his folks came from over there way back, in Scatland? He intends to go over there one day—and dig them up, I say, whimsically. He has no interest in word play, it is childish, beneath notice. I sound him gently on Watts and Vietnam and he guesses both problems make him anxious, the whole damn mess the country is in.

"You want to go up to your room now? I have some calls to make."

When an American says 'do you want to?' he's not asking, he's telling. I was just reminding Howard that General Westmoreland's pleas for more troops paralleled the same demand from General McClellan, about whom Lincoln said that giving him reinforcements was like shovelling flies across a room. Howard says he is not a history buff. If you don't specialise in the subject you're not expected to know *anything* about it. I have the squirrel brain for such nutty snippets. I even know that Pinkerton was a Chartist from Glasgow and only went to America to escape the British police. Anyway, Black Ava is working the lift. I would have sworn before a Grand Jury (so called because their price is a thousand dollars each) that Howard did not look at her once. He gets out at the seventh. We are alone, Black Ava and Young Lochinvar!

"Nice weather you're having," I say, kinda shy and shucks ma'am, Gary Cooper in Mr. Deeds. She gives a good imitation of deafness. We could have run away together to Chicago and miscegenated all night while by day I researched my definitive biographies of Albert Ammons, Meade Lux Lewis and Pete Turner. I wonder if fat-bellied, straw-hatted, panama-suited, high-hogging senators from the sweaty southern states pay her top call-girl's fees for private exhibitions. Congress is sexier than Parliament. Screwing versus chatting. Does she go home to a frame-house and fry up chicken and black-eyed peas for a handsome young blackie who calls her baby and/or momma? Negroes are impenetrable. I feel like the good Gestapo guy in Occupied France. Love me I am no racialist, I yearn to plead. She sees only my white death mask.

I get the whiff of the evil sniff in the corridor of the ninth. I brush my teeth and drink several glasses of iced water from the drinking faucet. I look at the shower cabinet. Both halves of the glass partition are sliding doors. I could easily have reached the tap. I had panicked, but I was maturing every minute. Should I sit right down and write my Sheina a letter? No, I'll phone her tonight. We celebrities do a lot of trans-Atlantic phoning. We have the mazuma, you see, the jake, the scratch. I could get an erection just phoning to London. We weren't all that poor back home there on Clydeside but we thought twice about making phone calls—when it was only tup-pence. Money is God in Scotland, too. The Scots save it, the Americans make it. I have always been a spiritual American. The whole of Glasgow is America daft. I switch on the radio and get Bobbie Gentry growling away about Billy Joe jumping off the bridge, dragging violins and a tragic air of sweet young death in some hill-billy never-never land. I wonder if Sally Weber and Grahamy Cameron will end up saying that line, we're just two crazy kids in a cock-eyed world. Precious American time slips by. Why am I like certain robust but low-class local wines? I don't travel well. At home now I could be listening to the lunchtime Archers, followed by Listen With Mother. Gideon Bibles are even more boring than the other kind. Is there life before death? Yes, if you are famous. People give you proper regard. There is always something to do. He followed signs to the pool, coming into a long, glass-walled corridor through which men and women passed in pairs and trios, some of them with towels round their necks, some like monks or boxers in the hoods of bathing robes, all of them wearing dark glasses.

"Hi—you afraid of a little sunshine?"

Milton wore a light blue robe, towel over his arm, bone-thin legs in canvas slippers, eyes behind the big shades.

"I didn't bring any swimming gear." Why *do* Americans make me feel guilty? "I thought it would all take place in smoke-filled rooms."

"Tell Linda your size, she can pick up a costume for you. We'll bill you later."

He had forgotten how hot it was outside. His shirt collar was instantly damp. In face of the assembled display of skin he took off his jacket, seeing himself, not without pride, as a figure he had always ridiculed, the street-dressed English dad paddling with his trousers rolled up a few grudging inches.

"So," Milton began, back propped against the upright angle of the sunlounger, "enjoyed your first morning as a huckster?"

"Not bad. The book buyers of America seem like honest, decent people."

"Did you expect different?"

Cameron's backside was being hurt by the tubular edge of the sunlounger but he did not feel like flopping down full length. He compromised, letting himself slide into the sunken middle, thereby bringing his knees almost up to his chest. Over Milton's bath-robed shoulder he saw a woman, tall white hat with broad brim, blue head-scarf knotted under her chin, dark glasses, one-piece black swimming costume. An older woman.

"I've been locked up with Goldcrest all morning. They are offering fifteen thousand dollars advance, the lowest of three reprint bids, but they have an escalator ceiling of a hundred and forty thousand dollars. The other bids are thirty thousand and forty-five thousand—but with very much smaller escalators."

"Excuse me for being dim but what is an escalator?"

The woman changed position. He was sure she was looking at them. He was going to be rich. She could sense his new glamor identity.

"The escalators give the contract flexibility. Basically they increase the amount you get in direct proportion to the success of the hardback edition. Goldcrest will pay you twelve hundred and fifty dollars for every week your book is in the *New York Times* best-sellers. Kromidas was in for forty-six weeks. They will also pay you an extra ten cents for every hardback copy sold above fifteen thousand. Kromidas has sold a hundred and ten thousand as of this moment in time."

"Hells bells! Milton, I didn't intend to get drunk last night. I just got carried away, I suppose. Were you—annoyed?"

"I am well aware that writers carry their own personal demons with them. And if you broke the ice with Sally Weber—well, let's forget it. Now then—you want to take one of the larger cash advances or do you want to gamble on Goldcrest's escalators?"

"I'm all for a gamble—especially if this Sally Weber lady is going to hold my hand, coast to coast!"

Milton gave him a cigarette. It was incredibly hot. The lighter flame seemed almost superfluous. The millions who came here before air-conditioning must have had a lot of guts. Or maybe they just didn't have the fare back home to temperate climes. Either way, previous Americans were obviously a race of meteorological heroes. You wouldn't have made it as a pioneer, Cameron, you have the soul of a sneak-thief and the guts of an actor. The face of the woman in the swimsuit was pointed directly at them. *Graham Cameron, like many great men, married too young.*

"If we go to Goldcrest it's because it is good business," said Milton. "I would not let you drop fifteen thousand dollars just for the possibility of having your ashes hauled. It would be fifteen thousand wasted come to that, Weber is not coming across for you, Graham, irresistible as you may be to some women."

The woman in dark glasses put a cigarette in her mouth and patted round her artistically splayed haunches for her lighter. *Like many great men, Cameron chose as his first wife a simple, affectionate woman who, sadly but inevitably, was unable to develop with him as his genius began to flower.*

"Before we move on to the film deal, let's see how your provisional itinerary looks as of now," said Milton, selecting sheets from his thin leather writing case. A black-haired woman of short stature and brilliantly scaffolded bosom stopped to say 'hi'. Looking after her, Cameron said: "Jesus H. Gentleman!"

"What does that expression signify, specifically?" Milton asked, taking off his sunglasses.

"I dunno. It's just something I find myself saying."

"It's a sad fact that we do not share the English tolerance of colorful speech, certainly not in the mass media, certainly not of anything remotely insulting to organized religion. The tour. The basic concept is to have you plug the book in as many major book-buying

cities as possible in the shortest passage of time following publication
—we have to move a lot of books fast if we are to make the *New
York Times* list. Now you start off with ten days in New York, T.V.,
radio, newspaper interviews ..."

There were younger women around, the show-off boys in the pool
were busily splashing Lee Remick's double at that very instant in
time, yet the older woman was infinitely more exciting. With an older
woman you felt you were gate-crashing knowledge and elegance and
mystery. *Like many great men, Cameron's hunger for life and experience was insatiable. To the small-minded, convention-ridden society of
his time he appeared merely a captive of his own excesses, a drunkard
and a lecher, albeit on a heroic scale. Yet these superficial traits were
only side effects of a phenomenal creative energy which, in its turn,
seemed inextricably linked with an overpowering sense of loneliness
and obsessional consciousness of approaching death.* The woman
looked at her watch, tanned fore-arm regally poised.

"... then early September through October the main haul, Boston,
Cleveland, Detroit, Chicago, St. Louis, Dallas, Houston, Denver, Portland, San Francisco, Los Angeles, Atlanta and then back to New York.
Now then, the movie rights. I have cabled full details of Two-World's
initial offer to your New York agency and your London agency,
recommending acceptance in principle. Two-World will give you fifteen thousand dollars, immediately, fifteen cents for every hardback
copy sold above fifteen thousand, ten thousand dollars bonus for a
book club choice, and a bonus of five thousand dollars for every five
weeks you are in the *New York Times* list. They might also be
interested in having you work on the script but your agents will
have to handle that deal. As of this moment in time that is the global
picture."

"God bless America."

"Spare a thought for your publisher. Two-World were tough—I
picked my hat up three times during the final negotiating session. All
right, let's go back to the store, start earning some of this money.
Move books fast, that's your new golden rule."

*Few young artists can have fallen in love so fruitfully as Cameron
did with Beulah Fruehauf, then a young and beautiful forty-five,
heiress to the Pfaffenbecker napalm millions; immensely cultured, she
turned Cameron from a ...*

He was dragging on his jacket as they crossed the poolside grass
verge towards the artist-loving Beulah. She saw them coming and
blew a little phallic puff of mushrooming smoke. Her toenails were

cut short and square and painted bright red. We kept men know well such toenails. A moment like this in literary history deserved a bit of style. Something incredibly romantic—Mrs. Fruehauf, our marriage awaits? He was within a yard of her. Jesus H. Christ! The skin on her arms and thighs was like tripe. She was seventy if she was a day! I may have a slight Oedipus complex but not for Pharoah's mummy.

"Hi, Milt," said a short, brown man with silver-frosted hair on his nutmeg chest.

"Hi, Irving. Meet my British author, Graham Cameron—Graham, this is Irving Balfour, an old friend."

"Hi, Graham." They shook hands. Irving Balfour two-fingered a thick brown cigar. He was about five feet tall with a monkey's wizened face. "Ya hear I was down in Mexico Ciddy, Milt?"

"Bernie told me."

"Yah, Jack Shapiro's kid, ya know, Ellen, the homely one? I say homely, she's plainer'n my ass but she's comin' inna fifteen million bucks when she's twenny-five, who needs to be bootifool? She's crazy about some Mex kid, Jack hears I'm doo a trip to Mexico Ciddy, he says will I see this punk's family, buy 'em off for Gawd sakes, she may be homely but she's comin' inna fifteen million clams, she can do better'n this jerk—Milton, he's a drap-out from Brooklyn Tech—*Brooklyn Tech* for gawd sakes! So I call on these people, ya won't believe it, the kid's old man is a dactor, a real dignified old guy, know what I mean, they ain't rich but they ain't a buncha bare-foot greaseballs. So whaddus the old man say, the Mex dac? He wantsa know from me, us bein' both fadders, he's worried about his boy, he asks me, is this some cheap Noo Yawk pig got her hooks inna my Pedro? Ya believe that? Ya know what I tell Jack Shapiro? I say, look, Jack, she's comin' inna fifteen million sure but she's no Miss America, know what I mean? She could do a lot wois. An' if ya oppose it she's as likely arunaway wit' the guy an' where does that get ya, huh? I mean she may be plainer'n a hoss's ass but she's still a female, right, she gotta mind of her own, know what I mean?"

"And how do Romeo and Juliet make out in this version, Irv?" Milton asked.

"I think Jack's buyin' off the kid, I mean, who needs a Mex drap-out? Ya doin' much good here, Milt?"

"I'm turning this young man into a rich author."

Irving Balfour pressed Cameron's arm.

"No disrespect intended, Graham, but by me authors should never get rich, they operate better from hungry. My kinda books they should make a fortune! But besta luck to ya. Ya enjoyin' the patties?"

"He thinks so."

"Really whoopin' it up, are ya, Graham? Hey—is this the one who got Sally Weber dancin' last night?"

"The very same."

"Well. Ya must have some secret ya could pass around. I always say some guy gets ta screw that broad they'll find she ain't got one! See you good people around."

He waddled off, two delicate fingers making a toasting fork for the fat joss-stick of his cigar.

"That little man is worth twenty million dollars," Milton said. "He came from Russia when he couldn't speak a word of English, all he had was a scrap of paper with the address of a rich uncle in Brooklyn. The uncle turned out to be a dishwasher."

"The land of opportunity, eh?"

"Don't knock it, Graham, it can do the same for you."

"Ah, says the creative artist, mere money is no yardstick."

"Once the escalators start rolling you'll become more dollar-conscious than the management of General Motors."

No, thinks Youngblood Hawke as they regain the air-conditioned safety of the hotel. Now that I'm due to become the H. L. Hunt of British fiction the magic has gone out of mere money. Ask any millionaire, getting rich is the trick. Afterwards you need more positive achievements. Just as dreary old Theodore Dreiser's most popular contribution to American culture is the chorus of *On The Wabash*, so the mark I leave on the Great Society will be to prove that Sally Weber had one all right, just waiting for my pubic statue to take the liberty!

"Will this Weber woman be at your party?" he asked in the lift.

"She has been invited."

Cameron hummed the tune of the Red Flag:

> *The working class*
> *Can kiss my arse,*
> *For I've been made a foreman ...*

Chapter Five

ULYSSES S. GRANT SAW VENICE AND SAID IT WOULD BE FINE
WHEN DRAINED.

Howard said this first interview was for a smallish but important networked radio show devoted to books. The nice lady had not read
Ladies' Man, regrettably, a scandalous admission she was determined
to rectify at the soonest, but in the meantime she had enough to go
from the press handouts. She said. I smiled a lot. She asked me a
question. My mind, so diligently stocked with laconic wit in the Mark
Twain genre, was a whirring alarm clock. Thoughts left it quicker
than a cinema crowd fleeing from the Anthem.

"I suppose you could say that," I said, several times. I kept blinking and shoving my head forward and concentrating and off she would
go and I immediately became one of those Thorne Smith men who
turn naked but invisible and do naughty things to nice ladies with fat
brown arms. I heard her coming out with some guff about me going
to exciting parties in Swinging London with Twiggy and Michael
Caine and Ringo and Tony and Meg.

"I once saw Mick Jagger getting into a taxi in Shaftesbury Avenue,"
I said, hopefully. I think she said my book was valid, although she
might have meant Mick Jagger. She was about forty-five and well-
corseted and freckled and broad-beamed, just my type. I suggested we
might have a drink together. It was getting close to fifteen days since
I last plugged in and in me was enough vital juice to jolt the national
grid. She put away her cassette and said she wudduvbingladtaennyo-
thutoime.

"How was I?" I demanded of Howard.

"You did just fine, Graham baby."

"But how did I come across?"

"Hit 'em with your natural charm, Graham baby."

So we turn up at the Tannenbaum Inc. suite for the party. Milton
is checking cardboard cases of liquor, gives Cameron a quick flash
of the essentially American know-how that used to get the weak-
backed Liberty boats rolling down the Henry J. Kaiser slipway twice
a day.

"Howard tells me you did not get in enough plugs," he says. "The point of the whole operation is to hit them with the book title. There is no question on earth Kromidas cannot answer without plugging his book. They ask him what the weather is doing and he'll say, 'As I've put it in my novel, *The Naked Supermarket*, the weather ...' Don't be hesitant, they all expect it, that's the only reason people go on the shows, for the plugola."

"I'll try to remember next time."

"Huckstering isn't so bad when you yourself are the direct recipient of the cashflow."

Milton went back to his appraisal of the viability of the liquor logistics. Cameron stood by the window. Brilliant sunlight flooded against the venetian blinds. The sinking American sun oozed through plastic slats with a luminosity that was downright theatrical.

For a moment, as the famous duo stood in the doorway, he could see only the tops of their heads, one white-blonde, the other grey-bristle. Milton brought them into the centre of the room, a plump blonde and a big, elderly man temporarily bereft of the magnetic field that stardom confers on its beneficiaries.

"Fred—this is Graham Cameron—our young London author?"

"Hi, Graham boy, gladda know ya," rasped the great man, shaking hands as if he meant to collect a souvenir. "Where ya wannusa rest our asses, Milt, I'm pooped, ya know that?"

Cameron could not speak. To direct great movies, write a best-selling novel *and* make a mistress of Stella Nelson? Move over, Leonardo.

"Fred—I want you and Stella and Graham should occupy the couch here—you in the middle, Fred—Howard, we'll have the coffee table in front of them—that's about it—very good." Milton stood back, an artist studying a composition. "Very good."

"Not too mucha the horse-shit, Milt," Kromidas barked. "Now then, ya think we can get a fucken drink, Graham'n me, the big writers?"

Howard jumped to it, gladly. Stella Nelson deposited internationally-acclaimed buttocks on the very same divan being sat upon by Humble Hotblood, Boy Scribe, he of the recklessly furtive eyes. She was plumper than on the screen, a svelte milkiness about her spectacularly bare shoulders and arms, fingernails a silvery-green, tinned peaches and cream, the eternal showgirl type, fuzzy pom-pom slippers, white nylon rugs, white and gold decor for dignity, a white poodle with a diamanté-studded collar, a giant panda-teddy in the bed and nothing on her face but make-up, the self-pampered, self-revolving, sexless sex goddess who wakes up at noon in a circular bed with black sheets and takes a pill or two. Revolting. Lead me to it!

"So, they givin' ya a hard time?"

"Oh, not too bad."

"Well, Graham, there's no way known to man to make a dollar without some fucken pain."

A big, grizzled man, aggressive in his movements, skin hardened as if in brine-pickle like the old prize-fighters, brown liver spots on tanned hands, voice from a sand-blasted throat, a dark blue chalk-stripe suit with wide lapels and turn-ups, the creator of universal myths, a truly great artist who had taken a short and historically dubious period in the evolution of American agriculture and made Olympians out of a handful of dirty cowherds.

"Milton told me to ask for tips on these promotion tours," Cameron said, not exactly nervous but certainly subdued, grinning for sympathy at Stella Nelson, who stared at him scientifically.

"Too goddam true, boy, I can give ya the whole fucken works."

The first guests arrived and were ushered across to the triple throne. They were introduced to Kromidas, who held out his hand but did not rise. Stella Nelson gave the tradesmen a curt, all-purpose nod. Everybody gushed a lot. Kromidas was called a fine human being to his face. He made no objection. The vassals had to be told why Cameron was worth being introduced to, but they could see he must be Somebody—they were not about to ignore such evidence of status as a place next to the great man. Kromidas closed audience by shutting off his face. One minute the gladhand, you wunnerful folks—next minute the glacial glaze, piss off you creeps. They moved on dutifully, telling each other loudly what a wunnerful person Kromidas was.

"Two things about tours, Graham—insist on a suite, ya'll need lotsa room ta innertain—and a bottla Scotch on the table when ya hit the hotel—after all the horse-shit ya'll needa Scotch, believe me. Hey—Stella, why don't ya haul yar ass over there and fix me'n Graham a fucken drink, huh?"

The body magnificent eased off the divan. She was very cool. She did not speak. She was very blonde and very striking in dazzling white, a lush cream bun. The critics say she can't act. The hell with them, your divine majesty, you just lie there and I'll make like Sir Larry.

"This right for you—Jeck Deniel's on the rocks?" Stella Nelson asked Tremble Hotflush, Teenage Tosser.

"Doncha use water with it?" Kromidas demanded. Stella Nelson did not sit down.

"No thanks, it's fine like that," said Cameron, throatily.

Kromidas held his own glass up to the light, suspiciously. "This Chivas Regal?" he demanded, truculently.

"Eccording to the lebel," Stella Nelson said, impassively.

"Yeah," Kromidas said, reluctantly. "The key to the whole bagga tricks, boy—sign every fucken copy ya can get yar hands on."

"Sign them? You mean autograph them? Why?"

Kromidas sipped his whisky, tentatively. He turned to face Cameron. The voice was loud and the face was powerful.

"Once ya've signed 'em they can't fucken return 'em that's why. I'll tell ya how it is. Ya go inna store, they give ya a few to sign, ya gotta outsmart 'em, boy, ya get a pen in yar fist and ya get yar John Hancock on the flyleaf of every goddam copy in sight—and then ya holler for more. I've signed books till I had writer's cramp in my ass but I kept telling myself—sign on, Fred baby, every one's worth another sixty cents, sign on."

"I see. Very good."

"Good? It's fucken hell—but ya keep telling yarself—another sixty cents. Ya read my book?"

"Oh yes—Milton gave me a copy. I thought it was fantastic."

"Lissen, we'll have a bull session, just you and me, none a this horse-shit, I'd like a hear what you as a writer really think it rates. I'm new to this fiction racket, I ain't ashamed a admit it. Hi—nice to see you good people."

"You've got a good memory for names," Cameron ventured at a lull in the flow of supplicants.

"That's something else, boy, ya get inna book store, ya have the manager and the under-manager and all those front office creeps nosing up yar ass—ya give 'em the slip, boy, ya get down there on the shop floor and ya give the gladhand to Henry the clerk, *he's* the guy that tells the old ladies in Omaha what they oughta be reading this week— make a friend a Henry, he's the guy who really moves the books."

"The common touch, eh?"

"That's good, Graham, I like a sensa humor. Hey, Stella, you wanna get us another coupla shots, me an' Graham? These goddam gabfests give me the fucken pukes."

I see it all now, the American artist fighting the mass hostility of a philistine people who regard the writer as effeminate, Hemingway with bulls and guns, Sinclair Lewis and Faulkner with the bottle, Kromidas with the truck-driver's tongue, Truman Capote with his death cell friends. The American artist must first and foremost prove he is a regular fella. Well, if that's what's needed call me Mr. All-Bran.

"So what does a tour involve I asked myself," Kromidas said to Cameron. "Meeting people is all. Am I frightened of meeting people? No, dammit, I've been meeting people all my life, I grew up with people, hell, I *am* people! And I enjoyed it, for Christsakes. Ya'll have a ball, boy. A healthy young guy like you—an author—from swinging London? Broads are mad for authors. Ya'll get balled in every city in the U.S.A.!"

So that's how we celebrities chat in private! If only I'd got here in time to meet Errol Flynn. Listen, you'd think people would retain some dignity, wouldn't you? I'm a sucker for fame, I know but here's a man actually kneeling on the coffee-table to get nearer to Kromidas. I think I'll slide away for a spell.

He poured himself four fingers of Old Crow and went to the window, strangely tired. Dusk over Washington. On the annexe roof he looked down on Big Al Fresco and the Society Mob hoisting a few, brilliantly tailored suavies from *Esquire* artboards, graceful lovelies laughing tinklingly at urban felicities. A faint undercurrent of rhythm ebbed from the terrace restaurant. What negro geniuses would be entertaining the Dow Index set tonight, he wondered. The rhubarbing crowd in the Tannenbaum suite was all white, pleasant, decent, serious. The key word was 'anxious'. They were anxious about Vietnam, South American poverty, the race question. They were all on the side of negro advancement but they all said that H. Rap Brown and Stokely Carmichael and the other black militants were pushing too hard, alienating liberal white opinion. Middle-aged ladies were warm and husky-voiced and, in general, seemed more worldly than their husbands. One young man in the mould of the Court of Kennedy—you know, like Arthur Schlesinger, men who are born aged thirty-nine and never get a day older—became slightly more abrasive.

"What is the real thinking behind your government's Middle East policy? We feel Britain is playing a tricky game over there. Is Harold Wilson deliberately giving comfort to the Communist bloc?"

"I shouldn't think so!"

"Don't you British realise but for the Six Day War the Airabs were going to drive the Israelis into the sea?"

"Cairo Radio hoo-ha! *The Egyptians!* They couldn't drive a nail into hot butter. Still, I suppose it came in handy for the Israeli economy—it all helps to keep the dollars flowing in, doesn't it?"

"I guess you British have always been pretty cynical."

"I suppose we have." Smile. "Still we're not currently dropping napalm on anybody."

"Only because you no longer have the economic resources—or the will—to defend the free world. No, you want to shelter under the American umbrella. We require no lectures on morality from the British Empire!"

"You don't, eh?" Your practised celebrity withdraws blandly about here. "I was interested to hear that Marshall Ky's hero is Adolf Hitler. I suppose we British ought to be thankful for Pearl Harbor —without it you might have come into the Second World War on the other side."

"Ky is irrelevant, the underlying issue is obvious to all but crypto-communists . . ."

"Sorry, Nature calls."

When he returned from the lavatory he got in with a group of pleasant folks who were happy to concentrate on his more lovable, tourist-type attractions, all that glorious pageantry shit. Being a celebrity his views on many issues were keenly invited. He blossomed.

"Oh yes, Mailer is pretty widely read in Britain—funny guy I always think, first of all he couldn't spell fuck—then he got delirious when somebody told him about sodomy—God help America when he discovers cunnilingus!"

Cunnilingus offended them. This was why they did not laugh. Like the great little trouper he was destined to be Cameron saved the act with swift reversal to folksy charm—that story about the impoverished duke who was asked why he went on spending three thousand a year on three pastry cooks. "Damme," whined the petulant old fop, "can't a fella have a biscuit when he wants one?"

Bang. A fist smashed into his back. Fighting for breath he turned and got another thump on the shoulder.

"Cameron you scoundrel," roared Chuck Brown.

It's in all the John Ford films, John Wayne and some other giant thumping each other manfully with hamlike fists as a prelude to brotherly love. My theory is that these big masculine brawls are symbolic substitutes for overt homosexual embraces. I mean, you couldn't have heavy petting between John Wayne and Ward Bond, could you? Symbolic or not, the punches hurt. America is a very competitive place. Chuck Brown looked like a born competitor all right, a big American in his prime, a handsome hunk of star-spangled virility. I wonder how I can symbolically beat the shit out of him.

58

"As your president puts it, I must have a piss," said Cameron. Kromidas was hidden behind a line of stooping backs. Never mind, dishonourable member, we'll soon find something better for you to do than pouring their hospitality into their sewers. Coming back through the crowd he came face to face with Stella Nelson.

"There's something I heve to explain," she said. Other faces watched them and admired him for being singled out by the cream bun goddess.

"I do not respond to people," she said, her face apparently serious under the pancake mix. "There is only one person in a million with whom I might possibly communicate." Her false eyelashes and display of succulent flesh did not match the dry, mutilated quality of her voice, which also had a tendency to squeak, Jean Hagen in *Singing in the Rain* when the talkies came along. "Most people want to reach me for negetive reasons. I shut myself off because I heve nothing to give them. I heve something to give but if I give it to all those who reach out for it then I would fregment myself." He didn't think she was drunk, and after all he was something of an expert. "When I do meet thet one person who creates a slight flicker of interest within me I make it a rule to give them no encouragement. The other person hes to make all the running. If he wants to get near me he hes to do it all by himself. I offer no help whatsoever."

"Oh." In his wildest dreams he had not imagined getting it into a real star! Nobody would believe him. He'd have to take back evidence! "When do I start running?" he said, grinning wickedly.

"I thought it would be worth explaining my ettitude to you," she said, snappily. "I trust Fred's judgment of people and I would not want you to think I em unable to relate to other humen beings.

"You'd better autograph my bare chest, or nobody will ever believe me," he said, impudently. He gave her a long but subtle wink. She turned abruptly and went back to Daddy. Might she be fetching her handbag prior to a quick elopement to a neighbourhood motel? She did not return.

"I presume I can depend on your good sense not to explore that possibility, if it was a possibility," said Milton, nervously eyeing Kromidas. "Fred would kill on the spot to keep his piece of young tail."

Chuck punched him on the chest, playfully as they say, almost dropping him to the floor.

"You crazy punk! You thought it was the big come-on, you thought she was going to lay you—"

"Lay me? Do I look like an egg?"

"You can't fool ol' Uncle Chuck, fella, you thought she had the hotsies for you—Stella Nelson!"

Cameron blushed. How brash and vulgar and aggressive these Americans are—and how perceptive. We—the scaredy-cat cousins who stayed at home—are elliptical and devious. Feathery nuances are our talk in trade. Like our boxers, we feint and duck and bob and weave—they admire our class and then they smash us to the horizontal. No, I guess we're not too well up on your boxers, said one sporty yank, but then who's to know one pair of soles from another? Infuriating, isn't it? Small wonder the rest of us find Vietnam so satisfying a topic.

Many fingers of hard liquor later Cameron decided there was only one way to prove to Chuck that British understatement should not be confused with incompetence.

"I think it's time to rejoin my good friends Fred and Stella," Our Hero murmured. "Us big authors have a lot to discuss—we can hoist a few, maybe Fred will take us to a celebrity nightclub—I'll ask Stella if she wouldn't mind giving you her autograph."

"You do that," said Chuck, nodding wisely. "Your bigtime friend didn't name the spot you were to meet up in, did he?"

Cameron shot round. The star couch was empty. Kromidas and Stella Nelson had gone.

"But he was quite positive about it—we were to have a few drinks and ..."

"You'll learn. A best-seller under your belt and you'll be shaking off the nobody people with the best of them. So brighten up, f'r fuck's sake—there's another little shindig on across the way. You think you can handle more liquor?"

"It's women I want to handle."

"You only screw movie stars, donchya?"

"Tom or Jerry, I'm not fussy."

Corridors, elevators, an evening lawn, a foyer, elevators, corridors, another party. Another definition of fame is that you don't have to go looking for life. I feel, somehow, aggrieved. All my nobody's life I've been chasing from party to party, searching desperately for drama, magic, *it*. America was going to be different.

Cameron got a glass in hand and listened to middle-aged men greet Chuck with genial insults. Chuck called out to one of the few young women on display, a dark lovely with a yewall accent. She listened awhile to their scintillating smalltalk; Our Hero saw the birth of a great romance and told her so, lyrically.

She shrugged and walked away.

"A proud southern beauty—too high clyuss for the likes of us, Chuck."

"Just another broad, baby."

"How can she be a broad when she's got such a narrow mind? Maybe she's one of the No-Fuck Broads. No? Don't get it? No-fuck, Norfolk. Broads. Stretches of water. East Anglia. No? Jesus, you Americans have no sense of humour."

"You're pretty juiced, fella."

"Ah bollocks."

In another room a couple of long-haired hippie types were playing guitars. Cameron wasted no time in announcing himself as a key figure on the London scene, close personal friend of Paul and John and Ringo and George. Great, man, we really dig the London scene, we met Eric in L.A. last week, that's where it's at, man. Says Our Hero; Old Eric's out there, is he? Thinks Our Hero: Eric who?

My new friends' names are Arthur and Wade. We are going to split this crummy scene and get over to their hotel where they have a few joints. Any liquor, I ask, not quite able to give up my middle-aged hang-ups. They guess they can lay their hands on a half-pint but basically their scene is pot.

"You guys wait along the corridor—I'll slip away from here in a couple of minutes—the guy I'm with is kind of important—I'll just disappear quietly."

Arthur and Wade left. The party was breaking up anyway. Cameron stayed behind, to lease-lend a bottle of whisky if you want to know. Somebody said they could have a hand or two of blackjack only for that asshole lush. Chuck handled that. He grabbed the paunchy, balding drunk and shoved him out of the door. There was no whisky for stealing, only a big quart bottle of Old Grandad, firm in the grip of an American gentleman with a Chinese face, and a Leo Gorcey accent.

"The bastard swung one at me," said Chuck indignantly.

"You were rough on him."

"That was gentle persuasion, baby, compared to when I get rough. Okay, you guys, let's play cards!"

Arthur and Wade are waiting in the corridor to free Cameron from this older generation stuff. He is torn. All his life he's wanted to gamble for big stakes in the American manner—remember that war film where Mickey Rooney won a huge bundle playing dice under the blanket? What do these long-haired weirdos know about Mickey Rooney, eh? The moment the lights went out, save for one immediately over the red table-cloth, and the glistening deck was cut out of the sealed packet, the decision was made for him. He took off his jacket and hung it over his chair. A man with a stand-up crew-cut, the kind you always imagine jabbing the palm of your hand in a million places, passed the quart of Old Grandad to Cameron, who ripped a half-pint or so into his glass.

Somebody hammered at the door.

The slant-eyed yank came back saying it was those two long-haired jerks.

"Dey say dey're waitin' for Graham."

"You wanta go with them Graham?"

"No."

"I'll handle it."

Chuck went to the door. Cameron felt a genuine stab of conscience. But the hell with it, his choice had been a gut reaction; he was whisky generation.

"You bastards holdin' Graham there against his will?" he heard Wade shouting.

"Piss off, freak," Chuck shouted.

"You fuckin' pig!"

Sounds of a scuffle. The door banged. Chuck came back into the room, wiping his hands.

"Swell friends you have there, Cameron," he said. "I busted that big weirdo on the nose."

"I'm sorry I caused so much bother ..."

"It's nothing, baby. Right then, let's play cards you guys."

Blackjack turned out to be pontoon. The way they played it you couldn't put extra money on for extra cards, which seemed, to Cameron, to make the whole game ridiculous. He explained British rules. They were not impressed.

"Them crazy British accents," said spike-head.

"Give you some idea how the language should be spoken, friend," said Cameron, dropping his shoulders, looking the man in the eye. All this busting and thumping was contagious!

"He's a fucking millionaire limey," said Chuck. "I beat my brains out all my life to make an honest dollar and this limey creep knocks off a lousy book and suddenly we're paying him more money'n he ever knew there was in the world. Isn't that too much?"

"You hit dat buncha Two-World tieves for every dallar you kin screw outa 'em, baby," said Shanghai Phil.

Cards were dealt and men said the same things they say wherever the pasteboards are riffled, who dealt this shit, heap of crap I got, how can I bet when I don't get the cards? Cameron had about sixty dollars and expected to be banging it down in wads, but the betting was careful, a dollar here and there, a five-dollar limit. Maybe they're setting me up as a mark, a live one.

"You know the greatest," Chuck said, "young Fauntleroy here thinks Stella Nelson made a pass at him! Hit me with a low one. With Kromidas right there in the room!"

"It must have been a blow to your virility when she picked on me."

"What say we dispense with the social amenities and do some fuckin' gambling, huh?" snarled a heavy-shouldered young man called Tommy.

Bills came and went on the red cloth. Dollars are grey on one side and green on the back, a functional sort of money, lacking the historical classicism of Her Majesty's scratch. You wouldn't imagine M'Lord John Wenchfondler paying, or not paying, his tailor in such utility stuff.

"This quart's dead," said Tommy, who might have been Aldo Ray after a throat decoke.

"Dere's plenny more," said Yangtse Doodle Dandy.

"No there ain't, them goddam party-goers din't quit till the last drop, we only rescued this quart because I had it stashed under the bed."

"Let's see the elevator jockey."

Cameron followed them down the corridor. Chuck banged the button. The door slid open. A dull-faced white man sat on a stool.

"Hey fella, where can we lay hands on a bottle or two?"

"Hit's hall closed hup now, gents."

Washington is, of course, a southern city. Cameron was puzzled. By day these menial jobs seemed exclusively reserved for negroes, and women at that. It would take him some time to grasp the subtleties of racialism.

"You can spring us a bottle, huh?"

"Ah tell yuh, suh, hit's hall closed hup this time a night."

Chuck held out a five-dollar bill. The man shook his head, face radiating apathy.

"This, too," said Tommy, holding out another note.

The man blinked slowly. He shook his head some more. Saul Yellow tendered some more currency. The tired face showed no spark of greed. Cameron felt obliged to display his contribution. It became a game.

"This is close on a hundred bucks, friend," Chuck snarled. "You'll haul your ass offa that stool for a hundred, wonchya?"

"Hit cain't be done, hit's all locked hup an' the managuh hus the key."

"Lissen ya half-assed jerk, for a hundred bucks I'd kick down the fucking liquor store wall!"

"Cain't be done."

No dumbcluck deadhead elevator jock was going to tell Chuck Brown what could or could not be done. He stomped into the lift.

"Ground," he snapped venomously.

"He sure can be mean when that old Irish blood gets up," said Tommy. They went back to the suite.

"Hey—we dug up Wasserman's secret stocks! He had it stashed in de linen closet—figured nobody would look dere, sly ol' bastart. Help yourselves, men."

Who Wasserman was Cameron never discovered. When Chuck came thumping back into the room they were all sitting at the table with personal supplies, Cameron's fist wrapped round the neck of a bottle of Virginia Gentleman.

"Where the fuck did all that come from?" Chuck demanded, banging down two bottles of Haig Gold Label. "This goddam stuff cost me twenty-five bucks and I was near to giving the night clerk one in the kisser."

A simple call to room service might have obviated the need for all this drama. Or would that have prevented Chuck from proving whatever it was he had just proved? Tourist Americans may seem a bit wide-eyed and naïve but on their own ground they are about as dreamy as a thundering herd of irritable rhinos.

After an hour or so the game broke down, various men saying they were pooped. Chuck said he would cut anybody high card for fifty bucks just to liven things up a mite. Some moaned and some jeered.

"I'll be in it," said Beauregarde Cameron, last of the Mississippi steamboat cardsharps, crooked but courtly with it.

"It's these itsy-bitsy deals at the end where I generally get cleaned out," said Tommy.

Cameron cut a nine of spades. Chuck cut an eight of hearts. Chuck threw across two twenties and a ten. Cameron let them lie there. They doubled the stakes. Cameron watched Chuck pinch the deck, middle finger and thumb. Cameron rolled his cigarette to the centre

64

of his mouth and let it droop, eyes squinting down his nose through the smoke. These guys only made movies, he lived them. Chuck drew a ten of clubs. As Cameron reached for the cards he experienced again his desire to flatten Chuck, to hammer him into the ground. He felt remorseless.

"King of diamonds," he said.

Moment's silence. Actually Chuck was not holding a Colt 45 on his lap, nor did he suddenly overthrow the table and blow a hole in Cameron's forehead, but just for a moment it felt as though he might.

"Judas Priest!"

Cameron collected the notes, careful to suppress any smirk or smile that might make the trigger finger itch. Chuck flopped full-length on a divan, propping his bottle of Haig Gold Label on his chest.

"You bastard," he said, "you never bet that much dough before in your goddam life."

"That's true," said Cameron, tilting his bottle of Virginia Gentleman. "I'd buy you gentlemen a drink if hit wasn't hall closed hup."

"They keep the bars open late in Maryland," said Tommy, pronouncing it as in Monroe.

"Fuck Marilyn," said Chuck.

Tommy took hold of Chuck's ankles and yanked him off the divan on to the floor.

"Come on, you old bastard Brown, no sulking, the limey cleaned you out—take it like an Ammurrican, boy. Let's hit the bars of Marilyn!"

A taxi took the three of them a long way in the dark. At five thirty they were in a scabby dive with a zinc bar, drinking schooners of beer, whisky bottles in jacket pockets, Chuck insisting he could beat Cameron at any goddam form of goddam cards he goddam cared to nominate. A U.S. sailor—or gob, as the natives say—was slumped drunkenly in a corner. Three girls played Rolling Stones records on the jukebox. A few elderly men swayed feebly on high stools. The bartender was the only sober person in the joint and he didn't seem any too happy about it. The girls looked as though they came from those mean streets down which only men with splendid guts might go. Cameron suggested to Chuck and Tommy that they, the gay blades, gentleman rankers out on a spree, might buy the girls a drink and give romance a chance.

"Yeah, get your goddam head kicked in."

"You'll wise up, son, if you live so long."

Cameron burst into song:

In eleven more months and ten more days
They're going to turn me loose,
In eleven more months and ten more days
I'll be out of the calaboose ...

Bettuh git yore friend outa heah! How laughable, you mean-assed bartending jerk, you got that fucking juke-box playing loud enough to burst ear-drums—but I'm not supposed to sing? Why's that then, you twit, is there no profit in it? Bettuh git yore friend outa heah.

Back at the hotel in a damp, blue dawn. They went up to Chuck's suite, where he flopped face down on the bed and snored. Tommy had to take a quick shower and catch the early flight back to New York.

Our Hero comes out of the west wing and walks jauntily under a sun that could melt British flesh. Spinning sprinkler heads gyrate manic walls of diamond water. A negro cleaning-lady is mopping some shiny red steps. He stops. Morning, he says, I'm lost, where's the front entrance to this hotel? She's quite taken by his accent. He feels the weight of Virginia Gentleman in his side pocket. She doesn't want a drink, she says, chuckling merrily. I'll just have a gargle myself then, he says, you need it in this heat. I shuah hopes yew's havin' a good time, Mistuh. In a glass hut at the entrance to the hotel carpark stands a thin white man in a grey uniform shirt and flat grey cap.

"Ah cud handle a shot Ah guess, mighty civil of yuh."

They pass the bottle to and fro in the pre-breakfast sun, wiping the top with the palm of the hand in the manner of men without women or glasses. The carpark attendant is from Kentucky, he only come to Washington to chase his dirty lowdown bitch of a wife, after she upped and run off with the man he thought was his best friend, taking his eight-year-old son, he hasn't been able to find them and he's spent all his savings looking and he's had to take this lousy paying carpark job, that bitch surefuckedup his life, that man she run away with is a mean bastard who's like as not giving the boy hell, still he might of known it would happen, his life has been fucked up all along anyhow by most things, especially the forces of Big Business.

Big Business? A grass-roots radical? A William Jennings Bryan populist? A Huey Long redneck? An old wobbly?

All Ah knows, Graham mah friend, is Big Business it's to blame for most everything going wrong these days, yessir, Big Business is

66

behind all this unrest, the coloreds and all, the forces of Big business and Commyewnism and all, it amounts to the same damn thing. Yessir.

Cold shower. Amazing what body can stand. All that porridge as a loon. Lay me down naked on top of bed. For a moment, only a single moment, my heart stops and my lungs lose interest. The bed is a tiny plateau surrounded on all sides by a dark abyss. I don't know if I'm going to throw up or flake out. I am a fool, I think, a self-indulgent, adolescent, suicidal fool. It could have been my last thought. Death is breathless, a gasping, choking rush to submersion. But a Cameron never can yield. I lower my chin on to my chest and shut my eyes and clench my fists and *force* air down my throat.

That's the great thing about being a narcissist, the ability to give yourself the kiss of life. I lie there panting. How could I possibly die, this close to fame? The cleaning-lady is out there in the corridor, waiting to rush in on my carefully-planned nudity. America is out there, I am beginning to get the smell of it, honky-tonk dreamland, can't you hear the honest slob singing I told you I loved you in thirty-two bars but all you did was drink my beer? Can't you see the sweaty men in undervests sitting on front stoops drinking canned beer from the ice-box listening to Paul Newman beating Tony Zale on the radio? Where is this damned cleaning-lady? She may be old, she may be fat, but we ain't got no miscegeneration gap.

Oblivion.

The noise of the door closing awakens Our Haunted Hero. He sees that the room has been tidied, his clothes neatly folded over a chair. He is still stretched fully naked on top of the bedspread. It is one of the most thrilling things that never happened to him in his whole life, poor wretch.

Chapter Six

MADAME, IT IS ALWAYS A MISTAKE TO KNOW AN AUTHOR.
HEMINGWAY SAID THAT, BIG EARN AS WE KNEW HIM IN THE
TRADE. FUNNY ENOUGH HIS OLD MAN KILLED HIMSELF TOO.

The evenings were good then. I was going across the foyer towards
the Waikiki Bar where I was due, at last, to meet Sally Weber, pronounced Webber, a descendant perhaps of long-dead Devonian
weavers. Outside white-walled limousines were oozing up to the
canopied entrance, disgorging expensive fun-people who got respectful salutes from flunkeys of both colours. Upstairs the Chinkley and
Bruntley T.V. news programme had been featuring negro riots, loan-
shark murders, the latest Vietgnome death toll, Bobby Kennedy
attacking hire-purchase extortion, but all was safe in this peaceful
little enclave of middle-aged do-wells hanging on to that happier time
when Katherine Hepburn made witty comedies about senators and
society gents in black ties rose to applaud Al Jolson and William
Powell preferred Shanty Town to the Ritz.

The Waikiki Bar was a glinting, shadowy place with mirrors for
walls. To be an alcoholic in America you'd need to know Braille,
believe me. Milton's party was sitting under a fringe of palm leaves
round a black, knee-high table. I recognised Howard and Linda and
Milton but in the half-light it was difficult to see more than their
silhouettes. There was a strange man and two strange women present,
one dark-haired and slim, the other fair-haired and wide.

"You've already met Sally," Milton said, gesturing vaguely towards
both women.

"Hi there," said one of them.

"And Fran—Howard's wife."

"Hi there," said the other woman, although I was not sure
which.

"And Dick Jordan of Goldcrest—your paperback house?"

"Hi, Graham, glad to have you on the team."

"Pleased to meet you." A fateful moment and I could hardly see
the woman, whichever one she was. I said I would have an American
whisky. My very teeth were tense.

"I've been coaching Graham all day how to be lovable American-

68

style," said Howard. "Tell us about London, Graham, it true you can get to hump every broad in sight?"

"I thought that man was talking about camels."

"Well, is this true what we hear about swinging London—miniskirts and permissive sex and all?" asked the fair, wide woman.

"Nobody in London ever heard of swinging London till *Time* magazine told them about it. Two days later every trendy idiot was breaking a leg trying to live up to the publicity."

I felt quite breathless. So this is what fame is all about. People actually listen to your lies.

"You people feel like eating now?" said Milton, impatient at the unprofitable pointlessness of just sitting in a bar, chatting.

"I guess I could use another drink," said Dick Jordan, Boy Hero.

"I'll drink to that," said the fair, wide lady, her voice having the hearty wheeziness of the avid social drinker. If she is Sally Weber —look out, America! We'll make Scott and Zelda seem a more sober duo than Moody and Sankey! The others began talking New York publishing gossip, full of men called Bernie and Al and Naussbaum, all of whom were dealing and chiselling and making out and losing out and being shafted and canned and screwed and buying houses they couldn't afford and needing to make thirty thousand a year for alimony before they had a nickel to themselves and taking vacations in whole continents rather than mere countries. Aren't there *any* Americans who go to the seaside with their kids and *paddle*?

"I was in London last fall," said the dark-haired girl as we drifted towards the door, Milton engaging the waiter in dispute of the check.

Which one are you, I wanted to ask.

"Were you staying at the Hilton?"

"No, Claridges."

"You wouldn't meet many germ-laden natives there."

"I wish I had," she said regretfully.

In the full light of the foyer I had a careful squint at Sally Weber. She had black hair in a funny pageboy style, rolled down over the ears but tied up at the back. Possibly she regarded her neck as her best feature. Like all the smart New York cookies that year she was wearing her spectacles pushed just above the hairline, scatty but fast-moving. A brownish sort of skin, not heavily tanned but not peaches and cream either, the slightest suggestion of a downy moustache. Her nose had a slight bump about half way down. She had cheeks common to many American women, just faintly rabbity. She

69

would be about thirty, I thought or guessed.

"I suppose you had a whing-ding time—publishers' cocktail parties and all that?" Again I caught the bad smell. My insides must be rotten!

"Not too much—I wanted to see London—all that historic jazz? I guess I did the whole tourist bit."

I saw it all and felt a warm pity for her, the bright-eyed American career girl alone in London, guide-book in hand, flat shoes and belt-less raincoat, intrepidly directing herself with a street map from art gallery to museum and lunch in the Cheshire Cheese with all the other Americans, handling herself bravely in the disease-ridden foreign capital, enjoying long, interesting talks with taxi-drivers, going to the theatre, alone, walking valiantly past the doors of shabby bars wherein strange locals did inscrutable things. It made me imagine tears, for I, too, know the deep despair of loneliness, as I was only telling the wife and fifteen children the other day.

Milton led us outside. Dusk was a deep purple. I held back to get a gander at her pins. Well, you couldn't have everything. Tillie the Toiler legs. Plucky, really, you ever heard of *plucky* legs?

A hundred or so people were queuing in a long, narrow space between trellis work covered by creepers. Through the foliage fairy lights were strung over three tiers of tables on a wide arc round an open-air stage.

"I should've booked," said Howard. "They have the Supremes doing the show tonight, I didn't guess they'd be so popular."

"Come on," said Milton, pushing into the crowd.

Muttering people tried to block our passage. I felt embarrassed. This sort of thing is easy for celebrities, with their tuxedos and sun-tans, people *like* being elbowed aside by the aides who always flank the greats. Snap out of it, Cameron, you are a celebrity, even if nobody else knows it yet. A floor manager stood at a small desk under a mini-floodlight telling angry men that all tables were reserved. Milton went straight at him.

"Your name sir?"

"Tannenbaum," said Milton. "There's seven of us. I hope there's no problem with our reservation."

As he said this Milton laid a ten-dollar bill on the open reserva-tion book. The head geezer palmed it smoothly, ran his pen down the list of names, turned to a lackey and said:

"Mr. Tannenbaum's table, number thirteen."

No white ropes—but you can't have everything. We followed the waiter. People stared at us, obviously wondering who the bigtime celebrities were. I tried to make myself invisible. I slumped low in my chair. We were on the ground level, a few feet from the stage. Near by was a table of negroes. I couldn't keep my eyes off them. They looked proud to have made it on the ground level. They had the same clothes as the whites and ate the same food and held their cigarettes the same way, and yet there was something stagey about them. Bullets were flying through the flames of Detroit and the long, hot summer was the thrillingly ominous cliché on every lip, and here were the assimilated blacks, separated from their white pace-makers by an invisible wall of soundproof glass. When the Supremes took the stage, three brown girls in shiny, floor-length gowns so tight you could see hip-joints fighting for room, the middle-class negro patrons seemed even more self-conscious and apart. Black was singing to black but in whitey's house. I felt like an impostor, for reasons unknown to myself. I drank a fair share of imported wine and for solids had a plate of cherrystone clams.

"You like this kinda stuff?" Dick Jordan asked, nodding up at the singers.

"It's not bad, for pop. Tamla-Motown's quite big in London."

"How's that?"

"Tamla-Motown—the Detroit sound. Actually I'm a King Oliver-Johnny Dodds man myself."

"I guess I'm not too familiar with all this rock'n'roll."

Black girls' bodies swayed stiffly in hampered stardust ... it happened to me and it can happen to you ... a regular rhythm, music for the half-remembered sadnesses of yesterday's adolescence ... I woke up, suddenly I just woke up ... haunting echoes for long-ago loves, and through it all middle-aged, middle-class white America went on talking about the new conglomerates, high interest fiscal policies, poor old Joe Harschfeldt got assholed from his own company, these kids make a lotta dough. I don't understand it myself, the kid's bedroom is full of these Rolling Stones albums, they're weird but *weird*. Not a head marked time, not a foot tapped, knives and forks, bottles and glasses, belly laffs, it's not new, they didn't understand it when it was Charlie Parker or Bessie Smith or Jelly Roll, or Poor Old Joe Oliver writing those awful letters to his wife, a really terrible dignity, couldn't raise the dough for a new set of false teeth, couldn't play till he got the teeth, King Oliver, true American genius, who didn't run away to the Deux Magots and whine about lost innocence but who only wanted to go on playing the music, here

71

at home, where he couldn't raise the dough for new teeth. I was going to cry there. Must be pissed. Watch Sally Weber, Milton passes her some papers, she pulls down her specs, little rabbity-cheeked matron face, poor Sally, men go round saying she ain't got one, men are brutes. Fran Abercrombie has grown a little louder. I can see it's a situation they've handled before, she must have a drinking problem. Howard says it's time to hit the sack, Fran says what for in God's name it's only twenty after ten. Linda Raskin says she's pooped. Milton says he has some letters he must dictate into the machine. Dick Jordan says he has to call his wife in Westport. Oh well the hell with it, even celebrities have to go to bed sometimes, dammit.

We rose and walked through the crowded tables. Clams and whisky and wine slopped like bilge in the scuppers of my guts. The girls on the stage swayed like black mambas preparing for the deadly strike, the notes swarming and the rhythm mounting. Busby Berkley would have had everybody jigging towards a mighty climax.

We stood together in the foyer.

"So, Graham, you've had a busy day," said Milton. "You'll sleep sound tonight, huh?"

"When it's bedtime." Boyish smirk. "I think I'll have a last drink —anybody care to join me?"

They all guessed not. He left them quickly, walking precisely in case of a slight stumble. He sat alone in an alcove of the gloomy Waikiki Bar and ordered Jack Daniel's on the rocks with a glass of water beside it, unable to remember the correct terminology. He lit his last Disque Bleu. The screen play didn't go like this at all, not him sitting alone in a hotel bar, moodily. When the hell was all this fame going to start? It might be more than I can cope with, all that pushing ahead of queues ...

"Hi there."

Sally Weber was standing by the table.

Chapter Seven

"You sitting all alone, thinking deep writer's thoughts?"

"So—you sneaked back. Didn't you want them to know you have
a drinking problem?"

"I'm sharing a room with a kook girl from the office—she has this
ridiculous man up there."

"Scotch on the rocks, Jack Daniel's for me," I said to the ever-
silent waiter, a Latin type but sour with it. I looked at her and nodded
slowly. "Why are American bars so dark? It's very depressing for the
lonely drinker."

"I didn't think you were the lonely drinker type, the other night you
could've sold tickets."

"We danced divinely I'm told."

"We swayed together some. I was a little high."

"A little high what?"

"You writers with your clever word play!"

"In fact all the guys were most impressed. They say you're the
unapproachable type."

"I'm also the frigid type according to sources. It's true, matter of
fact. Christ, I must be high again. I suppose everybody wants to
reveal their darkest secrets to authors—you understanding people
and all that psychological bunk?"

"Nobody ever tells me any secrets."

"You don't sound like an author maybe."

"Can I ask you a very personal question?"

"No. I never fall for the old personal question trick. I really am the
frigid type."

"How interesting. Does my breath stink?"

She leaned her face towards me and I blew gently, just a whiff.
I felt the warmth of her face on my cheeks. The spectacles gave her
a brainy look.

"Smells like good old-fashioned hooch to me," she said.

"Ever since I've been here I've had this rotten stink in my nostrils,
you know how a decomposing rat smells?"

"I'll take your word for it, rats I am happy not to know about. Anyway, it's the hotel stinks."

"The hotel?"

"Convention hotels, they're all the same, too many people I guess. I find I smoke a lot at conventions, it masks the stench of the carpets."

"Christ—a glamorous place like this?"

"You kidding? This—glamorous?"

"It is to me, Miss Weber, I'm just a great big simple country boy."

"I never fall for the great big simple country boy trick either, buster."

"I've been trying to decide who you remind me of. Sometimes it's Jean Peters—with touch of the Farley Grangers. Lovely but a little sad. And we're going all the way across America together! Did you volunteer or were you pushed?"

"It's part of author promotion. I went part of the way with Kromidas. I hold hands real good. That's all I hold."

"Like the Doris Day film where she was the slick career woman who had to play mother to Rock Hudson, he was a dim hick from out of town only all the time he was from another advertising agency trying to steal the account?"

"Is that crazy accent for real? How come Sir Laurence Olivier doesn't use it?"

"What a bizarre idea. You might as well ask why Jack Kennedy didn't have the same accent as Jelly Roll Morton."

"Jelly Roll Morton? Who he?"

"You never heard of Jelly Roll Morton's Red Hot Peppers? Some say the greatest jazz band of them all? He wrote down all the notes for the first time. He had diamonds in his teeth and thousand-dollar bills sewn on his suits. He actually claimed to have invented jazz but ..."

"Was this in a movie?"

"Dear oh dear. Words fail me."

"I know. I sure hope we can improve your communication potential for the American public, they're going to have a problem understanding you."

"I see. Maybe you could have me dubbed—like the way they used to dub American dialogue on to British films? Naturally we British are expected to understand every thick bumbling idiot from Brooklyn or Tennessee. It's *our* bloody language, mate! Pardon me. Let's have another drink."

She laughed and her glasses slipped down her nose and she took a delicate gulp of Scotch and I thought, you've got her going, Jock.

"How much do you earn a week?"

"What's that to you?"

"I feel a great curiosity about you, Weber. After all, we'll be practically living together as man and wife for two months."

"Oh no we won't, buster. You might as well get it straight now, I do not bed-hop."

"Bed-hop? I must get a notebook and jot down these quaint Americanisms. You can educate me in American euphemisms and I can tell you about Jelly Roll Morton. Bed-hop, indeed! It sounds like bloody kangaroos. Talking about sex, there was a woman in our town who had three children, then her husband died. She married again and had four children by the second husband. He died. She got married for a third time, had two children—and then she died. At the graveside one of the mourners said to the next man, 'Aye well, they're together at last.' The other man said, 'You mean the first or second husband?' The first man says, 'No, her legs.'"

"Oh. You know before I got into this racket I had this image of authors, egg-head guys with pipes talking about streams of consciousness and mental blocks?"

"So did I."

"You want to hit the sack now?"

"Your room or mine?"

"Look, Graham, I don't want to get all uptight about this but I mean it, I do not bed-hop."

"What does it mean?"

"Things may be permissive in London, but if you get to be known as a sleeparound in New York—it's not good."

"Sleeparound? What picturesque sex-slang you Americans have, all this humping and screwing and balling and getting laid and getting your asses hauled."

"What do you call it?"

"Ah well, I'm a lyrical writer, I mean, it's all dahn to yer romantic imagery an' that, innit, the sacred communion of the flesh and that? What was it Byron said, there's nuffink makes a bloke so hearty as hanging out of some young party."

"Byron? *The* Lord Byron?"

"Nah, Gerry Byron. I think I am getting a little high, Weber."

"What are you planning?"

"Oh I'll just sit here in the gloom and hoist a coupla more shots—I get claustrophobia in hotel rooms."

She lifted her glass, looked at it, chewing her lower lip, then tilted the rest of her whisky down her delicately gulping throat.

"Come on," she said, "I'll show you another bar a mite more lively than this."

I went with her through the foyer winking to myself in sly triumph. It had all been ordained. We would bed-hop together all round America and already I felt the warm poignant sadness when Cruel Fate decreed we had to part, knowing It Could Never Be. Shadowy people were dancing to music that sounded like rock played by Bavarians in *lederhosen*. It was what they called a discotheque. Everything from London was in that year. She found an empty table. A waiter appeared, obviously the man with infra-red eyes. Weber did the ordering. We danced. My right hand went round her back, which was firm to touch, and my chin pressed hard on her forehead. She smelled of perfumed soap. The music was old-fashioned but that just proved how little kids know today, for this was what dancing was all about, holding a woman close, knee to head, just enough movement to make it legal.

"Now you think you want to turn in?" she asked. We were sitting down. I leaned my head on her shoulder and fondled her knee.

"Have you seen anything at all of Washington?" she asked, moving away with a brisk little movement.

"Not a thing," I murmured, looking deeply, knowingly, longingly into her eyes.

"All rightee. If you won't go to bed I'll show you the town. Pick up the check and let's go."

She knew all about America, how much to tip a waiter and how to negotiate with stupid cabbies, and I drifted in her brave, girlish wake, just a great big simple country boy from the bed-hopping backwoods. In the cab she let me hold her hand. We saw the brilliant floodlight gold of the Capitol Building.

"Very interesting," I said, snuggling closer. "Can we go home now?"

She told the driver to go on to the White House. We stopped, despite the cabbie's reluctance. She insisted on getting out. I gawked through the railings.

"It's quite small. You think L.B.J. is in there right now, turning off the lights?"

"It's bigger than it seems. There's more in back."

The long stretch of pavement was deserted. I gripped the railings with both hands.

"L.B.J., L.B.J., how many kids did you kill today?" I chanted, not too raucously. She grabbed my arm and pulled me back to the cab. I pulled myself back to the railings and roared:

"HANDS OFF VIETNAM YOU BASTARD!"

"Ya crazy?" the cabbie snarled, gunning the motor for a jolting blast-off. Not a single F.B.I. man with ominous bulge materialised in defence of the free world's guardian. The driver told Weber he wanted them outa the cab, the guy nuts or somethin'? Weber told him sharply to take them to the Lincoln Memorial. The cabbie mumbled but went on driving. He grumbled some more when she told him to wait beside the broad pavement in front of the memorial. We went up some wide steps. I walked slowly, blinking a lot to get my eyes in focus, body crying out wearily for bed.

In a green light from the ceiling of an open-fronted temple the Great Emancipator sat brooding in the warm night.

"Father we have sinned," I said, looking up at the great folds of the stone trousers. I was a smart lad and I knew that Lincoln did not start the war to free the slaves, nor did he consider the black man his equal in the sight of God; yet the cheap pun that came to mind (the Ghettosburg address if it matters) did not reach the tongue; this was no ludicrous London monument to some long-dead military fool or face-grinding aristocrat, this was the soul of the America that could have been truly great, this God-statue staring out with sightless stone eyes over the endless American darkness—guarding, watching, omniscient. Other couples moved silently under the rock face and the eternally creased legs. There was a rope to keep worshippers at a respectful distance but we stepped over it and walked round into the darkness at Lincoln's back, looking up at the changing profile. I kissed Weber on the forehead ...

"Ya hadda nuff, huh?" said the cabbie.

"Drop us at the next bar," said Weber.

"Maybe there's some joints still open."

We had still not spoken to each other when the big-bellied, sullen-faced bartender put two beers on the table. It was a dark, dirty place. The only other patrons were three youths at the far end, motionless figures in sunglasses, feet up on chairs, short-sleeved T-shirts bulging out biceps, greased hair glinting in a weak light. She said they just might be muggers so let's hustle. I saw us as a pair of little figures in a big black forest. I held her round the waist as we walked in the shadows. No taxis came. I stopped by the bright window of a gown shop. I kissed her on the nose.

"What say we run all the way to the hotel?"

She blinked up at me. "Oh the hell with it," she said. "What harm's in it?"

Four blocks on she changed her mind. I had been admiring a car stopped by traffic lights, a big, wide, low American car, light blue with green glass and Martian tail-fins and radio masts and rear lights which were not red bulbs but bars of slow-burn red fire. The man at the wheel peered up at us, elbow resting on the open window, fingers drumming the roof.

"Nice going, fella," was all the man said. The lights changed and the car oozed away.

"No—I won't," Weber exclaimed, pushing me away.

"You won't what?"

"I don't even know you for God sakes!"

"Come on—you know we've both been aching for it all night. Let's live a little, gorgeous."

"I will not become involved in a relationship that can only have a negative conclusion."

"Come again?"

She went on about relationships and negative conclusions. I persisted against her tirade of analyst's jargon, giving her choice and well-tried lines in chat-up patter as we walked in the soft, warm air of the empty night streets of America's capital; every fibre of my being ached; what did Wilde say about denying pleasure's kiss? As soon as I saw you I felt I'd been waiting for you all my life; what will it all matter when we're on our deathbeds; isn't it the finest compliment one human being can pay another?

"You're a plausible bastard but I do not bed-hop."

We had to walk through a small park. I plonked myself down on a small bench, moodily ignoring her pleas to move before a cop came along. She sat down beside me. My eyes were blinking of their own accord and taking longer about it each time. I let out a little sob and put my head on her shoulder. Before she could push me away I swung my legs up on the bench and lay back with my head on her lap, seeing her chin and nose and glinting spectacle frames against the night sky.

When I awoke her hands were holding my head close to her

stomach. Through her coat I could hear pipes gurgling and spluttering. I rubbed my eyes and then sat up.

"You feeling better now?" Her voice was quieter.

"I don't think I'm cut out for all this glamour."

The hotel foyer was lit but deserted. It was four thirty. A scrawny-necked white man operated the elevator. She got out at the sixth floor. I went with her along the corridor, prepared for the quick peck and sincere remark at the bedroom door, as practised in movies of the pre-permissive era. *You are a very wonderful person, Graham, I wish it could all have been different.*

"Let's hope Sandra has pissed off," she said.

Sandra was kneeling on one of two single beds, wearing only a pyjama top, yelling drunkenly into the phone, which she held between chin and shoulder leaving both hands free to hold the vodka bottle and glass.

"Come up to your room?" Sandra shouted, snorting maniacally. "Up yours! Jerk! Motherfucker!" She slammed down the phone, saw me, pulled a pillow over her blue-veined thighs. She had dirty blonde hair. Her face was well greased. "Who's this long-haired creep?" she demanded.

"This is Graham—you intending to move outa here, Sandra?"

"I'm stoned! Jeez, that prick Stanley! You kids wanna drink? It's Stanley's lousy vodka. Screw him. I'm really stoned, you know that?"

I went into the bathroom-lavatory. As I sat on the seat I could hear them talking, although not what they said. It took ages to empty myself. A door slammed.

"What the hell were you doing in there all this time?" Weber demanded, peering at her face in a mirror, specs pushed up on her hair. Sandra had gone!

"Having a shit."

"Peasant!"

She pushed past me into the bathroom. I sat on a bed and examined my dirty nails. Come to think of it, a bigtime New York career queen would have unimaginably sophisticated ways of perpetrating sex. She came out of the bathroom wearing a short blue mini-nightie. She had brown thighs and knobbly feet, square, like mini-shovels.

"Don't gape at me," she snapped, reaching for the light switch by the door. I was pulling off my tie as she made a little dive for the safety of the sheets, which she pulled up to her chin. "I suppose you are incredibly experienced with women," she said in a little girl's voice.

"Just a great big country boy, ma'am."

I slipped naked under the blankets. She insisted on switching off the bedside lamp. My hands went to her body. She was hard and slippy to touch. She mumbled things in American. I could have fucked the accent apart from anything else. The door opened and Sandra switched on the main light.

"You making it with that long-haired weirdo?" she bawled. "Christ, I'm stoned. You kids wanna fucking drinka Stanley's vodka? Jeez, that motherfucking asshole, I'd as soon get laid by a real pig I really mean it."

Weber's body was tense and motionless. Sandra ranted and raved and then fell on her bed and passed out. Weber jabbed her elbow into my chest.

"My God get the hell outa here," she snarled in a vicious whisper.

"My darling one," I murmured, forcing away the blankets and twisting down to kiss her soft, white hip. She tweaked my ear savagely.

"Go on, disappear, get lost," she hissed. I didn't move. She twisted round to put her feet against my stomach, her back against the wall, shoving me over the edge of the bed. "Out!"

"Are you trying to tell me something?" I said, knees on the floor, chin on the edge of the bed, hands caressing her knobbly feet.

"Will you fuck off outa here!"

She pulled the blankets across the bed and sat in the corner of headboard and wall, eyeing me with desperate hate.

"All right, my darling," I said, standing up, giving her a full frontal aspect of great British dick. She closed her eyes and shuddered. When she opened her eyes again I was still standing there, arms flexed in the Charles Atlas manner.

"You pig—if I had a death ray machine right now I'd turn it on you and make you shrivel up and disappear! I would vaporize you!"

I saw her specs on the little table. I threw them on to the bed.

"Put your goggles on, Weber, see what you're missing."

She put them on and became the rabbity matron—Dugs Bunny, I thought of saying.

"Come to my room," I said casually. Pulling up my trousers I lost my balance and crashed on to her bed. I lay on my back, grinning up at her.

"Get lost," she snarled.

"Let's have lunch today and discuss ways to improve our sleeping arrangements," I said, buttoning my shirt.

"We have no sleeping arrangements! I'm going back to New York first thing."

I made a sincere face. "I want to thank you for tonight, Sally. I'll never forget it, honest."

"Yeah, yeah," she said, "just beat it."

Broads are mad for authors, said Kromidas. All over the U.S.A. milk-fed nubiles are shouting Make Me an Author. Every American burg big enough to have a dog-catcher is crawling with Friedas waiting for my D. H. Lawrence act. And I have to get landed with that frigid bitch? I crawl into my lonely pit knowing exactly why Lonesome Rhodes was such a bastard when he became famous. And if you haven't read enough or seen enough movies to know who Lonesome Rhodes is you can go to hell, all of you, take bloody Sally Weber with you and rot for all I care. I'll have my revenge, don't worry, I'll make you all pay, you miserable bastards. When I'm a star I'll bloody well crucify the bitch!

They left the convention hotel around ten thirty on the last morning of the book fair, Milton driving, Linda Raskin in the front passenger seat, Howard and Fran Abercrombie and Your Hero in the rear. Milton was in a relentless hurry. He had no time for boring route discussions. Quickly and efficiently he got them into the wrong part of the inner Washington road system. There were no signs saying BLACK GHETTO but in the open windows and on the front steps of the brownstone houses sat or stood listless negro men, by the dozen, by the score; there were trees in these avenues and the houses were not, to the trained British eye, glaring slums, but there was no doubt that this was no-hope territory; these men had nothing to do but kill time—or is it time that kills the unemployed? Gangs of long-legged black boys stampeded about the sidewalks under the slow eyes of their unwanted fathers and uncles. The sun was up and the car windows down and it felt good to be sitting there in a slick suit headed for the bigtime in New York, knowing you had also come from slums but had achieved something with your life. Then they were stopped by traffic lights and a dozen black boys interrupted their endless, mindless throwing of baseballs into baseball mitts and surrounded the big blue estate wagon, grinning in the windows, first of all touching and then banging the bodywork, raggedy boys in battered baseball boots and dirty T-shirts; Milton quickly pressed the button that silently raised the windows; two boys brazenly tried to open the back of the car where the luggage was crammed under coats and jackets. Linda and Howard said nothing, staring grimly ahead. Four or five black noses and distorted, pink mouths flattened against the glass, the bangs on the bodywork getting louder all the time, a dozen or more grown men watching impassively from the street corner, whitey's big automobile whale-stranded on a hostile sandbank. Then the lights changed and Milton gunned the motor. For a moment the car strained but did not move, as though held fast by black hands. Then the faces were falling away from the windows, some laughing, some strained and ugly with hate. Cameron turned to look through the rear window, ducking his head involuntarily as he saw a boy's arm catapult something at the retreating car. It was a bottle and for a moment it was caught by the sun and became an incandescent meteorite. Then it fell short and smashed on the road. Soon they were on to the correct exit route and heading north for Baltimore.

"Phew," said Cameron, fingering his collar, looking at Milton's eyes in the mirror.

"It's worse all the time in Washington," said Howard, shaking his head. "You have to admit it, Milt, we must have the sloppiest road-sign system in the world."

Chapter Eight

THE ONLY SNAG ABOUT BECOMING AN OVERNIGHT SUCCESS
IS IT TAKES SO LONG.

I will give the parks back to the people, Mayor Lindsay was promising that week, fearlessly turning his back on the mugger vote.

A race riot in Bedford-Stuyvesant, over there in Brooklyn, was narrowly averted when the cop who shot dead the running negro youth turned out to be black himself, a stroke of luck for the London insurance companies.

A man sacked from a Bronx garage went straight home for his gun and returned to give his late employer the bullet between the eyes.

Cameron had been awake since five a.m. all alone in the gloom room of his unpretentious but inhospitable New York hotel. He didn't feel like a man whose smash-hit, all-time, best-selling supernovel would hit the stands and the headlines tomorrow. He felt like the man who put the ereal in Fun City. Tentatively flexing his new money-muscles, he phoned Sheina. It was mid-morning over there in London, England, the weather was lovely, the babies were fine, Sheina was fine, the money had arrived, everybody missed him, he missed everybody, kisses were smacked under the Atlantic wastes and he was alone again. At eleven he was due to meet Howard at the Rockefeller Center for something called a pre-interview. Howard had asked if eleven wasn't too early. Nobody expects to see big stars before eleven, celebrities always sleep late, it's well known, exhausted by the relentless pressures of fame. So why was he here alone at six thirty, wide-awake and naked, flicking from channel to channel in desperate search for distraction? Seven American days gone. Don't panic, he warned himself, just relax and gather strength for the bigtime. On a breakfast talkshow a former girl dancer plugged her best-selling book on how to lose pounds and stay slim without time-wasting exercise or needless dieting. Later came one of the new sporty doctors—those witty T.V. medicos always suspected of squiring top models to flash nightspots on the proceeds of aborting top actresses in famous but mysterious clinics—plugging his best-selling book on fitness without time-wasting exercise for top executives.

"As soon as men hit the shores of America anything becomes possible," he said, picking up the phone and asking the duty dipsomaniac for Weber's number. "And this is the kind of thing we celebrities do—isn't it?"

As he heard the phone ringing at her end he held the phone between chin and collar-bone and started dragging on his underpants.

"Sally Weber," said her sleep voice.

"It's Cameron of Lochiel here. You may remember me from Washington."

"Graham you bastard. What time is it for Chrissake?"

"The early worm catches the bird. I'm alone with the breakfast show, I think I'm having a bad attack of the lonelies. Sorry if I woke you up."

"S'okay. Why don't you drag your inner resource problem over here for a cuppa cawfey? I don't leave for the affis before nine."

This fame game sure is a quick cure for shyness and inferiority complexes!

It was about twenty past seven when he waved down a cruising Yellow Cab outside the hotel. It was driven by a smart young cookie whose licence plate, affixed to the back of the driving seat, said he was Harold F. Fankel, a Tony Franciosa type with a wet duck's arse and a leather jerkin. He knew he was a smart young cookie and made with fast patter in colorful cabbie fashion. All New Yorkers behave like this, acting roles. Soon they won't have a mayor but a head scriptwriter. The President will be known as the Executive Producer. You'll get up an hour earlier to study your day's lines. Harold F. Fankel said his meter was bust but he would trust Cameron to pay him whatever he thought was the right fare down to 12th Street in the Village.

"Have a gamble, friend, ya pay me too much I win right? Ya pay me not anuff I lose, right?"

They zoomed into 12th Street, old-fashioned houses with high front steps, trees, window-boxes.

"This is it, friend," said Harold F. "Say, are you Asstraylyen wit' that accent?"

"I'm British, sir."

"Thank God ya ain't Polish."

"I see. Well, here's two dollars. How much do you overcharge Egyptians?"

Harold F. turned in his seat. He took the two dollars. "Be honest

84

wit' ya, I'm skinnin' ya forty cents this fare. Ya look like ya won't go hungery. Me I'm the Rabbin Hood kinda hackie, I take from the rich—be honest I take from the poor as well ony they don't use cabs."

They separated, laughing heartily. Everybody in Noo Yawk is laughing or fighting or hustling, none more so than Cameron, Lord of the Tiles, calling on his American mistress at an hour thought suitable for bed-hopping only by international hell-raisers and milkmen. Call me Dawn Juan!

He went up the steps into a small lobby, seeing a bank of zinc-fronted mailboxes and a console of bell-buttons. He checked the names. No decent British stock in the damned building at all? Greatest Jewish city in the world, of course. Muffled voice from grille. Loud buzzing sound. Nothing happens. Ring the bell again.

"What do I do now?" he addressed the grille.

Came the dull voice of Rapunzel: "Push the door when the bloody buzzer goes."

No stairs, only a lift. Security conscious. Linda Raskin says she's been burgled six times in four months. Junkies with fifteen-dollar habits. No Welfare State. When do you start calling it socialised medicine? Elevator? Well-known that British starlets, songsters, disc-jocks, band-leaders adopt strong American accents moment boat sights Statue of Liberty. Yet Charlie Chaplin lived here all these years and never took on slightest trace. Strength of identity?

She was wearing a dressing-gown, grey silk, knee-length. Her face was puffy, washed but not made-up, the eyes looking vulnerable and exposed without her specs. She had a small apartment, a jumbly living-room with record covers on the walls and odd-shaped McLuhan testaments on the table, a cupboard-sized bedroom, a kitchenette without a window. Cameron stood back against the wall while she fried some bacon and eggs. He made no move until they had eaten and she was pouring more black coffee. He put his fingers lightly round her wrist.

"This coffee is very hot," she said menacingly. He removed his hand.

"We've had breakfast together. You're compromised already. Nobody is ever going to believe we didn't."

"Look, Graham," she said, sitting at the far end of the table. "I'm 32, I've been through my messy years with men, I need something more meaningful—you can't play emotional piracy with my

85

life so for both our sakes just stop trying to parlay yourself into my bed. Right?"

"Check. We go coast to coast like brother and sister, that it?"

"Finish your cawfey and I'll be dressing."

Her taxi dropped him off at the Empire State Building. It was just after nine. As he got out of the cab she pressed his hand and gave him a poignant look, full of knowing and wanting and fearing. He stood in the blinding sunlight watching her head in the rear window of the zooming car. Isn't this typical of the creative artist, no commonsense, getting hooked on a frigid neurotic when the whole nation is jumping with lusty broads just desperate to wrap their thighs round young authors? Neurotics attract neurotics, they always say. Am I a neurotic? How can you tell?

He took the rocket elevators all the way to the top of the Empire State Building—the corny tourist bit, as Weber had called it, all those dentists from Omaha? He moved round the observation platform, not exactly scared of the height but all the same not resting his weight against the plate glass. New York's five boroughs were hidden by a smokey-orange smog, out of which poked a few skyscrapers looking like cacti on the painted desert. Buzzing-bee jetliners left black trails as they climbed out of the yellowy fog, as if from the sulphuric steams of an outer planet. Far away over the smog there was land and water, misty and blue. The earth seemed to be swimming in the sky. Moving his head slightly to see round a heavy spar which jutted out into space under the window, his eye momentarily fixed on some nuts and bolts. He had just been trying to remember how many feet the Empire State is said to sway—fourteen, is it—and idly he thought of fixing the end of the spar on to some landmark, just to find out if it was swaying at that moment. His eye kept latching on to the nuts and bolts, perfectly ordinary they were, inch and a half maybe. Wouldn't fancy going out there to tighten them up, he thought, stepping back a little from the glass. *Who tightened them up in the first place?* Oh my God!

His feet could sense the building moving rhythmically from side to side. Trying not to scream in panic, holding his breath, grimly forbidding his legs to run, he got back to the elevator door and kept his teeth tightly clenched until the bottom section elevator hit the deck. Out on the sidewalk in the sunshine he covered his gasping mouth with the palm of his hand. He looked up and felt giddy. The building was definitely falling towards him. How many blocks would you

86

have to run to be clear of it? A body would be less than a midge-stain under a mountain of concrete.

He caught sight of a big, healthy-looking guy in a window, dark hair, dark shirt, dark suit, you remember Jack Palance as Blackie the waterfront hoodlum in *Panic In The Streets*? That's what neurotics are looking like this year.

He went into the souvenir shop on the ground floor and picked up a few postcards that would stimulate the imaginations of his grand-children into trying to visualise their grandfather as a living, breathing man. He took them to the paydesk, where the girl asked for a dollar forty-five. He got out a single and a quarter and two dimes, quite pleased to be handling their currency so expertly. He got out on the sidewalk and started along Fifth Avenue.

"Hi, mister," a woman's voice yelled. In a flash he saw it, without having to turn, a typical New York broad daylight murder assault and he was going to be one of the fifty-seven passers-by who totally ignored the stabbed woman's frantic screams for help. "HI MISTER!" Jesus, it's easy to sneer in disgust when you read about it back home, but when you're actually *here*, you think you really would wade into three knife-wielding gorillas to defend some broad you never even heard of? "Hi, mister, wait a minute!"

The salesgirl came panting towards him.

"That was a twenny you gave me, mister," she said. "You got nineteen dollars to come."

She gave him the wad of singles. She had a nice, fat face, darkish, Italian stock maybe.

"They shouldn't let me out alone," he said, "this is the second time. Thank you very much."

"You're welcome."

"Let me buy you a ..."

"Sokay, I gotta rush back."

"Thanks again."

"You're welcome."

Twelve blocks' walk to the Rockefeller Center. Temperature about right for sidewalk egg-frying. Just for a moment Your Hero is dimly aware that by returning his nineteen dollars the salesgirl has shown him up for a fool. He is not sure why. He tells Howard about the incident, Howard in a fawn suit and Polaroid shades.

"Women take to you, Graham," says the sales vice-president, tak-ing his elbow and steering him to the elevators, "you'll just have to face up to it, boy, you're dynamite."

"Nah, it wasn't like that, Howard, I ..."

"I'll take your word for it. Now, Graham, this is the big one. We're seeing one of their top men, Anhalt, this is your pre-interview, it's very important, if Johnny Carson picks up a book in front of the cameras and says he likes it there's ten thousand people beating on shop doors next morning—if Carson says it's good America buys it. You just give this Anhalt guy a sample of the Cameron wit and charm, hit him where he laughs, baby."

"You mean this is an *audition*?"

"They like to have a chat with you, give Johnny a line on how to handle you. He's the tops in the talkshow game, he really knows how to handle people."

"That Mickey Spillane, he sure can handle women?"

"Can he?"

As the elevator climbed hypertense teevee veeps with clipboards got in and out, the kind who stare up at the lights on the numbers panel and click their fingers just to let the rest of us know they are too important to be wasting time like this.

"That English guy with the beard—Ustinov? He's been on Carson's show. You familiar with him?"

"Peter Ustinov? He's the one who says every time he goes to America he feels like an ancient Greek taking culture to Rome."

"Yeah, that's right, Peter Ustinov, the fat mimic."

They were shown into Mister Anhalt's office by a girl with very large breasts. She laughed a lot, but didn't explain the joke. It was a cluttered office, metal desks, no carpets, walls pinned with ratings charts and schedules.

"If I'd known I was auditioning I'd have brought my music and my pumps," Cameron said to Howard, who winked back, encouragingly. Mr. Anhalt came in, a very long man with dirty-blond hair long enough to be unAmerican, wearing a polo-necked fawn sweater and slip-on brogues which, after the usual amenities, were presented sole-on to Cameron as the lanky Mr. Anhalt got into the horizontal.

"Okay then," he drawled, "let's hear the kinda things you say."

Cameron looked at Howard and then at Mr. Anhalt, moving his head slightly to peer round the brogues.

"Graham did a coupla taped innerviews at the Washington book convention," Howard said eagerly. "They asked him about this swinging London bit, the permissive society, mini-skirts, all that jazz. He came across real good."

"What do you have to say about the mini-skirt?"

"Take it off, darling," Cameron said, patting pockets desperately for the fags. Lucky Strikes, this time. They seemed to amuse the two Americans. Howard didn't smoke. Mr. Anhalt was on Salem mentholated. Offering them around is not an American custom.

"How does Queen Elizabeth view all this permissive sex?"

"From the balcony of Buckingham Palace, I imagine. Wouldn't I be asked questions about the book?"

"Oh sure—you see authors aren't always good performers. Johnny has to have something he can bounce off."

"Why doesn't he get a trampoline?"

"You catch the show where he tried that new slippy polish? His audience loved that. Here's a question—is it difficult for a married man to stay faithful in London?"

"It depends who he's staying with."

Howard laughed, looking hopefully at Mr. Anhalt, who was staring straight ahead—at the ceiling. Mr. Anhalt looked like the kind of man who has not had a hearty laugh since the day he split his sides at Mom's funeral. Once he said 'not bad' as if they were having a script conference.

"Okay, I guess that's fine," he suddenly said, spilling his lean frame into the normal sitting position, at the same time jabbing at the buttons on his phone. "We'll be in touch with your office, we have the number."

He was in conversation with the party at the other end as they waved goodbye.

"They have to play it tough," Howard said in the descending elevator. "The whole world wants on Carson for the plugola."

"I'm beginning to feel like Dan Dailey playing a third-rate hoofer trying to break into Broadway." They were crossing Broadway at the time, stopping for a hamburger and coffee in a corner cafeteria staffed by tight-faced blacks and patronised by dead-faced whites of the middle generation.

They went on to the radio studio for the Harve Jackson show. A tough lady in dark glasses introduced Cameron to the other guests, two lady librarians who would be plugging their best-selling book on how to win at the dating game. Howard chatted easily to them, probably with the aim of gouging out vital trade information, sales-wise, outlets-wise, promotion-wise. The tough lady in the shades nodded for Cameron to follow her to the other end of the studio, a big dark room with a table and four tubular chairs and a control room behind plate glass. She had very good legs, this studio lady, real tension in the calf-muscles, lots of tendon play round the ankle. Her name was Betty.

"You look like a turned-on sort of guy," she said, voice low, "you wanna make a score?"

Jesus Christ, if they're this quick with unknown me, what are they like with Sinatra?

"Sure," he said, eyes crinkling knowingly, smilingly. "I'm on another radio show tonight—will I meet you afterwards?"

"Here—this is the number to call," she said, slipping a fold of paper in his palm. He put it away inside his passport, which he intended to carry at all times as magic token for warding off evil spirits and club-happy cops.

Harve Jackson arrived, a busy wee man with a checkered suit, the jacket draped over his shoulders, and dark glasses. He kissed the two librarians and let Cameron know with a quick 'shit' or two that he was a regular fella beneath all this Italian film director bit. They sat at the table and talked into mesh microphones, getting voice levels. Is a radio station really part of show biz? It may sound very glam but it's all down to spilling ashtrays and shirt-sleeves and guys making obscene gestures through the plate glass. Still, you gotta start somewhere, baby. Harve wanted them to talk about the different male-female relationships in America and Europe. The two lady librarians said that American man regarded woman as a boost to his ego, a sex-object, and a screen on which to project his own neurotic inadequacies. They said that in Europe gallant men were actually interested in women for their own sakes.

"In Britain," said Cameron, "I think it's true to say we regard women like good paintings or symphonies—the more you study them the more rewarding the experience."

"That's very significant," said Harve Jackson.

"You got in eleven separate plugs for the book title," Howard said as they left the building into the noisy heat of Broadway. In Fifth Avenue a group of enthusiastic people were holding out boxes for the Israeli fighting fund. Even in that heat there were two men in off-white raincoats.

"I'm a pacifist," Cameron said to the young man who was trying to collect.

"Tell that to Nasser, he's the goddam warmonger," said the young man.

"He's not very good at it, is he?" Cameron said, doing a matador's shimmy round the box.

90

"No, we punched the goddam fascist right on the snoot—and we'll keep on doing it!"

Howard took him to a Fifth Avenue bookstore. The manageress was delighted to meet him. They had two dozen copies of the book and tomorrow, official publication day, they would give him a nice display, with cards and all. Cameron signed all two dozen copies. Before the manageress could put them away again, a prosperous woman in her forties picked one up and had a look at his John Hancock. She looked at his photo on the jacket. She looked at him, then back at the photo. He froze internally. *The spotlight is on you!* The woman put the book down and took a copy of *The Confessions of Nat Turner* to the paydesk. He wanted to go after her, demand why she hadn't bought his book, the stupid bitch.

Howard left him in Fifth Avenue, arranging to meet him at eleven thirty for the Barry Gray show. Cameron walked back towards Hotel Lugubrious. The temperature was in the nineties. Tomorrow he would try to see U.N.O. building and the Statue of Liberty. This fame business is very tiring.

"I thought it would be one big round of cocktail parties," he said as he got undressed. "Artificial, superficial, soulless—right up my street."

"Your true writers do not crave for the starlet life," the other voice said. "J. D. Salinger has never been interviewed and hardly photographed. B. Traven had so much self-respect he didn't even admit to John Huston that he was B. Traven."

"As Rocky Marciano said, it's easy to be polite when you're heavyweight champeen of the world."

He had a cold shower. It was about four thirty. He lay naked on the bed. *Let's hear the kinda things you say!* Lift your skirt, girlie, ya wanna part or donchya? Your true writers have lots of pigskin luggage and go for cruises out of which come Somerset Maugham-type book club choices. They always travel alone and get to chat to all sorts of interesting people. I just hate being alone, that's all. You're never alone with the *New York Times*. You think I came all this was to read bloody newspapers!

The *New York Times* comes in sections, on the principle that if God had meant us to read American newspapers he would have given us hydraulic arms. The typography, if that is the word for thin type in thin grey columns, is like the dullest ever edition of the *Daily Telegraph*. The headlines are written by failed authors of park notices: The word fiscal was used a lot. MILWAUKEE WHITES JEER RIGHTS

MARCH ... WAR FOES TO TRY TO SHUT PENTAGON ... WILSON ASSUMES REINS IN CABINET SHIFT ... Takes Direct Responsibility In Hope Of Easing Spurt In British Unemployment ... JOBLESS REACH 559,000 ... From here it smells of Ruritania, an Ealing comedy. Dead U.S. Nazi leader Lincoln Rockwell was to be buried in a National Military Cemetery at Culpeper, Va, shot dead by one of his own blackshirts. Joe Namath of the Jets was accused of punching an editor in a bar. Charles B. Darrow, inventor of Monopoly, had died at 78. They sold forty-eight million sets. We played on one of them in Aunt Jean's house in the tenement, New Year, uncles arguing whether if the air raid siren went was it better to get under the table or run down the stairs to the street shelters? Boston Red Sox slugger Carl Yastrzemski was honored at Yankee Stadium when neighbours from Bridgehampton L.I. presented him with a T.V. set and a convertible. The Red Sox beat the Yankees 3-0, keeping them only one percentage point behind Minnesota Twins at the top of the American league. There was a whole-page ad for the National Guard:

> *The tragic and violent events of this summer have no parallel in the history of our country. Shots are fired from rooftops and houses. Stores are looted. Cities are aflame. The law is ignored ... If snipers shoot the Guard is prepared to face it. If armed territories must be flushed out and disarmed the Guard is prepared to face it. If battle-plans must be made for city streets the Guard is prepared to face it. The horror of American firing upon American is almost too grim to contemplate. We hope that day will never come again. We pray our cities will not become battlefields. But if it does happen, if havoc is repeated in our streets, the National Guard will, as always, respond.*
>> *Order will be maintained.*
>> *The people will be protected.*
>> *The laws of the nation will be upheld.*
>> *Rest assured.*

The soft bleep of the phone woke him from a short doze. It was Howard. They had an unscheduled radio show at seven. Could he make that?

"I'll try to tear myself away from the giddy round of cocktail parties."

"I like your style, Graham."

He took a cab to the address Howard had given him in East 57th

Street and found himself sitting at a round table in a cable-strewn room. The other guest on the show was an assistant from the King's County D.A.'s office. The host, a small man with silken grey hair, wanted to know why the D.A.'s office couldn't break up the Brooklyn Mafia. The Assistant D.A., a plump man in a double-breasted blue suit, looked like a bookmaker. Sitting close behind him was an aide, a younger man who muttered occasionally in his superior's left ear. They were both in possession of fat briefcases. The Assistant D.A. said there was only one problem—getting people to talk. He delved into his briefcase and brought out a sheet of paper, from which he read the names and addresses of the top six Brooklyn Mafia families. These known criminals were so fiendishly unscrupulous as to refuse to provide the necessary evidence for prosecution, but the honest people of Brooklyn could rest assured that relentless war was being waged on the forces of organised crime, at this very moment in time. Cameron was so interested he didn't realise for a moment that they were now on to the subject of his book.

"Your novel—published tomorrow by Tannenbaum Publishing at six ninety-five—is set against the background of the swinging London of mini-skirts and permissive sex and rock singers like the Beatles. Whatever happened to the England we associated with bowler hats?"

"This is one of the themes I was trying to cover in my book, *The New Ladies' Man*," said Our Hero. Behind the host Howard was holding up a copy of the book, tapping the title and nodding furiously. "The British have always been the most sexually active people in the northern hemisphere," Cameron went on, watching their faces for laughter. "Well the idea with my hero, *The New Ladies' Man*, was to show that beneath the bowler hat there always has been this sheer cauldron of raw lust and passion." His palms were wet. Nobody smiled. In fact the Assistant D.A. was nodding in corroboration. "I suppose the thing is if you're ruling half the world you can't afford to let the lesser races find out how truly immoral their masters are."

"That's most significant."

Seven plugs for the title was Howard's count. "Is that true about Kinsey—you English being the great Casanovas?" he asked. They were in the street headed for the Barry Gray show.

"God knows, I hadn't heard it before myself. It just came out."

"You said it with conviction, that's what matters."

"Unless Dr. Kinsey was listening in."

"I believe he's dead."

"We're all right then."

They waited in a corridor while Barry Gray interviewed an earlier guest about silver. Howard kept saying the Barry Gray show was one of the most important in New York but not to worry, he was a real nice guy. Cameron kept going to the water faucet farther up the corridor and wiping clammy hands on his trousers. He smoked so much his tongue and lips became numb and painfully hot at the same time. They could hear the other interview on the tannoy. Big stars don't happen by accident, you know. The tension behind the scenes is killing. All the time you're thinking you have to plug the book and sound witty and pleasant and justify the money they've spent bringing you over and not offend anyone and, worst of all, the real killer, *you must not dry up.* Howard thinks it's easy. Jesus Christ, I can't remember *anything.* Stop grinning at me Howard or I'll kick your teeth in. I should have stayed home.

Barry Gray has read the book. He likes it. He is tall and ruggedly handsome. He can be rough on people who use his show for blatant plugging but Cameron, an instinctive trouper, realises this and falls into a country cousin routine. Barry Gray is amused to see how many times Cameron the shambling but peasant shrewd hick can slip in a plug for the title. *The technicians laugh.* Front pages of *Variety* roll off the presses in a montage of thundering trains and stamping audiences.

Barry Gray comes over and says he liked the show. He says Cameron ought to take two weeks out of the tour and see the greatness of this country and the only way to do that is by car. He says his father was a Russian who left home to avoid the czarist draft and just kept on travelling west till he reached America. He says he would be happy to have Cameron back on the show after the tour and give his impressions of America. They shake hands. The elevator takes the new star down to the night street.

"Okay baby," says Our Hero, snapping finger and thumb, "where do we go to unwind—champagne and showgirls at Sardis, huh? You really thought it was good, did you?"

"Fourteen plugs in twenty-five minutes, Graham baby," says Howard. "That's plugging, in my book."

It's only one fifteen a.m. and he's rushing off home! He'll have to buck up a bit if he wants to stay on this ballsquad. Never mind. I have an ace in the hole. I let Howard drop me at the hotel. We go in a cab driven by elderly negro Junior Maggs. As American cabs are not direct descendants of m'lord's carriage or sedan chair, there is no

94

glass distinction between driver and passenger. Junior Maggs, great shoulders hunched over the wheel and head stuck forward to avoid contact with the roof, hears Howard tell me not to go wandering at this hour and me replying that not everybody in New York is a thief, witness my nineteen dollar incident at the Empire State. I see this Junior Maggs itching to get in on the discussion so I ask him if he thinks everybody in New York is a thief.

"Yessir, that's a safe assumption," he says, his deep voice quaintly formal.

"Cabbies know the score," says Howard, not quite addressing Junior Maggs but not entirely ignoring him either.

"Muggers, is it?" I ask black and white.

"Yessir," says Junior Maggs, "but I have myself insurance against them now."

"What's that?"

"This, sir," his free hand coming up from the seat holding a big black pistol. I duck sideways.

"You wouldn't actually use that, would you?" I say, sounding like Dame Dimity Daffodil.

"Not in the cab. I have been stuck up by bad mens three times and as we only carries fifteen dollars or so the punks always get sore and they raps you on the haid. So I got myself this insurance. Next time a punk takes to busting my skull I'll let him get out on the sidewalk then I ventilate him."

He tells us that very afternoon he's been in a bookie parlour up in Yonkers and he sees the precinct captain coming in and going into the john with the manager and coming out smiling.

"It's pay-off day for the cap'n. Five minutes later in comes the sergeant and he goes to the john and he comes out smiling. Then the patrolman goes in and comes out smiling. It's pay-off day for everybody in blue! I tell you, gents, my considered assumption is that everybody in New York is a thief."

They drop me at the hotel. Howard takes the cab on to Grand Central. I get to the phone and dial the number given to me by Betty at the Harve Jackson show. All this action after midnight makes me feel like Tony Curtis hustling around for J. J. Hunsecker in *The Sweet Smell of Success*. A girl's voice.

"Is that Debbie? My name's Cameron. Betty told me to ring you."

"Betty's here's right now."

Okay baby, give with the address and Hotshot is on his way over.

"Hi."

"Hullo. Graham Cameron here, the Turned On Kid."

"Lissen, sweetheart, Debbie's connection didn't show today, you ring again Thursday, okay?"

She rings off! I stare at the phone. It becomes clear to me the lady is pushing cannabis resin for money! Sirens sound in the street. I bang down the phone thinking it's the Phone Tapping Squad of the Narcotics Bureau. The night clerk gives me a phone message. Chuck Brown is in the Oak Room of the Plaza Hotel. Who needs sleep? I think momentarily of tipping off the cops anonymously about the Debbie and Betty drug ring. It was her gams I was after not her joints. I grab a cab outside the hotel. The foyer of the Plaza is a home-going outflow of coat-fetching, fur-draped, hand-pumping, silver-haired extras from those films where stuffy bankers finally nodded gleefully and tapped their feet to previously despised jive bands. The Oak Room is cathedral-heavy and brown and empty apart from Chuck. He is big and towering and glassy-eyed. He says he thought I might just be on my ownsome. I say I've been too busy becoming a celebrity to accept the many offers of quick screws Manhattan has been throwing up. We get them down very fast. I wonder if he'll take me to the penthouse suite of hundred-dollar-a-night call-girls. A cheap Puerto Rican whorehouse on the lower East Side will be just as acceptable. He says nothing in that direction. He stares at me moodily. I try not to smile too much. I don't know why. The waiter says they are closing up. We get another two double shots out of him. Chuck suddenly asks me if I've got peace of mind.

"Piece of ass would be more like it," I say.

"No, man, peace of mind."

"What a bizarre notion. What does it mean?"

"You've a lot to learn, fella. I read your book, passable stuff, a mite derivative but still okay. And you don't know a goddam thing."

Chuck's eyes are glassy and his head tends to hang sideways but he's articulate enough. Anyway, he says do I want to come back to his place in the Village and have a last snort or two? I visualise hippy girls looking like Red Indians. I'm sure this Chuck has a real scene going for him. Milton told me he's the youngest vice-president Two-World ever had, forty thousand a year and an open expense account. These bigtime P.R. guys are nothing better than filthy procurers. Lead me to it.

The cab shoots off down Fifth Avenue. Steam leaks from manhole covers. Gotham City is still boiling up a storm. The cabbie's name is

Angelo Piscari. He wears a flat leather cap and a brown jerkin. He guns the cab from one set of red lights to the next, swooping from lane to lane in vicious competition with the one or two other cars still cruising the dark wet avenues. Angelo Piscari's picture on the licence card is that of a hard-eyed rat, the kind that normally goes with a side-profile and a stencilled number. We stop in front of a modern apartment block. The way Angelo Piscari stops it's like a jet catching on the carrier tripwire.

"Dallar fifty," he snaps.

"My ass a dollar fifty," Chuck snaps back.

"Wanna checkameeder, mac?"

"Screw your meter, fella. It's a dollar twenty fare."

Their strained faces are so close I think they're going to take bites out of each other. I get out on the sidewalk. Money presumably changes hands. I keep well away. Chuck comes out of the car. He bends down and shouts in the window:

"Up yours ya pig."

Angelo Piscari replies in kind. The cab shoots off.

"All that for thirty cents," I say.

"You never give a goddam inch in this man's town," Chuck says. We go up in the elevator. There are no girls looking like Joan Baez in Chuck's apartment. It is where he lives during the week. He has a wife and children in a house upstate, too far to commute daily. There is a sitting-room with a couch, two chairs, a table and a sideboard. Out of this Chuck gets a bottle of John Jamieson. He wipes out two glasses with his finger. Ice and water seem irrelevant. He belts a big one into himself and starts taking his clothes off! Then I realise his intentions are hygienic. Twice before he gets into the shower, which is off to the left in a small bathroom-lavatory, he tells me about his Irish ancestry. It seems to mean something special to him. Not only are there no Greenwich Village hippies or high-class film company call-girls or halter-necked mistresses, there is nothing personal in the apartment at all, no pictures, no books, no knick-knacks of any kind. Feeling bitter I say that Jack Kennedy might have made Irish origins fashionable in the U.S. but back home among the Orange Lodges we wouldn't boast about bog beginnings. He doesn't like this. He comes out of the shower in a knee-length robe, white. He looks a little like Jack Palance in *The Big Knife*.

"Jack Kennedy was somebody special, fella, don't you ever forget it," Chuck says, three times. He rams down another big one and says he's hitting the sack so goodnight.

"Great party," I say, churlishly.

So I'm on the sidewalk in Lexington Avenue. I see a brightly lit glass and metal phone-box. In London it would have been vandalised to the nth degree and stinking of piss and last week's halitosis. I don't know what time it is but I've had enough not to care. I get into this bright phone-box and get through to Weber's number without effort.

"Hi," she says. "I caught you on the Barry Gray show. You're beginning to sound like the other half of a vaudeville act."

"I'm in Lexington Avenue. Where's that?"

So the next thing I know I'm in her apartment again. I may have taken a cab, I may have walked. Anyway, I'm there. She's in a nylon nightie. I think it's the one she had on that time in Washington. She gets quite motherly about me not having eaten all day. She gives me a cold can of beer and I lean in the door of the kitchenette and watch her cocky American movements and I think of teeth-braces and bobby-sox and junior proms and crushes on Dick Haymes and heavy petting in Pop's Packard and *Forever Amber* read by torchlight under the blanket at summer camp and sophomores and freshmen and alumni and girls most likely not to. My brain is zinging. I move into the galley and slap her bottom, saying in her ear that my real name is M'Lord George Thighfondler.

"Down boy," she says firmly.

"I'm in love with you," I say, with sincerity.

"Down boy."

"We almost did it in Washington," I say, protestingly.

"That was a big mistake."

"Look, why do I keep coming here for bacon and eggs if I'm not going to make love to you?"

"Maybe I'm a sucker for lame dogs. But that doesn't mean bed."

I am not a lost dog I keep telling Thomas C. Deems in the cab. Telling him quite angrily as well. This Thomas C. Deems was in Shaftesbury, England—during the Hitler war? Friendliest, nicest folks he ever did meet. What's the hell's that got to do with her calling me a lost dog, I demand. He's so friendly I could clout him. He won't take the money, says folks in Shaftesbury, England, were real decent to him, during the Hitler war? Course you gotta hustle to make a buck in Noo Yawk City but if you can't repaya kindness here and there wotsa point, huh? I give him up as a noddy. I think the next thing I know is I'm in bed. I don't even think there's any T.V. to be found at whatever hour of the day or night it may be. I am half drunk and totally perplexed. Is it something wrong with me? Ridiculous!

I made a false start, is all. Tomorrow I'm coming back fighting!

So there's this blonde babe works in Howard's section, about 25, sallow complexion, flat nose, big chest and beam end so wide she looks like one of those little doll-men who wouldn't lie down. She caught me on some show or another and told me, in the corridor, how amusing I had been.

"I'm better in the flesh," I said. "How about having a drink with me?"

"I'd *love* to."

So we meet in the bar of a restaurant round the corner, sitting on high stools, half the battle won.

"I don't use liquor in any form," she says.

For all its mighty flow of exported culture America has kept some domestic secrets. She explains that a Doctor Pepper is a bottle of pop. While we're on this subject I tell her I've always been puzzled by something called The Good Humor Man in American novels.

"The ice-cream vendor."

"Is *that all*? I thought he might be some semi-mythical harbinger of spiritual hope to the tenements."

I have a couple of Jack Daniel's but it isn't the same with a tee-totaller beside you. Roxanne is wearing a Russian peasant blouse that shows off enough chest and arm to make the drink unnecessary. We talk about this and that, mainly that man Milton Tannenbaum. She is crazy for Milt! By the time we get to the cafeteria by the Central Park Zoo we are talking about sexual relationships with all the un-hibited zeal of professional panderers. Tonight I will be Stilt Cham-berswain of the Harem Globe *Frotteurs*, I think, eyeing her mighty knockers.

"What's your sign?" she demands as we take our trays to the out-side terrace. She is not referring to the ominous bulge under my left navel—no, she is an astrology buff. From a floppy leather bag possibly gussetted and tooled by Navajo Indians she produces a very large, leather-bound tome and six weighty pieces of brass. It's some Chinese sage's mystic key for peeking into the future. She proceeds to chuck these pieces about the table, checking each random juxta-position in her book. Brass clatters against crockery. I see several straight citizens watching us uneasily. I have only three radio shows and two Jack Daniel's behind me that day. I don't feel like a celebrity, I don't feel drunk, I just feel like *me*. I freeze internally. The woman is a nut. It isn't so bad when we get off the terrace and walk through the bushes in the dusk, taking a chance on Mayor Lindsay's word that the parks are back to us. We hold hands. She tells me a great deal about astrology, macrobiotic diets, meditation. We agree that Peace and Love are imperatives. My hand steals round her waist. Shall I take her here in the heart of muggersville, my first American fuck, under a Manhattan bush?

"You ought to know I only screw with father figures," she says chattily.

"I am the father of two children," I murmur passionately.

"With younger men I have a role conflict," she says confidingly.

Gabble gabble. Two more drinks and I might have tripped her up and banged into whatever section was uppermost but even a sex maniac has his pride. Besides, she might spread it round the office. We part around ten o'clock. I ignore her hints about some macrobiotic carrot bar in the Village. I get over to a place called the Absinthe House where Chuck has told me he hoists a few of an evening. He is there with some of the film crowd. It is dark and smokey and toxic. We play spoof for rounds of drinks, fourteen of us, each round costing about twenty bucks. Some of us go on to the Oak Room of the Plaza. I ask Chuck straight out where I can find a New York whore. He says forget the whores, he'll fix me up with a great broad. The waiter brings the phone to the table. I find myself speaking to some cheery-voiced charmer called Mary. Sure, she'd be reely deloited to meet me. I'm at the Plaza, I say. I'm in Scranton, Noo Jersee, she says. I hold my hand over the phone and hiss urgently at Chuck. How long will it take me to get to Scranton, New Jersey? With my credit card I can hire a car and drive the sixty miles or so in less than an hour. But I have no credit cards and cannot drive. Chuck declines to chauffeur me. Goodbye, Mary, see you when I next drop by Scranton. I bomb out of the Plaza and go up to the first cabbie and say where's a place a man can get a whore in this town? Son, I cud take ya ta cheap hookers but whassa prafit in gittin' the clap an' yur head kickt in an' rolled, huh? Go home an' sleep it aff, mac; stay hellty.

Lost lamb is pressing Weber's button. Passes out on leather couch. Wakes up in darkness, thinks fast, blearily but craftily pads through to her bedroom, arms crossed in front in the clever fashion of the blind, whacks toe on chair leg, stifles agonised yelp, slips daintily into her bed, grabs hold like limpet. Commotion. Lights go on. Blink and mumble. Sorry, sorry. Won't happen again. Dress as best I can, crash off into night, cab to Hotel Mortis, find sleep possible only with lights on, television on, bed vibrator on....

For at least half a day Cameron was prepared to face the fact that he was an inferior being, worthless by average standards let alone fitted for elevation to fame. The cure came in a radio studio. This show was an hour-long dabble in nostalgia. The host was a gentle little man in his middle forties. He had very small, white hands and a sad little smile. Give him his due, he was the only American so far to have heard of anything pre-dating Danny Kaye. They discussed Busby Berkley, Harry James, the Andrews Sisters, Bessie Smith, Laird Cregar, the Three Stooges, Spike Jones and the City Slickers, Phil Harris—ad-libbing cut-offs and new openings to allow for the splicing in of old records and bits of film soundtrack.

"That was a genuine treat, sincerely," said the host. "I believe we could do a whole month of shows with you."

"That's very flattering of you to say so."

"Can we have a moment's talk, alone?" He's going to ask me to join the studio gang in the bar at the corner of the block, Cameron thought quickly. It'll be a crowd of witty, cynical downbeat writers from T.V. and radio—Walter Matthau in a *Face in the Crowd*—I always did fancy the Patricia Neal type. They went out into the corridor and stopped by the faucet. The little man looked up and down.

"I envy you, you know that?" he said, making the effort to look Cameron in the eye. Our Hero was immediately alerted. "I know this town, how it works. You have it all over you, Graham, success. You're going to make your mark on this town."

Aw shucks, fella. It's true but what's your angle?

"You know, Graham, my life isn't what it might seem to you. I work in these studios, radio—you don't get to meet a lot of people— it isn't like teevee—no glamor. You're going to be a big celebrity, you'll be asked to parties, the whole world will want to know you. There's one helluva big favor you can do for me."

"If I can, of course."

"Graham, you'll be asked to so many parties—you think you can take time out to remember me? A short phone-call to the studio here? Really, I never get asked to parties, you believe that? So many doors will be open to you. It would be nothing to you but so much to me. It isn't a lot to ask, is it? A quick call—say, Bill, you want to come along to a nice party with me tonight? I could come as your friend. My life is so dull."

"I haven't been asked to any parties yet—"

"Success is written all over you, Graham, New York's most exciting doors are going to open wide to let you through."

"Okay, Bill."

"Thanks, Graham, I mean it. From here."

He patted his chest, left.

It felt great to be back on the fame train again.

Maybe so, but that night ended in the usual fashion. You go through such hell in your pre-recognition days I'm surprised we big stars have even a spark of decency left in us by the time the autograph books are out.

I slept on Weber's couch that night. My hotel room had become a place for which Tannenbaum Inc. was paying fifteen bucks a night toothbrush-storage rental. I told Weber about the sad little interviewer, over breakfast. She came on all strong with compassion for New York's lonely nobodies. I think—okay, Miss Bleeding Heart, let's turn a little of this abstract humanitarianism in my personalised direction. I put on my sad spaniel eyes and move quickly round the table, not overplaying it, just a little sob or two.

"Jesus Christ, Graham, what do you wanna shove your hands down my boobs for? What's with you for Gad sakes? Now sit down and finish your cawfey."

"Thanks for the mammary," I say, grinning stupidly. Frankly I'm beginning to understand why we sensitive writers drink so much.

Chapter Nine

IT SHOULD ALWAYS BE REMEMBERED THAT WHEN DIAMOND JIM BRADY WAS THROWING THOSE ORGIES WITH BROADS LEAPING OUT OF CAKES HE WAS ACTUALLY DOING SALES-PROMOTION FOR RAILWAY ROLLING STOCK MANUFACTURED IN BRITAIN. AT LEAST IN THOSE DAYS WE WERE MAKING SOME PROFIT OUT OF AMERICA'S MORBID ATTITUDE TO SEX.

So here was our mixed-up hero on Friday afternoon waiting for Chuck on the lover level of Grand Central Station, instead of squiring his best American gal to somewhere lovey-dovey like Coney Beach or Yankee Stadium.

"I cannot see you over the weekend, Graham,' she had said. "My mother is coming across from New Jersey."

"I'm glad somebody in your wretched family knows how to come across," he had muttered savagely.

Then Chuck had asked him to spend Labor Weekend with the Brown family in upstate New York and our keen student of celebrity shennanigans accepted with alacrity, knowing full well that upper income-bracket show-biz Americans screw around like mad things, once the kids are hustled off to bed and the barbecue ashes hauled. You find his attitude immoral, unfeeling, disgusting? The way he saw it, he was just a normal married man given the chance of a life-time to live it up a little—if you're going to have a bit on the side, where could be safer than the other side of the Atlantic? In fact, he had even comforted himself with the thought that the first Mrs. Tanqueray would be positively proud to know he had not just succumbed to the temptations of faceless flesh-pressing, not just gone rubbing bellies with nellies, but had fallen for a woman of taste and dignity. Sally Weber isn't going to be just another nautch on the gun, he thought, oh no, she's got class, the frigid bitch. He lit a cigarette and watched whole populations of successful New Yorkers knocking off for the holiday weekend. Several hundreds of these affluent hedonists—it was only three thirty in the afternoon—took time from the homeword *blitzkrieg* to check market-price adjustments on a closed-circuit T.V. screen which links the station with Wall Street. Whole fortunes might have been wiped out in the duration of a cab-ride. Like Ol' Joe Kennedy I got mine in cash, Our Hero thought, superciliously scanning the tense faces of the stock-market puppets. *I got mine* ... a neatly murderous phrase remembered from a book about Chicago by Nelson Algren, America's only living novelist worth a fart, he mused, bleakly amused by his own awareness that two hundred thousand bucks can buy an awful lot of socialist ... a smaller truth became clear from study of the American male in droves; the reason even a deaf European can always spot an American is that their tailoring is based on right-angles—shoulders, sleeves, trousers, heads even—all corners square to the ninetieth degree. The only exceptions to this national geometry were the two lounging cops, one young and Italian dark, the other fat-bellied and Irish red; perhaps it was the uniform, more likely the guns, but they seemed superior to the commuter race, noncomformist, even artistic, the superficial indolence of their stances pointing up the whiplash intensity of their eyes. The artist and the policeman, both watch the mass, and who is to say which knows the greater truth? This city looks fast at first but soon you find you can beat all the sheep across the street from a standing start, when Big Brother changes DON'T WALK to WALK. The cabbies talk tough but you just tell them to drive to the nearest pre-cinct station and the meter suddenly works again. Look at that pathetic little bastard who wanted to be taken to parties. What does he drag down a year—twenty or thirty thousand? I could out-hustle most of them, knock off a block-buster best-seller once a year, wow 'em on the shows, get a penthouse over the park, some decent clothes—give me a couple of weeks to suss out the scene and I'll be passing on my old telephone numbers to Warren Beatty. There's plenty of it about—look at that mother and daughter team, for instance, New York's full of mother and daughter teams, the girl is bare-legged and milk-toothed and ripe-fleshed and berry-brown and highly pluckable, the mother is formally elegant in a severe suit and hard-tanned skin that might have been made from lampshades, you'd have to marry the girl to gain entrée but the main course would be mother-in-law, the old vampire queen, I'll show Tennessee Williams what depravity really means—

"Let's hustle we got but a minute," Chuck snapped. They raced to the correct platform—or track—and bustled to the top end of the open carriage. The train started. A little man came up the carriage and plonked a large, battered suitcase on the floor beside them. Chuck jumped out of his seat. Cameron had a blinding awareness that Chuck was now the Hero of Mad Bomber's Commuter Train Mass Slaughter

Bid. He shut his eyes in anticipation of the blast. The little man told Chuck to hold it a minute. Cameron opened his eyes. Out of the open case the little guy was pulling bottles and paper cups. Ice cubes came from a plastic sack. A bad-tempered queue of strong, noisy men stretched all the way down the gangway. Out of the case came whisky, gin, bourbon, rye, vodka. Chuck was the first to be served. He handed Cameron a paper cup of bourbon.

"It's the only way to fly, fella."

"I thought you had club bars where tensed-up Madison Avenue execs got plastered before getting home to John O'Hara country. I often wondered—are these club bars for members only?"

"Not on this train. I got you the stuff, dint I, what's your beef? Uncle Chuck won't let you die of thirst."

The train came out of a long tunnel. The line was on the same level as the top storeys of dark old tenements held together by skeins of fire escape ironwork. Negro women leaned out of open windows. In the concrete playgrounds of the new blocks and in the wide, dirty streets the long-legged children were all black. If New York is integrated, he thought, the deep south must be something else.

The little man beside them ran out of ice. Large men with button-down collars and boyish crew-cuts over gin-glowed faces said bad-tempered things that in placid Britain would have caused fist fights. The little man showed no emotion. He got off at the first stop. Chuck said he would catch the next train back to Grand Central, doing it over and over again.

The train had green windows to shade the commuting hordes from the sun. They went up the side of the Hudson, seeing the red cliff-face of the Palisades, on top of which cool conifers shaded the elegant mansions of Mafia overlords.

"Fancy another?" Cameron said.

"No more now till we hit Albany. Sorry."

"Ah ha." From his travelling bag, top grain cowhide, thirty-eight dollars from Fifth Avenue, Everybody's Hero produced a quart bottle of Jack Daniel's. "I thought there might be anxious moments between bars."

"You son of a bitch! There's a pickle of brains under that fungus."

They drank the bourbon out of the paper cups and hardly noticed that the air-conditioning had failed. The farther north they went the more the scenery looked like the Highlands of Scotland and the more relaxed Chuck became. By the time they reached the station they were both as relaxed as newts. Chuck's wife was there to meet them with the car, a decently battered old wreck with one door that wouldn't open and another that wouldn't shut. Chuck's wife was about 35, plump and dark. They all sat together on the front seat, Chuck driving, a good pint of liquor in him but giving Our Hero no cause for alarm, especially as his eagerly furtive eyes were revelling in her tightly-skirted thighs and nyloned kneecaps. She was that kind of Italian woman who accompanies a joke with a pull at the man's ear or a slap on his knee. They drove on and on across the rolling tree country of upstate New York, Cameron making with the wit, Maria bashing him heartily, Chuck steering and singing like a *Wages of Fear* truckie coming back empty with the loot.

The Brown residence was a wooden, two-storey house with a field and barn at the back. They had dinner that night with some of Chuck's neighbours, eating round an old kitchen table. The floor was of red flagstones. There was a long black kitchen range. He woke up in a little farmhouse bedroom with the windows open and a slight breeze moving white net curtains. Looking out in the dazzlingly clear sunshine he saw Chuck in blue denims and a white-shirt sitting on a power-driven mower. Cameron dressed, thinking that with all his new money he ought to buy at least one change of clothes.

When he appeared in the kitchen Maria was in a red blouse and white slacks, working at the sink unit.

"Morning." Cameron stood back, diffidently.

"Sit down for your breakfast—have you had genuine American pancakes with maple syrup?"

"Oh ... well, not exactly, I—"

Chuck came in, loud and cheery.

"Feeling kinda brittle this morning, Graham?" He opened the tall fridge, bringing out two long cans of beer. "This will straighten you out."

Cold Budweiser and sweet pancakes covered with hot syrup, four thick slices of bacon on top—not the drunken introvert's usual breakfast but anything less than hearty relish would have been churlish not to say subversive. Sheer bravery carried him past the first mouthful and after the beer and a few cups of black coffee the hangover, stupid European self-indulgence, was gone.

At one end of the patch about eight or nine assorted youths were chucking an American football about. Our Hero, onetime sportsman and no mean performer with the round ball, sat on a deckchair to watch. One of the boys would take the oval ball, bend down, then backheel it to a line of three others. They would slash it quickly to each other while the rest tried to block and intercept. They all used the slow galloping stride of the American gridiron and it was not hard to imagine them, in ten years time, with heavy shoulder padding and helmets and calf-revealing tights. Some of them could have been only eight or nine but they worked at it seriously as if under the eye of a stern coach. Cameron felt very British and amateurish. He walked down to the bottom of the lawn, waving to Chuck on the mower. There was an old wreck of a barn at the bottom of the Brown property. He flung his leg over a sagging wire fence and walked into a rough, hilly meadow. He came to a small pond. He heard several splashes and kept still among the weeds until he saw a large frog jump into the grassy shallows. He climbed a small knoll and sat down.

To his left was the tilted wreck of an old wooden cart, the long narrow kind with four high wheels, the wood bleached from years of American weather. Looking round to make sure he was not being watched he went forward and lay on his stomach in the tall, blue-grey grass growing round the long-silent cart. From that angle it could have been a pioneering wagon; he could see absolutely nothing of the twentieth century. He raised his head and peered through the feathery forest of dancing grass ears. Those must be the Catskill Mountains, a misty blue against the lighter blue of the sky, just as the first explorers must have seen them, a view the Indians would have known a thousand years ago, the rustle of grass and the buzzing of the insects, the cool brush of delicate grass feathers against his chin, a black horse grazing steadily in the pasture ahead, a white cloud travelling east, the air as clear as he had not remembered it since he was a boy back home; he lay and stared at the sheer size of the far mountains and the unbelieveable height of the white-traced sky. It was not his imagination—he had never been able to see so far or so high in his life. Yet how *could* the sky be higher over America than over Britain?

Then, in the afternoon, driving with Chuck along rough country roads, the sun so undiluted that Black Aberdeen Angus heifers in a sloping field became two-dimensional cut-outs back projected on to an electrically green screen ... to a town that was clean and white, no billboards or neon signs allowed on Main Street, whose liquor store had bullseye windows ... not the America of Greasy Thumb Guzik or Blue Jaw Magoon but a dreaming afternoon of a town with an old coaching hotel from whose timbered entrance might emerge Red-coat officers in powdered wigs ... a small black and white dog crossed

Main Street in leisurely fashion, disdaining its road drill ... a car moved out of a shrub-bounded parking lot and the eyes got a slight shock, as if something from the next studio lot had crossed over into the wrong set ... we keep calling this a new country, yet they were using this Main Street before Johnson and Boswell toured the Highlands by stage-coach and Mayfair was a footpad's swamp ...

They parked on the other side of the deserted street from what could have been a middling-old Devon inn. Chuck said there was no need to lock the car. They laughed at some recollection of big city excesses as they crossed the empty road.

I CAN'T GET
NO—OH
SAT—ISFACTION

Bang bang bang.

Out of the dreaming afternoon. Into the pounding beat. Two mare-headed G.I.s dancing merrily with two girls. Booths, with bits of old leather and harness brass. Men in shirt sleeves. A college gang packed shoulder to shoulder, their life and soul half-standing as he shouts something that makes the guys guffaw and snigger and avoid the eyes of the patient waitress. Two middle-aged women, heads almost touching over the table. Through to the darkened bar at the back. A right-angled bar and a solid line of hunched shoulders. Men on stools.

"Hey, fella, willya haul yar ass over here and give us a drink!"

So this is where the dreaming people are.

Take the schooners to a booth. Talk about books and various topics of common interest to men. Drink slowly. Chuck in jeans and white T-shirt, unshaven.

"Hey, honey, over here."

Hand on tilted hip, tray dangling down aproned thigh.

"Whatsitabee, gents?"

"Ehm, two beers, please—and—what do you want to eat, Chuck?"

"Two jumbo-burgers."

"Hey, does your fren come from England?"

"That's right."

"You know the Beatles?"

"The name is familiar. What do they look like?"

"You must be a teevee comic."

"Why?"

"You don't make me laff, that's why." Departs.

Returns. Several times.

"What's a nice girl like you doing in a place like this?"

"Waitin' for Mister Right."

"Okay, what time do you finish—I'll take you to a nightclub, show you the town."

"A nightclub? In this burg? Anyway, you look kinda tricky to me. Would a girl be safe?"

"No, but I'll give you my Ringo Starr autograph."

"The real nitty-gritty, huh? You English guys know the way to a girl's heart. Two more beers?" Departs.

"That approach of yours has all the makings of a novelty item."

Beer isn't drinking. Didn't F. Scott seclude himself in hotel to write and stay sober? And didn't he succeed, even if room-service was sending up thirty-two bottles of beer a day?

Sit on stone patio reading *New Republic*, their *New Statesman*. At this level Americans do not joke. British long ago turned death into carnival to maintain equilibrium. Americans haven't been killing people long enough. Teddy Roosevelt's rough-riders charging up San Juan Hill to Nagasaki in one lifetime. Saw old lady in T.V. documentary, crossed the West in covered wagon, now her favourite teevee watching is the moonshot. All happened very fast. But black horse still grazing steadily in soft evening light. Catskill Mountains a dark blue. Sky like cathedral ceiling in glorious Technicolor. Boys still working on gridiron tactics. Read article about Tennessee alcoholic. Spent thirty of his fifty-three years in gaol on minor drunk charges, no single sentence ever exceeding thirty days. In court eight hundred times. Freed in the morning, totally drunk again by evening. Alcoholism an illness. Gaol meant deprivation of civil rights. Chuck brings out two large Martinis. Maria joins us on porch. Guests not due for half an hour. One man with wife equals peace of mind. I am grafted on to this family, for a weekend. It doesn't feel good. Loss of status. Should have wife here, prove equal, feel good. Maria goes inside. Wander, glass in hand, to bottom of paddock. Black horse comes across to guzzle. I don't understand how you can endure the week in New York, Chuck, when you've got all this ... Oh yeah, but the thought of getting up here on Friday nights keeps me going. You like our place? ... Great, fantastic, what was all that crap about not having peace of mind? ... I guess we all talka lotta crap when we're juiced ... well, I could be outa Two-World on my ass tomorrow, it's that kinda set-up, no security. We owe about thirty grand on this place—I got ahead of the pack, forty grand a year at my age? I'll tell you, Graham, success is all in this man's country but just when you think you've made it to the top you find they've shoved your balls in a dresser drawer and slammed it shut ...

We go into the old barn. Chuck drags stiff body of dead fox from a dark corner. Must've been poisoned and crawled in here to die. Glasses still in hand. Have a piss against barn wall. Hear first cars. They all had their wives and they were all convivial. Chuck was a big, easy-going host, balls in a drawer notwithstanding. You can look at men with their wives and see how thin the magic has worn, how much bitterness there is beneath the safety-valve joking, how eager he is to be charming to the other women; yet you are jealous. Does Narcissus care how the water *tastes*? I know I wasn't going to drink so much. It is sealing off the nerve ends. Stored-up juice is turning to acid. Take a trip to the john. See phone. Chance quick call to Weber. No answer. Fresh drink. Another trip to john. Shove forehead against wall. Am I lucky that I have not spent thirty years in gaols? I carry my own gaol with me, is that it? Sit and listen to the Americans. If I keep quiet they'll forget I'm here. That old man with the Bugs Bunny teeth and frizzly white hair is a doctor. He speaks with a slight European accent.

"If the whole country is so litigation mad what else is there to do?" he is saying, hands turned up in a small shrug. "I am driving past the scene of an auto smash, right, my whole instinct as a human being and a doctor is to stop and help. But the moment a qualified physician touches an injured person he becomes legally liable for any fancied or real after effects. If a broken leg doesn't set properly I am hit for damages, even if I only offered aid and comfort."

"You would actually drive on by a situation where maybe somebody is lying bleeding to death?"

"I'm sad to say it, I have no option. It happens all the time to doctors in this country, they stop to help and then the sharp lawyers get hold of the injured person and who do they sue—the doctor. If you lose one or two cases like that you don't find you can get insurance coverage. Without that you can't practise."

"Well that is about the sickest thing I ever did hear," said the interrogator, a sharp young man with a shiny black suit. "Don't you realise that is exactly the attitude that took our people into the gas chambers? You turn your head the other way and hope the world ignores you? I'll say it to your face rather than behind your back, Doctor, frankly I think you should examine your conscience."

The old man made another of those middle European gestures, the upturned palms, the raised eyebrows, the rise and fall of care-weary shoulders.

"It is painful to me but it is the situation I face. Perhaps I was always a coward. I ran away from the Nazis—one of the last ships they let sail from Hamburg. Most of my family decided to stay and face it, it can only get better, they said. I didn't stay to fight then and I'm too old to fight now. It is the way things are."

The young man intended to press home his attack, pushing off a restraining hand from his wife, who tried to hush him up at the same time as she gave the rest of them silly little smiles. Chuck stood up and began filling empty glasses.

"In my book Dr. Feldman is no coward," he said. "I guess I wouldn't have the guts to spell out my own compromises. You never done any tricky real estate deals, Myron? We all have our secrets. Except our British cousin here—he puts all his personal dirt into his books. Isn't that right, Cameron?"

Heads turn. Isn't this what you always wanted—to front the band, hog the mike, score the goals? *To make up for what*—that's the question that now seems important.

"It takes real cowardice to spend your life typing out silly little fantasies."

"You have a talent and you should thank God for it," said a middle-aged woman. Heads nod. Why do I feel like an undetected carrier of leprosy? The cars ooze off into the great American night. Milton driving two hundred miles. A last drink. Husband and wife go to bed. Stranger in their midst undresses in farmhouse bedroom. Buzzing noise in ears. Shoes won't come off. Listen at window for croaking of bullfrogs in creek, or distant wail of trains, or howl of coyote. Hear nothing but desperate rustling of pages. *New Yorker*, only reading matter in room. Not likeliest source of erotic stimulus but—ah, towards the back of the book, a single-column fur-coat advert, she's about two inches high, showing a bit of knee. Use one eye at a time, easier to focus . . . these good folk think it's art but it's only occupational therapy, the typing I mean, keeps your fingers off your cock. It is a disgusting word that rewards fools with gold.

The next day they drove to a party given by friends of Chuck and Maria. The house was on the banks of the Hudson, an old stone barn the interior of which had been gutted so that the main living area was a vast well, roof to ground, with bedrooms leading off a

111

balcony. The action took place by the pool, twenty or thirty eagerly pleasant, decent, liberal folk hoisting cool shots from a trolley. The host had swimming costumes for those who came unprepared. Cameron felt brown enough now to take his place in the water. He did a couple of idle lengths on his back, noting that the pool was cleverly designed to give a view of the Hudson and the purple hills beyond from water-level. He floated on his back, watching the brown, laughing people living out the American dream. The water washed away the hot eyes and the thick tongue. He was the luckiest man alive, to have accepted Chuck's invitation, to have failed in his jackanape scheme to find young love with Weber. Not many idiots are given such second chances.

You think this could last? Didn't Fitzgerald say there are no second acts in American lives?

One minute he's all but submerged, the quiet visitor who was only going to sip a beer or two and make polite, evasive noises.

Then this chick arrives. She's about seventeen. She comes with her parents. Dressed, she's just a big, teenage girl. She comes out of the changing room, six feet tall if she's an inch, smooth teak thighs and breasts that seem likely to tear open the seams of her one-piece costume. She comes into the water with a running dive so reminiscent of Johnny Weismuller it's a wonder she doesn't beat her chest and bawl a mighty challenge to the creatures of the jungle. She comes forging up the pool, does a back-flip turn under water and shows only great arms and brown legs as she churns back to the other end.

So what does our new, mature, dignified Hero do? He takes a deep breath and slides under the water and gets a bleary glimpse of her great knees driving bubbles into the blue depths. He's never had the guts to open his eyes under water before, it might be added. We all have our secrets? This demented fool even took a sip of the water. It had caressed her body. Some of it might even be *from her body*!

He got out and towelled himself vigorously and sat on a canvas chair watching Jane's mighty arms smash down on the water. Then she got a pair of goggles and floated face down, her buttocks curving out of the water like a heavenly Loch Ness monster. He went to the john. By standing on the slatted bench and craning a trifle he could see her from about ten yards distance, albeit with his head in the horizontal position ...

112

The sun shone from a clear blue sky and the Hudson sparkled like shattered mercury and a tall, fair woman sat beside him showing maddening yards of lightly browned thigh and even his toes felt randy. The amount of sexual heat these people could generate in a crowd was enough to melt granite. It was a wonder the pool was not boiling. It turned out that Jane in the pool was the daughter of this lady with the maturely muscled thighs. Our Hero had changed by now to whisky. After all, the ladies mustn't think he was a beer-slopping peasant. Juicy king-size beefburgers were cooked on a mobile barbecue spit and slapped between crisp, floor-dusted rolls. Jane from the pool and her mother were keenly interested in all things British. Dusk approached. New buckets of ice were produced to cope with the inordinate flow of liquor. He and the mother grew gracious. She was deeply impressed by the fact that he was a creative writer. Yes, he said, shaking his head in contemplation of tortured inner depths, but it's a sad and lonely life. She could very well understand that. The warmth of sympathy these middle-aged American matrons exuded was amazing—and no sign of varicose veins! She was still there waiting when he came back from the changing room. To make a point against the noise of a Sinatra long-player piped from the house in some affluent manner he pulled his chair closer to hers and even ventured to tap her exquisitely large, bare, perfect knee with the tips of his middle fingers. She listened intently to whatever subtle nonsense he came out with. Other people moved around them under a soft light from a wall-bracket lamp but they had no faces. She had big and beautiful arms. Their knees were almost touching. A great love story of our time was about to be born. Daring things were said, expressions of great passion too magnificent to be constrained by petty moralities. Drinks were fetched and downed excitedly. Her hand rested gratefully in his. Husbands, wives, children, these are Lilliputian strings, you divine creature, let us throw off the shackles of the tiny minds that have cramped our lives, let us depart—immediately!

There was a crashing noise. Yes, crashing. A man was standing beside them, shouting. Yelling, indeed. A strangely wild man.

Cameron pushed him into the pool. It seemed a good idea—at the time. He turned, beaming triumphantly, to sweep up his buxom prize. He raised his hands and gave the Tarzan yell, beating his chest with both fists. Back he toppled, so slowly he could plainly see all their eyes widening, their hands shooting forward to grab him.

That's funny, I can still hear their voices but I'm under water.

Where are you, light of my life?

He was in Chuck's house, sitting in the kitchen in a pair of strange underpants. His hair was wet. His feet were bare. Maria was standing over him, shaking her head.

"What happened?" he asked, thickly.

"It hadda be the biggest shock of their cosy little lives," Chuck roared. "He was standing right there beside you and you were trying to hustle Hannah behind the garage for a quick bang! 'I would die for one moment with you, Hannah,' you were saying. With John right there!"

"Oh my God."

"You're propositioning her with her old man standing beside you! Ha ha, he was fit to burst."

"Oh my God. I'm going to be sick."

"Again? That goddam pool's two parts puke to two parts neat bourbon by now, boy!"

"She was going to run away with me, you know that?"

"Yeah? She was going to run away from you, you mean! John heard you—he smashed his glass on the ground! Jesus Christ, Cameron, when you go a-calling on folks they really know they've been called on! Here, have another belt at this. I ain't laughed so much in years. I mean, there you are one minute making like Mr. Charm—you had 'em eating outa your hand, fella. Next minute all hell's let loose. Want a beer to chase that down?"

"Let's go back and I'll apologise, Chuck."

"The hell with it. Have another belt."

He awoke at ten thirty. Everybody had slept in. The only train had left an hour earlier. Chuck was deeply apologetic. There was no way to get back to New York for the show at one thirty. There has to be, said Cameron. It took six phone calls to find a local cab company that had a driver on duty. The man said it would cost forty-five dollars being Labor Day. Cameron shaved and drank a black coffee. Chuck drove him to a filling station on the highway.

"Don't fret, fella," he said, "I'll explain to Milt it was my goddam fault."

"I'd rather he didn't even know we had this little emergency."

"Okay. Here, you want my shades? Give the sun an equal chance against those big red eyes of yours?"

"Thanks. You can't lend me a couple of cigarettes, can you?"

"I can do better." He handed over a solid, six-inch cigar. The cab lurched on to the parking lot. The driver was a thin, rural-style man with the usually whippy neck and tartan shirt and tight, whining mouth. He wanted the fare in advance. He didn't think it was possible to make New York in two hours. Cameron shoved forty dollars in his hand and told him he would make it another forty if he got to the studio in time. He shook hands with Chuck. The driver said he had to call the office to tell them the destination.

"Let's just fucking go, eh?" Cameron said. It's shades for menace, folks! Percy Kilbride Jr. was suitably obsequious. Off they went, smoking the cigar in the back seat, the Hudson sparkling, the mountains shimmering, the rich houses clean and white, the big car occasionally slowing down to the legal seventy, the big silent guy in the back, dark shirt, dark glasses, dark suit, two hundred thousand dollars at stake, not a game any more, on his own now, trusting nobody, looking for nothing out of this country but its money, telling the punk who was driving that they had no time for bloody coffee, sliding into the shabbiness of Yonkers, fathomless gaze showing no emotion as aimless negro jumps out of way of car, a hard man on his way to a big bundle. This is how it would be from now on, hard as nails, trusting nobody. On the way up you meet all sorts of guys who say they're your pals but when it comes to the crunch, baby, you gotta set your own alarm clock.

Subway from Cortlandt Park at the end of the Broadway line. Negro families in Sunday best, picnic happy. That's something we top guys have to leave behind. Sprint across Times Square and Broadway.

He stopped running as he slammed through the swing doors. A uniformed commissionaire phoned through to the Mal Parsons studio. A keen young studio assistant got him to his seat at a semi-circular table during the commercial break.

"Our third guest has just arrived—kinda breathless I'd say," said Mal Parsons. Cameron squinted against the lights and gave them the old Ernie Kovacs smile, all teeth showing.

"Tell us, Graham, for a lot of people must envy you deeply— what does it take to become a successful author?"

"That's a good question, Mal. Forgive me for being breathless, I had to drive three hundred miles in two hours to get here. The secret of success in creative writing depends entirely on luck."

"Luck, is that all?"

"Yes. You must have the luck to be born with a great talent and also to be better-looking than Gregory Peck."

"Why do you have to be better-looking than Gregory Peck?"

"Would I be on this show if I was a club-footed dwarf with a hunchback?" He heard a cameraman laughing somewhere among the dazzle of lights. He grinned wolfishly. "My publisher, Mr. Tannenbaum, wrote to me in London—we live in a slum that makes most of Harlem seem like the Diamond Ring—he wrote and said, Graham, I can make you half a million dollars doing the shows to plug *The New Ladies' Man*—but send me a picture of yourself so that the producers can see how devilishly handsome you are."

There were other celebrity guests round the table but not being pepped to the follicles with last night's booze they didn't stand a chance.

"And you sent over a picture that did the trick, huh?"

"To be honest, Mal, I sent him a picture of Gregory Peck. That was where the luck came in—Mr. Tannenbaum never goes to the movies."

Thirty minutes went in a flash. Mal Parsons wound up by telling the good folks that these new Beatle-type Britons were just unbelievable and if they wanted to hear more of Graham Cameron's great sensa humour they could tune into his radio show tonight.

They went straight upstairs and taped the radio show. A laff a minute, said Mal. A star is born. Fame is easy. All you have to do is become three different people. One, the genial, camera-hogging show-off. Two, the nervy prize-fighter who cauterises his soft spots in a pickle of whisky so that he can play the genial show-off. Three, the tough middle-man who manages to get Whisky Pickle to the Studio in time. The guy who said to the rural cabbie at Van Cortlandt Park:

"You mean you won't take me right into New York to the studio?"

"You'll be there faster on the subway, mister."

"You won't take me to the studio door?"

"I get caught in the downtown traffic? You'll be faster by subway."

"Okay—here's the other five for the fare—and here's five for yourself."

"Dint you say you'd make it another forty if I got there in time?"

"If you don't want the five give me it back."

"Okay, I'll drive you down to the studio."

"No thanks, you said I'd be there faster by subway."

"Christ, that's all the thanks I get, coming out on Labor Day?"

"Write to Johnny Carson—he needs the laughs."

As he raced up the ancient iron stairworks of the terminal station

116

he kept smiling. The more he thought about Labor Day by the pool the more he wanted to laugh. There was not even a trace of guilt in his guts. America had done that much for him already. No more boyish fantasies, no more shy yearnings, no more tormented intro-spection—above all, no more shame. He was a writer, wasn't he? In fifty years time the pool-side fiasco would be used by definitive bio-graphers to show how he had scorned the deathly inhibitions of the petty bourgeoisie. Was Jack London a teetotaller? Didn't James Joyce's shoulders know the feel of every gutter in Europe? Was William Faulkner a Doctor Pepper addict? How about Raymond Chandler and Sinclair Lewis and Thomas Wolfe ...

Let us leave our Apprentice Genius to his rabid musings. What I find really worrying about young Cameron, on the eve of his trip across the length and breadth of the U.S.A., is that out of his whole weekend the thing that registered in his mind, the truly significant memory, was the thrill he experienced when being told that he had the ability to get them eating out of his hand.

Chapter Ten

HERE LIES THE REPUTATION OF MR. BRINNIN
WHO MADE A SHROUD FROM DIRTY LINEN.

On the train from Penn Station to Philadelphia there was a dark-haired girl wearing the same heavy-frame spectacles as Weber, in the same way as Weber, tilted up above her hairline, presumably so that they would not interfere with her reading. The effect of the spectacles on Cameron was so powerful he stared at them throughout the whole journey, feeling somehow that when she lifted her eyes from the magazine she would smile at him in recognition. Not only that, every American voice around him in the crowded evening train had echoes of Weber's voice. From the railway track New Jersey was a belching chemical plant fringed by wasteground. The girl with Weber's spectacles went on reading ...

They'd been sitting together in an Italian restaurant on 50th Street. At the next table, at least six inches away, a large-boned New York woman was being wooed, one might call it, by an incredibly ugly little man with pebble lenses and a pitted skin under a greasy black crew-cut. A real troll, in local parlance.

"I'm unique, I'm the greatest," the little nasal foghorn proclaimed. "Ya won't meet anudder like me, I'm unique."

"Ey! Pointy Head! Ta me ya're nuthin—I cud cut ya aff just like that—whack!" his true-love snarled, slicing the air with a karate palm.

"I ain't got conventional good looks—I know that f'r God sakes!" the man had said, perching forward on his chair, the broad-cheeked female sneering audibly. "But I got pep—I make tings jump!"

"Ya make me sick that's what ya make me do," said the woman. "Ya ever think a drappin' dead?"

"Ya're not receptive ta me, honey, what's wit' all this hostility? I bought ya dinner, dint I?"

"Ey, ya make me sick."

They had laughed all the way back to Weber's apartment in the Village. At times her chortling became so hysterical she had to lean against him for support. She was delicate and feminine and vulnerable
118

and for the first time he began to feel sick with something other than pure lust. Just for a moment it seemed she would be happy to lean on him all the way into bed, but just at the last, when the hand round her waist began to make more urgent movements, she gulped down a few sobering breaths and became frigid Sally once more. Still, it was another link in the chain. It was now firmly implanted in his head that Weber was indispensable to Fate's Great Scheme. The Guiding Hand had made him write the book at a time when Swinging London was all the rage in America. The Guiding Hand had provided the title that excited the moguls of Two-World pictures, and thus brought about the tour. It was all pre-destined. But is it love or romance, he wondered. I know it's real because of the intensity of passion I feel for the spectacles of this unknown woman across the carriage.

The station at Philadelphia needed only an organ to give it cathedral status. A cab took him through slanted evening sunlight to the hotel. The most historic city in the U.S. was a mixture of recognisably European buildings and the usual bank and insurance company slabs. His room was so far up it might have been in the sky. He read the official handbook for visitors, all the time composing dialogue of such transparent sincerity that Weber would break fingernails tearing off her chastity belt. The U.S. Mint was here. He was glad at last to discover who Benedict Arnold was: he had sold out to the lousy British, the treacherous bastard, tried to hand over West Point to the Redcoats. He threw the handbook at the mirror. The room was of modern hotel design, planned by environmental computers, light alloy fittings, folding chairs, not an inch of wasted space, a maximum-profit per square inch layout for broiler humans. He ate in Ye Olde Cheshire Cheese restaurant, whose genuine English authenticity was proven by the inclusion of Guinness on the wine-list. He asked the red-waistcoated waiter with the *lederhosen* for a bottle of Liffey water but the man said, in a Spanish accent, that they had run out of German beer.

Backstreet Philadelphia was not unlike the quieter parts of Chelsea. Walking in a strange city, killing time, alone, was not suited to his temperament. He tended to speed up all the time, get hot and flustered, find himself on street corners he had passed already. He thought what the hell and went into the first bar he came to. It was not so dark as those in New York. The T.V. was on, full blast. The barman was a heavy-flabbed Slav in a brilliant sports shirt. The other customers were three elderly men drinking beer. The bartender put down the glass he was gouging into with a dirty dishtowel and drew off a beer. The old men cackled gleefully at a Phil Silvers joke. It was a show dedicated to the memory of oldtime burlesque. Silvers was not Bilko but the desk clerk of a sleazy hotel. Jerry Lewis walked across the foyer holding a small glass which he filled from the faucet. He walked back to his room. He did this three times. Finally Silvers had to speak.

"You must indeed be thoisty, sir," he smarmed.

"No," said Jerry Lewis casually, "my room is on fire."

The old men laughed so much they worried the bartender, who took a heavy stance before them, gouging mechanically into another glass. One of the old men had a bald head and a neck like a dying daffodil stalk. His flesh was pink and slack. The neck and the skull formed a question mark. He had a hooked nose and a receding chin. He was like a newly-hatched chicken. Cameron tried to visualise the American life story that had brought this skinny old buzzard to the pathetic conclusion of slurping beer down his narrow old chest while cackling spastically at the sharp wise-cracks of Phil Silvers on television with the sound at full volume. Was this The Audience? Chicken-head got off his stool. The middle man was revealed to be an old woman. The other man had his wrist on the back of her neck. Her face was a falling slab of pale putty. She banged the old guy on the chest. Chicken-head came back from the john. Phil Silvers was in great form. Messalina made a joke at Chicken-head's expense. Suddenly the two old geezers squared up to each other, a decrepit display of rage on their faces, childishly exaggerated. Before they came to whatever they were capable of in the way of blows, the bartender leaned over the counter and flicked their faces lightly with his dishtowel. Chicken-head began to cry. The woman put her arm round his waist. He burrowed his pink skull into her neck. The three of them left together, swaying a lot. Phil Silvers did a slick routine with Danny Thomas. Laughter battered the walls of the empty bar.

The radio show took place at one end of a café, friendly host Fraser Buchanan sitting at a table on a dais. The other star celebrity guest was a woman dancer who had written a book on how to keep a husband happy by staying honeymoon slim through six simple dance routines. The only member of the public present was a fat man who ate chocolates from a big bag and made loud interruptions. Friendly Host Fraser Buchanan and the two celebrities ignored him. Friendly Fraser gave the book the usual introduction—title, price, hearty endorsement of its best-selling entertainment value—and immediately asked how European poverty compared to American poverty. Cameron said, truthfully, that he'd known British slums that *looked* a lot worse than anything he had seen, so far, in America.

"I hope our so-called liberals and progressives hear this," said Friendly Host. "We all know things are not perfect in America but by heck they're a lot worse other places."

"I don't suppose it's any consolation to poor Americans to know that a lot of foreigners are doing worse," Cameron remarked.

"Is swinging London really as permissive as we hear?" Friendly Host said quickly.

"Not everybody in London is an immoral swinger," said Cameron. "There are thousands of immoral squares. Mind you, I was brought up in Scotland, which is pretty old-fashioned. We're still shocked by sex after marriage."

Eight plugs in twenty minutes.

"That was a top interview," said the studio assistant, a young guy in his twenties. "My name's Jack Garrity. You handled that fascist motherfucker real good, man."

They arranged to have a drink in a bar on 13th and Pine. It was eerily similar in layout and clientele to Henekey's in the Portobello Road (London, England). Tall, bearded, middle-aged men in corduroy jackets spread out a lot of mature charm for the benefit of young girls with straight blonde hair. Cameron got talking to a young black guy at the bar. He said Philly was rough. Five guys had jumped him for cash last Friday. He carried a blade for such eventualities. He had it stuck down the inside of his trousers. They ran when they saw the blade. He pulled it out an inch or so to let Cameron admire it. He guessed he was going to move up to New York and live with his brother in Harlem. Some white intellectuals behind them were dissecting the layers of meaning in 'Sergeant Pepper'. Jack Garrity came in. Cameron bought two whiskies and two beers. The bar closed. They brought a dozen cans of beer and went back to the hotel. Jack Garrity said he didn't know any spot in Philly where there was any action at this time. They sat in the broiler-cage in the sky and drank the beer. Jack Garrity had held down different jobs since quitting college but mostly he liked to travel. He'd hitched first time to Alaska, then back to Philly, then down to Mexico, then back to Philly, worked a year in a garage, hitched his way to Frisco, went all the way up the coast to Alaska again, got a deal that meant driving this rich guy's car to Denver, worked there for a while on a newspaper, came back to Philly, couldn't sit still, had a look round Texas, came back, saved some dough, met a guy who was driving to Mexico City, worked there for a while in a bookshop, got the chance of a lift down to Guatemala, didn't care much for that, came back to Philly, got this radio job with motherfucking Fraser Buchanan, thought he would quit next week and head up Montreal way. He was 24. He left about half past three. Cameron was bunged up with beer. He went into the bathroom and got rid of it by sticking his index finger against the back of his throat. He slept quite well. Getting along without drink was easy, when you were in love.

Chapter Eleven

HENRY FORD TOLD HENRY OLDS HOW TO PREPARE FOR A RAINY DAY: SHOVE A HUNDRED MILLION DOLLARS OR SO IN A SPECIAL ACCOUNT AND FORGET ABOUT IT.

"You don't drive *at all*?"

Weber was steering the rented Chrysler through downtown Philadelphia. She pronounced it at-all. Listen carefully—in Britain it's a-tall.

"No. Something kind of non-masculine about that, eh?"

"You never wanted to drive?"

"It's very sexy, being driven about by beautiful sophisticated women. Look at slim little you handling this veritable juggernaut. I think I'll nibble your left ear and finger your womanly bosoms, driver. Now we're on the super highway parkway beltway thruway expressway turnpike you won't have any hands to defend yourself."

"Ey—ta me ya're nuthin'—I could cut ya off—just like that!"

She made the karate gesture with her free hand. He caught it and pressed it back on to the wheel.

"For God's sake keep 'em both on it, woman!"

"You're nervous! You big goof, you're too goddam chicken to drive a car!"

"That's true." He put his stockinged feet up on the window ledge. "Could you ever find it in your heart of hearts to surrender your body to a craven coward?"

"You're nothing but an auto virgin, Cameron. A big lunk like you can't drive a car?"

"Lay a finger on me and I'll scream."

"Would you believe ninety miles an hour?" she murmured, hurtling diagonally across two lanes and rocketing past a mighty trailer-truck. He presumed she was smiling cruelly behind the big dark shades.

They drove through flat lands to Baltimore. He had his stockinged feet out of the window to give them a cooling blast.

"Isn't it romantic, just you and me alone in this steel capsule?"

"If you say so. Keep talking. I was up awful early. I might doze off."

"Why don't we stop in the middle of this scrubby wilderness and lie down in the long grass and forget this whole cock-eyed world, baby?"

"Can't we discuss trends in literature? You're the big author—tell me what's selling over there in England these days."

"The usual rubbish. Listen, if we're having a complete role transference, why don't you pull in to the side and maul me and rip the thin fabric off my ivory-white shoulders with your brutal fingers and take me, ruthlessly, totally, until my very being is crying out—Oh God, at last, you make me feel like a *woman*!"

"Why don't you kiss my ass!"

"That's not original. It was in a novel called *The Moviegoer* by Percy Walker."

"Walker Percy. You read *The Sirens of Titan* by Kurt Vonnegut?"

"Nope."

"You ought to. That would tell you something about America."

"You'll find me a willing pupil, miss. Where the hell is this, anyway?"

"I thought we'd take the back roads, show you a slice of America that isn't all super highway."

"You know which slice of America I want to see, sister."

"Why don't you kiss my ass!"

"That's right."

They pulled in at a filling station. It had the usual plastic bunting. The moment the air-conditioning went off with the engine the heat inside the car made the whole body sweat. They opened the windows to let in even hotter air. Out of a glass kiosk came a very fat man, wiping his neck with a rag. He had not shaved for a day or two. His short-sleeved silk shirt was stained dark wherever it touched his massive body. He grunted with each breath.

"Yeah, lady?" he rasped.

"Fill her up would you?"

They could hear his grunts as he pulled the pipe to the rear of the car. Nothing moved in the wide, silent, country suburb street. Weber scratched her left ankle with the toe of her right shoe. She was wearing a white blouse, grey skirt, nylons with seams, flat-soled canvas shoes. The man came back to the window.

"Seventeen gallons, lady," he growled. She handed out her credit card. "Ya wanna glass? It's the free offa."

"I guess so."

The man rolled back to the kiosk.

"It's the promotion offer," she said. "You can take it home as a souvenir."

"I'll drink your bathwater from it."

"That's obscene."

The man came back through the glare, a small glass gripped in each Neanderthal meathook.

"One f'r bothaya," he snarled, scowling, relieved to complete the stupid little transaction, a fat man in a glass box in a nowhere dump.

"My Philadelphia drinking pal told me Baltimore has the wide-openest street in the U.S."

"Baltimore? This is the stuffiest damn city in the nation."

She was surprised. Everything and everybody was for sale. Rock pounded out of dark red caverns. Strange men moved in shadowy doorways, every other of which was a walk-up palmistry emporium. Hard-looking touts rapped out short, sharp spiels from the dangerous foyers of strip 'n' rock joints. Then, at a corner, there was a little man with a cigar butt between finger and thumb, black shirt and yellow tie.

"Hi, folks," he chirped, "come on and see da show—we got twenny-one noo voijins—how do I know dey're voijins? Dey just got aff de boat from de Voijin Oiles!"

"You don't really want to go into one of these joints, do you?" Weber said, hopefully.

A dark, booming place. A horse-shoe bar with stools. Girls mount bar at one end and strip to rock while undulating round to the other end. Drinks a dollar a shot. Throw leg over stool and sit at a canter, eye level with strippers' shaven shins. Ask the unsmiling bartender between hard-veined fetlocks for two Scotches on the rocks.

"Light a match so I don't give him a hundred dollar bill," I murmured into Weber's ear. "I wouldn't fancy arguing with that guy about the change."

"Change? They don't make change in a joint like this. Whatever you give them, that's what the drinks cost."

Eyes get used to light. Most of the customers are grey-suited men wearing lapel badges. Oh no, not lapel badges again! Overhead a wide-hipped blonde whirls her titty-props in different directions. The conventional men pretend to each other not to be interested. Amazing how many glasses are ruminatively twirled as swishing thighs

125

zoom by at twelve o'clock high. Trust agile American brains to think up new twist—here we drink showgirl's slippers out of champagne!

A stripper comes off the far end of the horse-shoe bar, swings on a silk robe and comes round behind the stools.

"Buy a working girl a drink?" she says in my left ear, pushing a gleam of white knee against my dangling leg.

"No thanks."

"Ya cheapskate bum!"

Another stripper finishes her bar-top grinding and bumping with a backward contortion that lets her boobs drop into some guy's glass. The master of ceremonies snaps his yellow braces against his purple shirt and blasts the apathetic audience through a screaming mike:

'A big hand for the bootiful Sophie Lorren, folks! We love ya, Sophie, don't we, folks?"

The working-girl in the silk robe nudges my elbow.

"Go on, cheapskate," she sneers, "give the girl a hand—ya get to clap for free." I look over my shoulder. She grins at me, black hair, carmine lips, white face. "Ya don't get *the* clap for free, that costs fifteen bucks!"

"My wife wouldn't like it," I say.

"Ya wife? Can't make it any other way, huh? Bye, cheapskate."

On the sidewalk.

"As well I did come along," says Weber. "You're just the big dope to pick up a tramp like that."

"She seemed rather witty."

"It's all been said before, sonny boy."

I decide to ditch Weber and then slip out again and find that witty working-girl.

We get back to the hotel. We go into the bar, where else. We get lumbered by the friendly waitress. She brings us one drink and then stands over us, hand on hip, tray dangling.

"I'm very popular with my customers," she says, by way of introduction. "I have made many fine friends. You see those two gentlemen over there—they are two fine senators—each Christmas they give me a hundred-dollar present. They are very fine people. I think the reason I'm so popular is I treat people as people, you know how rare that is today."

God, she does go on. Then Weber says she's going to hit the sack. I make my joke, your room or mine.

"Down boy," she says, sporty aunt style. It's the most revolting expression I've ever heard. I couldn't get an erection over her if she

126

was a hole in the ground. I leave her in the corridor with a laconic goodnight. I think she's a mite surprised. Well she mite be. I sit on my bed, noting that the room is the same one I occupied in Philadelphia. I check my money—a hundred and seventy dollars and two bits. A bit is twelve and a half cents, only there aren't any single bits, only two bits. It's the same as a quarter. I put thirty singles in my little waistband money pocket and head for the door. The phone rings. I walk over the bed, Groucho Marx style. It's Weber. She's going to have to beg for it now, I decide, I'll have her eating out of my lap.

"I had a call from the local book rep," she says. "They've cancelled your appearance on the T.V. show—they think your book is too pornographic for Baltimore."

"I don't believe it!"

"It's the title more'n anything."

"What a load of bollocks."

"We'll get a bigger play from the other channel. They hate each other's guts. I'll see you for breakfast?"

"Only a thin wall will separate you from the sound of me restlessly pacing the floor, nervously killing the night hours until next I see your maidenly knockers."

"Why don't you ..."

"Love to, sweetheart."

That's the new me, playing hard to get. I bet she tosses and turns all night. I just toss. No, I didn't go out. When I'm sober I'm really quite sensible, like most cowards.

A radio studio. The interviewer is a big, genial woman, about 45, just my type. She thinks I'm some kind of European gallant whereas I'm only trying to find out if she's game for a quick shafting in back of the control panel. She tells me Baltimore is the most hypocritical city in the nation. Wide Open Street is Mob-controlled. The respectable chamber of commerce gang ban a lot of films and books but they don't meddle with the Mob. The same people who ban books and films spend their Sunday afternoons watching cockfights on the lawns of colonial-style mansions. The interview? Mini-skirts, the Beatles, how shaky is the institution of marriage in the new, sexually frenetic Britain? I say we Londoners perpetrate casual sex on each other as readily as Americans shake hands. She lets me shake hands.

My first autographing party. I have seen this expression on the itinerary and have imagined champagne with the city's culture vul-

tures, most of them randy young wives of impotent, billionaire non-
agenarians. It consists of me sitting at a table in the book department
of a large store. On the table are two hundred copies of *The New
Ladies' Man*. I get my John Hancock into every fly-leaf. A girl comes
up, short, dumpy, pimply, greasy, four-eyed, hairy-legged. She buys a
copy and asks me to dedicate it to Anne Hofstader. My very first fan!
I'm sure she'll be game for a quick shafting in back of the children's
shelves. I give her a flowery, personalised dedication.

"What was it particularly about the book that interested you?" I
ask, standing up, smiling crinklingly if that's a word.

"I buy all the best-sellers," she says. "Is it a novel or something?"

Another fan turns up. He is wearing denim trousers, tartan shirt,
zipped jerkin, all stained. He sways a little.

"I am buying your book because I also too aim to be a real writer
you know?" he says, blinking slowly. 'How long did it take you to
write it, the book? What I got to do to be a big writer like you you
can tell me the secret way in?"

"Dedication is everything," I say.

"Yeah, dedicate it to Don, will you?" he says. He almost loses his
balance as I personalise my John Hancock. The manager hovers near
by.

"That'll be six ninety-five," he says to Don.

"I don't have that much money!" Don says accusingly. The manager
takes the book out of his hand.

"We'll put it by for you, sir, until you call again."

"You do that," says Don. He glares at me. "Is anything to stop
me being a big writer, huh? Am I so repulsive a personality I can't
be a big writer too also?"

He reels out of the book department. The manager says it's always
kinda slow this time a year, book-wise. But I have the girl from
the Baltimore paper waiting to interview me. I'm taken into the
manager's office, a square yard of glass with a desk and chair and
standing room for one adult. The girl is on the chair. She is fresh-
faced, petite, about 25. Her name is Ella Staebler. I sit on the desk,
keeping my knees out of her face. She asks me about my ideal
woman.

"The nearest one," I grin wickedly. She writes this down in long-
hand. "No, don't write that, I'm supposed to be married."

"Supposed to be?"

"That's what my wife thinks anyway. You not married?"

"I have this steady but he's kinda dull. I had an affair last fall with a naval officer. I had an affair this spring with an army officer. I guess I'm irresponsible, I'm always having affairs with married men, you think that's irresponsible?"

"Of course not. You're young and beautiful and intelligent—who says you have to be tied down by petty rules and conventions drawn up by elderly fuddy-duddies who're jealous of young, warm blood? You doing anything for dinner tonight?"

"What about your manager?"

"My manager?"

"The lady out there who's with you. She looks kinda possessive to me."

"Oh—*her*? She's a lesbian. She likes watching other people doing it. Isn't that disgusting?"

"I don't know, I never tried it."

British soldiers have a gesture for conveying to each other the impending certainty of a good rattle. You clench the right fist and slap the right bicep with the left hand, while pumping the right arm up and down, face puckered in a chimpanzee grimace, pouting lips blowing a silent whistle, the whole producing an effect so vulgar and obscene it is only legal during world wars. Being in Baltimore I risk only the silent whistle. The door opens. Weber looks in. She has the tight face and beady eyes of a wife who suspects that her husband and her old schoolmate have been groping each other while she was in the kitchen.

"Sorry to hustle you two but we have to get moving, Graham honey," she says, giving Front Page Ella, Girl Reporter, a quick bitch smile. "We're due in Washington seven o'clock."

I look at the young sheilah Graham would like to dive his dick into. How slender are my chances of a crack-up night? I could stay on in Baltimore and catch the morning train. But is this chick going to come across? Why did Weber say we have to be in Washington by seven? Has she realised my relentless sexual advances are no mere hobby horse? Paradise is potentially on both sides of me. I'm torn and bewildered, the answer doesn't come pat. Call me the lost decadent.

"It's the price of fame," I say to the girl, shrugging sorrowfully, expressive eyes conveying longing, sadness, regret, waiting for her to grab my zip and take my problem out of my hands. She looks at me blankly. "Give me your address," I say, "I'll drop you a postcard with my views on American woman."

She writes the address on a page from her notebook. I have this

129

half-formed notion that I'll get to Washington, see if Weber is up for grabs, if not catch a quick train back to Baltimore and provide a meaty column for the young Lewd Ella here, as I now affectionately know her. She leaves. Weber goes silent until we are stopped by traffic lights in the shabby torrid zone of Baltimore's negro section. I'm watching a man having an argument with a woman in front of a cut-price liquor store. He is as wide as he is short, with a neck like a bunch of ebony bananas. I'm thinking he looks like Jimmy Rushing the blues singer or Louis Armstrong before he dieted to an elf of his former shadow. I'm wondering if I'm not getting just a little tired of negroes agitating my conscience. Their continual self-pitying is all the more obnoxious because I haven't actually heard any of it yet. But I know what they are thinking. I'm getting into such a state I might soon burst out of this gleaming automobile and grab that fat guy by the breasts and scream at him that I was brought up in a worse dump than this and I haven't been sitting on my fat ass waiting for the bosses to confer equality on me as if the class war was some kind of field for bloody charity! I'm breathing very heavily, I may tell you. Why the hell should I be dragged through their ghettoes and continually be reproached for their misery? I'm going to roll down the window and scream at that black lard-barrel—do you know that the American negro has a better chance of going to university than the average Briton? I'm ...

"Sorry I butted in when you were making time with that hot-eyed little bitch," Weber suddenly snaps out of the silence, her voice shrill with venom.

"You're jealous," I say, triumphantly.

"Piss off," she growls.

Boy, am I going to lay her when we get to Washington! It'll be the biggest hauling of ashes since the great fire of London. And guess who'll laugh longest and loudest when she discovers she's in the Pudding Lane club! I ease my tight trouser crotch off my sweaty groin, laughing out of the window at the dingy black masses. You niggers don't know it but the next white American bastard you meet may be *mine*!

Chapter Twelve

ASKED IF IT WERE TRUE THAT HE ONLY WHISTLED WHEN NERVOUS, HINDENBURG SAID YES. ASKED WHAT TUNE, THE OLD SQUARE-HEAD SAID I HAVE NEVER WHISTLED IN MY LIFE.

The dining-room is heavy and dark and red. There are three of us present, The Wounded Hero, the black waitress and Graham Cameron, third-rate fiction's answer to Elisha Cook jr. I started out to be the Kirk Douglas of the writing racket. Women don't walk out on Kirk Douglas but as soon as we hit this bloody hotel Weber just disappeared, leaving a note at the desk to the effect that she's having dinner with relations. I kicked the wall. I mean, she just pissed off. I'm likewise. They always used to slight Elisha Cook or sneer laughingly at his twisted little face and he always betrayed the gang and then got shot. I don't have a gang to betray. I sit eating my deep fried butterfly gulf shrimp and thinking of Irresponsible Ella back in Baltimore and getting into hot flushes of cold hate for Weber, until I'm probably more like Neville Brand than Elisha Cook. Neville Brand is a burly, ugly brute who harbours deep grudges and generally leads the revolt in the big house, the one who chucks the first tray at the warders. Weber knew that Ella meant to try me, that's why she dragged me away. Is she now punishing me for looking at someone else? I'm beginning to think I am just a big simple country boy, when it comes to women.

"Richard E. Galt, Special Air Service," says the voice of The Wounded Hero. He leans across two tables, thrusting out his hand. He limped in here on a stick, left leg stiff, aluminium rods running up from the heel of his glassy black boot. His green beret hangs over the back of a chair, like the resting gunfighter's belt. He is in his middle twenties, blond head almost shaven, spine, neck and head in a line as straight as a hanging rope, both flanks of his chest blazing with medal ribbons, one gold bar on each brick-wall shoulder. I introduce myself and move over to his table. I idly note how easily I make friends with strange men. Still, it's better than masturbation, at least you have someone to talk to.

Richard E. Galt, lootinnant, is in Washington to see a senator. He may be getting a second Silver Star. He is on his second tour of

Vee-ate-nyum? Charlie ambushed his patrol and he got a round, in the laig? He has the Purple Heart. This I have to see—I remember Dana Andrews getting it in some film where all the brave G.I.s were shot by the slant-eyed yellow fiends. Richard explains that it is *not* their Victoria Cross but an award for any U.S. serviceman who sheds even a drop of blood on foreign soil. You get it, he says, even if you get a round up the ass, never mind if you were running away at the time. He says he likes Vee-ate-nyum, for the action? He has a wife and two fine kids in officers' quarters, down there in Fort Benning? Georgia is his home state. He is due to fly out on Sunday to Laos, as an adviser to the Laotian army? He hopes it will not all be training. He's been in the army since he was nineteen? The second Silver Star would be a real career booster—this senator is working on it, that's how it goes in this man's awrmy, if you have a connection in Washington you sure as high-ull use it. He guesses you sure need a lot of brainpower to write books. He has been thinking of hitting a few bars?

We go to the Gilded Parrot cocktail lounge where a bustier version of Anita Ekberg is dealing them off a silvery tray. She's in a microskirt, fishnet tights, black strapless bodice. I don't think I'm man enough to try. Richard goes to phone his senator's secretary. I slug my Jack Daniel's down in one and ask Anita to fetch another. She brings that. I smile sadly. At school I was the one boy in the class who actually liked ladies' preferences—you know, the two dances where the girls pick partners? Was this some early pointer to my future career as weaver of dreams? I watch her serve some convention delegates, biggish men in standard business suits, the shoulders square and pinched against the outer arm, the skirts of the shiny jackets riding up and down elephantine asses. They horse around some with Anita. She laughs a lot. The convention men greet some newcomers with sound and fury.

"Jees-zuss Ker-ist! Al McDaniel!"

"Dammit! Mike Fuhlendorf! You old son of a!"

"Denver! Sixty-four! You ain't changed a bit you old!"

Hands are gripped, arms pumped, backs pounded, chests thumped. Richard comes back. His senator's secretary might pick us up later for a drink.

"What say we haul our asses downtown and find some action?" His neck is stiff in the officer's collar. "Man kin soon find himself a piece of tail in Washington."

"Isn't that waitress fantastic?" I say, thinking maybe a Silver Star hero might bring out the patriotism in her and then some for the hero's best buddy.

"She ain't interested in us poor guys," he says. "They git them jobs in high-class bars to set a trap for big fat ol' capitalists. You stick with Dick, he'll make your dang sing."

I swear it, the way he pronounced it, sing rhymed with dang. Or was it dong?

The cabbie knows some several lively spots where we can have ourselves a good time. We go to all of them. People stare first at Dick's stiff leg, then his medals, then at his long-haired companion. So I'm a behind-the-lines guerilla fighter. Custer had long hair, dint he? In one cocktail lounge we tell the waiter to offer two drinks to these two tootsies. They shake their heads. The waiter tells us they are waiting for dates. At one joint we are even turned away because we have not booked a table.

"We only got back from Saigon yesterday," I snarl. "How the fucken hell could we have gotten reservations?"

"I regret it, sirs, but without a reservation ..."

"I don't see why these bureaucratic Pentagon expense-account pigs should sneer at you, Dickie," I say as we find yet another cabbie with a list of the sure-fire action spots. "It's their bloody war, isn't it? You didn't volunteer to go out there and slaughter Vietnamese babies, did you?"

"Only for mah second tour," he says.

"Exactly. Hey, how come you don't speak like an officer? All British officers are shits."

"What's a British officer sound like, Graham, mah old buddy-buddy?"

"Like a pain in the ass, Dickie you ol' son of a. If giraffes could talk they'd sound like British officers."

We ask one cabbie if they don't have good clean all-American brothels in this goddam city.

"They haid," he tells us, "but the new chief of police, he closed 'em all dow-un."

By midnight we are down to neighbourhood bars. We are getting nowhere. My militaristic friend knows how to get the bartenders running—he raps the zinc bar-tops with his stick. It's good for getting service but it tends to create wide spaces around us. We come back to the Gilded Parrot lounge, arm in arm, singing 'The Eyes of Texas Are Upon You'. Some crabby old doll in a floor-length cocktail dress is tinkling the ivories for a bunch of elderly civilian shits who don't know the hell of war. Give us Temptation is the sort of thing we yell. I think we may even have offered Anita Ekberg two hundred dollars to come up to Dick's suite, I dunno, it's all bloody Weber's doing, here I am, or was, sitting with yet another man in yet another fucking hotel room drinking out of a quart bottle and droning away joylessly. He lies on the bed, boots and stick and beret and all, and goes to sleep. I leave him there, genocidal Prussian butcher that he is.

Next morning, hangoversville. Weber:
"You have a strictly limited concept of leisure time activity."
"Leezure? It would be too much to expect you to behave like a normal woman when you can't even speak the language."
Eleven a.m.; interview at the *Washington Star* on Virginia Avenue; tell the clean-limbed, bright-eyed, feature-writing health fetishist that the underlying theme of my book is the English retreat into fantasy. One a.m.; lunch in the Rib Room of the Mayflower Hotel on Connecticut Avenue; tell the bow-tied, middle-aged, calory-counting book columnist that the underlying theme of the book is the universal dilemma of middle-aged men panicking over loss of youth. Three thirty p.m.; interview at Station W.G.M.S. on Wisconsin Avenue; tell them the underlying theme of the book is urban man's sense of alienation. So what the hell, I don't know what the underlying theme of the accursed book is, I only typed the damn stuff. I don't know what the fuck I'm doing half the time, except getting the carbons in the right way up.

Are you beginning to wonder how an idiot like Cameron could ever have written a book that might merit this trans-Atlantic circus? Believe me, so am I. Weber keeps whizzing me round Washington in this rent-a-deathtrap and I'm as hungover as hell. When the windows are closed and the air-conditioning on the temperature—at least round my knees—is below freezing. As soon as we get out of the bloody car water flows from every pore. Then we go into air-conditioned foyers and goose-pimples rise as the seeping sweat is quick-frozen. Washington by day looks like Paris, from the brief glances I give it, wide avenues leading nowhere and packed with foreign bodies. Things are so bad I think yearningly of our little basement flat in North Kensington, where the loudest noise you can hear is the hungry wail of yet another shit-smelling infant. Their names are Gavin and Amanda, now that I think of it, little English buggers. I'd have sent Sheina to Scotland to have them—so that they could play football for Scotland, *of course*—but that plan petered out. Indecision. Been my problem all along. Writing crummy fiction is just my meat—sit in a warm room all day *making the bloody stuff up*! Call that work? When I was twelve (in the school holidays naturally) I was shovelling shite on farms for sixpence an hour. You think writing crappy novels in a warm room, sitting on your fat arse, is work? I'm ashamed to take the money. Naturally none of this comes out in the plugola interviews. I go on a T.V. show that night. This guy wants to know why British pop groups and writers and actors and models and other assorted parasites are taking over America.

"Since we gave up fighting wars we've had time to become experts in rubbish," I say. He is reading the questions off a sheet and does not listen to the answers. I'm shagged out and thirsty and randy and don't give a monkey's fuck what I say. Nobody notices. I get the title in five times in four minutes. As we leave the studio the monitor screens are showing the face of Lyndon Bane Johnson plugging the Great Society's War on Poverty. I sit in the car with Weber and seriously think of smashing her over the head and cruelly raping her inert body in Parking Lot Mad Dog Sex Fiend's Virgin Outrage. I didn't really mean that writing books is easy. It's a monumental grind. Grind means fuck in Britain. God, if I put half the energy into grinding rich women that I put into *The New Ladies' Man* I'd be the Porfirio Rubirosa of Powis Square.

"So what fun-packed plan have you for the rest of this balmy evening?" I remark bitterly. We are both drawing neurotically on glowing cigarettes.

Well, I wouldn't have credited it from Weber. She doesn't say much but drives to some section where they have narrow streets crowded with strolling gangs of hippies. She leads the way to a quaint olde English bar. She has a double shot herself. I have a double shot and a beer chaser. I intend to get *rotten*. I order the same again and glower at her defiantly. One word from the bitch and I'll smack her kisser.

"Look, I am sincerely sorry for leaving you alone last night," she says. "I just didn't see you enjoying the company of my relations— they are very stuffy people."

"Forget it," I snap. "I'm a big boy. I can find my own fun. In fact, if you want to push off back to New York and let me do the rest of this bloody trip on my own I don't give a fart."

I'm really mean to her. You know why big stars throw fits of temperament? Once everybody says they love you how else can you tell if they *really* love you except by spitting in their faces? It seems very logical nay commendable, sitting here, far from home. I might add that I have always suspected that a strong feminine streak is necessary for the writing of novels.

"I'll take you a place you'll dig," she says. I shrug. We go across the street. Talk about role reversal—I'm now Miss Sulky Pants and *she's* Van Johnson, my faithful high school beau who's willing to wait patiently until I get my dreams of big city fame out of my system and come back to settle down in Nextdoorsville and give him a whole ballsquad of wunnerful freckly-faced sons any man could be proud of.

She pays our dollar admissions to go down into a long cellar packed by Young Folk listening and dancing to a rock group. It's real teen territory, bare wood, trestle tables, prematurely-shaven waiters working nites to pay their way through college. The rock group is short-haired and blazered and hygienic but they do recognisable imitations of Chuck Berry. There are, of course, no coloreds present. Weber has, of course, never heard of Chuck Berry. The Russ Tamblyn-type boy waiter is suitably impressed by my order of double shots of Scotch and beer chasers. Nobody is actually wearing a long white tuxedo with a bow tie but otherwise they are the Sons of Andy Hardy set who jitterbugged at the junior proms of Hollywood's yesteryear. The girls—well, they may be teensters but already they look like loyal wives. I see one boy who is mildly drunk. His co-ed date's pretty, freckled face is anxiously solicitous as she tries to stop him making a fool of himself on the little dance-floor. I don't think I was this wholesome at the age of ten. It occurs to me that all these upright, well-scrubbed lads are just about the age for Vietnam. Flies to be shovelled across the room! I examine Weber over the rim of whatever glass I am currently draining. I have one of those flashing insights that we big writers are prone to. She hates this place but she thinks she's doing me a favor! Me being a rock'n'roll buff and all! She thinks I'll feel at home among all these gidgets and teen-guys! She is *catering* for my eccentricities! Oh my God, how daft can anyone be? I pat her hand gently and say we might feel more at home with slightly more senior citizens. We drop into a middle-aged bar across the street. I tell her about Chuck Berry.

She doesn't say 'down boy' once. In fact, she begins to talk quite revealingly about herself.

"I know you think I'm a moralistic prude but I'm not like that underneath. All the time I know I would like to—you know what I mean—but something freezes me up. I want to stretch out my
136

hand—but I can't? Not on my own."

I am not totally without sensitivity. I recognise a call for help when I hear one. A few more Scotches is all the help she needs. When we get back to the hotel we head for the bar, my hand steering her elbow. Our moment is at hand. I feel great. We take stools at the bar. Also on stools at the bar are these three men. They want to talk to anybody who'll listen. In my elated mood I feel like chatting to the whole world. They're Omaha delegates to a national Kiwani conference, Joe and Al and Mike. They have never met a real live author before. That calls for a real live drink.

"Wait till I tell my wife—she's crazy but crazy about books. What d'you say the movie's called?"

The bar closes at two a.m. but they have plenty in their suite. Weber says she's kinda pooped. Maybe she says it tentatively, giving me a cue to come upstairs and defreeze her. Maybe not. Anyway, I've got the taste in my mouth now and Al and Joe and Mike are laughing at my various jokes and in any case I'm a married man with two kids, so I say, I'll just have a couple with these men. All right, I know what it sounds like, I'm always ending up in rooms with men, maybe the faggot in me isn't so sublimated as my sexual ravings make out.

Get lost. I need a bit of cheeriness. Weber will probably turn frigid. In any case I have two kids to prove I'm normal.

So did Oscar.

Jesus wept, I'm only going to have a couple with Joe and Al and Mike. Maybe I'm a bit nervous, like the honeymoon husband, I admit it, I've made such a big thing about it Weber is probably expecting the greatest shaft-job since the Simplon tunnel. Just a couple of drinks, then I'll be knocking boldly on her door ...

Anyway, I finally manage to stagger to my own room, number 86 on the 8th floor, or is number 8 on the 86th floor? I don't remember Weber's number. I try to get the night operator to put me through but she, or he, is very obtuse. Anyway, in the morning, when I haul the receiver up from the floor on the end of the line, it is dead.

"I'm sorry about last night," I say in the car on our way to the morning radio show.

"What is there to be sorry about?"

"I didn't really want to go on drinking with those blokes, I just got carried away. It's the tension. I tried to find your room ..."

"Thank Christ you didn't."

"Come off it, you know very well you were aching for it."

I'm sure that's a blush. By making us wait she has brought us to
real love. She is too full of wonder and delight to speak. When we
get to the studio she stands behind the engineers in the control box.
I take my seat at the studio table and pout a little kiss at her through
plate glass. One of the shirt-sleeved backroom boys thinks it's him
I'm in love with. He seems kind of startled. Weber tries not to look
at me in case her heart bursts. Our Friendly Hostess is middle-aged
and husky and brisk. The other Guest Star is a negro civil servant
who is on the show to plug a wonderful new Federal food stamp plan
by which the deserving poor will get ninety-five dollars worth of
groceries for sixty-five dollars, provided they are skilful enough to
find the office that issues the necessary forms and provided their
city or county authority is implementing the scheme and provided
they are literate enough to fill in the hundred or so forms and provided the guardians of the public purse find them eligible and provided they have sixty dollars in the first place. The black bureaucrat
is no Cassius Clay when it comes to the verbals. Furthermore I hold
very advanced socialist views, among which is that all food should
be free at least for children. Futhermore his bumbling is eating into
my plugola time. When our chain-smoking Friendly Hostess interrupts
his turgid stammerings to ask me how this compares with socialised
British handouts I am glad to pour merry scorn.

"It sounds like a good idea," I say, smiling coldly at Food Stamp
Fats, "that is if the poor don't die of starvation before they get the
forms filled in."

Everybody laughs except the big federal butter and egg man. I get
in a swift seven or eight plugs for *Ladies' Man*. I am very witty.
The black brother from the red-tape belt is generally ignored. Did
somebody mention advanced socialism? Like many of that self-styled
ilk, Cameron has no time for petty amelioration measures. Until the
revolution he sees charity and welfare as mere sops to keep the
oppressed from seizing power. The poor people of America should
be glad that Cameron is making two hundred thousand dollars or
whatever ridiculous sum it is. Such lunatic grotesqueries are only
hastening the coming of heaven on earth.

"How was it?" he says to Weber in the car.

"A laff a minute, baby," she says.

"You sound exactly like Howard Abercrombie. Let's not get too
facetious, eh?"

"You were kinda rough on that welfare guy, weren't you?"

"That bumbling idiot? He deserved all he got. Now then, let's have a beer, I'm dehydrated." He stretches his arm along the seat and lovingly presses her shoulder. "Just a beer—I'll be clear-eyed and bushy-tailed for tonight, I promise."

Again she is too overwrought by newly-awakened romance to give utterance to the maelstrom of passionate hopes, fears, wishes, desires racing through her tremulous woman's mind.

"The Federal Communications Commission is pretty strict on drunks getting hold of mikes. A lot of stations won't let you in the door if you're even smelling slightly of the stuff."

"In Britain it's the other way round." We have so many wonderful things to learn about each other, and about our countries. "Our airlines only survive financially because they pour booze down your throat as soon as it's chocks away. Our navy floats on gin. The House of Commons is the best drinking club in London. Back home I'm not even considered a serious social drinker."

"Bully for you, buster."

The world does not understand people like us. We're called neurotics by clods who wouldn't know the difference between an inferiority complex and a coconut shy. We hide our sensitivities behind façades of laconic mockery. I look at Weber and admit to myself that until now she has been merely the physical manifestation of vague ambitions. Now I'm beginning to see her as a person. She is neat and clean. She has a blouse with a high collar and lacy ruffs at the wrist. Her nylons are not rucked up in little folds round her ankles. She is a little bit like Tula Ellice Finklea the movie actress. With a touch perhaps of the Joanne la Cock. Who is Tula Ellice Finklea they are asking in a million free libraries. And surely there never was a movie queen called Joanne la Cock! There was but she changed it because people would have been shocked by a marquee billing Joanne la Cock in *All The King's Men*. The very thought buggers description! As for Tula Ellice Finklea, she was said to have the most beautiful legs in the world. It's a shin to tell a lie, they used to trill when she paddy dude with that Irish hoofer. Want more clues? If she'd been in *El Cid* she'd have supplied most of the missing charisma.

"You realise that compulsive word-punning is an early indication of schizophrenia?"

"Word-punning? Is that different from gun-punning? You Americans with your verbose jargon. What happened to the lean, shrewd yankee trader with his laconic monosyllables between thin jets of yellow tobacco juice?"

"Has this streak of insanity come to the surface before, Cameron?"

"I'm feeling great so let's celebrate I'm the guy who found the last chord. Dey said Uncle Louis was mad!"

Our Hero and his current Love Object are passing within sight of the Capitol Building during this exchange. It does just cross Cameron's mind that on T.V. this morning, through the only eyes in medical history to develop overnight hernias, he saw an item about a huge anti-war rally planned for mid-October. Give him that much, it does cross his mind.

We came into the studio behind this young program-assistant, a stocky Jewish guy in horn-rims, very tense. He pointed to where the program host was taking five in a shaded corner, lying on a leather couch, an ice-pack on his forehead, sunglasses shielding his eyes from the glare. The monitors were showing a networked newscast. Weber and I sat with the audience, six or seven women who had about their pasty, aggressive faces an air of desperation, as though they were only present in a last-ditch effort to beat the Bored Housewife Drinking Problem. Television looks fairly glamorous on the screen, especially the talkshow with its important-looking desk and ultra-modern chairs. I've often watched these shows and imagined all the star guests poncing about in mink-lined splendour for the benefit of us dull-eyed rednecks. What I have realised since I started appearing was that the luxury extends no more than an inch past the range of the camera lens. Zsa Zsa and Raquel and Hermione may look as though they have trailed their sequined gowns across Persian rugs but the fact is that the talkshow action is taking place in a corner of a large hangar. If the camera could move one more degree you, the slob-viewer who falls for all this fake glamour, would see bare walls, often sweating with dank moisture, enough cables to re-stock Western Union, and bevies of unshaven union guys defying the bosses to implement the no-smoking stickers. Also, it is very draughty. Outside in America it is appointment in Sahara by John of that ilk but inside the show must go on in frigid air.

Then Mr. Ice-Pack got off his couch and came across to meet us, a clean-cut gent in natty blue blazering, young in outline but a trifle waxy round the eyes.

"Very glad to have you on the show," he said, shaking hands as if I might be a cholera-carrier. "Quite a book you've written there, Graham, quite a book. I respect talent—" He is now talking exclusively to Weber. His natty blazer is draped over his shoulders. "This," he gestured round the studio, "is transitory, a communication plant.

140

However, creative talent must be disseminated. We in the television medium have this responsibility to the community and to the artist. This is the vital service we can and must fulfil. We have an obligation."

The monitors showed that the newscast was over and we were escorted across to the interview table in the aforesaid mink-lined corner. It was brightly lit and reminded me of the ice-cream and over-priced confectionery stall you see in most cinema foyers. The mike was hung round my neck by a man with a simian knuckle-tonsure. I twisted a little, remembering the golden rule about not swivelling. They always tell you this on T.V., but they always provide you with swivel chairs. As always, before the fingerjab signalled transmission, I felt desperately empty and totally unfit to be appearing on an American T.V. show. I licked my lips and squinted through the solar-bright light to see if I could spot Weber. Did the American viewing public but know it, I spent a lot of time on prime American time seducing my manageress. Somehow I was finding it easier to tell her what I really thought of our inter-personal relationship with a million or so citizens listening in or looking on. She couldn't answer back.

Mr. Ice-Pack got his cue. His orange make-up crinkled in a big hullo folks smile. He gave the usual introductory guff about the successful new young author from swinging London. I listened modestly, not swivelling, not screwing up my haemorrhaging eyes, not picking my nose nor chewing it. I hoped the neck-mike wasn't picking up the plonking and gurgling that was going on down there in my corruscated pipes. Mr. Ice-Pack turned towards me.

"Now, Graham Cameron, what I would like to know about this book of yours"—he held up a copy and I glanced quickly to make sure the camera was getting a good visual plug—"why does a reasonably talented, presumably normal young man with a wife and children, as it says in your blurb, why does he have to write a filthy book like yours?"

There are times when I have doubts about myself, when I take the pessimistic view that I am a shambling nincompoop with the brains of a hutch-rabbit. Funnily enough, this does not apply, I have been noticing, when I'm within a hundred yards of a microphone or camera.

"You think *The New Ladies' Man* filthy? Mmm, you're the second person who's said that. My mother was the first. Mind you, her standards are pretty severe—she always thought Walt Disney's *Bambi*

141

was a bit stag-night. What parts of *The New Ladies' Man* did you find particularly sexual or obscene?"

I knew he was trying to make what these media-hounds call good television. You flatter the guest beforehand and make him think you're his friend and admirer and then you spring this trick in front of the camera, hoping to enrage or fluster him. My genial act—and act it was, for I had a momentary impulse to kick him in the slats, an American expression which means either the teeth or the shins or the balls; it turns up a lot in American fiction but I never heard an actual American using it—flummoxed the smooth bastard for a second.

"I started to read this novel and frankly after two chapters I had to put it down. I was physically nauseated. Did you write it with the intention of making money from dirt?"

"Yes."

He frowned, as though I'd forgotten my lines.

"You admit it?"

"Oh yes," I said airily, shrugging nonchalantly, keeping a beady eye out for which camera was showing the red light, "my agent told me if I hoped to make a name for myself in the United States I'd have to write pretty good dirt to compete with all your domestic filth-merchants. Good title, eh, *The New Ladies' Man*? It's been banned in Baltimore already, you know."

"I believe—I wonder if you do, too, despite what you say—that creative artists, with God-given talents, should be helping Mankind to look at the stars. Your gaze seems firmly stuck on the gutter."

"That's true," I said cheerfully, turning my head casually, slowly, to let the other camera get my full-face. "But just think—you want us all staring up at the stars—" I covered an impeccably timed pause with a hammy hand gesture towards the ceiling "—and falling down manholes."

Yes folks, the technicians laughed. I saw the guy with the earphones slapping his thigh. I turned on my inquisitor and beamed innocently.

"On this show we try to get at the truth, Mr. Cameron. Why should decent American lovers of literature be asked to buy this kind of stuff? For instance, in the first two pages you have your so-called hero—and I may say, he's one of the most repulsive people I've met in a lifetime's devotion to classic literature—you give a prolonged account of his urinary tract problem. Is that what you feel Mankind should be concerned over at this crucial juncture in history?"

"His urinary tract problem?" I frowned at my own ignorance. Then my face lit up. "Oh—you mean where he needs the john and can't find one and does it in the telephone box?"

Somebody sniggered. I began to see why top entertainers need a live audience.

"Is that an important aspect of modern society? Is it important to our understanding of the great issues facing us right across the board of human society?"

"It would be pretty important if you developed the same urinary tract problem here and now in the middle of this broadcast. What would you do, raise your right hand and ask teacher for permission to leave the programme?"

The guy with the earphones bent double, hands on knees, his ill-suppressed snorts probably damaging his career prospects.

At the end of the interview—five title plugs and two pornographics later—he shook my hand and said we'd achieved some real television. The last I saw of him he was back on the couch with the ice-pack. As I was having a gargle at the faucet in the corridor one of the floorhands stopped to say:

"You hit that crummy ratfink right where he lives, Scotty. You shoulda seen the cocksucker's face when you mentioned the john!"

Weber refused to agree that I had been a sensation. I put this down to jealousy. She was a bookish kind of person, educated no doubt to incredible degrees—and here was the unknown British nobody not only writing the next big best-seller but also holding his own in the mindless demi-monde of the plugola circuit. To her I must be some kind of new renaissance man. The understandable awe in which she regarded me was responsible for her nervous insecurity and I only laughed when she said:

"You sure you weren't born in a trunk with Judy Garland, Grahamy baby? Soon as you get in front of the cameras you come on like a real vaudevillian."

"I thought this tour would be all bookish culture programmes and educational television. Still, I don't mind the crap, as long as it brings in the dollars."

And as long as I'm never more than five minutes away from my last or next drink.

Weber had been talking about spending another night in Washington but when we came out of the T.V. building she said we were setting off back to New York. I would have liked to hang around and pick up some reactions to my performances but if she wanted to inaugurate our lifetime of romance in her own bed back in the Village I was not about to complain. I kept asking her about certain things I'd said and trying to find out if they'd come across but she was too preoccupied with our coming nuptials. I got my shoes off and stuck my feet on the air-conditioning vent and went over the show in my mind, selecting various gags and comments that could be worked up into a slicker routine. We came to a roundabout with a plethora of signs to countless small towns of which only the residents have ever heard, but no sign pointing to New York. Weber drove round about it five times rather than stop at the filling station and ask for directions. Then she made her choice and we cruised on to one of four highways.

"Dammit," she said two hundred yards from the roundabout. "This is the road to Harrisburg."

"Is that bad?"

"It's way off our route. Jesus."

I suggested a quick U-turn over the grass and a dash back to the roundabout but she said the highway patrol would emerge from the trees and come after us all sirens screaming. I think she said our little error added seventy-eight miles to our journey. I enjoyed the ride. Imaginatively channelled, the terror that grips thinking people (i.e. non-drivers) in motor cars can produce sexual euphoria. Around the time we were passing exit signs to Gettysburg my ostensibly sleeping eyeballs were slithering up and down Weber's nethers, from skirt-splayed thighs to pedal-pressing ankles. Her morbid fears of bodily communion, it occurred to me, might be an inhibited person's self-defence against strange perversions. One night in New York one of Chuck's male friends told me that American women are incredibly aggressive in bed. His phraseology was disgusting, as is all American profanity to the British ear, but the gist of it was that the American female has a compulsion to straddle her submissive male and brutally rape and screw and shaft and gouge and spur his body, immediately prior to whipping the knackers off him with a pair of electrically-operated hedge-trimmers from Sears Roebuck. On the other hand, I've heard that the American male's idea for his big horn's last stand is up and on and wham-wham thankee ma'am. From a nation whose phrase for cunt is 'a piece of ass' one might expect backward notions.

A great idea hit me as Weber tooled our rented passion wagon into the parking area of the Valley Forge Howard Johnson. I stood for a moment under a grey American sky, stamping down my trousers and
144

waiting for my blood to get back in the proper veins, thinking—I'll show these hucksters how to publicise *Ladies' Man*!

I waited until we were seated at the counter among the truck-drivers and lingerie reps and convention-circuit Kiwanis. Weber ordered two king cheeseburgers and two coffees, Sanka for herself and genuine Nescafé for me. She lit a True cigaret. Behind the counters there were half a dozen white girls and some black skivvies, boredom and lethargy writ large over their listless, greasy faces. What we had here was a standardized oasis on one of the featureless camel trails that cross the great desert of middle America. Outside you could see the drawn-faced people reluctantly leaving their mobile hidey-holes, stamping down their creases, coming inside, gulping down their standardized portions, staring disinterestedly at the souvenir display-racks, solving their urinary tract problems, bolting back to their standardized cars and disappearing down a grey highway under a grey sky. A suitable setting, indeed, for the birth of an idea that would take one of us out of the standardized ruck. Color that man *famous*.

"*Confidential Magazine*," I said to Weber.

"Come again?"

"*Confidential Magazine* is still being published, isn't it? We have to get our title across to the American public, don't we? *The New Ladies' Man* is a natural for *Confidential*, isn't it? All right, we get Tannenbaum Inc.'s press division to leak a story about me to *Confidential*. Any old lie will do—Stella Nelson is carrying my child—you and I have been screwing backstage on all these family talkshows. Can't you see it? I'll be a Sex Scribe! Success scandale! Want to hear my song—From the balls of mount and screw me to the whores of Dodge Cit-ee ..."

"Good God. It's the most crummy, vulgar—"

"No doubt. Is it any more vulgar than these crappy, mindless T.V. shows you're putting me on? Of course it's vulgar! Vulgar—of the common people. Once you accept the principle—huckstering—what's the difference between clowning on T.V. and turning yourself into a virility symbol? Eh? Huh? The Errol Flynn of British fiction—we'll sell a million books, baby!"

I sat back on my stool, triumphant, eyes aglow. She shook her head slowly. I imagine the young Jimmy Watt got the same reaction when he rushed to tell his mammy her kettle had given birth to steam radio. She was going to need a lot of convincing. That's half the fun of inventing devastating new concepts.

"You wanna wash up while I pick up the check?" were her actual words. I made a note of them for posterity. I had future generations firmly in mind when I stuck the shiny Howard Johnson menu down inside my trousers, risking laminated castration for the sake of a priceless exhibit in the Graham Cameron Memorial Museum. I had a giddy turn in the john but splashed my face with alternate handfuls of hot and cold water until the black clouds stopped looming over my eyeballs. We drove through Dutch Pennsylvania. It had mountains and white farms and tasteful fencing, the kind of place you expected to see the young Elizabeth Taylor astride a paddock rail watching a glossy filly with white bandages on its fetlocks. I had my stockinged feet up on the dashboard, sometimes out of the window to evaporate the sweat. I hummed and sang and counted the snake-farm signs and kept Weber generally amused, especially when we saw a giant hoarding for a hotel chain. *Unwind with Us.* Picture of a worried man with a giant key stuck in his back.

"Very relaxing image," I chortled to Weber. "Stay at our restful haven and get a fucking great keyhole cut into your guts. What do you think, kiddo?"

"It must get results."

"Cheer up then. We're on the threshold of great things."

"I'm all washed up."

"You don't need sleep when you're famous, I'm finding. I was brilliant on that show today, wasn't I? Go on admit it. So it's crap—it still needs talent. You're a cool one, Weber, but you don't fool me—underneath you're just one big quiver! Here we are at the birth of a star! My little nervous precious!"

I leaned across to plant a smackeroony of a kiss on her wispy-curled nape. Without taking her eyes off the racing concrete ribbon, she smacked me quite hard across the nose. Bending forward quickly, I pressed my supplicant lips on the exquisite sheen of her nyloned knee, nudging up the hem of her skirt with my virile cheek. She got my right ear lobe between finger and thumb and jerked me off, albeit the wrong organ. I slipped a hand under her guard and delved my fingers between the buttons of her blouse. She nipped at my wrist, catching some fine hairs between her nails.

"Ohh—that hurt," I said reproachfully, kissing my own skin.

"Just quit that stuff or next time I'll scratch your eyes out," she snapped. I'll buy her jewelled rowels for our honeymoon night, I thought. Rhonda Fleming had a very cruel face as well. Lead me to

146

it. I curled up in my corner and slept through most of New Jersey, safe beside my gentle love.

Twilight on the turnpike. Fiery red sky to the west, purple-black to the east. The silver glint of the evening jet. Four lanes of ghost-silent cars, ribbons of slow-burn reds rising and falling gently. Giant trucks sailing majestically, outlined by strings of fairground lights, carnival wagons, outriders of a mighty circus, the great chemical complex, white steam and red furnaces, miles of it in the dark, mighty industrial America blasting and billowing and fuming and pounding. And the holy city against a black-ink sky, lit as if by golden fire, the Empire State Building and the ethereal honeycombs of the Wall Street skyscrapers. It is like a foggy night in November going through the Holland Tunnel, but the mega-city is warm and cosy. It welcomes me back. Out there is endless night and lonely desert but here is bustle and light and raucous humanity. *And shelter.*

"I'll drop you at the hotel then I'm going to hit the sack for forty-eight hours," she says. The shouting is over. She is a stranger. We are shyly polite to each other. I get my bag out of the boot and stand on the sidewalk watching her red lights merge with the Fifth Avenue traffic.

Chapter Thirteen

YOU'RE *PEOPLE*, SAID THE BOOK STORE LADY. TO BE CALLED
PEOPLE, HOWARD EXPLAINED, WAS A GUT COMPLIMENT.

Have five days' rest, they tell me. Relax, sleep late, eat well, we'll
fix you up with tickets for the theater. The theatre? Jesus Christ, I
couldn't be bothered going to see all that middle-class crap in the
London originals.

I slept till seven fifty-three that first morning back from Washington. I was rested already. Relaxation-wise, I could have told them,
I have to take a book to the lavatory otherwise I get too bored to
finish shitting. I don't tell them this because Americans do not discuss shit, sweat or death. Mental illness they love. They call it analysis.
Weber has it once a week, Milton has just stopped, Howard is thinking of stopping because his angina problem is taking up too much
time as it is. Weber pays twenty-five bucks an hour for some Jungian
charlatan to listen to her frigidity problem. She gets angry when I
ask how long the cure will take. Boy, what a racket—there is no
cure. As long as you've got the money the analyst will go on listening.
Does the Pope know? By comparison his lot are giving it away. Weber
accuses me of requiring analysis. I say I'll give her twenty-five bucks
for an hour on her couch. We could split the lolly and both be cured
for twelve and a half bucks. She says I'm more neurotic than anybody she knows, despite my pose as uncomplicated peasant. I tell her
I regard life as just stuff that happens. She says I'm so lacking in
motivation it's a miracle I ever got to 33. How come Weber and I
are having such intimate chats after all that groping and grappling on
the retreat from Valley Forge? I don't know, I think the bloody
woman is beginning to get a thing about me.

"The signs are good, Graham," said the disembodied mouth and
chin of Milton Tannenbaum.

"Oh?" said Our Man Cameron, squinting into the darkness where
Milton's nose, eyes and upper-skull presumably were. Outside it was
ninety-two degrees and the glare so intense he had almost joined the
policemen and all the other personality defects by investing in sunglasses, yet Milton had the curtains drawn, his twenty-first-floor office

148

lit only by an angle-arm desk-lamp. It was a corner office, a top status symbol in a large corporation. You had to admire the subtlety of a man who made it to the corner and then refused to look at *either* view.

"I spoke with Sally Weber, she says you did excellently in these early shows."

I must make a gesture to Weber, Our Man thought, something that will restore my simple, lovable image.

"Now what I suggest you do now is rest up for a day or two. You're flying out of La Guardia on Tuesday morning, and the schedule we have for you from there on in will leave little breathing space."

"Yes, I'll get some rest in," Our Man said, nodding wisely. A bunch of orchids in a long, cellophane-topped box, with a note signed simply, *Graham*? A string of pearls worth ten grand from Tiffany's — chuck 'em casually in her lap while she's making up in front of the mirror for the first house of the Boston try-out? *Try these for size, honey ... oh, Graham, how did you know I've always yearned for pearls?* In comes William Demarest. *When you two love-boids stop slobbering over each other there's a full house out dere and dey're gonna tear the joint apart if the coitun don't open as of now!*

"You screwed her yet?"

"Ha ha. What a funny question. You told me yourself she never comes across."

"I thought your dynamic approach might have swamped her."

"I don't know where you heard about my dynamic approach."

"We've been getting tapes of your shows in the office. They'll be putting you in the sexual hall of fame."

"That's what you told me to do, wasn't it?"

"Are you trying to tell me it's an act?"

"Course it's an act."

"The stage missed a great talent is all I can say."

"I'll phone my wife and get her to send pictures of the kids and flash them about in front of the cameras if you prefer that."

"So long as you keep plugging the book title I'm happy to go along with whatever personality you care to project."

"They're obviously not interested in books as such so I thought I might as well take my cue from you — those placards on the Pan Am roof? You don't think I enjoy making a fucking idiot of myself on moronic television shows making out I'm the randiest bastard in London, do you?"

"If you weren't a swinger you couldn't have written a book like *The New Ladies' Man* with such conviction."

"It's fiction! Swinging London is a lot of crap. There's no such place. Surely you realise the point of the book—the guy has read all this swinging shit in the papers, he is going mad thinking everybody else is having a ball, he starts living in fantasy! It's fiction, Milton, *I made it up!*"

"I guess I owe you an apology."

"You really thought it was thinly-disguised autobiography?"

"It does come across that way."

"I'm glad I didn't write about a pederast then."

You could tell Our Man was nettled by this exchange. All the time he was walking to the offices of the agency which handled his American rights he kept thinking the crowds on Fifth Avenue were looking at him and sniffing in disgust. Get a load of that brothel-creeping sex-dog, they were saying. All the way to the Chase Manhattan Bank with the cheque for five hundred dollars he could hear them muttering threats against any slimy foreign debauchee who cast his filthy bedroom eyes on their daughters. By the time the girl-teller counted out his five hundred in tens and twenties he was a skulking figure of loathing and disgust. His first decision was to call off the tour. He went back to the hotel and, after eleven false starts, composed a tersely-worded note to Milton apologising for walking out but saying his dignity as a man and husband and father and his integrity as a writer might both be destroyed by fresh exposure to the vulgar huckstering required for best-sellerdom, which in any case he despised.

He sealed the note in a hotel envelope. He then put through a call to London. Sheina was giving the babies their tea. She seemed surprised to hear him again so soon after his lovey-dovey call of the night before. He told her angrily that he was sick of the whole thing and would be home by the next night. She told him not to do anything stupid but he said his mind was made up. She said he ought to go out with friends for a few drinks and calm down. He slammed the phone down on her and then threw the Manhattan directory out of the bathroom window. He packed his case and left it by the door. He went downstairs and headed towards the Tannenbaum Inc. offices. At a DON'T WALK sign he shouldered through the sheepish people and strode across the road, defying the cars to run him down. Going up Fifth Avenue he saw the exquisitely-draped window of a high-class
150

confectioners. He went inside. The lady assistant was soft-voiced and over-perfumed, no doubt making out she was a temporarily impoverished Hungarian countess. He bought a chocolate elephant for seven dollars. The old whore gave him a lot of breathy charm for seven bucks. She gift-wrapped it. It made a parcel about the size of a football. He went back to the hotel and sat at the writing-table in the palm court foyer.

Dear Sally, You can eat this as a little memento of our travels. I'm glad you turned out to be a neurotic, frigid bitch. It saved me betraying my wife for the sake of a quick and no doubt forgettable fuck. I hope when you do meet a man to bed-hop with he is kinky about old maids. Graham.

Right, he thought, no second thoughts this time. I'll deliver these time-bombs and be on my way.

"Mr. Cameron?" the desk-clerk called across the floor.

"Yeah?"

"Phone call for you, Mr. Cameron."

He had the chocolate elephant under his arm, the two envelopes in his right hand. He stood sideways in the phone-box.

"Yeah?" he grunted.

"Hi," said Weber. "I thought of taking in this movie *Bonnie and Clyde* tonight. You wanna come?"

"Oh yeah? Hold hands and eat popcorn and a goodnight peck on the front porch?"

"Christ, have I caught you in the middle of one of your moods?"

"What d'you mean, *moods*? I don't have moods! It's you who has the moods!"

"Okay okay, so I'm having a good mood. You wanna come to the movies or don't you?"

Fingers drum.

"Yeah okay."

"It's on Second Avenue, I'll pick you up at the hotel around seven."

They ate the chocolate elephant in the movie-house. Smoking was prohibited and there were no popcorn trays. Neither were there any adverts, trailers or Tom and Jerries. Weber read the elephant note during the short wait for the lights to down.

I hear you are a hard tusk-master so here's piece of tail you can chew without recrimination. Howdah and farewell, Sabu.

She didn't object when he took her hand, nor when he kissed her

151

knuckles. She didn't object to anything until, in the middle of a cosy necking session on her leather couch, during a commercial break in the Johnny Carson show, he took her hand and placed it accurately on his zip. Her face was buried in his neck at the time. She shook her head, or tried to. He persisted. She twisted her face to murmur up at his ear:

"Not yet, Graham, don't rush me, *please*?"

A lesser man would have strangled her with her own nylon or brazeer but Cameron was no slavering-mouthed hyena, no Jack Elam in *Rawhide*. He behaved with great dignity. He didn't even slam the door behind him. In the Oak Room he found Chuck jolting back a few shots with Tommy, the guy from that night in the bars of Marilyn. They engaged in manly conversation. Any slimy, tomcatting lech could fool around with bevies of faceless broads, Our Hero told himself. Only a man with the soul of a poet could endure the waiting and the longing, the yearning and the hoping, the hurting and the wounding ...

"Let's raise a little hell," said Tommy. "I know, let's hit Toots Shor's for a blast or two!"

"We're hell-raisers," Cameron said as they shouted down a cab. He was impressed. Twenty minutes later, during the shouting match between Chuck and an under-manager in the foyer of Toots Shor's establishment, he felt more like his own maiden aunt. The trouble was that he had come out in *the* dark shirt without *the* tie. Chuck was persuaded to leave before the cops came. Our Hero tried to console himself with the thought that Errol Flynn, in fact, died not of too much booze and screwing but of drug addiction.

Waken in Howard's guest suite in Westchester County. Very hot and damp. Sheets twisted. Listen to deep male voice from outside.

"Tammy?"

Feels good to come to without hangover. Learning to cope. Temporary, fame-induced neuroses now behind me. Brentanos asked for three dozen extra copies. Solus review in *New York Review of Books*. Highly favourable. Said I'm better than Donleavy. This is favourable? Success coming smoothly, as planned. Must think deeply and seriously about personal situation.

"TAMMY?"

Always *felt* I was man who needed two wives. Sheina not as prudish as Weber but probably won't readily agree to sharing home. Sheina hates Americans.

"TAMMY!"

Sheina will have to realise I am not a bank-clerk but a *writer*. Dickens had two, didn't he, under the same roof? Something like that. Joyce encouraged Norah to have it off with other guys. We writers are like that. Bigger than petty rules.

"TAMMY, WHERE ARE YOU, TAMMY?"

Better to have honest menage à trois than mistress on sly, tell Sheina. Menage have seen the glory of the coming. Great writers of past had powers of personal magnetism, brainwashed wives and mistresses into accepting folderols. Did Dosstoffhimselfoffsky's missus keep nagging him? Come away from the gaming floor, Fyodor?

"COME HERE THIS INSTANT, TAMMY!"

Hemingway needed new wife for every book. Romantic bastard. Who the hell is that bawling down there? Get out of bed and pad nakedly to open window. Ever hear of total sunlight? Pool looks cool. American living standards very high. Howard said to have bought this mansion on Fran's money. Couldn't afford it on pay as mere vice-president. Tannenbaum Inc. has thirteen vice-presidents. Remember L.B.J. as vice-president, gave away monogrammed ballpoints in Berlin. Only a heart-beat from presidency. Hard lines, Howard, Milt ain't got one. More appropriate to move Weber to London than us to move to America. Have rota system for fair shares in bed. It's Howard who's been shouting. Small boy in check trousers and sports shirt standing before him on lawn. Must be son. Thought Tammy was a girl's name.

"No sir," he is saying. Must be about eight. Howard has hands on hips. Doesn't look at all genial. Boy standing almost at attention. I will be august but wildly tolerant patriarch, multi-mothered sons can be layabouts or admirals as they desire, so long as I get to screw the girl-friends.

"Where have you been, Tammy?" Is this the same Howard who gladhands at conventions?

"I was playing ball, sir."

"I was calling you, Tammy."

"I didn't hear you, sir."

"Okay, Tammy, now you want to get busy and police the hedge?"

"Yessir."

"I want you should pick up *all* the leaves, Tammy."

"Yessir."

The little soldier in his mini-adult trousers breaks ranks and bends his back under this hedge. It's okay, Tammy kid, I'm beaming down

153

from my window under the eaves, ten years from now you can reject the bastard where it hurts. Mine used to beat me with a leather belt. I've been rejecting him cruelly ever since. It's been a long campaign with many a sweetly vicious victory, and hardly lessened in ferocity by the irrelevance of his death. Wait till he hears down there I've come home from America with quarter a million dollars and an extra wife!

A few friends and neighbours stop by for drinks at the poolside. I am in a swimming costume, brown and slim now, no longer the great gutsby. I do a few underwater dives with young Tammy's goggles. It is green and misty down there. I get out and join the middle-aged set on the sunbeds. My immersion makes me feel virile in an effeminate sort of way, the bathing beauty who did get wet. Little Tammy keeps on swimming, possibly he's crossing the Channel in his own backyard. Even at his tender age he has to do the masculine thing. The pressure on American males to comport themselves like American males must be hell. During the night the humidity was so bad that twelve hundred dollars of new paper slipped off the walls of Howard's reading-room. This was because of a power failure, due to the goddam Con Ed electricity monopoly. It's so hot in the house I feel like Jackie Patterson sweating off the pounds in the furnace-room for the Rinty Monaghan fight but seemingly they can't switch the central heating off in summer otherwise the humidity rots books and carpets. I think that Sheina and Weber and I will live in one of those cool, white Spanish-style houses like the ones Picasso keeps his inspirations in. Young Tammy has just about reached Cap Griz Nez and looks set to be the first under-twelve to attempt it both ways without a break. Wasn't there a guy who ran all the way across the Atlantic on the deck of the *Queen Elizabeth*?

In deference to my visiting author status, no doubt, they start talking about culture. We hear general condemnations of sleazy urban politics, the goddam Con Ed monopoly, again, big city graft. These well-to-do, intensely civilised, east coast Americans seem to despise all things intrinsically American. I imagine their dream was raped when Adlai Stevenson didn't make the White House. Even their 'liberal' views stem not so much from any desire to have negro sons-in-law as from their distaste for the graft-happy demagogues who run the country.

Anyway, there's this big guy who looks a bit like wise old Jay C. Flippen. He's culture mad and to him culture means England. We

154

hear how courteous and fair-minded and law-abiding are the English. We hear many a sincere compliment to Her Gracious Majesty and all the stable, time-honoured virtues she personifies. Young Tammy is out of sight, possibly doing a few lengths under-water to escape the relentless face-bruising slaps of the choppy waves. I am not drinking heavily. In fact I initially asked Fran for a beer. I won't say my asking for a Schlitz or Budweiser created the same excitement as did Alan Ladd's request for sarsparilla in *Shane* but it did tend to make me noticeable. Americans of the middle and professional classes regard beer as stuff for working slobs to slop down dirty vests in crummy neighborhood bars. I toy with a half-pint of yet another of these brilliantly-named export whiskies which have so much prestige for Americans. Tammy surfaces and I wonder if the little devil has been jerking himself off under the water.

Oh yeah, Jay C. Flippen. He is describing, lyrically, the great sense of peace and continuity and timelessness and cultural values he felt while walking round Stratford-upon-Avon. You'd think Ann Hathaway's cottage might be on a par with Bethlehem the reverence he gives it. The visiting author is asked which of the Bard's masterpieces he finds most satisfying, *ultimately*. The visiting author is fairly evasive. He once took part in class readings from *As You Like It* and this little acquaintanceship with Shakespeare makes him glad his country's ruling classes did not think him worthy of further education in all that blank-verse mumbo-jumbo.

"But as a writer you cannot afford to cut yourself off from the basic wellsprings of your society's cultural bedrock," says Jay C. He's the one in the monogrammed blazer and natty cravate. (Did I say I'm still in the same dark shirt I flew over with? It's been laundered a couple of times, of course.) Is this guy after culture? Like dogs after hares. Naturally he has never heard of W. C. Handy or Huddie Leadbetter, let alone Chick Webb.

"Culture is what the middle-classes call anything that is dead or from another country," I remark. It is not so insulting as it sounds because I smile a lot. "Anything immediate or relevant is dangerous to bourgeois property values and therefore has to be dismissed as popular crap or mere propaganda. Now my idea of culture, your honour, is what people *do*. *Last Exit to Brooklyn* is culture. The fact that we are sitting in the area administered by the Ossining School Board is culture. What the hell has Henry James to do with the men who're waiting in the death-house a mile or two from this very spot? I read a con's history of Sing-Sing once, did you know what they call
155

the shed where the electric chair is? The Dancehall! Do you know the first guy they ever electrocuted was given three different voltages and eventually they had to put a bullet in his neck—how can you guinea-pig an electric chair? Do you know the ambition of most men in the death row was to beat the State by taking their own lives—even if it meant gnawing through their own wrists? Nelson Algren put it the right way when he said American literature is the young guy telling the judge who sentenced him to death, 'I knew I'd never get to twenty-one anyhow.'"

Believe me, I'm beginning to feel a little sympathy for Dylan and Brendan, hopeless drunks and child-men as they undoubtedly were. It's a lot easier to play the know-nothing clown with cultural Americans. They only care about Jane Austen and Thackeray and all that dusty old bollix. They see no possible interest in the crowd in the street in the city they have escaped from. *Hamlet*, if you please, is a continual testament to the potential grandeur of man's spirit. Young Tammy's just about crawled round the Cape and shows no sign of flagging. Jay C. Flippen, regrettably, has to bow out in the middle of our meaningful conversation. I'm just as glad, for I have every intention of drinking little and saying less, and he seems to be provoking me. As soon as he has gone, Howard says to Fran:

"It's sad about Grant, isn't it, honey?"

"I'd say he's taking it pretty well," Fran replies.

Grant Harper Fowles. 51 years. Vice-president of a large cosmetic corporation. Sixty thousand a year plus stock options and top hat pension scheme. Big wheel in Westchester social set. Wife on many charity committees. Corporation falls foul of government trust-busters on price-rigging rap. Unloads executive fat but fast. Grant axed. No chance of comparable job in New York at his age. Mortgage in the 100,000-120,000 dollar bracket. Didn't have long enough in upper exec. grade to take up all stock options. Five weeks now without a job. Telling neighbours he is taking a prolonged vacation to reappraise direction of future career. Resigns from country clubs, golf clubs, etc. Lets chauffeur go. Tells neighbours he is rediscovering joy of driving. Used to give lavish parties, now says wife is under medical supervision for hypertension, mustn't overtax herself. Only job offered so far is $17,500 p.a. in Reading, Pa. Might just take it, tells neighbours, to get out of New York rat-race, enjoy country life. Neighbours know truth. Mrs. Fowles devastated at losing friends, roots, social position. No friends in Reading. Howard and Fran only couple who still see Grant regularly. Other neighbours say they don't invite them

156

to dinner parties to save them embarrassment. Embarrassment? Yes, they can't afford to reciprocate.

Tammy comes out of pool.

"How many lengths, Tammy?" says Howard.

"Twenty-five, Dad."

"You can do better, Tammy."

"Yes, Dad."

Tammy goes up lawn to house where home-help has dinner ready. Howard looks after him admiringly.

"That's my boy," he says. He looks at visiting author, winking broadly, smiling. "Great little kid, isn't he?"

His name is Tommy!

It was a pretty quiet party. Nothing much happened. Forty guests consumed about a hundred and fifty dollars' worth of booze. One of Howard's friends, a magazine writer, brought along his latest date, an ethereal blonde who had just signed a seven-year contract with M.G.M. After only three drinks she had some kind of fit during which she bit her lower lip. Blood ran down her twitching chin and tears dislodged make-up. Two women helped her through to the john. The visiting author could already hear himself telling the blokes back home about this revealing incident when she became a big star. But would he ever again see the blokes back home? All the time he was watching the door for Weber.

She came in wearing a white summer frock with shiny brass buttons. It contrasted strikingly with her dark hair and tanned skin, giving her a Romany look. Cameron had a swift seizure of heart and lungs, an involuntary inhalation followed by a panicky sensation of drowning. He went to the john. Two anxious-faced men by the locked door told him he, too, might as well cross his legs and play shakes and bladders. The star-to-be had passed out. He went back to the party, helping himself to a stiff shot of Scotch on his way round the room. Weber was with two brisk-looking men, one of whom was laughing disdainfully.

"Hi Graham," she said. "Do you know Saul and Kenny?"

Hi they all said. Cameron gave her a meaningful glance, nodding imperceptibly towards the French windows. She smiled faintly and looked back at Saul, who was telling them the amusing story of how he'd travelled to the coast to break the news to Leon Irving, the best-selling author, that his new book had bombed, sales-wise.

"He just doesn't have it any more," said Saul, authoritatively. "I mean, he always did have a drinking problem but now I guess he's a grade-A lush."

Our Hero again tried to signal Weber over to the French windows. She hardly seemed to notice him. They went on discussing Leon Irving's falling sales graph.

"What he does now I can't imagine. With two lots of alimony and the kinda life-style he's got for himself out there in Malibu he has to drag down about eighty thousand a year before he gets a dollar for himself."

Cameron found himself hovering. He kept staring at Weber. To think that a working-class nobody from nowhere was the one Fate had chosen to change the life of this beautiful, worldly, *important* New York lady—it was frightening. Having prognosticated every permutation of humiliating failure that lay ahead for the wretched Leon Irving—"none a the movie companies will touch him any more even—" Saul and Kenny decided to spare him a little time.

"Things look pretty good when you're going up, huh?" said Kenny.

"Things look pretty good," Cameron said, eyes fixed meaningfully on Weber's face. "Sally, there's something I wanted to speak to you about."

"It's a cinch he wants to tell me more about some jazz musician I never even heard of," Weber said to Saul and Kenny. "Graham is one of these European jazz buffs—and movies! I never knew Hollywood made so many movies as he tells me about."

The Americans grinned. I've been in your bloody bed, Cameron wanted to say. I know you better than these stainless-steel bastards. But he found he could not speak. Maybe she didn't even remember. Maybe she didn't think it was worth remembering, just a bit of the pawing and groping to be expected from whatever crummy author she was currently humoring.

Feeling hopelessly excluded, he went to the john. The door was locked. He slipped through a side door on to the payteeoh and stood at the far edge, where a low stone wall overlooked the lawn. In case anyone was looking through the half-drawn curtains, he raised his glass to his mouth, at the same time unzipping and pointing his cock at American sod. As filtered whisky flooded out into the darkness he looked westward at the limitless black vault of the night. He shuddered. Tomorrow he was starting out on a journey that would take him to the end of that American night. As he shook off the last few drops and shoved his unloved member back into the folds of his Y-fronts,

158

wiggling his backside, knees bending slightly outwards, he heard the inscrutable coughing of some furry creature in the bushes. Racoons in the culvert, Howard had said. Racoons! What am I doing here? How did I get here? That black sky has no end. You mean I sat at our shaky kitchen table typing among the butter and jam and now *I'm in America?* It can't be true.

He sat down on the little wall. He was shivering, although it was by no means cold. Through gaps in the curtains he saw heads and shoulders and heard laughing voices. The shivering quickened into uncontrollable trembling. The glass fell away from his hand. It did not break. He clasped his arms across his stomach and crouched forward until he was almost doubled up.

The pale-faced, wary-eyed man who skirted unobtrusively round the fringe of the party and helped himself to a whole glass of neat whisky and drank most of it in one heart-stopping gulp was a thousand years older than the Graham Cameron who had left his home in London less than three weeks before. That's what he told himself. He had been to the brink of disaster and had pulled back in time.

"Hi, you having a withdrawal mood?" said Weber.

"Mood?" echoed Our Hero disinterestedly. "Nah, I just don't like this kind of thing. Nothing ever happens at cocktail parties, does it?"

Chapter Fourteen

ORGASMS GALORE!

For our flight out of La Guardia to Cleveland Weber was wearing a blue woollen dress and pearl-hued nylons, white shoes and gloves — and a shiny black raincoat. With her hair down in some fancy new style, pinned up above her ears, I have no doubt she thought she looked pretty alluring. I said very little to her. She had come within a hair's breadth of wrecking my home and family and I had decided to treat her with cold disdain.

"What is that you're doing—toting up the loot?" she asked when we were airborne.

"I'm working out the money my wife will get under this Death and Dismemberment policy," I said, keeping my knees together and my legs jutting out in the gangway so that there would be no chance of any of those accidental little touchings she had been using to tempt me.

"Jesus Christ, you got the spooks for real."

"No, I'm merely being practical. If I get killed the pay-off is twenty-five thousand dollars but I've taken out a double idemnity thing. That's fifty thousand. If I lose both feet, or both eyes, or a hand and a foot, or a foot and an eye, I get the straight twenty-five thousand. A hand or foot or eye on its own works out at about ten to fifteen thousand dollars—"

"Aw, for God's sake's! Put that creepy thing away!"

"When I've finished."

"Jesus! Would you seriously object to me having a nap?"

"Do whatever you want."

"Thank you."

"You're welcome."

The sky was dark with heavy rain-clouds as we touched down in Cleveland. To the west the sunset was red. The bus that took us into the city was incredibly hot. I reached up and wound down the window an inch or two.

"Keep the windows closed," the driver barked through the loud-speaker system. "The air-conditioning don't work if the windows are open."

Faces turned to stare. I stared back. Weber, with typical female lack of nerve, reached up and wound the handle until the window was closed. One man kept on staring at me. I crossed my eyes and rolled them at him. He blushed and looked away. The drive to the city centre took about an hour. I wondered if we had deplaned at the wrong airport. At the hotel I allowed Weber to handle the details of booking in. She tipped the bellboy. We had adjacent rooms but there was no connecting door, something I had no doubt she had not bargained on. I got my washing things out of my case and then lay on my bed to read *Why Are We In Vietnam?* I had decided to buy enough books to keep me occupied during all the free time I would have between T.V. shows, radio interviews, press conferences and autographing parties. I had made up my mind to cut out drink altogether. It made me too vulnerable.

Naturally Weber's nerve broke first.

"Hi," she said on the phone. "You settled in?"

"I'm reading," I said, coldly.

"I have a friend lives here, from college? I've told her we're both going out to their place for dinner."

"You go ahead," I said, "I shall read and perhaps watch some television. Let me have a copy of the schedule before you go."

"Jesus."

I put down the phone and went back to Mr. Mailer's desperate strivings. There was a knock at the door. Reluctantly I put my book down and got off the bed.

"Are you having one of your moods?" Weber asked. I behaved with calm dignity, leaving the door open but going back to the bed and lying down with my book. She checked her complexion in my dressing-table mirror—or meer as it is inexplicably pronounced in their version of English. I sneaked a look at her over the top of my book. She had one leg up on the dressing-table chair, pulling at the seam of her nylon. Her skirt was pulled up enough for me to catch a prolonged glimpse of the inside of her thigh, brown skin partially scaffolded by a black suspender.

"You sure you don't want to come with me to my friend's home for dinner?" she said, still looking down at her seam.

"Oh, all right," I said exasperatedly, throwing down my book with a sharp sigh. "If it's going to bother you I'll come!"

Not many celebrities would do this, I thought, as we boarded a local train and trundled off into Cleveland suburbia, little of which I could see for interminable goods trains passing in the opposite direction, the wagons bearing massive lengths of steel and machinery.

We were met at the local station by a chirpy lady with bright blue hair and diamanté-studded red spectacle frames of devil's horn design, another bejewelled chain hanging loosely round her neck to prevent the spectacles from falling off her person. Personally I should have thrown them into whatever polluted lake was nearest. She drove at about fifty miles an hour through typical American suburbia, post-boxes at the ends of paths, lawns with no hedges or fences, family groupings posed in apparently motionless compositions for Rockwell covers. The old lady was the mother of Weber's college friend. She talked and we said 'yes' or 'imagine' when required. Her conversation was exclusively about the wonderful things her grandchildren had done or said.

The house we drove to was in a tight little cul-de-sac where a horse-shoe of burned lawn served all the detached houses indiscriminately. There were a few trees, so well-trimmed they suggested newly-shorn convicts. Sally's college friend, Joanna, came down the path to meet us. She was heavily pregnant, her freckled face pale with tiredness. She already had two girls, aged 8 and 10. Her husband greeted us at the door. He had a double chin and a gut made all the more prominent by the thin, stooping quality of his shoulders. It did not take long for patterns to emerge. Joanna's theme for the evening was to be the different turns their lives had taken since leaving college, hers for the duller. Weber kept saying anybody would think them-selves lucky for God sakes to have two lovely daughters and a home and all. And a husband, she pointedly omitted from the list! This amused me. We were taken out back to see the swimming pool, not a sunken, tiled job as in the homes I'd been violating up till then, but a circular plastic affair held up by means of small-scale scaffolding, giving the impression of a temporary fairground erection into which some foolhardy young man might soon dive from a hundred-foot tower. It had recently developed a slow leak, Jack told us. We examined the leak at some length. The company was being difficult about implementing the guarantee. It had been empty all summer and the amount of space it occupied made it difficult to sit out on the lawn. I learned that Jack was an engineer. We went inside to enjoy one of his sweet Martinis. He had his own special recipe. Grandma told us this while Jack worked with the shaker. Joanna told us Jack might not be good at much else but he was a whizz with sweet Martinis, isn't that right, honey? Family joke. We all laughed with as much enthusiasm as we each found possible. Glasses were eventually handed round, small liqueur glasses. Isn't that the greatest little Martini you ever did taste? You ever taste a sweet Martini that good? It was, indeed, very sweet. I polished mine off in two swallows, smacked my lips appreciatively and said it was first-rate, holding my empty glass at an angle. Jack was glad I liked it. No refill was forthcoming. We were given an opportunity to admire the color teevee. We sat in a small back room with a fine mesh frame-door leading to the backyard. As Jack fiddled with the controls, under the helpful guidance of grandma, the two girls kept coming through the little room to and from the garden. Each time they let the door slam jarringly behind them. Each time Jack barked at them but although his voice was loud enough to make me blink, it had little effect on the girls. The color balance was a little shaky, Jack said, that was why Judy Garland was coming over in a bluish haze. The teevee maintenance men had been messing about with the set ever since they'd brought it home but the balance was still not right. Jack was going to have to light a fire under them. That's Jack's trouble, he's too easygoing, both grandma and Joanna told us. They all said how much they admired Judy Garland, with the life she'd had? Occasionally, during lulls in their comments on how tired she looked, I heard snatches of the interview. Judy Garland sounded like a punch-drunk boxer and looked like a sick child. Now and then her face lit up with a guilty little smile. She kept looking off-camera, as if for reassurance. Most of what she said was lost against the door bangings and new suggestions about improving the color balance.

Dinner was steak. Grandma did most of the talking. Jack sat at the head of the table, but he kept very quiet, except when the two girls made yet another appearance down the stairs and had to be told forcibly to go back to their bedroom. Once he caught me looking at him and gave a bright little smile and pulled himself out of his day-dream with a perky little twisting of his shoulder. Grandma told us she had not decided how to vote in the mayoral election. Stokes the negro was a fine man, well respected by the community. She said he would make a fine mayor but she had not yet made up her mind whether she could bring herself to vote for a negro. Joanna made an attempt to broaden the conversation, participation-wise, by asking me what kind of writer I was. I made a self-deprecatory moue and said Sally would be better to tell them that. Grandma said losh she used to read all the books there were but who had the time these days? Anyways, it was mostly all dirt today for people with empty heads and no spiritual values. Present company excepted, of course, she was sure things were a lot healthier in England. She said she had made a trip to Paris, in fifty-eight? She did not like it too much and had been glad to get home among her friends.

At last I could stand my thirst no longer and asked if I might have something to drink.

"Water will do fine," I said, apologetically, counting on somebody to say, you'll have no such thing, here's another of Jack's very own sweet Martinis. I got water. I asked Jack a question of peripheral relevance to Grandma's latest pronouncement on the Kennedy assassination. He gave a little start and then stared at me blankly. It was obvious he had not been listening to anything. Around half past ten Weber said we had to go. I had been rapping her ankle smartly with my shoe for at least an hour. Grandma protested, saying how early it was and how seldom she got a chance to talk with interesting, travelled people. Jack drove us to the station. We parked beside the flat track-platform, in the dark. For a few moments he came to life, describing the cycle of chemical pollution that had killed all organic life in Lake Erie. He became quite animated. Then we saw the lights of the train.

A young couple with a baby in a carry-cot were the only other boarding passengers. I gave the guy a hand with the baby. Even on suburban local services American trains have the high step associated with saddle-toting cowboys alighting in dusty western towns. One cannot imagine the royal family, with corgis, lifting regal legs two or three feet in the air prior to Christmas at Sandringham. Weber and I sat three places behind the young couple. He was wearing a white T-shirt, his hair wet-combed in a neat parting with a quiff. They had no obvious signs of poverty, their clothes were not dirty or threadbare, yet there hung about them a kind of guilt—the quick, darting look up at the conductor, the joyless, head-averted murmurs between man and wife.

"I forgot to get Jack's recipe for sweet Martinis," I said to Weber. "Damn it."

"Are you sneering?"

"I thought you had special communities for your senior citizens."

"Joanna says she can be a problem—but she's a fine woman."

"A truly wunnerful human being. Kinda people, in fact."

"You're sly, Cameron, I don't care for that."

"I'm also as dry as a dead-man's armpit."

"You're revolting!"

"You're a prude, Weber, a bigtime New York career lady and you

164

have all the censorious impulses of a priest-loving bog Irish spinster."

Weber said nothing. The train battered along between suburban halts. The young couple in front of us were unlike any other Americans I had seen so far. Certainly there are millions of American poor in New York but that city casts such a stagey light on its inhabitants even the vagrants always make you think they are about to tear off their soiled masks and reveal themselves as stock company hopefuls. There is no glamor in a local train in outer Cleveland late at night. The young couple were working-class whites and intensely joyless. Outside, the darkness gave way to explosions of fiery light as the train went past the open volcanoes of steel mill furnaces, all of it pounding and blasting and steaming, the industrial heart of the great production machine, more and more goods wagons roaring past the windows of our glumly-lit carriage. *They didn't own a car.* In three short weeks I had assimilated so many American assumptions I had instinctively and subconsciously assumed that any healthy, non-drunken, *white* American who had to take his wife and sleeping baby by public transport must be *deficient*, one way or the other. I was not surprised, at the city terminal, to observe them carry the baby past the cab-rank and walk off into the night streets. When Sheina had Gavin we were living on about ten pounds a week and we used to wheel the secondhand pram considerable distances at night, on the few occasions we went out. But London, or Britain, is a cosy place in which to be poor and besides, we had reason to hope that my kitchen-table typing might one day hit a jackpot. I felt very depressed for that young couple.

Weber asked me if I wanted to have a drink in the bar. From her tone I knew she was humoring me again. You think I'm so thick I didn't know why she flashed her thigh at me? Or so lacking in self-awareness I didn't know why I let a glimpse of stocking-top propel me off into Cleveland suburbia? But not again. I learn slow but good, as they say, in America. From now she'd have to do a lot more than snap her garters to get me to heel. I said I wanted to get to bed. She thought that was very sensible. We parted formally in the corridor. I gave her two minutes, then slipped out of my room and got the elevator down to the lobby. I sat at one end of the bar, watching the guy stacking glasses. He looked along at me but did not approach. We were the only two people present. I raised my hand but he went on working.

"Is there some problem about me being served, mac?" I said loudly.

"We're just about shut."

"Just about get me a Jack Daniel's on the rocks water on the side," I snapped back.

I deliberately took a long time about drinking it, smoking two cigarettes and returning his questing gaze with my own ominously blank stare. Then I went outside to taste the nightlife. How could I go home and tell people that all I'd done in Cleveland, Ohio, was get a good night's sleep? I found a joint near the hotel. Nightlife in Cleveland's city center seemed to consist of a zinc bar being leaned upon heavily by morose men given to little conversation except the odd little snarl at the bartender. I had a couple in there and then went to the cab rank.

"You know anywhere lively I could get a drink?" I asked the driver of the first cab in the line.

"It's all closed up right now."

"Nothing at all? Surely there's something going on around here?"

"Only nigger spots still open now, mister."

"Fine, take me to it."

"Ya kiddin'? Git a knife in your back? I ain't takin' you to no nigger spots, mister."

Two other drivers said the same thing.

I got a good night's sleep in Cleveland, Ohio. My bedmate was a luscious blonde Californian art student who was writing a novel and hoping to study painting in Paris, France. She had staples where other women have belly-buttons.

Things began to pick up pace in the morning. First there was an autographing party. I sat at a table in the book department of a large store getting my John Hancock in the fly-leaf of approximately four hundred copies. The store amplification system gave my personal appearance a lot of play. Two middle-aged women bought copies.

"I can't understand it being so slow," the kindly manageress said. "The last author we had on a personal appearance they were lined up on the stairs all the way down to the mezzanine floor, we had at least three thousand people in the store to see him."

"Must have been some author," I quipped, taking advantage of my celebrity status to light a cigarette in defiance of many no-smoking signs.

"Bob Hope," she said.

Weber and I walked to the W.K.Y.C.-T.V. studios on East 6th Street. It was sunny but not so hot or humid as in New York. By

166

day Cleveland, Ohio, was a bit like a temporary version of Manchester, England. At a fourway crossing the green WALK sign was on the blink but Weber said we still had time to make it to the other side. I wouldn't have risked it myself but this was, after all, her country. We were just on to the street when we heard the blast of a whistle and a short but shattering bellow. We had not seen the cop standing in the middle of the intersection. He was a small man in a white crash-helmet and dark glasses. He had round, narrow shoulders in a dark blue shirt, plus gun and the usual metal accoutrements round his grotesquely wide hips.

"Ya stay right there!"

He pointed with his short, white stick at the part of the sidewalk we had just left. His voice came over the roofs of three lanes of heavy traffic, loud and clear. When the red DON'T WALK changed to the steady green of WALK he gave us another bellow and pointed with his stick at his feet. We started across. He edged towards us through the moving cars.

"I'll do the talking," Weber said. He addressed us from about two yards, hand on hips.

"Ya lost? Ya noo to Cleveland? Where ya goin'?"

"We're looking for the W.K.Y.C. studios, officer," said Weber.

"I'll show ya, lady."

He gave us directions and waved us on with his white stick. The lights, meanwhile, had changed but no car moved until he regained his stance. He glared at them, presumably he glared, the most you could detect about him was the way his helmet was facing.

"Jesus H. Gentleman!" I exclaimed when we had put his pistol range behind us. "I thought he was going to smash us into the ground!"

"Chicken! Hell, boy, that was a *friendly* cop."

Weber left me alone in a dingy dressing-room while she went to phone New York. I knew it was a dressing-room from the number of bulbs round the mirror above the little table where Thespians apply greasepaint. I was sitting forward, elbows on knees, blowing smoke at the floor when a small, middle-aged woman with grey hair came into the room. She smiled at me, motherly-fashion.

"You on this show?"

"Me and my nerves," I said.

"You don't have to worry, son, they're all very friendly here, you'll do just fine."

"I always feel like running away just about now."

"Just be natural, boy, that's all anybody asks."

Other people came and went, giving me quick glances and then retreating without speaking. A tall man with spectacles introduced himself as the last-minute deputy host for the regular host who had been taken sick. He got my name, eventually, and checked me on a list. Yes, I was definitely on the show, he was glad to see. What could we profitably chat about? Mention your book by all means, I really would've liked to read it first, but could we discuss all this new London permissiveness—the mini-skirt and such? Phyllis Diller would be the other guest, isn't she outa this world? Phyllis Thaxter was the only Phyllis I could remember. A be-smocked make-up girl came in, studied my face and asked if I wanted a toucha powder to cover the dark parts of my chin?

"No, leave it," I said. "I'm not running for President." All teevee tyros say the same things to make-up girls, they all wish to make it quite clear they are too ruggedly masculine to endure faggoty cosmetics.

"Who is Phyllis Diller?" I asked.

"That Phyllis Diller—she's a killer," the girl said. "Wow!" She snapped her fingers and wiggled her shoulders in time to her own rhyming rhythm.

"But what is she?"

"She's that crazy comedienne—you're not familiar with her in London? Does she ad-lib but fast! Wow! If she doesn't like you—wow—she'll cut you to ribbons—wow—just like *that*!" She clicked her fingers again and smiled evilly. I wanted to run away even more. What madness is all this, I kept asking myself. I have nothing to say even when I remember it. Another girl led me through the shadowy plasterboard canyons common to all teevee backstages. We high-stepped over all the cables and walked out into the white dazzle of the lights. They put me in a seat and fixed on the neck-mike. I grinned a lot, hopelessly. When the searing kaleidoscope of garish purples and vivid oranges stopped using my eyeballs as a screen I got a look at the live audience, serried ranks of middle-aged women on banks of bleacher seats. Did *they* look hostile! Who is this long-haired guy in the dark suit and dark shirt and crazy tie? They fobbing us off with star guests nobody ever hearda? Then they clapped and huzzaed like mad. The host was walking to the table with the small, motherly, grey-haired lady on his arm. Only now she looked like a female demon! She made a Jerry Lewis face and pulled at her hair with both hands. It stuck up in many directions. Phyllis Diller she's a

168

killer gave me a warm smile. Like the fourth Marx Brother I wanted out.

"I thought you and Phyllis Diller made a great team, Graham," Weber said as we left the studios and hurried to the W.E.W.S.-T.V. building on Euclid Avenue. "Perhaps she'll find a spot for you on her show. You could be the new Fang."

"May I never go through another ordeal like that in my life."

"You came across hot and strong. You even upstaged her—once. She took real kindly to you, buster. That plug she gave your book—a guy who can hold his own with Phyllis Diller is destined for stardom!"

"I don't remember a single thing that was said!"

"Don't fool around with me, you're beginning to get hooked, you egomaniac."

We met Phyllis Diller in the corridor of the next studios.

"Watch out," she yelled for all to hear, "it's that sex maniac from London again. He's trailing me!"

We shook hands, old troupers meeting again for the first time since way back. I had passed into that warm world where cheeks are kissed in public and everybody is darling.

Miss Dorothy Fuldheim was middle-aged and warm. She ran a sincere show, I was very sincere.

"No, my wife wasn't annoyed about the sex in my book," I vaguely recalled saying, "I think that when a marriage is based on strong foundations you can afford to joke about it, don't you think so, Dorothy?"

We got a taxi back to the hotel. Weber seemed a little withdrawn. I wanted to hear how I'd come across. This wasn't ego, it was common sense.

"I'm so glad your marriage is based on sound foundations," she said drily, looking out of the window. "That must make you very happy and secure nights."

"You ought to try it some time," I swiftly rejoindered.

"You're a performer, Cameron, a natural *performer*."

"What would you prefer, I should go out there and make like the Delphic Oracle?"

"You're wasted, Cameron, you want to come out from behind that old typing machine and let the whole world enjoy your act."

I could see she had a jealousy problem. I told her to stay in the hotel and listen to my late-night broadcast on the radio. (I said wireless, actually, and she said that was very cute. Considering the damned thing was invented on the Isle of Wight I didn't see why *we* shouldn't determine the terminology and told her so, with acidity.) The host for the two-hour open-end show was a fast-talking, non-nonsense man called Jack. He introduced me to Dr. Allenby, a marriage guidance expert.

"Without too much horse-shit I try to run an aedult show here, this is the real battle in the media today, for the right to talk about aedult subjects at an aedult level. If this idea grabs you I suggest we give the show some shape by having Dr. Allenby defend marriage the institution and you Graham to knock it. That's in line with what you say in your book, right?"

It was the usual smoky little studio room with soundproof plaster-board walls and cornucopic ashtrays and paper cups containing half a cold inch of that afternoon's coffee. We each had a little wire beehive to talk into. Jack introduced us—as far as I could tell the doctor wasn't plugging anything, which seemed a little suspicious—and for a minute or two we mouthed cliché-ridden generalisations about husbands and wives.

"Let's not pussy-foot round the subject, gennelmen," said Jack, cutting in on the doctor, who wore rimless glasses and pink make-up. Make-up? For a radio show? It had to be make-up, they don't have faces that pink in this evolutionary phase. Oh yes they do, in America. "The nitty-gritty of this question is whether marriage makes people more or less happy. I'll tell you about my mother. She had nine kids. When she knew her condition was terminal she wanted to speak to me, I was the eldest and I was going through a crisis-period in my own personal life. Jack, she told me, I was sitting by her bed, Jack I was married to your father for thirty-nine years and I had nine children and you know, Jack, I never had a single orgasm all those years. Don't make the mistake I made, Jack. Marry for love. Get happiness out of it. Graham Cameron, what's your reaction to that one?"

Jesus H. Gennelmun!

"Anything I say would be an anti-climax," I said. Neither party smiled. "Aye, well, I can't say it's something my mother and I have ever discussed to any great extent." Was this going out on public radio? By the sacred eyebrows of Sir John Reith!

"You must have known lots of women—is it the common thing for them to have orgasms?"

"Modesty almost forbids me to tell you I have left a trail of totally

170

exhausted women in my wake," I said. "My own feeling is that it's
entirely the man's responsibility to make sure his wife and girl-
friends have orgasms—I made this point in *The New Ladies'
Man* ..."

"You are married, are you not? With children?" This was Dr.
Allenby. He looked and sounded most sincerely worried.

"Oh yeah," I said carelessly, "we all have some handicap or another,
don't we?"

"Does your wife have orgasms?" Jack butted in quickly. Fuck it, I
thought, I can out-orgasm any bloody American.

"Yeah, all the time," I said. "She's actually the nympho in *The
New Ladies' Man*, the one who gets orgasms just from looking at
mounted policemen."

The doctor kept making sensible, decent comments but Jack wanted
orgasms and I kept thinking of that frigid bitch in the hotel and saying things that would sizzle her shell-likes. Late-night Cleveland heard
how swinging London had given up cricket and morris dancing for
group gropes, gang bangs, mob mauls, ruck fucks. I put a little cross
on my pad for every title plug. Another verbal spasm sends its spunky
load of surrealistic hogwash into the great American night. We are all
madmen! It's the Clitoral Truth Show, folks! Hi gals, hymen! *Love*
that medical dirt! Hi, fun-loving Sally Weber out there.

We had a break while Jack read the commercials. Then we went
into the second hour, open-end. In the control booth Jack the engineer
had a bleeper to knock out obscenities. The show was live but there
was a four-second delay between us speaking and our voices reaching
the citizens. I could see why when Mr. and Mrs. Joe Doakes started
phoning. The calls came from some communal melancholia where
booze-brained men stammered incoherently against the shrill cacklings
of their women, most of them Bible fetishists. My God, but they
could talk! They didn't actually *say* much but what word-power! A
woman with a southern accent had heard the first half of the show on
the car radio and had hurried home off the turnpike to get down on
her knees and say a prayer for the poor misguided soul of that Graham
Cameron, may the light of Jesus lead him to everlasting salvation. She
was, by comparison, quite reasonable. At least two callers said all
book writers today were known Communists. A near-hysterical man
accused me, in violent tones, of being *godless*. I replied cheerily that
I was, indeed, an atheist and would be quite willing to discuss it with
him, when he sobered up ...

Jack and Frankie drove me back to the hotel through Cleveland's dark, wet, empty streets. I said I thought the telephone calls were a trifle bizarre.

"You better believe it," said Jack. "Frankie'n me do this night drive home five nights a week—you know what conclusions we come to— every night, sitting together in this car? Maybe, the good, sensible folk don't call radio stations. I don't know. But we get 'em every night and all we can report is that when we look out into this big black night all we can visualise is a great big sea of human shit."

A couple of regular fellows, I thought, watching the slow-burn red lights cruising off down the shining street, just two nice guys pulling down an honest dollar or two.

I knocked on Weber's door. She let me in. She was wearing a long, pink, nylon nightie. She got back between the sheets.

"That was a fine old slice of razzamatazz you gave the folks," she said. She was reading *Nicholas and Alexandra*. I sat on the edge of her bed. Her fore-arms were firm and tanned and fuzzy with soft black hair.

"Give 'em what they want," I said morosely, staring down at my big, scruffy, cut-price, empire-mades. "You know something? I haven't polished my shoes since I left London."

"The star without polish."

She looked at me heavily. We stared at each other. She made an upwards movement of her face. I let out a terrifying sob and buried my face against her folded arms. She stroked my hair and held my face close to her breasts. I kissed them frantically through nylon. She ran her nails up and down the back of my neck. I raised my face and kissed her chin. She kneaded my ears. I kissed her bare shoulder, moaning ecstatically. I twisted round quickly, bringing my legs up on to the bed, lying half on top of her. I pulled the nightie straps down over her shoulders.

"Oh my precious wonderful darling," I gasped, several times, beginning to tear off my jacket, trousers, shoes.

"Uh uh," she said, pulling at my ears with entrancing savagery.

"Oh my sweet precious love," I moaned, keeping my face on her breasts but raising my arse to the ceiling to get my trousers past my knees.

"No," she said, not quite firmly enough.

"It'll be much better with them off, my darling wonderful Sally," I murmured.

"No! I know what you want!"

I smiled endearingly, no mean feat in that position.

"Yes, my precious, I want you, all of you, for ever and ever and—"

"What you want is just a mirror for that big outsize ego of yours!"

She scrambled off the bed and stomped across to the door, holding it open, glaring at me threateningly. She looked fully prepared to start yelling. I saw more *Confidential* headlines. Orgasm Author In Hotel Sex Rape Hassle. Midnight Screams Stampede Sleeping Elks.

I dressed with dignity.

"You only want to hump me to give your success story the missing ingredient," she railed.

"Drop me a postcard when you finally achieve an orgasm," I retorted icily. "I'll give the nation a fire-side chat about it."

"Get out you louse."

At least I'm certain of the Pulitzeroff Prize, I thought, wryly.

I went downstairs but the bar was closed. I went back up in the elevator. From no discernible direction came very faint voices, but life was all behind closed doors. Somewhere people were being liked and loved and touched and comforted but I was totally alone in the hell of the dead hotel corridor. I stared up and down its full length, fists clenched, chest heaving—nostrils, no doubt, dilated. I knew it looked like an act but I wasn't acting, and there was no audience. I wanted to kneel at a door, any door, and beat on it with my fists and grab at a hand and kiss it and beg for help. I'm not this much of a failure, I kept shrieking at myself. I'm not a freak! Please God, tell me I'm not a freak. Other women have loved me. Tell me other women have loved me, Dear God. I wanted to run at the walls, smash down the doors, tear up the red carpet, destroy the ice-cube dispenser.

I heard the elevator pinging. I went into my own room and locked the door. I stood there breathless, listening for accusatory voices. In the silence my ears roared like seashells. I saw my disordered face in the mirror. We stared at each other and could feel only contempt.

I phoned Sheina. The hell with the cost, Two-World and Tannenbaum Inc. were splitting the tabs and they had got me into this nightmare. We spoke for half an hour, at a cost roughly comparable to the return fare, Cleveland-London. My conversation consisted exclusively of one question—you do really love me, don't you? Sheina thought I was drunk. When the phone went down I was alone again with the silence. I put out the lights. I felt no more like sleeping than dying. I put the light on again and rummaged in my bag. I took the blonde art-buff from California into my bed. This staple-navelled bitch had the cheek to sneer at me! I got up and after some ferocious

173

banging managed to get a window open. I chucked the bitch miles down into the Cleveland night. I lay in the darkness listening to faint but unmistakable party noises, voices and music and the heart-rending laughter of a throaty, lusty woman.

Hours passed.

I had lots of time to think during that endless night and it became more and more obvious that my only chance of coming out of this tour alive was never again to be sober enough to feel the pain.

Chapter Fifteen

SUBURBAN HUSBAND OPENS DOOR TO CHEERY BIG GUY
WEARING BLACK GLOVES.
HI, SAYS CALLER WITH A WOLFISH GRIN, I'M THE BOSTON
STRANGLER. HUSBAND SNARLS OVER SHOULDER — IT'S FOR
YOU, DEAR.

We had an hour to kill in Cleveland before the Detroit flight. Weber
said we should stop by some book stores. I said, wouldn't it be as
easy to go inside while we're at it? Of course we go inside, she said,
appraising me with a puzzled frown. I opened my mouth to explain
and realised I was too tired. It must have been bloody lonely for
Dorothy Parker. In a garden square in the city center groups of
earnest young committed folks were handing out leaflets boosting
Stokes the negro for mayor. The young men wore bleached raincoats
handed down from grandfathers who rode with Jesse James. The girls
had Joan Baez hairstyles. It was more your liberal activist college
gang than your actual hippies.

"This tour is taking us through the old Babylon of sex'n'dollars," I
said to Weber. "One really should be joining the new Jerusalem movement—flower power and love-ins and Bob Dylan. Fancy a drink?"

"What—at nine-thirty in the a.m.?"

"Oh well, later then."

In one bookshop the saleslady said Mr. Schwartz would see us as
soon as he had finished with the Bible rep. I found a dozen copies of
Ladies' Man stacked anonymously behind Catskill ranges of *Nicholas
and Alexandra* and *The Confessions of Nat Turner*. These bastards
always favour their own. Doesn't every intelligent, objective British
sportswriter know that Tommy Farr was cheated out of the Joe Louis
verdict? Weber had a hard time convincing Mr. Schwartz that this
was a genuine spontaneous visit by a genuine visiting author who
did not want to cash checks or borrow money. He said novels were
harder to sell each year, although Nat Turner was moving well. I
tempered Weber's aggression with a line of self-deprecating charm.
Mr. Schwartz agreed to let us put my dozen up front. I did the
arrangement myself, cleverly hiding stinking Nat Turner.

In another shop they had no copies of *Ladies' Man*, had never heard of *Ladies' Man*, didn't think it sounded like their kinda book anyways, greeted my charm-act with blank faces. Weber was stubbornly forceful. She insisted on being allowed to use the phone and soon found out that the shipping company had slipped up. Three dozen copies were on their way as of now, express-freight. The apologetic manageress promised us a solus display.

"That was a useful morning," Weber said on the airport coach. "If you sit on your fanny in New York you never get to hear about these snafu deals."

"We can have a drink or two on the plane," I said.

Lake Erie was the colour of lead, the sky being black with rainclouds. The plane was full of men with heavy briefcases and anxiety-problem faces. Many of them had their jackets off, no doubt to hide all those bloody lapel badges. The standard business shirt was cotton, with short sleeves, chest pockets holding pens and cigarettes and even wallets. Your American man feels better with a good load on his chest.

"Yeah, I'll have a Jack Daniel's," I said to the stewardess. "What'll you have, kid?"

"It's only but midday—oh hell, I'll have a dry Martini on the."

On the. If they're not swamping you with jargon they're trying to cut out words altogether. They don't even say sunnyside up when they're ordering eggs. They just say 'up'.

"You were a mite frisky last night, Cameron," Weber said, in her archest. "I find I can handle you better when you're juiced."

"We must both drink more."

"Mature people should be able to have a coupla drinks without turning it into *The Lost Weekend* you know."

"My God, you've actually remembered a film, Weber! How mattoor can you get?"

"It was a book, Smartypants."

"I'm beginning to think Americans are ashamed of Hollywood. Films and jazz are your only original contributions to world culture you know."

"I guess in those economically underprivileged countries you go to the movies more."

On the airport bus I read her extracts from a tourist pamphlet, Welcome to Beautiful South-east Michigan. Detroit was founded in 1701 by Antoine de la Mothe Cadillac. Whites of Weber's type tend to regard Cadillacs as synonymous with *nouveau riche* negroes. Uncle Tom's Caddy, I say, digging her in the ribs. She stares out of the window. I tell her I feel like one of the Red Cross people who used

176

to visit with concentration camp inmates. She tightens her lips. I gurgle with gallows mirth. The city is served by nine railroads, more than two hundred motor carriers—whatever they might be—seventeen freight and passenger airlines, a public bus service and five private bus companies. Entertainment ranges from Broadway shows to the symphony, jazz combos to main headliners. She had her specs in position number two, in front of her eyes as God intended. She looked very much like a brisk businesswoman. We had adjoining rooms with a connecting door on floor twelve. I washed my face and hands and changed my socks. She knocked on the connecting door. She had her shoes off. Her feet were really quite knobbly. We had a newspaper interview, then another friend of hers was picking us up for dinner.

"We'd better get a bottle of whisky up here. God, I know I've got it made now—*me* dispensing free booze to reporters!"

"I feel privileged to have known you during your humility period."

"Give us a kiss then."

"Stop it, Graham! Look dammit, you've mussed up my hair."

They knocked on the door at that moment and I subsided. Weber answered in her stockinged feet, hands patting at her coiffure. I bet they thought we'd been indulging in sleazy celebrity morals. When I was a reporter I always imagined that's what the stars got up to. Maybe all fame is a sham.

The photographer was a short man in his sixties with an expensively red face. The reporter was younger and quieter. Like press photographers of any nationality the little guy won the race for the first Scotch and then dominated the conversation. The only Scotchman he had photographed was back in the twenties, Sir Harry Louder?

"I went about Noo Yawk with him a coupla days, each time the cab hits the hotel he says he's fresh outa change, handle the fare willya? So I pay all the cabbies and he's inside at the bar and I hadda pick up mosta them tabs as well."

When he subsides into the comparative reticence of actual photography, interrupting us only to push my chair about to get light from the window, the feature-writer and I get down to the interview. He doesn't care for a second whisky. He wants to discuss the mini-skirt some. It's a last-minute assignment and he hasn't had time to read the book, so I have to give him a resumé. It sounds hellish. Weber says she will leave us to it while she makes a call to New York from her own room. I tell the two press guys the mini-skirt is just propaganda, a visual con like most stuff today, all it does is show you more of what you aren't getting. Two-World is picking up the tabs so why don't we get this interview over and move out in the bars?

"I guess the industry has changed a lot," says my interviewer. "We don't have the same characters any more—we've gone all respectable —very few of the guys go off on bats these days. I guess we all have to worry more about holding down the job. They're cutting down on the city desks—all the readers have moved out to the suburbs, so that's what the papers print, home editions, suburban stuff, lawns and P.T.A. meetings. You don't think the mini-skirt is symbolic of the new sexually uninhibited England?"

Like all great men I have this fantastic ability to put my head down and my feet up and recharge my batteries with a ten-minute nap. Half a bottle of whisky is great battery fluid. Weber comes into the room with this man, shortish, fairish, bright-eyed. His name is Bill Udall. Weber worked with him in a New York advertising agency before she went into publishing and he joined the P.R. department of General Motors. The first thing he suggests is a drink in the bar.

"You don't have a special recipe for sweet Martinis, do you, Bill?" I ask innocently.

"You bastard," Weber hisses as we leave the room. I grin at her sweetly.

We smash a couple of big ones into our faces and then we get into Bill's fine big car and head off for suburbia, all three of us in the front. I always imagined Detroit as a lunatically modern, technological city but the inner suburb we drive through is flat and shabby and dirty. This is the place they had the riot, with the fire and the National Guard and the snipers. Wooden shop fronts are seared black and planks have been nailed across smashed windows.

"It's crazy," says Bill, "most of these are negro businesses. Why did they loot and burn their own people? I think too much is being made of the negro question as such, know what I mean?"

"Not exactly, Bill."

"There's a hardcore criminal minority latches on to these riot situations and takes advantage of them."

Some minority, I think, staying politely quiet. In the newspaper I'd read it said the damage came to around one hundred million dollars. Five hundred people were injured. More than a thousand people were arrested. Two brigades of paratroopers were flown into Selfridge air base. (I thought Gordon Selfridge came from Chicago? Wasn't that why they couldn't name the airport after General Marshall? It would have been Marshall Field, you parochial English know-nothings.)

"I'd better tell you, Bill, cousin Cameron is a radical and a socialist," says Weber. "He doesn't object to hustling round the nation playing the dollar millionaire but he reserves the right to tell us what a bunch of fascist racist war-mongering capitalist swines we are."

"Yeah, I know you've all gone pretty far to the left in Britain," says Bill.

"In what way?"

"Well you have your socialist Labor government."

"Socialist? Harold Wilson?"

"Graham says God Bless Fidel Castro before he goes to bed nights," says Weber. "I heard him say once Chairman Mao is a mite reactionary for his taste."

"He sure is socialistic enough for me," says Bill. "I always found this with creative people, the tendency of radicalism."

"Until they've gotten themselves a big best-seller," says Weber, "then they start equating income tax with the Anti-Christ."

"At last I'm getting close to genuine grass-roots American reaction," I quip. After all, I am a visitor. I even try to say something nice about the place. "S'funny, I always imagined negro ghettoes would be narrow streets of crumbling tenements but these houses don't look so bad."

"The houses are okay," says Weber, "it's the numbers who pack into them."

"They come up from the south by the hundreds of thousands," says Bill. "Even if they have to live a family to a room they still think it's better than Mississippi. I guess I'd maybe feel the same. Although, on a pure stomach-filling basis they do better down south, they can get four crops a year down there—they don't have too many rights but they do have full bellies."

With no perceptible boundary line the wide, flat, tree-infested street became a white suburb and then a rich white suburb. We turn into this leafy suburban avenue and come up the gravel drive. Would you believe a spanking new Tudor castle with leaded windows and a neo-medieval door with black-iron adornments? My shoes are much too shabby for the palatial carpets. These rich Americans live in rooms that are so splendiferously formal I always expected a hand-rubbing salesman to come out and try to sell me the three-piece suite. You never see yesterday's newspaper lying on top of last Sunday's newspapers. Bill's wife, Grace, is a vibrantly warm young matron, wittily self-deprecating. She apologises for the mess! She may mean the two little girls in their pajama suits. They show me their new story-book with the three-dimensional pictures. I sit on a wide sofa and sip a beer. Weber is interested to see that another of my multi-facets is the ability to charm kids. I wonder how I'd rate as an American father. Like most unmarried women of her age, Weber no doubt has very firm ideas on the bringing up of children. As I do my avuncular bit with the two little girls I manage to make a new appraisal of Weber's legs. Also Grace's legs. I am beginning to get perverted impulses as regards women's legs. I make my funny rolling eyes and the little girls think I'm the cutest. It is very tiring, especially when you have these hideous thoughts as regards incipient ankle-fetishism racing through your skull. I'm glad when Mom packs them off to bed, enabling me to free both hands for domestic American booz-ing. Not only do you get the actual glass with the magic ingredient but you also get a paper napkin to wrap round the bottom of the glass, to stop condensation liquid messing up your lilywhite meathooks. You also get a little round tray, or coaster, which fits neatly round the bottom of the glass, thereby protecting the furniture from unsightly rings. When I accept our host's offer of a Scotch to go with the beer he gives me a duplicate set of this equipment. If the Lord had meant us to drink at home with Americans he would have given us more hands. Weber sees me clumsily juggling all this gear and makes a patronising little remark insinuating that I am some kind of lush. Right, I think. From then on every remark I make is brilliantly cal-culated to make Bill and Grace think Weber and I are lovers. I call her darling a few times and put my arm round her shoulder as we go to the car. I'm not getting any sex but I'm getting the publicity. Weber's getting the needle. She gets in the front with Bill. I play the hammy, over-polite Briton, closing the door behind her with a lover's solicitude. I can tell that Grace thinks I'm sleeping with Weber.

"Oh yes, the riots were a scary time," she says, relaxed beneath my arm in the back of the car. "We could hear the rifle shots, they were coming nearer all the time. Honest to goodness, I said to Bill, we should pile the kids in the car and just take-off, you know, just drive *away* from here—but Bill has good strong nerves, he said to sit tight, they wouldn't get this far. It really was a most awful experience."

"You poor dear," I say, pressing her hand. We flirt a little, mainly for the benefit of them up front.

"Sally will be jealous," Grace says, skittishly. Weber stares straight ahead. Bill gabbles away with gruff good humour. Most middle-aged hubbies are downright glad to see their wives flirting. It makes them feel less guilty about their own little secrets. It occurs to me I might even get to screw with Grace on account of the fact that she thinks I'm screwing with Weber. It's not a serious proposition but I keep hold of her hand. Bill doesn't seem to mind. We go to this restaurant with a head flunkey who's sporting a rich European-type accent and exquisitely old-world manners. He lights candles with a flourish and snaps his fingers to materialise wine genies and sprays hand-tooled menus at us—wherever good books are appreciated they're collecting first editions of these menus, red-leather hand-tooled bindings and *prose*—wait till these menu-writers get to work on boring old novels, them and their flavor-drenched and dew-fresh strawberries dawn-picked in sparkling goodness bloom! I order a shrimp cocktail or Pacific prawns or something and a coupla dozen cherrystone clams.

"I guess you like seafood, huh?" says Bill.

"I read this notice in a fish shop window in New York, it said shellfish is tops for helping the body dispose of alcohol," I say.

"There ain't enough clams in the ocean," says Weber.

"We're just good friends," I smirk to Grace and Bill. I must be the first celebrity who ever said that and meant it. Of course they think I'm joking and smile understandingly. I blow Weber a little kiss. She averts her eyes and shudders.

"Basically it's madness to try and make a public figure out of a writer," I say to Bill and Grace. "His only claim to fame is that when he's actually at the typewriter some magic chemistry, alchemistry, takes over. He's unusual only while he is actually working. I can't explain what the chemistry is—objectively speaking I'm just a guy with a fairly good memory for snippets of useless information and two typing fingers. I'm not a philosopher with great thoughts to impart—in fact I sometimes think the chemistry is Nature's compensation for lack of actual brainpower."

They were such nice, warm, intelligent people I felt it was important they should understand something about the real me behind the tomfoolery.

"I only ever knew but one writer," says Grace. "He lived near my mother's place in Maine. Gosh, I forget his name. He drank a lot I recall. Is it an occupational hazard?"

"A fringe benefit, ma'am."

"Graham has this drinking problem," says Weber. "There are only twenty-four hours in the day."

"You have this suburban wives' afternoon drinking problem in England?" Bill asks.

"Yes, we can never get enough suburban wives to drink with in the afternoons."

Everybody laughs, except Weber.

It's a restaurant where the auto rich go to show each other how wealthy they are. Whenever a wrist, male or female, stretches forth in the direction of green-pasture-fed black Angus steak you can hear gold jangling and see it glinting. Tight faces above white silk ties. The platinum women look as though they are inflation-hedging acquisitions from private auctions held at billionaires' conventions in sun-soaked Miami. The service is such that the waiter is fawning over you before the raised hand can snap a finger. We are all witty and pleasant. Ten minutes away black children are being nibbled by rats and black men are rotting their lives away. Meanwhile even the waiters are all-white. I shouldn't be here. What can I do? Throw over the table and shout the slogans of the oppressed? There's nothing I can do. I mean, this is what it was all for, isn't it, this gorging and gurgling and guzzling—and making out that I'm a big lover boy when all the time I'm shambling through a great big lie?

There is one thing I can do.

It's an occupational hazard, by gosh.

"It's not morning," he croaked into the phone.

"It is so."

"I've only just got into bed."

"That was two hours ago, Graham honey. Time to get this show on the road."

In the mirror his eye was red and crusted. The other one was gummed shut. He opened it and saw that somebody had dragged barbed-wire across the eyeball. From his throat to his balls his insides were one big disaster. The razor blade was a rusty iron bar dragged across tearing skin. His hands were useless trembles. Weber steered his useless, shivering hulk downstairs. They got into the cab in the dark. It was raining.

"Station W.X.Y.Z. at two zero seven seven seven West Ten Mile Road and we have to make it by seven," were Weber's incomprehensible, ear-shattering words. The highway was the descending road to hell. His face was a dying thing through rain-spattered glass. The road was a tunnel without a roof. The headlights of an on-coming army water-haloed moons across his retinas.

"What are all those lights? Am I dead already?"

"The morning shift starts early at the auto plants."

"Good God. There are millions of them. Why are they standing still? Why are they not moving?"

"It's the early morning traffic snarl-up, happens every day," said the driver.

Hicks from the Styx?

"You see those chains hanging down the sides? If your car breaks down you get up on the catwalk and pull the chain and it brings down a folding ladder and you climb up top and go look for help."

Can this be for real? I am sitting in a cab in the dark in a sunken road with chains hanging down the sides with mile after mile of headlights facing the other way and rain bouncing off the windscreen going to participate in a television talkshow? In Detroit, U.S.A.? At six thirty in the morning? Beside an American woman? I think I'm going to die. Oh my Gawd!

They stood among technicians in a backstage gloom of concrete and cables. Weber got two boiling coffees from a vending machine. He saw a man in a suit of brilliant emerald green. He saw a man with a face of brilliant orange reading the news and local weather. He shook hands with a very healthy, tanned man in a blue blazer. He shook other hands and sat with other people round a low table. He lit a cigarette and thought he would faint. The familiar face of a Hollywood star was only a few feet away. Not on a screen, either. He was saying he had turned his career into the area of independent productions. The man in the brilliant emerald suit started talking. He was Mr. Grow It All, the Detroit gardening expert? He had the initials monogrammed on his blazer to prove it. Mr. G.I.T. in a flowery scroll. A lady spoke next. She was an Illinois State food board hygiene inspector?

And Graham Cameron, brilliant young author of the new best-selling novel, *The New Ladies' Man*, from London?

"Hullo."

"With due respect, the movie industry is in trouble because it's stopped making valid entertainment films and is trying to cash in on what a lot of old studio hacks think are the new trends. The movies have got to find their soul again."

Too true. Nod wisely.

"I read in the trades about Mr. Cameron's book being bought by Two-World. *Alfie* made it big for Paramount so now they all want in on the new swinging London bag."

"I beg your pardon." Opening mouth was a mistake. Stomach may fall out on floor. All eyes on. Make effort. "Swinging London wasn't even invented when I wrote my book."

"But they'll adapt it to suit the trend."

"They can make a Tarzan movie out of it for all I care now I've got the cash."

"That's a refreshing thing to hear from a writer. Most writers in my experience regard their stuff as sacred, they don't realise the movies are an art form of their own."

"I don't."

"My my." Healthy Host. "We really got something good going there, huh, something pretty deep for all us breakfast folk, huh?"

Who was watching this crap at seven forty-five in the morning, huh? Don't they have nightmares of their own to look at?

A radio interview, live, by a disc-jockey who leavened the boredom of consecutive sentences by spinning new waxings and platters on the turntable.

"I don't care if they make a Tarzan movie out of it now I've got the money."

Cab back to the city.

"Where did we go last night?"

"Bill took us to that nightclub? You don't remember?"

"Not a bloody thing."

"Partial amnesia and memory gaps are an early warning signal."

"What's total amnesia?"

Interview in the hotel with reporter. Sit on edge of chair, keep hands between knees, look boyishly shy. Reality keeping hands together in same spot.

"I can't give you an exact figure but I think it'll come to well over a hundred thousand dollars. For that money, Al, they can make a Tarzan movie out of it. You fancy a drink, Al?"

"Sorry, Graham doesn't have time for a drink, we have to be at the Fisher Building."

"Sally is playing Budd Schulberg to my Scott Fitzgerald. Her book will be the real one."

No time for a drink, she says. Giantburgers in coffee shop. Go to john. Go past john and get into bar. Knock down Jack Daniel's straight and beer. Hold on to bar-rail.

Grab a cab to Canada. Driver cocky young guy. Says we'll make Windsor on time providing them Immigration bastarts don't louse us up. Raining again. Slickered Immigration officer says I have to check in at Passport Control. Weber and driver can stay in cab. Don't they know Canada belongs to Britain? The Dominion looks exactly like Detroit. Fly-posted, neon-cluttered, liquor-store mess. Drive along river into teevee carpark.

"Hullo there," said the Big Ham, raising both hands. "How do you like my hair?"

"I could take it or leave it," said Cameron.

"It's really my armpits. I had the operation, they graft the hair from your armpits on to your skull, a hair at a time. All the big teevee personalities have had the same operation only they keep it secret. It makes you look ten years younger and helps you when contracts are up for renewal. You must be this daring young author from London everybody's talking about. Delighted to have a brilliant young man of culture on the show."

"Ya big ham," sneered a passing technician.

"Have that underling canned and blacklisted," said the Big Ham.

"Ya big prick!"

They sat at a raised table.

"I never heard of this hair operation," said Cameron. "Does it give your head a bit of an aroma?"

"Yeah and he has dandruff down here," sneered a lounging technician, scratching both armpits like the chimp from Tarzan.

"Okay, let's go."

The Big Ham had once been a Hollywood face. Swinging London intrigued him. Also he could have written books himself but for lacking the sheer patience and guts needed to sit there year after year batting out the words. Specially in swinging London with all these mini-skirts?

"Albert Pierrepoint is the only real English swinger, believe me."

"Who's he?"

"The public hangman."

So who wants all that doomy old guff about literature? You think at this level they knew William Faulkner from Big Chief Sitting Eagle?

They were back through the river tunnel and slowing into the

U.S. Immigration gate by three five precisely. Cameron had not seen a single mountie. The big Immigration cop in the slicker came up to the window. He told Cameron to report to the office. His passport was stamped. He had emigrated to Canada for an hour and thirteen minutes. The big cop asked the driver for the official cabbie's border pass. The cabbie showed his driver's identification card, with picture.

"Ya come through here without the pass one more time, son, I'll have ya bustet," the big cop snarled. "I could haulya outa the cab as of now. And don't give me no funny looks, punk, before I bust ya! It won't bother me none at all if yahaffta stay over there the restaya life. Beat it before I change my mind."

"Up yours, ya big pig," said the cabbie—when the window went up. The big cop stood in the drizzle, watching them for false moves. "He knows me, that big bastart! None a the hackies carry the dam border card. You know what it is, I don't call the big bastart sir, that's for why."

The airport coach left the hotel at three thirty. There was too little time for a quick shot. Cameron slumped down in the seat and shut his eyes wincingly against a headache. Weber made notes in a little book. She kept a careful tally of the dollars and cents. She said they were about eighty dollars ahead because, somehow, they didn't seem to be having all the allowed-for meals. Suddenly the loud-speaker crackled into life.

"Good afternoon to all of yew good folks." It was the driver, a thin man in a grey shirt. The coach was doing about fifty on a four-lane race-track road. "Ah trust yew all kin see what bad drivuhs theah is on the highways. Thet big Ford jist crossed two lanes without lookin', d'yewall see thet? Now thet could huv gotten us all ky-ulled. Ah don't know why—hit's all simply a mattuh of followin' *the signs*."

People smiled at each other. Cameron looked down through green glass. Immediately under the coach was a beaten-up old pick-up truck driven by a pair of hairy arms. On the side window of the truck was a sticker, VOTE FOR WALLACE. The driver picked up his mike again. They could see his eyes in the mirror.

"Yew know, mah frens, many people in this heah wuld jist don't follow the signs. Now how many times yewall heard folks sayin' how easy it is to git lost on a big arrport? Yet an arrport is jist like life hit-sigh-ulf, the signs are theah iffen yew have the mind to look for them. Life has hits signs because they were put theah for us all to follow by a great man. Yew all know to whom Ah refer to?"

Weber smiled at a grinning passenger.

"Ah'll tell yewall. Thet man was Jesus Christ our Saviour. He put the signs theah for all us sinners to follow. An do we? No suh, all of us are like thet bad drivuh who jumped the lanes. Ah ain't one of yore educated types but Ah drive this heah coach in and out of the city to the arrport most every day and Ah kin tell yew—no man ever went wrong iffen his mind was set on followin' the signs. Well now, heah we are, mah friends, remember the signs and the man who gave yew this little talking-to."

"What was that all about?" Cameron weakly asked Weber as they entered the airport by means of a glass catwalk suspended in mid-air.

"Why now, suh, that's whut we could call a real good ol' fashionet southern Buybul nut," she said. "Yewall jest follow the signs like the man said, y'heah?"

"Yeah, let's see if there's a sign to the bloody bar."

"Ah'm sorry, mah fren, the arrport is dry."

So she's started to make jokes, I think, standing in a locked stall in the john. I'm gulping down the last inch of Scotch from the bottle with which I entertained the gentlemen of the press. She can do a one-woman history of burlesque for all I care. I leave the empty floating in the lavatory seat. It's the first time in the history of shipwrecks that the bottle has thrown the castaway into the sea. I bob away from the Isle of Detroit, hopelessly adrift, at the mercy of the tides. I contain no message.

Chapter Sixteen

BIG BILL THOMPSON GOT ELECTED MAYOR OF CHICAGO ON
A PLATFORM OF PUNCHING KING GEORGE ON THE SNOOT.
TAKE THAT, YOUR ROYAL SINUS, HE SNARLED, OBVIOUSLY
A FRONT MAN FOR COSA NOSTRILS.

Two drinks on the plane. It's a different airline but the same plane.
And the same passengers. It's a different state but the same hangover.
Weber's had two Martinis. She doesn't seem any randier. Just as
well, I think I'm impotent, I didn't even get a lift when the stewardess
leaned across the opposite row of seats and I got a close-up of buttock-
hugging knickers. All I could think was, her cheeks are a lot rosier
than mine.

We walked off the plane. Chicago. My old man's favourite film was
Dillinger starring Lawrence Tierney. All his life I think he wanted to
be able to see the spot where Dillinger got it outside the Bioscope.
Okay, Dad, I'm here in your place. I see no O'Banions, Capones, H. H.
Holmes, Bunnies, violin cases, James Stewart on the northside, Alan
Ladd holding the front page, King Oliver sending telegrams to Louis
Armstrong. Mind you, we are still in the corridors of O'Hare Air-
port.

Remember the old days when you had to walk twenty yards or so to
and from an aeroplane, often in the rain? Today passenger comfort
is all. They brought the buildings out to the plane, with expandable
chutes that latch leech-like on to the side of the mighty jet. So you
no longer have to hold your hat and run across the tarmac. Now you
have to walk a mile or so along a corridor, but you are totally protected from fresh air. I go to the bath-house john. I can see in the
mirror that I'm suffering from tired hair. My follicles are listless, as
are my bollicles. Still, each new city is a new lease of life.

There's a queue for cabs. But we have to make this studio in
twenty minutes. I have long ago lost all my British sense of fair play.
I go past the queue and speak to this black cabbie. For five quickly-
palmed bucks he opens the door and we get in and he tells some irate
pedant to go peddle his queue. We ignore the angry eyes of peri-
patetic computer salesmen, lingerie reps and Kiwanis. We slide away
from O'Hare—like a couple of o'tortoises? The sun is darkly intense,

as if in anticipation of a thunderstorm. These aren't thunderclouds but the normal pollution base. The driver is so big he has to lean forward so his head won't dent the roof. He's wearing a blue wool jersey with a turtle neck. He knows which show we are due to appear on. He knows all the teevee celebrities. Rather than have to explain my own claim to stardom I ask him about Chicago taxi-muggers. Inevitably he brings this big black pistol up from the floor and says, negro-hoarse:

"If the next punk takes the money but don't whup me on the haid he gits it in the laigs. If he bops me one he gits it where his heart uset a be."

They learn this at the cabbie acting academy.

We make the studios on time, the usual American single-storey rectangular building with white walls, set in an acreage of featureless lawn. If nobody else has thought of it, I'm calling it the neo-laboratory school of architecture. We are taken along corridors to a cool, dark room with curtains pulled. People stand around a long, shiny table, drinking coffee, looking glamorous. Weber also looks glamorous.

"Good of you to come on the show," says Al Wolfe, our Friendly But Nervy Host, a smiling man with a thin, sallow face and the kind of hair they used to call patent leather, in the same kind of book where the hero had his own way of making excellent coffee. He introduces us to this obvious gangster. In fact, he's a juvenile court judge. I think he's wearing corsets. Just a feeling I get, I have no real evidence. All the other glamorous people, I realise, are hangers-on. Then the celebrities start arriving. There's The Comedian, a short, ugly man with a dark-haired girl on his arm. He is in his seventies, at least. I can now spot an armpit graft job at fifty paces. He is also wearing bright orange make-up. Maybe the girl put it on for him in the car. She is in her twenties, leopard-skin coat, black stockings, high black boots, pale-faced. The Comedian has a voice like an adenoidal corncrake. He is one of those Hollywood luminaries who rarely appear in films but issues witty cracks for syndicated columnists.

A big voice comes from the corridor. Into the room the voice is followed by The Cowboy, a face I've known from a thousand B-westerns, six feet six inches of him, both arms raised in effusive welcome. This is known in the trade as Presence. He has it. The whole studio has arrived at him. If you follow my meaning. He has the same sports coat Chandler described Moose Malloy wearing, with golf balls for buttons? Plus a Sherlock Holmes hat.

"Hullo you ol' bastard!" He roars this at The Comedian. Suddenly the room is full of men called Al and Irving in dark shiny suits, lots of women called Betty and Billie, in figure-hugging suits. I think Weber and I are the only parties present not wearing corsets. Weber recoils from this mid-American, Hollywood-orientated corn. She is a cool, sophisticated New Yorker, cultured even. I admire her!

"This all you're offering your guests for Chrissake, Al?" roars Cowboy at proffered coffee. "I need a very big shot, Al, believe me, otherwise no show."

"Me too with that for a shot," croaks The Comedian, Old Orange Face.

"It isn't company policy to have liquor on the station but Henry will see what he can rustle up," says Al Wolfe, nervously. He looks like the kind of man who'd be happier running a shoe shop in darkest Iowa. Henry slithers back with a bottle of Haig. Cowboy grabs at it. The bottle is a pencil in his fist.

"How about our limey friend?" he bawls at me. "You know the Red Lion pub in Mayfair? I know 'em all there, boy! Just mention my name next time you're round that away! Great folks! Love 'em all!"

We sit down. Cowboy roars some more. Orange Face begins to dominate. He is a pneumatic drill. Other conversations disintegrate as he tells us a story about General Dayan.

"One of the great, great guys," bawls Cowboy.

It's nothing to his story about Abba Eban. Bald heads are confused with women's breasts, that kind of story. U Thant, Bishop Pike, Rita Hayworth, Cardinal Spellman, Nasser, Joseph E. Levine—the world is a happy little circle of Hollywood stars and Israeli politicians. Hollywood stars? They are all Orange Face's very closest and dearest and finest human being friends. And he is willing to tell us all the dirt he knows about them. This big star pays his elderly, God-fixated wife fifty grand every time she catches him screwing young tail. That big star patriotically entertains the G.I.s overseas like any good American would, especially as his T.V. sponsors pay him a hundred grand every time he touches down in a combat area. Yet another global figure is nothing but a Mafia creature used by The Mob to publicise their legit hotels and Las Vegas nightspots. I stare at the grotesque face of this armpit-grafted, creamed and powdered old rat-bag and then at the faces of the ladies and gentlemen and all I can see are mechanical dolls laughing. Canned laughter. I'm half-canned but I'm not laughing. Why am I not laughing? I'm thinking, how in

190

the name of hell am I going to get in any plugs against this sort of competition?

"What is the attitude of the panel to the hippie generation and the anti-war movement?"

Orange Face presses his heart and raises his face to Old Glory. Hippies are filthy, degenerate, criminally ungrateful to this wonderful country of ours, greatest free nation in the world. There is a live audience of some forty or so people. They applaud. Cowboy is marginally less fascist, if only because he tends to grin a lot while describing how he'd beat the shit out of any of his kids who dared come home looking like a hippie. The juvenile court judge says we all have to make a big effort to understand the new generation. The audience applauds. He goes on to say, however, that strong discipline is the only way to save American youth. The audience applaud that as well. I see Weber sitting by herself, face totally blank. Al Wolfe looks at me but Cowboy remembers something else he forgot to roar:

"I want to tell the good folks of Chicawgo that our fine American youth isn't all unwashed hippie degenerates, no sir. Last night something happened to me and I'd like to share it with you good people out there, I was walking back to my hotel in good ol' Chicawgo—the finest, most American city I know—" the audience applaud that energetically "—I mean it—and I saw this nice, clean, upright American soldier boy headed for the bus station—he was carrying his packs and all and I could see he was on the Vietnam draft. And I looked at that fine young American boy and I felt a great big thrill in my heart. And I said to myself—*on you go, son, you go on out there and defend me and mine*. America can be proud still."

"That's true," rasps Orange Face. "I wanna tell you, we lose out in Veetnam we're gonna have three million red Chinese on the beaches of California. You know what's wrong with this country right now— all this permissiveness and protests and riots and drugs—*there's too much goddam free speech*. Our good clean American boys are out there defending us against the forces of filthy international Communism and here at home we're allowing every long-haired commie drop-out freak to talk a lotta treason! Our society is being eaten away from the heart! We gotta crack down on these Commie-loving freaks. When I was young we knew we were the luckiest people on earth—to be Americans! When I see Old Glory up there I get a sob in my throat and a pain in my heart. I ain't ashamed to admit it—

191

every day I get a big bang outa being American. This is a decent, God-fearing country and we gotta keep it that way!"

The audience are applauding well by now. I glance across at Weber. She is keeping aloof from her fellow Americans. The embarrassing thing for her type of New Yorker is that they despise this Old Glory crap but basically they believe it. Her and Orange Face differ only on style. We are asked a question about marijuana. Again I say nothing. The girl in the black stockings—who is some kind of showgirl or dancer, I never listen to other people's plugs—tries to come in with a mild defence of youth but Cowboy and Orange Face and the hanging juvenile court judge know all there is to know about Youth without some stupid young person butting in. I listen blankly, thinking all the time—does Weber take me seriously—as a man and a writer? Personally I feel not so much drunk or hungover as atrophied, a partially preserved specimen floating timelessly in a bottle. The judge advocates hard labor for life, I didn't catch which particular section of society for. Orange Face thinks the gas chamber is too good for The Enemy Within. All right, Weber you patronising bitch, I think, here goes. I raise my hand. Al Wolfe is relieved to know I can speak. My previous silence is money in the bank. Cowboy gives me a reassuring nod and wink.

"Maybe as a visitor to your country I don't have any right to comment on these matters—"

"We'll be very interested to hear the British viewpoint from Graham Cameron, brilliant young author of *The New Ladies' Man*," says Al Wolfe. The audience clap. I see no applause board being held up. Maybe they're a trained audience.

"I'd just like to say that on this show today I have heard the greatest load of unadulterated fascist rubbish of my life," I say. I can sense Weber holding her breath. She knows how much booze I've been putting away. "Why did we bother to fight Hitler at all?" I go on. Wide eyes appear in slack faces. They all stare at me. What do I do now? The hell with it. "I'm sure most Americans have too much sense to listen to the ravings of a lot of elderly show biz lunatics," I hear my dulcet Scottish tones declaim. "This hippie generation is going to wipe all you old hypocritical homicidal fools off the face of the earth. You're moral imbeciles! You consider a harmless marijuana cigarette as a weapon of the Anti-Christ, yet you pin medals on men who drop napalm bombs on Vietnamese babies? It's your clean-cut, law-abiding, property-loving, decent men who have patriotically slaughtered a hundred million human beings this century—who is the flower generation killing? And—"

"I gotta tell you right now," Orange Face snarls, twisting in his posture belt.

"You haven't quite killed free speech yet," I say, icily, allowing the general hubbub to cover the fact I can't think of anything else to say. I look across the shiny floor and see Weber doing something with her spectacles. I feel full of zing. I am a sensation. From that moment on they all wait to hear what I'm going to say. I get witty yet. Views—I gotta million. More teevee violence I hear myself advocating, the old argument, show the real stuff and psychopaths will be sickened. It's like a pub debate, anything goes, except it's going out to millions. I presume it's going out to millions.

"Incidentally, my mother is your greatest fan,"—I tell Cowboy. He nods and winks to the audience. They laugh eagerly. I cough. "Yes, my mother told us all about those films of yours."

"Hi—you sneaky—" Cowboy roars. "His mother told him—why I oughta bust you on the—" he throws back his head and laughs.

"We'd better get out of here fast," I mutter to Weber as we drift along the corridor. I am wrong. Orange Face shakes my hand and offers us a lift downtown. The girl in the black stockings says she wanted to cheer me, it was what she'd been trying to say only she was scared. Cowboy squeezes my shoulders and says things like you danged sneaky young devil. Al Wolfe says he will take Weber and I out to dinner, introduce us to the columnists, be our host in Chicago. A GIRL RECEPTIONIST ASKS FOR MY AUTOGRAPH. I am red-faced in triumph. Instant fame—I won't say it's better than sex but if my memory is reliable it feels strangely similar to the preamble to maximum penetration.

"You were wonderful, Graham," Weber says in the cab. "You came across blazing with sincerity. You'll be a big hit with Chicago's Commie minority."

"You think I'm developing all the slick, superficial impulses of a show biz rat?" I ask, grinning widely.

"I heard Al Wolfe telling the director you turned out to be the sleeper of the year."

"Great. What does it mean?"

"You were so quiet at first they were writing you off, personality-wise. But then you came across with real impact. Fantastico!"

"You won't of course believe this but I believe in everything I said."

"Sincerity is always effective."

We are driving along a tree-lined street. I can't see any hood-infested jungle. Weber says the big wooden houses are the negro section. I think Chicago's negroes are doing a lot better than Glasgow's white folk. I know something good is going to happen in Chicago. I give Weber a swift kiss on the cheek. She smiles and vaguely pats at my arm.

The hotel had class. The staff had exquisite manners. They had two chairs with plaques to say they had been sat upon by Queen Elizabeth and Prince Philip. I was glad to see we still cut a bit of ice. Feeling positively ambassadorial I wandered back to the desk.

"They've screwed up the reservations," Weber said. "They only have one vacant room in the main hotel. One of us will have to take a room in the annexe across the way."

"Why?" I said, smiling down at her, devastatingly. "Let's both go to the annexe."

"Quit horsing, Graham—I'll go to the annexe."

"Of course not. There is some gallantry left."

So there I am in this small back room by the broom closet on the ninth floor of the goddam annexe. For a star I was being sickeningly humble, I told myself. Still, something exciting was going to happen in Chicago. I could *feel* it. I looked at myself in the meer. My hair was flatter and greasier. My dental plate rubbed dully on my gums. My trousers seemed to be sandpapering my legs. My shoes looked as though they'd followed the Joads through the dust bowl on foot. The phone rang. It was sure to be this nymphomaniac society hostess who'd caught me on the Al Wolfe show and wanted me to grace her table. It was Weber.

"We have nothing on the schedule for the rest of today," she said. "It's twenty after six now, you want to meet me in the foyer for dinner—say eight thirty?"

"Eight thirty," I said.

When two people are in love silly things like that make them laugh. When only one person is in love—well, she made me feel childish. I lay down on my bed. Come on, I silently yelled at the bloody phone, ring you bastard, I'm famous! Celebrities, you'll find, are always rushing in late for appointments and trying to pack too much into their crowded days. I'll tell you why. That's why they wanted to be famous in the first place, to escape all these dull minutes of mere living. I thought—come on, you twerp, get out of this crummy room and give the hotel's resident nymphos a chance. In my whole life I have never picked up a woman in a public place—is this some clue towards my predisposition towards the weaving of dreams?

Half an hour later I come up in the elevator again carrying a shampoo sachet, twenty Disque Bleu and the *Chicago-American*. I saw no woman to accost. My suit and I had a shower—I mean, I hung it in the glass cubicle to steam out the wrinkles. We touring celebrities pick up little dodges like that. I lay down in the bath with the paper. NEW HOFFA SENTENCE—5 YEARS. A man called Danny Escubedo was out on a hundred-thousand-dollar bail bond on a charge of selling marijuana and heroin to an undercover Federal narcotics agent. This Escubedo was well-known. In 1963 he was doing a twenty-year sentence for slaying his brother-in-law when the Supreme Court ruled as inadmissible a confession made when he was not legally represented and had not been advised of his constitutional rights.

Dean Rusk was offering his resignation as Secretary of State in case his daughter's marriage to a negro might embarrass the Johnson administration.

MILK-SHAKE MARY GETS 2 TO 6 YEARS.

Mary had laced her husband's milk-shakes with arsenic. Hurricane Beulah had caused billions of dollars damage in Texas. Che Guevara was reported in Bolivia. Armed guards were riding steel trucks as a wildcat teamster strike caused violence in Gary and Chicago. A ten p.m. curfew had been imposed in Aurora following a night of disturbances by bands of negro teenagers who had thrown bricks and looted a food store following the city council's failure to consider an open-housing ordinance.

So I'm lying in a bath in Chicago reading a bloody newspaper. So I'm going out of my mind. So I get dressed in my sharpest and beat it down to the bar. It's all men. I understand why travelling salesmen need to foster this sexual myth, poor bastards, they never *see* any women.

A crowded restaurant. Lively—if you like 'em aged sixty with tannery faces. I'm really getting with the booze, I think, the only time I don't feel sick and numb from a hangover is when I'm getting drunk. Weber says, bitchily, that at least she can take a drink or two without it leading to the Bowery. I examine her scientifically. She might have been lush ten years before. The hardening lines of her shin bones told of a golden girl growing older. I saw her shins when I

195

went under the table to pick up my napkin. For some reason this reminded me of Gary Cooper.

"I'll tell you a story," I said, eyeing her dispassionately. "In 1436 King James the First of Scotland was spending Christmas at Black-friars' monastery in Perth. They were junketing merrily, the royal entourage, the king the only man present, when around midnight they heard noises and saw torches and the King realised that his sworn enemy, Sir Robert Graham, had come to kill him. The doughty monarch got a pair of tongs and ripped up a floorboard and jumped down into a secret vault. Meanwhile the baddies were at the door. One of the ladies of the court, Catherine Douglas, shoved her arm through the staples where the bar went. They bashed through the door, break-ing her arm quite drastically. The escape hole from the vault had been bricked up, only the day before. When the marauders discovered where the king was they started dropping through the floorboards. He disposed of the first two—then Sir Robert Graham jumped down and hacked his majesty to death. Catherine Douglas was henceforth known as Kate Barlass."

She looked at me expectantly.

"That it?"

"Yup."

"Should I see some significance in it?"

"In Scotland women are willing to chance their arms."

"You're being oblique, Graham."

"Yes, my next book will be called Oblique House."

"Why do you always retreat behind bad jokes, Graham? Are you frightened to tell me what's in your mind?"

We went back to the hotel. In the bar the pianist thought we were honeymooners or lovers and kept playing romantic slush and smiling and nodding at us. He might have got this idea from the fact that my left hand was resting heavily on Weber's nearest shoulder. At home I am always touching my wife—for comfort, reassurance, you tell me. I had five shots of the stuff they were putting in the glasses.

"You're turning morose," she said.

"Sally, if you don't let me sleep with you tonight I'm going to kill myself."

"That approach went out with garrets. You never know when you're beaten, do you?"

Oh Jesus.

So I agreed the sensible thing was to get an early night, consider-ing our heavy schedule and also the fact that the goddam pianist was now winsomely dedicating The Honeymoon Waltz—to us! Oh Jesus. I actually went all the way across the street and up in the elevator to my broom closet. I took off my jacket and trousers. I put through a call to London. I have a wife, I kept telling myself, I already met Miss Right, she loves me, if she gives me the slightest encouragement I'll get on a plane tonight. This bloody tour is not a joke any longer. So she doesn't answer. Doesn't *answer*? Where the hell is she at this time of night? The dirty bitch, if she's out with some bloke—just my luck, my American sex orgy is a flop *and* I lose my lovely wife. Oh Jesus. I go out on the ironwork fire-escape platform. Chicago looks like a city at night. I go back into the room and start dressing. Take twenty dollars, singles, I think, positively yearning for an unexpected blackjack to blot me out. I hear somebody screaming. I get scared. I take off my trousers again and lie on the bed. I admit it, I can't think of anything else to do but pull myself off. There are no naked women in the *Chicago-American*. I try to remember what naked women look like. I succeed only in almost pulling my arm off. This is disgusting, I think, getting off the bed and dressing again. I go out into the big bad dangerous city. The bars are full of other morose men who look like Mafia heavies and talk, if at all, about coin collecting. I find myself in Well Street. There are stumble-bums and winos in the shabby doorways of cheap dosshouses for men. I look in bars for the terrible O'Donnel twins, who told people—be missing. All I see are white men drunk and black men drunk and all of them hopeless. They fall about like dying bulls in the ring, jerkily. I get back to the hotel in a cab. I go into the lounge bar. The bloody pianist is smarming at some other couple. I put the drinks on the room number. I seem to have even lost my knack of picking up stray men. I go back to my room. The screaming is still going on. I go along the corridor. No other doors open. I trace it eventually to the service elevator. Somebody is trapped down there. I shout something and go into my room and phone the desk. No joking, the girl says I have to take it up with the bell captain. *He's* as dense as Sherwood Forest so I slam down the phone and call Weber and explain it to her and she insinuates I'm pissed but I scream at her that somebody may be dying and she says she will pass it on and I am then compelled to stand at the open door of my room waiting for the screams to end. They do, though whether this is due to rescue or death I never know. So, I go to bed. I keep seeing the lurking shapes of prowlers at the window. I get up and put on the lights and look outside. Chicago is roaring away down there in the twinkling night but the fire-escape is deserted. I get back into bed. I put the pillow over my head to shut out the light. Then I get up again and put my shoes outside in the corridor for early morning cleaning by eager and mercifully anonymous black valets. I try to phone Sheina again. This time she answers. She says the last time she was sleeping and not to call her in the middle of the night, wakening the babies.

"You'd better fly to America immediately or I'll kill myself," I say many, many times. She says:

"I'm just giving the babies their breakfast. Try and get a grip on yourself, you big baby."

"All right, I'm coming straight home. I just can't live parted from you and the kids." So she says:

"You'll feel better if you go out and have a few drinks with your wonderful American friends."

No joking!

I get to sleep around five a.m.

In the morning my shoes are still in the corridor, untouched by human hand. I rush down to meet Weber for breakfast in the basement coffee shop. I have four cups of black coffee. We see the girl in the black stockings from the Al Wolfe show. She stops by our table. She says:

"And did you catch that old freak—he didn't touch me till we were in the station, then he takes my arm and tries to make like I'm his new piece of pussy! Jeez, he's creepy. Honest, I thought you were great."

"You're not so bad yourself," I hear my vocal reflexes responding. "Perhaps we could have a drink later in the day?"

"Sure, love to. Wish you'd asked me last night, I was stuck in this museum with nobody to talk to—jeez I hate these middle-age hotels, I'm from Frisco—"

"We're going there."

"Ring me. You'll *love* San Francisco."

"Everybody says that. So, we'll have a drink tonight, eh?"

"If we have the time," Weber suddenly says. Quite coldly. The girl looks sharply at her, then smiles knowingly.

"See you kids around," she says, going off. I turn to Weber, moving faster than my stomach cares for.

"What the fuck's the matter with you?" I snarl. "You're not going to lay me or whatever the ridiculous expression is—so suddenly you're possessive?"

198

"She's not going to lay you either, big boy. She's saving it for some old Hollywood freak with a coupla million bucks to leave her. Come on, Casanova, let's take a walk."

Oh Christ.

So we have to pass the Hefner residence. It looks dark and dingy to me, one of the customers, those ugly air-conditioning boxes on the outside of the windows. I suppose it's very apt, me coming all the way to America and compensating for my failure with women with the wretched man's magazine and then getting a look at the actual editorial office. You mean it's big enough to hold swimming pools and circular beds and hundreds of bunny girls who are really sociology majors yearning to write novels in Paris, France?

"What say we hang about and see if they draw the curtains and give us a tantalising glimpse of an orgy?"

"Gawd, Cameron, if your public only knew."

"What public? You heard from the office lately? We haven't hit the *New York Times* list yet I bet."

"It's early days. Wait till we get this show on the road round a few more cities."

We reach an esplanade. They call it a lake but you cannot see the other side. It's a big sea, with real ships. The Chicago skyline is a curve of high income bracket apartment blocks and then skyscrapers. It looks a bit like Bournemouth. I get down on the sand and shuffle my shoes in it, always a good way of removing the old lot of dust.

"Remind me to buy shoe polish," I said, moodily.

"There's a shoeshine in the john."

"So *that's* what those nigras are doing. I thought it was ritual foot-kissing. No man is going to bend his back over my shoes, matey."

"It's how they make a living. Your socialistic ideas will starve them to death."

"Better dead than servile. Look—what's this?"

I dropped on my haunches and picked up a spent shotgun cartridge, the red bleached white by wind and water.

"That's the kind of shell I expected to pick up on a Chicago beach," I said, looking up past Weber's looming pelvis to her firm chinline. She stared down at me from a dazzling blue sky. A breeze made gentle movements of her skirt. I just went mad. I dropped on my knees and kissed her foot. Grovelling in the sand!

"Just a great big country boy," she said, and there was a considerable hint of viciousness in her voice. Then she kicked a little sand in my face. I felt utterly humiliated. I mean, sickeningly humiliated, not masochistically, not erotically humiliated. The dirty, selfish, miserable bitch. I grabbed her ankles and yanked them towards me. She sat down heavily. Her skirt rode down her splayed thighs — okay, up her thighs, only her knees were pointing up so the literal direction was *down* her thighs. Anyway, for a moment, an awful, stomach-gripping moment, I was looking close-up at a widescreen presentation of her nicely tanned inner thighs and dark pubic hair pressed flat by light blue nylon.

"You going crazy, you bastard!" she hissed, scrambling to her feet. There was a man walking a Cairn terrier about twenty yards away. I knelt there, defiant in my public humiliation. He just walked on, the indifferent bastard. I looked at my Chicago sea-shell. A great memento of a fun-packed trip. I could see it on our mantelpiece at home and me telling friends and them laughing at the peculiar humour of it and me thinking, yeah, I remember what the circumstances were when I found that little conversation-piece. Revolting. I threw the damn thing into the water.

"This was all going to be so beautiful, too," I said to Weber. I thought I sounded quite sane. She simply refused to acknowledge what I was talking about. We walked along that sunny Chicago beach and saw an actual sandlot baseball game close-up, only wire-mesh separating us from the catcher in his mask, dust spewing up from their spikes, sweat running down dark faces, a man selling ice-cream from an old-fashioned pushcart, uncles and older brothers and fathers smoking and shouting, T-shirts and Coke bottles, I could have watched it and maybe got talking to some of the men and gone for a beer but we had this next teevee and off we have to go, back on the plugola circuit, back to the lapel badge crowd in the hotel and I know nothing magic is going to happen in Chicago, I mean it's all action, radio shows, newspapers, Al Wolfe even takes us to a celebrity opening night in this swanky hotel, a big deal they all say only the lady singer is a drag and even when I get to shake hands with Gene Tunney, on the sidewalk, something I know my old man would have taken as a real sign that I had succeeded in the world, I'm still thinking — yeah, this is the success circuit so why am I the most inwardly depressed man on earth, it's all a big lie, and we whizz about in taxis and all the time I'm looking out from behind glass wondering where Albert Ammons and Meade Lux Lewis and Pete Johnson might be, or have

200

been, and Oliver and Dodds and Pinetop Smith and Greasy Thumb Guzik and all the other old men or ghosts whom they never heard about on the plugola circuit, knew not and cared not, I was in love with an America that nobody else seemed to have heard of, making me doubt my own existence, knowing only the chase for today's dollar, promotion of self, performing, for plugola, for money, the big money is at stake and where the big money is that's where you'll find us show biz ratfinks, on the Big Lie Circuit, sitting with the hottest columnist in town at the best table in the smartest lounge in town and the Sharp Set drop by the table, precisely casual, dropping in nuggets of secondhand nonwit for the favor of A Mention. The Plug. The white phone rings all the time on the white table-cloth and unseen plugsters wheedle and flatter and boost, everybody's boosting something for a profit. And I am so far gone on the booze it doesn't really seem to be happening and next day Weber is telling me, cheerily, how we got back to the hotel just in time to meet this crowd of ermine-clad Daughters of the Revolution, a lot of corseted old matrons with liver-spotted forearms, and I'm trying to *dance* with them, and then we're in the taxi rushing us to O'Hare and I'm trying to read the *Chicago Tribune*, maybe just to try and look like a normal man in a taxi with a woman. Weber says we did very, very well in Chicago. We sit in the airport waiting for our call. I think I may slide to the floor unless I keep a grim hold of this newspaper. This is the one the anti-British colonel owned. He's dead now. For him the Grim Reaper turned out to be a McCormick Harvester. I would chortle if I had any illusions left.

Historical Scrapbook Corner. Col. Theodore Roosevelt, in one of the most strenuous speeches of his life, delivered in the stock-yards last night, demanded henceforth in this country 'one language and one devotion' ... pacifists were scathingly denounced as cowards. Raising his clenched fist and looking into the 12,000 faces of his great audience, Roosevelt shouted 'Liars!' at the pacifists and others who have characterised this as a rich man's war.

They call our flight. We walk down the endless corridor. Weber's shoe comes off and she has to steady herself against me while putting it on. Lapel badges part to pass our little island. We must look like a married couple. I feel like shouting at the pleasant-faced men.

Then we are back on the same aeroplane with the same passengers and off we go into the blue horizon. Sorry, Dad, I never did get to see where Dillinger got it outside the Bioscope.

"You're going to hate St. Louis," says this woman beside whom I seem to have been for as long as I can remember. I think—if I die, will they bother taking the corpse all the way back to Britain?

Chapter Seventeen

WEBER AND I MAKE UP PUNS TO PASS AIRTIME.
YOU HEAR ABOUT THIS SHYSTER LAWYER WHO KEPT MOVING
FROM HOUSE TO HOUSE, CITY TO CITY?
HE WAS AN AMBIENCE CHASER.
WHEN SHE LAUGHS I STARE HOPEFULLY AT THE ROOF OF HER
MOUTH.

Meet me in St. Louis, Louie?

The song is wrong. Cabbie tells us locals pronounce it Lewis. As, indeed, did Armstrong. It is dark. I bitterly regret wasted opportunities in Chicago. I am determined not to let introverted nonsense stop me *seeing* St. Louis, it's one of those towns I feel I know a lot about, gateway to the West, meeting place of the river giants, stopping place for old steamboats all piloted by Sam Clemens, staging post for great jazzmen forced out of New Orleans when Navy Department closed down Storyville.

"By going south we will keep a jump ahead of October's temperature drop," says Weber. Her knees are looking particularly bewitching. I didn't know it was October. The hotel is full of Kiwanis and other conventioneers. Know now why they need lapel badges, to tell each other apart.

"This is one American city you are going to see something of apart from its bars," says Weber, hustling me back down from our rooms to cab-rank. How did she know I had been thinking exactly the same thing? Maybe this denial of life-giving body-contact is in itself a fiendishly refined sexual pleasure? If I knew American rules I could play the game, too. Maybe I should propose marriage, fake a letter to Sheina telling her I'm not going home ever. Then screw Weber, maybe even go through form of marriage at midnight before sleepy-eyed judge as in movies? Maybe she'd be receptive to pleading? Maybe she wants me to crawl? Whip me with wire coat-hanger?

Does the lady cabbie know this kind of filth is running through the head of tall, lifeless British passenger?

We see this high arch by the river. Four hundred feet high and hairpin thin, although it contains a sightseeing cable-car currently out of service through mechanical fault. It can be seen for a hundred

203

miles. We see a moored steamboat, smaller and dingier than the movies. A restaurant now.

A lady cabbie? She'd been bored with household chores and they don't have any children. When she applied for the job the cab company had been kinda floored but they gave her the chance. She didn't have any trouble from men passengers. Her husband worked nights so they didn't get to see each other too much but the money meant they could afford little extras, especially at vacation times. Last fall they went to Florida? In her forties, with grey hair. A grey evening. The downtown section has broad, empty streets, the banking and insurance company fortresses punctuated by heavily formal windows of silent department stores. Downtown St. Louis just dies when the offices close up.

Back to the hotel.

Ate on plane, don't want to eat. She does. I look at her face. I don't even know her features. I know her spectacles better. Heavy dark frames grained to look like wood. Rather than have her bumpy nose marred by a red mark she has them a size too large, which is why they often slip down. When she takes them off, WHAM, Superweber appears from cloud of smoke in tight tunic and cloak. Robin, boy wanker, says,

"I'll just nip up to my room and change my socks."

"Would you fetch my raincoat? Here's my key?"

She hasn't slept in this bed so no point in smelling sheets. Her case is open. Ferret about. Panties, girdle, nylons. Don't think she'll miss one pair of soiled nylon panties, will she? Hold daintily to protect musky odour. Put them in writing-table drawer of my room. For later.

"Now, for dinner I suggest we go down Gaslight Square?"

"Okay, Fanny."

Her raincoat is gaberdine, black, beltless. In ten years she'll have a blue rinse and polythene rainbags round her shoes. Oh God, at times I think Americans are *hopeless*.

We ask the desk clerk for directions. It is only seven blocks away. I say:

"We'll walk then, get some fresh air in our nostrils."

Our pantie-sniffing nostrils!

"I wouldn't advise walking, sir, with respect. Take a cab. We have this after-dark street problem here, *certain elements* have made our streets unsafe for walking at night."

He means niggers.

In the foyer of a restaurant the under-manager clips a black bow tie on to the collar of my dark blue shirt. Ties are compulsory. We descend into gloom. The black bow tie is invisible against the blue shirt. The style, she says, is Kansas City Renaissance. I just sit there and frizzle in my own acid. If I could only touch her body, rub up against her, push my face up her skirt. How do I get to this bloody woman? Get her drinking, of course. That's no trick, she'll drink all right, see me under the table. Maybe if I pretended to be sloshed and fell under the table I could flash my tongue up under her girdle and taste her juices before she could scream for help?

We find a joint where there's an integrated Dixieland band. The pianist is white. I have Jack Daniel's with beer chasers. She has Martinis. The people are only half of them conventioneers. The others are from a dustier, cruder America. Four men and a woman are drinking heavily round a table quite near us. One man is already drunk, a big guy with the kind of face that is never clean-shaven, and a suit that's hanging six inches or so off the left shoulder, the pocket weighted down with something. A gat maybe? He shouts violently at the waiter and one of the other men half-carries, half-knees him outside. This leaves a big guy of about sixty with grey hair cropped short up the sides and flat-combed straight back on top, a younger man whose drunken head lolls face-down, and the woman. She is wearing a beltless overcoat, fawn-coloured, with the padded shoulders and voluminous drape of the forties. She also wears a stiff little black hat. Her face is flabby and white. In ten years she will be Marjorie Main. She says something to the waiter, her white, podgy hand pulling at strands of her straight, wet hair. The waiter points at the pianist. The musicians are middle-aged and professionally in-different to the audience. They are playing an almost note-perfect copy of Kid Ory's 'Savoy Blues'. Two of them have gold-rimmed spectacles. I keep feeling better because of the jazz and then I look at Weber and remember that I am starved of affection. The woman gets up and moves, coat flowing behind, towards the corner of the stage. She speaks up to the piano-player. To be the only white man in a black band must be something else. Yeah, yeah, he nods, all in good time, lady. She taps him again on the back. Yeah, yeah, he nods.

She is annoyed. She reaches up and gets hold of his right wrist and pulls it off the keys. She wants to hear 'Georgia'. Now. You play requests in this joint donchya? Huh? Here's a dollar to play 'Georgia'. Yeah yeah, lady. They finish 'Savoy Blues', reach down for glasses of beer behind their stands and sip delicately with instrumental fingers.

They wait for the tap and launch into 'Georgia'. We go to another bar, with a juke-box of Elvis records. Naturally, being an East Coast sophisticate, Weber doesn't reckon Elvis at all. I needle her a lot. She takes it calmly. She's tolerating me. I can't stand for that.

"You're a Germanic bitch," is one of my choicer lines. "You need soul to appreciate Elvis, it offends the Prussian in you."

"Prussian? You kidding?"

Dang me if she ain't Jewish!

I never even guessed.

"You antie-semitic? It figures."

"Who me? Just because I still got my foreskin don't mean I'm prejudiced, honey chile. You want to see it again? Don't look nervous, mah lil sweetie-pie, Ah'll be gentile with you. Ha ha."

"You seen enough lowlife for one night?"

"Meet me in St. Lewis, Jewess!"

You can call me a pantie-wrassler. Trouble was, I breathed so much whisky and smoke into her panties they didn't smell of her at all after three minutes. Also they burst at the seams when I put them on.

So I lay in my wanking chariot in St. Lewis and thought what the hell.

We're at breakfast when Judy Garland comes in. She's clinging resolutely to the arm of a much bigger man. She stands about four feet high, in a tweed trouser suit.

"At last I've seen a real live star."

"I spoke to her last night on the phone."

"You did *what*?"

"I was booking an early call and the operator says Miss Judy Garland is in the hotel and can't get to sleep and is feeling lonely and wants to know if there's anyone else awake she can talk with. So I talked with her some."

"What did she say?"

"She was very nice, she was doing a charity gala and had come ahead of her manager and was all on her ownsome. I told her about my tour with my wild British author and she said she wished there was somebody she could have a beer or two with in Gaslight Square."

"She did?"

"I said as far as I knew the joints were all closed up. She said she had plenty of liquor in her room, why not bring my wild author round for a coupla shots?"

"Christ! What did you say?"

"I said we had a heavy program and had to get some shut-eye. That was it. We said goodnight and hung up."

"You—you mean—you told Judy Garland we couldn't have a drink in her room because we needed sleep?"

"Why yes."

"I don't believe it!"

"Go across, ask her."

"I've heard it all now."

I flushed her torn panties down the lavatory.

We did a show there with a big cheery lady who livened up the live audience by turning her back on the ladies, lifting her skirt and poking her big ass at their faces. When the show started she told us about negro children whose heads were swollen bigger'n water melons. I told her I, too, believed in helping people.

"That's the most refreshing thing I've ever heard from a modern young author. You go back home to Britain, Graham Cameron and keep writing—we'll keep buying your books, won't we girls?"

"Yes," the girls chorused, after a bit of cheer-leader waving from our friendly hostess.

We got to the airport about five. The flight was delayed. The airport was dry. The convention crowd wheeled about among the rurals. We sat next to an army private. His wife was pregnant and her freckled face was pale with exhaustion. They had three children, one in a harness. The G.I. uniform does not look quite so glamorous inside America. The exchange rates aren't in their favour.

Weber said she must get a cheque cashed in Dallas. I said I was down to about twenty dollars. She told me the office had allocated a thousand dollars for my spending money. I said, Christ, I wish you'd told me. Why, what would you have done with it, she asked. I bet you if I offered a cabbie a hundred dollars he'd soon russle up a nice little brothel. You're *low*, you know that. And sinking fast, I said. I am a rumour, lay me. I am a clinker, haul me. I am a sack of coal, hump me.

You really *are* low, Graham.

Blacks sweep the floors, whites serve the tables. Weber doesn't even notice. I get at her again.

"You drink coffee that has no caffeine and smoke cigarettes that have no nicotine. Aren't you a little worried you have to eat food that hasn't come out of the Du Pont chemical complex?"

"I wish you would drop dead."

"I thought I had."

We took off around nine. Great place, St. Lewis, especially the dry airport.

Chapter Eighteen

THE STATE ATTORNEY WAS EXPLAINING THE LAW TO THE
CITIZENS OF TEXAS. HE SAID HE KEPT A LOADED GUN AND IF
ANY INTRUDER CAME INTO HIS HOME HE WOULD GIVE ONE
WARNING THEN BLOW HIS HEAD OFF. THERE ISN'T A LOT OF
BURGLARY IN TEXAS. LOTS OF DEAD BURGLARS, OF COURSE.

So we flew into Love Field in the darkness and Dallas is a clutch
of golden towers against a midnight-blue sky and the air is moon-
clear and we slide into the Cabana Motor Hotel on the edge of the
Stemmons Freeway, decor a heady blend of Hollywood Baghdad
and neo-Martian, coloured in sci-fi variations of purple and
orange.

"As residents you are honorary members of the Bon Vivant Club
and you can buy liquor by the glass on production of your membership cards," says the Personality Manager. Following the bellhop
along the corridor we pass a tall, lean-hipped youth wearing a Stetson
and toting a guitar case over one shoulder and a bedroll over the
other—with high-heeled boots. This is more like it. Wonder what he
meant about joining the club to buy liquor by the glass. If you're not
a member you have to buy it by the bottle?

"I never thought I'd have to join a drinking club in Texas. What
about all those mean-eyed range-war gunslingers pushing through
swing doors and calling for a bottle of rye? I could hardly believe it
when the air hostess said you aren't allowed to drink flying *over*
Texas."

"The Sovereign State of Texas is a mite peculiar about liquor,"
says Weber. "Even in the wet counties you can buy only beer across
the bar."

We are comparing rooms. In mine the wall beside the bed is a
mirror. In hers the ceiling is a mirror. Just the thing for reviving
the sexual appetites of jaded cowpokes. The local bookshop has had
a bottle of champagne in an ice bucket put in my room. *Welcome to
Texas* is the scrawled note. Star treatment at last. I'm going to like
Texas. We drink the champers out of bathroom glasses. I catch her
eye and ogle up at the ceiling-mirror. She has the good grace to
blush.

"Dallas is famous for chili con carne and tortillas, Mexican cuisine," she announces. "Shall we?"

"This is turning out a chilly con without carnals, you tortuous neurotic," I think of saying, if anybody appreciated word play about here.

In this restaurant they serve wine with meals *at the table*. That's sophistication for yuh. Party of four comes in, men in silk-fronted tuxedoes and brown, high-heel boots, women in Berkley Hunt ballgowns. The waiter puts down liquor glasses, water, ice. Man lifts brown paper bag on to table and pulls down top to reveal neck of whisky bottle. Pours large measures. Bottle stays in paper bag. Texas law. Streets empty. Most of the action takes places in the private houses of the rich.

A new city, a new lease of hope. Surely *here* something glamorous and exciting will happen. Not tonight.

Morning. Cab downtown. Drop in on bookshops, pick up schedule from champagne-donating book manager. Usual plugola stuff. Weber picks up street-map. Start walking to other bookshop. Feel air baking my hair. Come to a narrow side street, cars parked both sides. Cool little chasm, nearest thing to a London side street seen in America.

"We can cut down here," says Weber, consulting street-map like American tourist.

"We'd better cross at the walk don't walk. The hotel guide-book says jay-walking is illegal in Dallas."

"Come on, chicken, there's no cops for miles."

"It's your country."

We put one foot outside line of parked cars. Whistle blast. Look down narrow canyon, see cop. Dark glasses, big silver cap badge, glinting metal. Whistling and pointing and bawling simultaneously.

"Let's make tracks," says Weber, withdrawing to sidewalk.

"Stand there!" bawls cop, maybe thirty yards away.

"We'd better do as he says."

"Come on, head for the corner. Keep walking. Don't look round. Don't run." Whistle keeps blowing. "This would be a bad time to sneeze, Cameron."

"Why?"

"Make a sudden move for your pockets and he'll blow your head off!"

"Suddenly I'm a hay fever victim. Oh my God."

"Ten yards and we're clear."

Pass a man who's staring back down side street to see what commotion is about. Turn corner.

"Break into a controlled sprint, men," says Weber. "Into the Marcus Niemann building, he won't follow us there."

It's Buy British week in Marcus Niemann. I intended to take Sheina back emerald-studded belly-button brush for wife who has everything else. Not going to take her back English-leather handbag. Reach other book store. Light up fag in relief. Told smartly no smoking allowed. Meet staff. Wait vainly for overwhelming hospitality offers of invitations to fabulous poolside parties. Have dry lunch in store restaurant. Sobriety is health-giving but lacks zing. Remember to phone Texas cousins.

"If we walk back to the hotel we can pass through Dealey Plaza," says Weber, consulting her street-map. It's the first time I've heard any American actually suggesting a walk. In the sun! Ninety in the shade and they have a city ordinance against shade in Big D. Such limited amounts of liquor as I managed to imbibe in St. Louis are oozing through my skin, thereupon to be quickly evaporated. It never drains but it pores! I tag along behind her in the scorched, rectangular, siesta-dead street, the only living things in sight, leaving the inner ramparts of the golden fortress city—did I come here to be famous? What is fame anyway but a way of getting unknown people to look at you twice? Who needs it? Us shadows, we need it. Only I'm not going to get it. I walk with my eyes down, noting how her sharp heels keep nailing the shadow of my head to the ground. Always the shadow slips free, only to be speared again to the concrete, again and again. Yea though she walks on my shadow I fear no evil, worse luck. All my life I wanted to come to America. Then they asked me to come, not as an immigrant bum but as a star-to-be. Then I was told this woman would take me all across America—three fairy tales in one.

"Fairy tales only happen to fairies," I hear my unAmerican voice say as we go across into Main and then across Houston.

"You deep writers—with your enigmatic pronouncements," she says, echoing some previous joke we made, when we first started out; only a faint echo for her steps are quickening now and it is only by increasing my effort that I keep the shadow of my head in place for her descending heel.

The Book Repository is easily recognisable, a square, red-brick building standing on the last bit of level ground before Elm drops down to the underpass. It's all there as in the teevee hashbacks, the grassy knoll and the wooden fence. It's all very small, though, average British marksman could spit the distance from Oswald's window to the car.

There is no need to risk causing offence to tetchy-tempered Dallasinians by asking directions. The precise spot where the President was hit is marked by groups of people taking snapshots, happy families posing with big smiles on the edge of the sidewalk, Pop bending down to get the Repository window between Mom's floral print and Junior's jug ear.

Weber is strangely moved by all this. My impulse is to get away from it but she's climbing the grassy bank to get a good look at the wattle fence. She then crosses the road to get a good look at the grassy knoll. She's looking for fresh evidence to confound the Warren Commission.

A big motor-cycle cop draws up beside the snapshooters and stares at them heavily through his helmet visor, one heavily-jackbooted leg angled like a stanchion from saddle to ground. He doesn't speak but the crowds nervously dissipate.

"I can see the motel from here," says Weber. "We can walk over, I don't feel like going back downtown for a cab in this heat."

We venture where the sidewalk ends. We wait for a red light and then sprint through a minor underpass, hoping to make the other end before the traffic hits us. We cross grassy mounds. We are the only humans in sight. The sky above is brilliant blue but the immediate horizon is dusty grey. White buildings are ominously silent. We reach the edge of Stemmons Freeway. The cars come up over a rise, four lanes of them. The horizon haze is a light smog from their exhausts.

"Right, after the little blue truck," she says. I'm trapped, scared to go back, terrified to go forward. She grabs my hand and we run to the middle. Down the other slope come another four, endless lanes of cars, tight-faced men behind glass, here and there a white Stetson or a denim jacket or a cigarette hanging dead center from slack lips, suits on hangers, big schooner trucks, dust on aluminium, hairy arms, all of it flowing and only us standing upright. Then we're racing over a road that no feet have ever touched and jumping on to a two-foot strip of grass under a white wall. We edge our way perilously along this thin ledge, cars vibrating our backs.

"You did all that just to frighten me," I said, accusingly.

She laughed. I saw myself in a mirror. I had the flat, lifeless hair of a corpse from the river. I knew then I had become a *real* writer.

212

Without it I was a nothing, just a big, shapeless chunk of unlovely, unlovable *ectoplasm*. I didn't weave dreams, I put stuff on paper to prove I *existed*. I didn't have any other evidence.

It was at this stage of Our Hero's travails across his onetime dream-land that his kin came driving out of rural Texas.

The Camerons were Scots Protestants who moved across to Ulster when the lands of the infidels were being red-handed over by King Billy, who slew the papish crew at the battle of Boyne Water and no doubt inspired the song, wha'll buy my caller herrenvolk. They lost the land and some of them even lost the religion that gave us our freedom, religion and laws, some of them married Papes and gave birth to dark tales of old aunts who called for *the priest* on their dying beds. Then, around the Boer War, there was only the two of the Camerons left, William who went to South Africa with the Inniskilling Fusiliers, and George, who went to Scotland to learn the cobbling.

William never came home from the Boer War. He went to Canada and then America. He was 93 when he died in East Texas. He used to write to George's oldest son, Fred, father of Our Hero. In his time he had seen the San Francisco earthquake and been flooded out of a chicken ranch in Colorado and seen a Communist get into the White House. By whom he meant Eisenhower. He lived in the United States for almost seventy years but never forgot to make his strokes light up and heavy down.

Both in Texas and in Scotland the men in the family tended to be self-taught mechanics, cobblers, never far enough from the land not to be able to grow their own vegetables and potatoes but never quite farmers, never educated beyond the statutory minimum but never illiterate, God-respecting but more or less as an equal. Cousin William in Texas and Fred in Renfrewshire both went to worship on Sundays, William to the Baptist Church in East Texas, Fred to the Church of Scotland in East Renfrewshire. Both had one other characteristic in common—neither had ever borrowed money in his life. They saw hire-purchase as a cheapjack indulgence for getting trashy folk into petty bondage for the sake of geejaws.

This was the first time, since William left for the Boer War, that any members of the two branches of the Cameron family had ever met. In a purple and orange stucco motor hotel on Stemmons Freeway, Dallas, Texas. Cousin Graham from London busily being interviewed by a natty little girl reporter from a Dallas newspaper, Auntie Mayrelee and Cousin Mike parking the '63 estate wagon and coming, a little hesitantly, into the foyer with the rubber plants and stills advertising the stripper in the club. All of it owned, the girl reporter was saying, by Doris Day and James Hoffa in partnership. Could that be right? It's what she said. Mike was short and dark in a scarred leather jerkin, with a zapata moustache. Auntie Mayrelee was grey-haired and cheerful, wearing a wool cardigan over a print dress.

Shake hands, Camerons from across the ocean!

Our Particular Scion parks Auntie and Cousin in his room, then goes next door to Weber's room to finish the interview. He is feeling fairly peppy, in comparison with recent days, credit for which must go to the Texas licensing laws. Not quite peppy enough, however, to impose his will on the somewhat complicated situation he now faces. For a start Auntie takes it for granted he is coming home with them for the weekend. It's what they agreed on the phone. But this girl reporter has been making it fairly obvious, over a couple of shots in the Bon Vivant club, that she might not be averse to showing him something of Dallas on a Saturday night. Somewhere downstairs there is the other woman in his life, Sally Weber, currently phoning the New York office. Our Hero knows enough about the family to be quite sure Auntie Mayrelee isn't going to 'understand' the propriety of an unwed couple travelling together and staying at the same hotels. Little point in explaining to her that nothing carnal is happening because Weber won't come across—it may be chastity in practice but hardly commendable by Old Testament standards.

On the other hand, to slope off with this girl—no certainty of her doing anything—is going to mortally offend Auntie and annoy Weber. He sat on the bed, trying not to stare at the girl's well-rounded knees, half-seeing his own dreary reflection in the mirror above, telling her more nonsense about Swinging London. A really good operator would have had her by then, he thought, a quick bang on Weber's bed and a hasty adjustment of dress.

Weber came in. As always she reacted with cold hostility to the other girl. Our Hero just sat there. The girl reporter closed her notebook and said she'd better hightail it back to the office. Weber held the door for her. Then they were both standing, looking at each other.

"Another of your instant conquests?" said Weber mockingly.

"I used to think you were saving me for yourself, wasn't I the naïve young fool? I've got my aunt and cousin next door, they want me to spend the weekend with them."

"That's nice for you."

"I'm sure they would like you to come as well—actually they don't really know you're a woman, if you know what I mean, it'll be all right though, I don't think they're actually hardshell Baptists ..."

She smiled.

"I won't intrude on family," she said.

"What will you do then?"

"I'll stay in the hotel."

"That won't be much fun for you?"

"What? A chance to rest up and keep out of bars and do a little reading? That'll be a lot of fun for me, Cameron. And it will do us both good not to have to stare at each other over restaurant tables for a day or so."

"I never see you staring much."

A true creature of our slick, immorality-orientated times, Our Hero did have enough true feeling, now that the decision was made for him, to be aware of the historical importance of this moment in the mythology of the Camerons. That it was Family he had no doubt. Faces that had been snapshots, voices that had been letters. So they left the mad rainbow of the motor hotel and got into the big dusty estate and set off in the late Friday afternoon for the Texas interior, two hundred miles to the Piney Woods, nothing at all by Texas standards grins Cousin Mike, hell man, we drive five miles for a piss in Texas. Aunt Mayrelee say's Mike's had this *low* streak since the army. He's to mend his language and show his cousin we're not all roughnecks in Texas. They stopped at a hamburger joint in a poor section of south Dallas, red winking neon against a purple sky, two girl waitresses staring blankly into middle distance and rocking their heads to 'Ode to Billy Joe', giant beefburgers with French fried, finger-licken-chicken in a basket, and then off into the Texas dusk, the high sky higher and bluer than any sky on earth but the land dark and flat, the houses and trees coming up out of the black horizon and looming past the car, silent and eery. Mayrelee drove while it was still light, hammering the big car over miles and miles of straight, wide road, shooting through little townships, Texas towns, single-storey wooden shacks round a fourways junction, hamburger joints, filling stations, odd glimpses of heads behind glass, never a human being by the road. Cameron went to sleep in the back. When he woke up Mike was taking the wheel. Mayrelee got in the back and Cameron moved up front. As he slid on to the seat his hand touched metal.

"What's this?" he mumbled, head aching from sleep in the heat.

"That's a pistol, cousin," said Mike. "Texas law says yew kin carry a pistol so long yew keep it on display on the seat."

"Is it—*loaded*?"

"Wouldn't be much good not loaded. Yew see, cousin, in Texas yew kin be a hundred mile from the nearest law, we have evil men who stop poor travellers on some pretext and then rob them. Yew'd soon get to appreciate a good weapon if'n yew lived here. Now this town we're acomin' to, the sheriff here is a scaredy cat, he don't go out to no murders 'less his wife comes along too, to hold his hand?"

Some of these itsy-bitsy towns don't pay their sheriffs but thirty cents a day feeding allowance per prisoner—no wages, just a feeding allowance—and the judge well *he* only gets paid by taking half of the fines, so you can imagine your chances of not being locked up—as for being found not guilty, well ... No, sir, despite Lyndon Johnson coming from Texas we don't care for him *at all*. A tawl! The big searchlights picked up giant moths dancing ghost-like in the warm light. Mile after mile of pale road raced towards them and disappeared into the maw of the big car.

"I'm right glad to meet yew, Graham, I always hoped we could meet the family. Mayrelee, yew aimin' to fix Graham a mess of beans or somethin'?"

"Well he isn't comin' all the way from the old country to say his kin gave him *beans*!"

"I don't really think I could eat anything."

"The poor boy's flat out. Graham, I've fixed you a bed in Mike's room, Mike's about due to leave for the plant—imagine one of your kin working in a common old foundry and you so clever, writing books and all? I put two blankets on the bed, it's turning a bit fresh now."

"Yew're lucky, cousin, it isn't hot by Texas standards. We have it up to a hundred and twenty regularly."

"Why I remember when the war brides came from England, some of them were jist a fainting away with the heat. Don't it *ever* get hot in Britain?"

"Why jist a month back the birds was fallin' out of the sky cause there was no oxygen it was *so* hot! But it's cooler now."

Visiting Cousin wakes in bath of sweat. Only soles of feet are cool. They're touching something cold and metallic. Lifts head, wincing in unnecessary anticipation of hangover ache. Sees naked feet sticking well past end of bed, resting on the barrel of a machine-gun mounted on a black tripod. Decides booze has finally got to brain cells. Looks again. Explores with foot. Hallucination or not, that is a machine-gun. Look round walls. Decor is neo-Armoury. Hardly see the paper for rifles and pistols. Sees Mike's head barely emerging from blankets.

"You wakened, cousin?"

"Yup." Mike throws off blankets and swings naked legs out of bed with peculiarly American abruptness.

"Am I delirious or is this a machine-gun at the end of my bed?"

"That's genuine First World War German water-cooled machine-gun. I collect weapons, as you can see, cousin. Under Texas law a machine-gun's about the one piece of artillery you ain't supposed to own, 'less it's been deactivated."

Dee-actuh-vy-ated.

"Dad and me we're reactivating it fast as we kin machine the parts."

The pawrts.

Thirty-nine working guns in the house. But most only collector's items. The house is wooden, single-storey. Stands in conifers with big lawn. Uncle Buster collects clocks, Cousin Mike collects artillery. Nothing sinister about it. Big family breakfast. Like a family house, like home, you know, rugs and a sideboard drawer bang full of papers that you can never find the right one of. Smallish rooms. No air-conditioning, nothing fancy. I mean, just a house. I can hear the silence but there's still a roaring in my head from all the planes and all the cities. There is no drink in the house and I'm glad, the very thought of a drink is revolting. I don't need the stuff, not basically, only when I'm in unnatural surroundings. I've never met these people before, we are, objectively speaking, foreigners, but we are Family and it is all very safe and I have to tell them lots about Sheina and the children and the folks back in Scotland. I am Cousin Graham from the old country, decently married with lovely children, making a name for myself. How could I possibly be that sex-obsessed clown from back there, on the plugola circuit?

Snap of Celebrity Cousin posing on lawn with rifle-bandolier over each shoulder, two revolvers stuck into top of plugola-circuit suit trousers, automatic carbine in hands.

"Like Bonnie and Clyde," says Gunwary Graham.

"I met Bonnie Parker once when I was a little-bitty girl," says Mayrelee, waiting for the Polaroid to bring forth instant family mythology. "We were visitin' with my mother's folks and I was playin' in the yard and this big girl looks over the fence and says what's your name little girl? And I said, Mayrelee Stirling, what's yours? And she said, I'm Bonnie Parker."

"Really? Fantastic! What else happened?"

"Mom called me inside and I didn't see her no more."

They put fourteen working guns in the boot of the estate car and drove to a passel of land Uncle Buster owned in the Piney Woods. The oil derricks and deserts were over in West Texas, they said. They carried the guns through thick conifers and bushes to a grassy clearing. There they shot off several hundred rounds of ammunition, giving him different carbines and revolvers to try, picking out twigs and flower heads as targets, the cracking and banging hammering his ears, cordite blue-stenching the woodland dell. This fear of guns is an affectation adopted by people who've never handled them, he thought. Barrel up slowly, target in sights, squeeze the trigger. Cut the head clean off a blue cornflower. Thin blue smoke hung in sunbeamed layers. Crack went the guns and soon the little clump of blue flowers was no more.

He tried several shots at a butterfly but missed. He found he was hardly smoking at all. His heart seemed to have shrunk back to its normal size. Funny about Weber, she says I drag her into bars when all the time it's her that's driving me to drink.

You know anything about okra, pronounced oakrey? It's a green vegetable. The coloreds eat it raw. Not a bad chew. They had nothing against the coloreds if they stayed on their own side of town. Old Grand-Uncle Willie came to Texas after his chicken ranch got flooded out in Colorado. He worked in the woodmill. When the plant closed down in '33 he just come home and set down on the porch and said he'd never do another day's work for other men so long as he lived. He just went setting there till he died in '55. Oakrey tastes like turnip leaves. The coloreds eat it raw but we cook it.

I'm so glad Weber didn't come along. Her being Jewish and New York, she wouldn't enjoy us. Sheina would. Sheina is Family, Weber is pornography. If Sheina was here I could really be myself, not just half of a person. The roaring in my ears is quietening down. I feel as if I'm coming out of a period of shellshock. I've talked so much about the kids I begin to *feel* like a proper father. My strength is coming back. I'll be a different man for the rest of the tour. Look out, Sally Weber!

They took Cousin Graham to see the Sam Rayburn lake, man-made by the U.S. Engineer Corps, four million acres of it. He and Mike scrambled down to a rocky beach and skipped flat stones across the water. They drove through more little townships where big T-shirted youths sat leggily under corrugated awnings, staring, motionless.

The coloreds are happy nuff but for all this agitation goin' on ... they have the same as us and that's how it should be, but they have it in their own section ... one day they jist might start comin' through town and up our road and the first one puts an uninvited foot on my land he gits his haid blown off ...

West Neches, a town. Concrete and glass but the silhouette is still recognisably western, low, rectangular buildings, none the same height as its neighbour, CASH DRUGS, sun-bleached fawns, each shopfront its own shape and color of neon sign, a fankle of telephone wires criss-crossing the street in such profusion they might be slack moorings that will hold both sides together in the event of a hurricane.

I'm beginning to feel better. Why was I getting so worked up back there, on the tour? Energy coming back. Bought a pair of fawn Levis in West Neches store. Five dollars. Get out of that bloody suit. When I see Weber on Monday night I'll apologise for previous insanity and then finish the tour in proper state of relaxed curiosity.
Is sex-madness manifestation of loneliness for family?

That night Mike drove him across the river into Trinity County, which was wet, a little-bitty drive of twenty miles or so. They crossed a bridge towards a semi-circle of waiting bars all bright with strings of gay lights and blinking neon.
"They're jist traps for them that jist want to fall over the bridge and git quick gallons of beer down their throats. Better class of place farther on up."
It was a long-fronted, wooden building with a wooden floor. In

one corner four large Texan youths were shooting pool, six-foot-plussers, newly-watered hair, white shirts, black trousers, white socks, red necks, literally, hulking farm boys out for Saturday night, one of them drinking beer from a bottle which he kept gripped between his teeth, like a cigar, as his massive back stretched low over the green baize. The bar was a zinc counter with a few stools. The barman wore a tartan shirt. He was in a little gangway between two zinc counters. On the far side there were tables and chairs and some girls playing rock'n'roll on a juke-box.

"Whut's yewr pleasure, gents?"

There isn't a bottle in sight.

"My British cousin wants to know what yew have to drink?"

"Wall, yew kin have yore choice, yew kin have Lone Star Ale—or yew kin have Pearl Ale. An' if yore really fancy—yew kin have a glass."

The pool game breaks up. The big one who can upstand a bottle of beer between his teeth comes across, puts man-sized hand on Cameron's shoulder.

"Yewall care foah gyame uv poo-ule?"

"I'm sorry, I don't know how to play."

"Ah cud teach yewall."

"We don't care to play," says Mike.

"Thet's okay then."

In all the bars the big strapping country boys were belting each other playfully in the guts and horsing around and sidling up to the girls and buying bottles of beer by the dozen, white shirts and open necks and box-cropped heads and freckly faces and milk-teeth in adult faces and juke-boxes booming out hard rock or country guitars or cry-baby ballads, in one there was a band in white Stetsons and fancy red shirts with monograms and white thong-fringes.

And outside, when it was time to go home, the dark shadows of the highway patrol cars waiting just up in the shadows a piece, waiting for the drivers to come out and whizz off in their old tailfin jobs with the crumpled fenders, Mustangs, Volkswagens, a white Jaguar, dusty pick-up trucks, an old-style Chevrolet Impala with corner fins, an old roundback Ford Pilot painted with red and white zigzag stripes. All of it under stars that never were so far away or so easy to see.

Uncle Buster and Aunt Mayrelee went in the estate, Mike and Graham went in Mike's red Triumph, with the hood down. Coming out of West Neches they came through the colored section. At first Cameron thought the little square cabins might be the American version of allotment huts. They weren't much bigger than beach chalets. But whole negro families sat out front, some on the tiny porches, some on the wooden steps, little girls with ribboned plaits, fat old mammies with huge arms, tired-moving men working on old cars, all of them watching the passing car.

They picnicked at a lay-by, Texas-style, with a massive stone table big enough for Aztec heart removals, a barbecue supplied with kindling wood courtesy of the State Highway Department. They sat on stone benches, half way up a little wooded slope. It was in the mid-eighties, fairly cool. Uncle Buster said that not far from here you could look out over Louisiana. Below them, on the grass, two young couples were picnicking on a blanket. They had a battery teevee tuned into a football match. Aunt Mayrelee brought out the pieces of fried chicken and the bread and mustard and pickles.

"I wish I wasn't going back to that tour."

"I reckon that would be a strange world to us. But yew'll be makin' a deal of money, I trust."

"That's supposed to be the idea. But I'm beginning to think it won't be as much as they said in New York."

"We never had what yew'd call a lot of money but we've always gotten by. We don't owe no man a single dollar—that's about good enough for us, eh Mayrelee?"

He had his machine-shop, built by himself. It burned down. He didn't have it insured, not reckoning on giving money to no insurance companies. He just set to and built it again in a better location.

"Sheina will be proud of yew comin' home with all these good American dollars," said Mayrelee.

"Yeah, I suppose so."

On through the town of Tyler and then they were in a slow-moving trail of cars coming up to the sloping parkland where the Canton Trade's Day Fair was held. Not a Kiwani in sight, just plain folks on a Sunday outing, milling about on dusty tracks between lines of traders' stalls, red-faced farmers in flannel shirts and braces, tired-faced womenfolks in faded print dresses, twelve-year-boys in scaled-down replicas of their fathers' Levis, miniature Stetsons, girls who gave a long-hair a quick look and then giggled, heads together, Americans of toil and dust and careful faces and hard-won dollar bills.

Mike bought an Imperial Japanese Army rifle for twelve dollars.

He carried it with the barrel lying up his right chest, right hand grasping the trigger-guard, index finger just touching the trigger, muzzle pointing straight at the sky. The men poked about the gun stalls, looking for collector's items, a San Francisco police department detective's nickel-plated automatic dated 1937, a genuine frontier Colt .45, German infantry rifles, a First World War Canadian officer's pistol ... men lifted them and balanced them and put them down and came back and examined them some more and squinted the question at the easy-spouting trader and spat in the dust at the ridiculous price and put their tongues in their cheeks and grimaced and walked and shook their heads and let the trader bring the price down, and when the money did appear it was with sudden movements, hands shooting to hip pockets, dollars pushed across quickly as if hesitation might be fatal.

There were stalls that sold nothing but barbed wire, six inch lengths of assorted kinds stapled on to flat board. There are hundreds of different thicknesses and types of barbed wire, different kinds of spikes, you'd never be done buying the stuff if you tried to collect a piece of every kind ever used in Texas.

There were stalls selling Texas antiques, tiny spirit kerosene lamps made out of old tobacco bottles, old anvils, pieces of harness, old fruit jars, Ben Franklin stoves, high-button shoes, old school dresses, Civil War recruiting posters.

Cameron bought four ice-cream cornets and they wandered on through the dust and the crowds. Here was a stall selling nothing but fancy rocks, geodes they were called, volcanic coconuts split in two and polished to bring up the rich blues and grey and silvers, rock and quartz.

You could buy anything at Canton, old clothes, new clothes, dogs, old fiddles, arrowheads, geese, rabbits, thirty-year-old movie magazines, DRAFT GEORGE HAMILTON lapel buttons, cattle branding-irons, sewing machines, canvas-fronted radios of the kind that once rasped out progress reports on police nets spread for Duke Mantee and Pretty Boy Floyd.

"Yew want to see yore first real-live Texas sheriff?" said Mike. "That's him comin' towards us now, the tall fella."

He was youngish, late twenties, a pearl-grey Stetson pulled down to the bridge of his nose, a white shirt and a tie, a grey sports coat and fawn slacks. He stood about six foot five, maybe more. The tails of his sports coat hung slightly back to give his hands free access to the pearl-handled pistols jutting from hip holsters. He walked with a stiff-legged lope, each hip apparently independent of the other, each two-inch heel coming down with precision. On his lapel he had a silver star.

He also wore executive-frame spectacles.

As he eased through the people he glanced left and right, hardly missing a face. He was hardly likely to miss a long-haired pasty-faced stranger to the parts. They came abreast.

"Yewall havin' a good time?" he said softly, just above Cameron's forehead, nodding solemnly and walking on.

Over the loudspeaker came a man's voice:

"All yew guys walkin' around with guns—be suah they ain't loaded."

And that was Canton and they shook hands goodbye on the slope of the grass carpark and Aunt Mayrelee cried a little to think of them living so far away and never getting to see each other and Uncle Buster could hardly speak as they held hands and Mike revved up the little Triumph and they zoomed away to Dallas, doing ninety on the flat, straight highway, the white towers of the city standing straight up from the plain, skyscraper walls of a medieval fortress-city, thirty miles away and as clear to the eye as the bonnet of the car, his face tight and red with the sun, the wind hitting the open car so hard it flattened the hairs on his arm, racing past golden oceans of corn, just a couple of simple country boys having a danged fine mind-blowing time.

Never thought *once* about that bloody woman.

The It Will Do Club.

Pronounced Hit Wy-ull Doo?

Pitch-dark, only light a soft purple glow over a small dance-floor. Waitress appears from gloom, takes orders for two beers.

"How are you supposed to know what the women look like before you ask them to dance?"

"The secret is to wait till they strike a light for a cigaret—you kin git a quick look at their faces."

Betty and Kelly Jo? Two bachelor gals?

Orr they hy-ell! Their husbands had gone to the Cotton Bowl for the big Cowboys game, they would now be on a two-day drunk?

Yewall cud come back to Betty's place, but Wayne and Art might jist arrive home all sudden like?

Cameron slept with Cousin Mike. Country boys do it all the time.

223

Neither of us ever had a bed to ourselves till we got conscripted-drafted. Sleep back to back, not quite touching.

In the morning, when they went downstairs, Weber was having breakfast.

"Hullo—Sally, this is my cousin Mike, Mike, this is Sally Weber from New York—she's handling me on the tour—my manager you might say."

"Right pleased to meet you, Sally."

"Likewise."

Mike took off his jacket, rolled it neatly and placed it on the floor under the table.

"It'll get crushed," said Cameron reaching to hang it over the back of the chair.

"No, don't move it," Mike said quickly, pushing his hand away. "The artillery might fall out."

He grinned at Weber, who examined him scientifically.

"I feel safer with it near me in the big city."

And then Mike Cameron was rolling off on to Stemmons Freeway in the little red Triumph with the Texas numberplates and Graham Cameron turned back into the motor hotel and Weber had their bags down at the desk and was settling the bill and asking for a cab to the radio station and as they stood in the foyer, among colours unknown to nature, she said briskly:

"Have a nice weekend with your country cousins? That Mike? With the gun? That's Texas all over. Mean-looking little guy isn't he?"

"Mean? You mean vicious mean, not miserly mean?"

"Carrying a gun into a hotel!"

"One thing, he isn't mean-spirited."

"Meaning I am?"

"Don't bug me with all that introspection jazz, man. Let's get this show on the road."

"How much of this new London permissiveness and moral decay," asked the radio interviewer, "is due to your socialistic Labour Government?"

"Speaking as a socialist I'd say you Americans should be strong enough by now to stop behaving like elderly spinsters looking for reds under the bed. Socialism is a bulwark against moral disintegra-

224

tion. Do they have B-girls and topless joints in China? Didn't Castro close the brothels? As I say in my novel, *The New Ladies' Man*, our traditional, religious, moral values will only be maintained ..."

So long Big D. So long Family.

Chapter Nineteen

TWO HOUSTON BROTHERS ASKED FOR A DOLLAR TWENTY'S GAS. BEFORE THE SERVICE-STATION ATTENDANT STOPPED PUMPING THE CLOCK SHOWED A DOLLAR TWENTY-THREE. THEY REFUSED TO PAY THE EXTRA THREE CENTS. THE OWNER CAME OUT WITH A RIFLE AND MADE THEM PAY UP AT GUN-POINT. THEY CAME BACK WITH TWO SHOTGUNS AND A RIFLE, FIRING AT THE FRONT OF THE GARAGE, WHOSE OWNER FIRED BACK. HE WAS WOUNDED, SO WAS ONE OF THE BROTHERS. POLICE CAME AND ARRESTED THE BROTHERS. THEY FOUND THE PROPRIETOR AND HIS WIFE BARRICADED IN AN OFFICE WHICH THEY REFUSED TO LEAVE. THE POLICE KICKED THE DOOR IN. THE PROPRIETOR SHOT ONE POLICE-MAN, WHEREUPON THE OTHER OFFICERS SHOT HIM DEAD. MORAL? IF YOU LIKE ARGUING WITH TRADESMEN OVER PENNIES DO IT IN THE RENFREWSHIRE HOUSTON.

Weber won't say much about her weekend in Dallas. I think she's been weeping quietly since Dealey Plaza. I tell her, non-committally, that I heard a typical Texan say his biggest regret was that Oswald didn't finish off Connolly as well. She gets tight-lipped and says she thinks I'm a spiritual Texan. I must say I'm feeling a lot healthier. Like many heavy boozers I probably would vote for total prohibition. I am physically and spiritually refreshed and enjoy looking down at the great forests and lakes of Texas.

So we hit Houston airport and the local book rep has his car to meet us, Arnold Carmichael, a tall, shy man in the late forties. I act with decent restraint. Houston is smoggy and humid and the sky is purple. Can this be right? No, it's the anti-glare strip at the top of Arnold's windscreen. Houston is a sprawl of caravans under pylons. If you look thru the windscreen you get dizzy, it's either a yellow glare of smog-diffused sun or the blinding purple of terrestial dazzle. Arnold is one of these quietly cynical Americans who live in a constant state of wry amusement at the childish vulgarities of his country-men. He says Austin now bills itself as the Funtier City. He's seen a firm of undertakers called Boxwell Bros. There's a good bookshop near the space center but the astronauts read only technical books or comics. There is no zoning in Houston—you can build a riveting plant in a high-class suburban avenue. Town planning is regarded as a dangerous socialist infringement of individual freedom, another

226

open invitation to millions of red Chinese to swarm up the beaches of California. I find all this mildly amusing but Weber grimaces and clams her lips and hisses her loathing of all things Texan. The Texans murdered Her Saviour and they are all damned. You'd think a Jew would see the fallacy in that!

Anyway, we hit the Hilton-Shamrock and Arnold buys us a drink in the South Seas bamboo bar—with genuine ethnic barmen—and the sun's shining through a glass roof and I'm sitting on a stool feeling pretty spruce and Arnold says I don't have too much of a schedule and I say calmly just let me get in front of a mike or a camera and I'll fatten that old schedule, Arnie baby, and Weber says, kinda sarcastically, you don't know what a master-showman you have here, Arnold, he's wowing them in every city and I decide that's the end of Weber, she can go paddle her atrophied fanny. I just tell her I want a couple of hundred bucks and sit there till she gets it from the cashier. So Arnie and she go off to arrange my Houston debut, media-wise, and I get another J.D. in and this big guy on the next stool, in string tie, turns his head and says:

'Yewall in waaldin'?"

"No, I'm an itinerant author."

"Yeah? Ah jist thought yewall might be in waaldin', thar's a passel a Canadians heah for the convention."

Get to a radio studio. Were we poor back there in Scotland, Mr. Pappenhacker? We were so poor my old mother used to go down to the railway line and make faces at the train-drivers so they would heave lumps of coal at her and then she'd pick up the coal and bring it home in a sack on her back and we would be warm, for a couple of nights anyway. Does the Queen like the Beatles? Well, Mr. Doofenbecker, she was only telling a friend of mine at a Buckingham Palace party—I was there but there's such a crowd you don't all get to speak to her—they're her second favourite group. Number one with the Queen are the Rolling Stones. As I put it in my book.

They want you quickly in a studio across town for a teevee, Graham, they caught the radio, what impact! Knock 'em dead there, ten plugs and did yewall know this book of mine was banned for being too sexy in Baltimore? And Boston? Course, Joe, that's only helped it jump into the best-selling charts. Back to the hotel to await important calls from high-placed Houston, pronounced Hewstin, teevee execveeps. Down to the club bar, let Weber do the wheeling and dealing, I'm the one they wheel on and off, a laff a minute, Grahamy baby.

So I'm in this smokey club bar drinking liquor by the gly-ass and

227

they're all watching baseball on teevee so I ask this convention delegate, lace manufacturers not welding, what's the game and he says the World Series and we get talking to the guy next to *him*, only this one is deaf and we have to shout, he sticks out hand across the lace manufacturer and says, Earl George Armstrong, glad tuh know yuh, and dang me if Earl George isn't by way of being an air freight millionaire, with his own airline? Now it's real convenient us meeting like this, Graham—say that again, yuh'll have tuh shout, Ah'm as deaf as a stone—I have this problem, Graham mah friend, my other millionaire friend was due up tonight for a party but he's stuck in Panama City and I have these two broads lined up, highly recommended, yewall like to make up a foursome? Shout a lil louder, Graham mah friend, Ah'm as deaf as assholes.

Do I want to make up a foursome!

So I go to find Weber and realise it's seven o'clock and there's a note under my door saying she's dining with Arnold at Maxine's so I think the hell with that, and meet Earl George in the bamboo bar and smash in four or five big ones and get upstairs to Earl George's suite and he has this cocktail bar there with all kinds of liquor, he's a short, stout guy with thin black hair and face you wouldn't sell a secondhand car to. I tried to tell him he looked a lot like Martin Balsam but he thought I said Martin Bormann, and wasn't too unhappy about it at that. We bawl at each other for half an hour till the broads arrive, Sue and Deedee? We have some inconsequential pleasantries, repeating most of it in yells at Earl George, who smiles a lot at what was said the time before last. He keeps staring at us, lip-reading. I think Sue is my baby tonight, brassy, blonde, vulgarly polite.

"Hey, anybody hungry?" Earl George yells, jumping to his feet.

Nobody wants to eat. He subsides, disappointed. I am subtly discovering whether Sue expects payment and how much, and can we hit the bedroom as of now. I can't get any joy out of her so I have another drink or six and follow Earl George into the john and ask him, at a mere shout, if they are call-girls.

"Really fine human beings, huh?" he says, nodding sagely.

"ARE THEY WHORES?" I scream into his ear.

We come out and they are packing to leave.

Nivuh bin so insulted in all our ly-ives!

Placate them.

"Hey, who wants champagne?" Earl George erupts.

Yes, we'll have champagne. He presses a button. The door opens immediately and two white-jacketed flunkies wheel in a trolley with ice-bucket and the rest. Champagne disappears quickly, quite a lot down my trousers.

"And how d'yewall like Hewstin?" Sue asks me, as I'm rasping my stubbly chin on her exquisitely bare shoulder. I'm subtly telling her any city can be enjoyable if a man's willing to spend two hundred dollars on the right little chickabidee, which I am, when Earl George leaps to it.

"Hey, anybody hungry?"

He presses the button and out of the snarl of waiters in the corridor appear two more flunkies pushing a trolley bearing four steak dinners, and I mean over the end of large platters type steaks. We all nibble a French fried or two, I think Deedee even cuts a fragment of steak, then we push the plates aside and get some more freshening into our glasses. Earl George is on his feet again.

"Hey, Ah'll tell yewall what—let's hit Galveston, huh? Ah *love* the beer in Galveston. Let's head for Galveston, huh?"

"Can't we just stay here and have the orgy first?" I whimper, running my prehensile lips over the buttons in back of Sue's natty little dress, but they are all leaping about for Galveston and Earl George is on the blower and when we go downstairs to the lobby there's this grey-uniformed chauffeur and this Lincoln Continental and we get in the dance-floor at the back and I pass round the bottle of Old Crow I brought from Earl George's liquor bond and we're off on to the super thruway in the dark, shouting merrily and kissing the nearest passel of skin.

We get to this waterside bar. It's midnight. Our entrance to the tavern is blocked by a large man with a towel over his shoulder.

"Hit's all closed hup, folks."

Now where have I heard that before? Everywhere. But I wasn't with Earl George before.

"Oh no yew ain't," he says, bringing out a roll that would break a camel's back and stuffing dollars into the man's shirt pocket, "yewall jist opened hup agay-en!"

"Well, okay then, yewall kin have a beeah."

There's sawdust and a wooden table. We get big schooners. It tastes nice and cold. I'm mesmerising Sue, wandering tongue tasting her ear-wax, when Earl George is jack-in-the-boxing again.

"Hey, let's git back to the hotel huh?"

"I haven't finished my beer yet!"

"Plenty of beer in the hotel, Graham mah old friend. Let's go."

Back to the mobile football field.

Sue passes out on my chest. Swiftly my enterprising hand is under her stiff corsage and firmly wrapped round a length of warm tit. Quite a length, too, I'd fallen asleep before I got to the bottom end of it.

A nap is good for you, they say. We're all bushy-tailed and beady-eyed when we get back to the Shamrock.

I think it's ninety miles to Galveston. We'd been there five minutes at least. This Earl George doesn't fuck about in boring places, I think. It's catching. In his suite, I say, brash millionaire style:

"Tell me, are you girls paid for already?"

"Graham honey, yew're a very dear person with a very fine sense of humor but Deedee and I will have yew know we don't jist bed-hop with *any* man, I have tuh like'n respect a man for I—"

"Bedhop?" I hear this Scottish voice bawl. I hold my glass so tight it squeezes out of my hand like soap. It rolls in a circle on the carpet. I kick at it viciously. Earl George is shouting something. He bounds across the room and hammers that button for more cham-pagne or new steak dinners or Lincoln Continentals—

"You lousy bitches," I hear myself yelling as I take off into the corridor, in a fine old state ...

I got downstairs to the foyer but the club bar was all closed up. I had no discoverable key nor any memory of my room number but after recalling my name for the friendly desk-clerk he was able to put me right. Then, in the elevator, I think—I'm mad. Earl George's suite is where it's at. Where is Earl George's suite? What floor is it on? I get out at the seventh and sway about until the car returns from the top. I go back down to the desk and ask the friendly clerk where I can find the short, deaf millionaire with the two broads? No, I forget his name, I had it a minute ago, he has a lot of champagne and cold steak dinners up there, where the orgy is, with the two broads? For Christ's sake! Of course you know who I mean you dolt! OF COURSE I'M NOT BLOODY DRUNK!

I seem to remember all these middle-aged idiots in the elevator, there's a vague recollection of speaking to Weber, but I'm pretty sure I never did get back to the orgy.

So in the morning, after she's hauled me out of bed, I'm on fire and those big red eyes are peepholes into the furnace and this time the hangover is no dragging misery but a crescendo of heart-implo-sions and I hardly hear her telling me how I was bashing on her door at three a.m., she's telling me as we get downstairs into Arnold's car and set off on the day's schedule, me sitting in the back holding on to my face, eyes registering excruciating images, WE TRADE ANYTHING THAT DON'T EAT, A Friendly Bible Church—an ANTIQUES SHOP with a window full of old fridges, this can't actually be happening, if I don't get a drink quick, oh my God the first call's a bookshop with piles of the bloody thing to autograph, I'm the zombie with the pen, I can even feel my heart beats in my fingers, boom boom, I think I'm going to faint, shuah hope the book does well for yuh, see yewall again right soon y'heah, is that bar open I want a drink, no time, Graham, we have a heavy schedule, you do the schedule I'll be in the bar, oh well I guess we've time for a beer, you ever see anyone breakfasting off beer, Arnie, it's like icicles hitting your guts, so we drive on another thirty miles and the Arctic Ocean is slopping about my insides, there's another bar, I say if I don't get something in me I'll die, Ye Olde King George, authentic English tavern, a wooden shack, pitch-dark inside, bare cement floor, five Stetsoned Texans leaning long-hipped against the dim glow of the bar, two big schooners and a feel round the walls till the palms push open the door of the john, suddenly as I'm pissing I snap out of it and feel okay, so I go back into the darkness and let them know with a merry quip that I've pulled through and off we go, Weber as tight-lipped as hell, Arnold quite enjoying it all, another bookshop where I'm signing copies and this friendly lady is handing out lapel badges advertising the new miracle window-cleaner—that's the plugola circuit for yuh, we're all making another dollar so don't ask questions—and then it's a teevee studio and I plug and joke and wow 'em and Weber is grudgingly impressed and then we're back at the Shamrock packing and Arnie is driving us to the airport and I make sure my Fifth Avenue leather-bag comes with me as hand luggage and off we go and boy, soon as that fun-flying machine is over the stratospheric border line into Oklahoma Drinking Territory I'm ringing for that lil cutie doll stewardess for my sippin' ration and the sun is shining and I beat the system by drinking Weber's two as well which means I have four federally-permitted drinks on the four hours to Portland and Weber is pretending she's asleep so she won't have to hear me cheering up the hostesses, who think I'm the greatest only we can't have a date for they don't stop over at Portland but fly straight on to San Francisco, and there's me chatting up these girls with my witty British humour and listening to taped rock on the personalised earphones and taking little trips to the john, with my jacket dragging down to one side where I have Earl George's contribution to fun-flying, the bottle of Old Crow I purloined from the orgy—Earl George! That was his blasted name!—and there's me tilting up the Old Crow sitting on the john and as long as I don't look in the mirror everything's just fine.

Portland here we come!

Where the hell is Portland, anyhow?

She opens her eyes and stares at me. I grin back, defiant in my madness.

"By rights you should be on your back," is the most she can manage in the way of sheer contempt.

"By night I will be, honey pie," I say, bravely smiling on through an inner convulsion that threatens to disintegrate me.

Chapter Twenty

DID YOU KNOW THAT WHEN MARK TWAIN SAID REPORTS OF HIS DEATH WERE GROSSLY EXAGGERATED HE WAS NOT ACTUALLY JOKING? YOU SHOULD LIVE SO LONG YOUR INNER FEARS SOUND WITTY.

Oregon Trail. Thirty-five thousand feet over Denver and Rockies. Leave Earl George's empty bottle in jet lavvy. Flight goes on and on and on. Wake up in state of panicky shivering. We are told we are about to touch down at Portland. It is an effort for me to look out of the window but I can't face Weber either, so I close my eyes for long periods of futile prayer. There is a sea-mist effect about this scene, I do notice there are hills. Main Street is a forty-eight-lane highway. Commotion makes me open eyes. Ahead of cab see drunk in tartan lumberjacket and lace-up boots trying to cross, slips back a yard for every sideways yard of toppling progress. Cars hoot, swerve, accelerate. One gets him. Spins a couple of times before lifeless form illegally straddles lane markings. Lotsa hooting. Lucky—we are in next lane, zoom past little snarl. Twenty Kiwanis ahead of us in line at desk of Cattleman's Hotel. Whatever Kiwanis are or do, home life not part of it. It was Rotary in the movies. It's ironic, really, all you do is write a crummy book and try to raise your head out of the anonymous crowd. You don't realise how dangerous it's going to be. I will pop into Weber's room and let her know I will be in the bar. Pop in? That's a laugh. My feet slide on carpet but the rest is statue-stiff. She is phoning. She smiles, points at phone to let me know she is phoning. She smiles and mouths glad tidings at me. Her smile is a surprise. It keeps me there, standing still, my vague sense of surprise. I'm amazed I still have these spontaneous feelings. No sexual attraction now, however. Keep seeing skull beneath flesh.

—well, I can promise you, Howard, Graham has become a most powerful performer—yeah, real impact ... true, every city he gets on one show and they all want him, you know, shows that gave him the shoulder before? ... yeah I know he bombed on the Carson pre-interview, Howard, but if they caught him now ... yeah, Gypsy Rose Lee, you call me back when you've spoken with the producer ... or I'll call when we reach Frisco ... Bye, Howard ...

I'm a sleeper, she says, had to find my feet, soon as we hit Gypsy Rose Lee show then others will follow, Joey Bishop, Merv Griffin, Mike Douglas, Carson himself!

She is picking at a snag in her nylons. She is a snag in nylons. Once I could climb Lee Jacob's ladder to delve angry hymen. No more. How come Warren Beatty's teeth got whiter and Faye Dunawaye's hair got silkier on run? Body mere receptacle for processing liquor. Skin turning grey.

—Coming down for a drink?

—I have to see the local book agent to pick up your schedule.

—Meet me in bar then.

—Why don't you wash up and get some shut-eye, Graham? And don't wander off, it's no fun for me hanging about hotels on my ownsome.

You made the rules, but I'll have shave, tidy drunks not looked at so suspiciously. At toes of shoes little areas of leather bleached white by sun and sweat. Lather and scrape so fast won't see face. Try to remember what it looked like, once. Mounting excitement of waiting bars. Won't feel crawling flesh rasping on suit. Deep psychological flaw? Mere chemical addiction? It matters? First time planned it consciously, in advance, oblivion. Hesitate a moment. Try to conjure up faces of Sheina and Gavin and Amanda. Can't remember own, what chance they got? Can't remember what I *was*, let alone how I looked. Voyage of self-discovery? Van Demons Land? Wasn't there, when we got there. Strip away layers of identity? Wrong direction, front page has all the news. Go to bar now. Hesitate. Look at latest staple fodder, buxom graduate of Alabama State, M.A. in Poultry Management and Oakrey Culture now fascinated by archaeology— gee but I dig that crazy old stuff. Stare at art-paper knees. Doesn't work any more. Switch on teevee. Blonde lady in black onepiece demonstrating balletic calisthenics for figure-conscious housewives. Physical jerk-offs? Maybe try to read Gideon Bible? Duller than regular edition. Go to door. Stop. The next drink is your last. Go back to centre of room. Bite thumb-nail. Think of wife and kids. Better off without me. Think of Weber, Milton, Howard, money, arrangements. Their fault. Bite translucent thumb-end. Rip body apart. When last eat? Thought makes sick. Booze only cure. Vicious circle. Switch on teevee, maybe see myself. How can you? All my faces gabbling away in sealed cans in cities back on trail, never to be seen. Archives for Martians. Switch channels. Quiz show, eight celebrities in little windows. Girls' talk, fat blondes, actresses, press another button,

234

grainy picture, rat-tat voice, baseball, statistical lingo, the Red Sox, the World Series, domestic tournament elevated to global rating, Americans express only in euphemisms or hyper-Hollywoodbole, look at them, Mickey Mouses in pyjamas, bunt-balls and fly-balls—they have shiny skidlid helmets now, not caps with skips, you can depend on *nothing* in this country—a lot of blacks, no wonder whites made so much fuss about Jackie Robinson, knew the coloreds were better at it, let's sit for a second, only a second, and watch this tomfoolery. That's a pitcher, Jim Londburg is he saying? Stands all nonchalant, chucking ball from bare hand to gloved mitt, takes it in both hands, swings up a leg, jerks back arm, bends at waist, uncoils body, jerks arm, wham. Strike one. Quite stylish, in a grotesque sort of way, come on let's have a drink, no, just a moment, this is dramatic, the man says, the Red Sox have no chance but Jim Lonberg is keeping them in there, he's the pitcher, nobody's hit a ball from him yet, is that a big deal? Folks were calling them the Dead Sox, until today the Cardinals were three-one ahead and only needed to win today to clinch the Series. Best of seven, is it? Cardinals expected to walk it but Londborg is pitching up a storm. He stands there all isolated in the middle, ground level shot by radio-camera, thinking, looking, flicking ball from hand to glove, then he takes his breath and coils and *wham*. He didn't hit that one either. I've heard of Roger Maris. Wasn't he bigtime? Here, that's that guy who got the presentation in the *New York Times*, Carl how the hell do you spell it, I remember, squirrel-brain, Yastrzemski, strike one ball two, new innings, experts explain, very dramatic, Lon Burg may be putting Red Sox back in with a chance, not bad, look at that, runner caught between two bases, fielder at either base zings ball back and forth over his head, they want him to run for one base so they can touch him out, he's on a shorter run each time, like a cornered rabbit, they zing the ball back and forward over his head, flat throws, they got good throwing arms, wham they got him.

Phone rings. Shit.

"Yeah?"

"Hi, we can do a little newspaper interview up the street in twenty minutes."

"Shit!"

"It won't take long."

"I'm watching the World Series—this Lonborg's pitching a fantastic game, the Red Sox are back in with a chance—nobody's hit a ball from Lonborg yet, you any idea how long this game goes on?"

235

"Baseball for God's sakes! I thought you said it was a kid's game played by morons in pajamas?"

"That was before Jim Lonborg entered my life. Hey, he's just struck somebody out. The Red Sox crowd is going mad."

He ran to meet Weber outside the newspaper office and gave the feature-writer a lot of fast quotes and said was there any chance of seeing the rest of the game on an office set? The literary-minded interviewer seemed wryly amused. He guessed a certain section of America came to a stop for the World Series. That's my section, thought Our Hero. The man told them there was a bar on a corner with a teevee. It had bagpipes on the wall, this bar with the tartan decor, the plump, thirtyish waitress wore a kilt (Royal Stewart tartan) so short it hardly reached the upper, outward slope of her black-mesh buttocks, but Lonborg was whinging them down again and he made Weber sit at the counter with all the other honest men and watch every ball, drinking beer only, I mean, that's what you drink watching the World Series in a bar, isn't it?

Jesus Christ, Lonborg didn't get his no-hit shut-out after all, some clunk Cardinal batter got a feeble touch about the second last pitch of the game. Still, Red Sox were back in the series. Now it's back to Boston!

"Where are we Tuesday?"

"Frisco. You'll like Frisco best of all American cities, Graham, it's my favorite, a lot of these places we've been, yah, deadsville, but Frisco you will love."

"Wear flowers in my hair? Look, let's check what time the game will be on, try not to arrange any stupid shows or interviews, huh?"

"You look good for Gypsy Rose Lee."

"Will I have to strip?"

"God, you know all the Americana crap, don't you?"

We get to this autographing party. I actually manage to hold down a hamburger beforehand. God Bless Jim Lonborg. At least ten people buy copies. So there's this couple hanging about, wanting to talk. He's a dentist, Joe Campbell, this is my wife, Arlene? She's plumpish, dark-eyed, forty, wide hips. Joe is a mini-Jeff Chandler. They read the advert, love books about Britain, always wanted to go there, interested in novels. They come with us to this radio station where this aedult host, oh well, you know the sort of stuff, he thinks flower-children should be defoliated, drug-takers whipped. I am very controversial, talking about flower-power presidents, etc. I say Senator
236

McCarthy was a Communist agent used cleverly by the Kremlin to discredit American democracy, it's all in my book, is it hell—it's The Manchurian Candidate—but I won't be here when the complaints come in, will I?

"We'll take Graham and Sally to Mary's Room, that would show them Portland at night, eh, Arlene?"

"Is London as permissive as we hear? Joe and I have been planning a vacation over there—you think we'd get to meet some swingers?"

"You sit in back with Graham, honey, I'll have Sally up front, all right with you, Sally?"

Oh yeah, I'll bet she's quivering with tortured emotions. I get my arm round Arlene's meaty shoulders and snuggle some. We park and walk down a bright street.

"Okay if I hold Arlene's hand, Joe, she reminds me of a woman. My God, she is a woman."

"I wouldn't want you to think we're hicks or prudes just because we're lost up here in Oregon."

Mary's Room is half-dark. The people sit at tables in a long room flanked by a bar. There's a narrow stage behind the bar. Girls are stripping to hot rock. Drinks come round off trays toted by girlie-girls in black mesh all the way up and velvet nearly all the way down. There's a lot of Greeks present, and farmers and maybe lumberjacks, all drinking hard, laughing fit to burst or threatening to beat shit outaya, a few young guys in college jerkins, a few hard-eyed doxies swinging legs. Lots of Swedes in Portland, says Joe. I sit next to Arlene and get my right hand firmly round her nyloned thigh. I don't know how Joe is faring with Weber's thighs but I wish him luck. Let's get four double shots and four beers. No, no, Joe, I got it, money to burn, have one yourself, darling. Thanks a lot. You're welcome, honeybun.

Swing doors open. Into dark smoke leans sky-high streak of young American manhood, face a dark shadow under pinched-in sheepman's Stetson, hands loose at sides, corduroy jacket, big-shouldered and hip-length. Five inches of high-gloss hand-tooled leather showing under cream trousers. Cigaret dead center of mouth. Blows smoke sideways up furled brim of big hat. Walks full-chested Robert Mitchum style to next table. Drags chair into position, drapes tree-like legs round it, eyes never leave girls on stage. Stretches out booted foot, hooks next chair, drags it close and bangs both heels on seat. Narrow eyes, drags on cigaret. Big redhead spins her tits in opposite direction, fluorescent nipple-paint making green catherine wheels. Sheepman takes cigaret out of mouth, stares waitress in the eye:

"No-Cal Cola and a pack of mentholated?"

Joe leans over to say Arlene has better gams than any on stage.
They feel shapely enough. This big redhead, she's stripping artistically,
she's dreaming of making it out of here on to Sunset and B-pictures
and thinly-disguised libels in Harold Robbins novels, that's what
success is all about in this country, huge anonymous masses going
nowhere, save yourself from the heap. Arlene presses her thighs
together, meaningfully trapping my hand. Throw more money on
trays of scantily-clad lovelies. Shots, chasers, partysville. I made it at
last. Jesus Christ, I was beginning to get doubts.

Weber says she wants to hit the sack. Poor old Joe, I think, helping Arlene to her feet with the judicious support of hand cupped under
lovely bum. She wiggles it a little. Will Joe wait in the car? That's
the only snag I can see.

He parks in front of the hotel. I take my right hand out of Arlene's
blouse and bring my right arm back round her neck.

"Well it's been charming of you to show us round," says Weber.
Natch she's copping out of any wife-swapping deal. The bitch prob-
ably thinks *marriage* is too sordid, if anybody's ever asked her that
is. Joe does offer to escort her inside but she's out of the car and *off*.
Bye bye you frump, I curse inwardly, you did your best to spoil
America for me, didn't you?

"She's a lesbian," I tell Joe and Arlene. "Now then, let's get a
drink and make our filthy plans."

There aren't too many places still open. Joe drives round the block.
I ask Arlene wittily if she'd like to come up and see my press cuttings.

"How about it, honey," says Joe, "you'd like to spend the night
with Graham, wouldn't you?"

Yoicks!

"Not in the hotel, I'd meet somebody we know."

We drive round the block again. Sin's easy in Portland—but parking ...

"You want to come back to our home, Graham?"

"Well, you sure that would be safe, Joe? I might have designs on
this juicy little wife of yours."

"I think Arlene would enjoy intercourse with you, Graham."

"Yes, I would, very much. You want to come home with us,
Graham?"

Clear throat, twice.

"Are you—ehm—serious?"

"Why of course we are. It wouldn't be the first time. You can have breakfast with the family and catch a cab back, our home is about twenty-five miles distance. We're not squares, you know, because we live in Portland."

"It's a long way. I've probably got an early show or something."

"We rise early, Arlene has to fix breakfast for the five boys, you know, to catch the school bus?"

Vision. Bleary-eyed guest, unshaven, stumbles through strange home, joins swapped wife in shiny, gadget-packed kitchen crammed with five freckly-faced brats munching their Wheaties and asking Mom and Pop who's this guy? Yeah, and what's with this Joe, a dentist offering his wife? I heard about these sex-murderers, they probably do this all the time, she screws me and he watches and when it's all over they ritually barbecue me and feed me to the bobcats.

"Look, why don't you come to my room, then I could get you a cab?"

"We know too many people. What do you think, Joe?"

We muse, scientifically. I guess big celebrities get this all the time.

"Dear, whatever you feel you want is okay by me."

"I really wouldn't be at ease in the hotel," she says.

We drive round the block again. I get a good handful of her knockers and she gives my dick a bit of rub'n'squeeze. We stop by the entrance. They still want me to come on out to their spread but I say I cannot. We exchange addresses and say we'll meet in London. I think, Sheina will like that. How many more Americans are going to be dropping in on us over the next few years?

So why didn't you go, I ask myself as I sink wearily into bed. Elementary caution? Good taste? Puritanism? I might as well admit it to myself, here in the dark in a hotel room in Portland, when her hand groped me there wasn't even the suggestion of an erection. Breakfast with those milk-fed teensters would have been bad enough after a night of illicit passion across the landing—but imagine if Mom was in a foul mood because The Visiting Stud turned out to be NO BLOODY GOOD ...

And in the morning it's hangoversville again only ten times worse and we have to drive to Salem and sign books and look at white-capped Mount Hood and draped signs such as JUMBO ORIENTAL DRIVE-IN and the Glendale ACTIVE ADULT LIVING Community, which doesn't mean an orgy township but Senile Inactive Dying for old folk, and trees and October sunshine and scenery and there isn't a drink to be had in Salem, just a lot of stupid books that nobody intends to buy, especially the lady who picked up a copy and said

239

she was looking for a present for her hubby only, chuckle, chuckle, she didn't want him catching any of my very advanced permissive London sex ideas, and then we drive back to Portland, do a newspaper interview and a radio show from a café, I still don't know why they have radio shows from cafés, Weber just wheels me to wherever I'm scheduled and I do my stuff and sometimes I have this odd sensation that I am being done to death by evil forces unseen by the nice, decent people I meet, only I can't shout out to them for help, they're too busy saying what impact I have, it's no longer a case of having nerves or worrying about plugs or taking care of my language, the impact is automatic, I once saw Behan drunk on teevee but with him it was more an excess of life force, I'm just a well-programmed robot-zombie, I don't remember what I said the moment I said it, or even while I am saying it, this book *The New Ladies' Man* sounds like a lot of gibberish and Weber says:

"We can list Portland as one of our successes, Graham."

And I say:

"You book out and I'll have a quick drink otherwise I won't last to the airport."

And it's another taxi, I mean the same taxi, the same flight desk, the same porters, the same corridors and hostesses and smiles and dinky hats and although they say this is the evening flight to San Francisco I know it's the same plane we've been sitting in for a month and the same dollar I give the same girl for the same plastic goblet of bourbon, and the same siren voices heard faintly through the noise of the engines, women's voices singing out there on the wings ...

"Hi, guys and gals, this is Big Bill Bradstock your driver, gladda have ya on board. It's prime weather for these here flyin' machines, folks, so sit back and have fun."

... and skin and flesh is rotting off my body and

Chapter Twenty-one

ALL ACROSS THE LAND THE PEOPLE WERE HARRIED AND
ANXIOUS AND TENSE. YEARNINGLY THEY LOOKED WEST TO
SAN FRANCISCO. FROM RADIOS AND TEEVEES AND JUKE-
BOXES CAME A GENTLY INSISTENT HYMN TO THE LOVING
PEOPLE THERE. WEAR FLOWERS IN YOUR HAIR.

my clothes and skin have become indescribably filthy and I rip at the
itches on my scalp with unspeakably black fingernails. Yet, when I
look down at my hands and trousers the dirt immediately vanishes. I
don't understand this and keep flicking my eyes to surprise it but it
is always too fast; I tell myself I cannot be truly dirty for never in my
life have I had so many baths and hot showers, sometimes thrice a
day. But I am, I can feel it, worms are nesting between my toes and
crutch-pheasants are roosting in my belly-forest and when my greasy
fingers rip furrows through the scales on my skull my dead hair comes
away in rakefuls.

There is a little girl in a white dress running up and down the
gangway. Her mother, a fair, freckled woman with blue rings under
her eyes, smiles parentally as I pat the little angel's head. The other
passengers keep their eyes averted. Weber, however, gives me a smile.
It is a very nice smile. Nobody is nasty to dying men. My stomach is
aching from lack of food yet the very sight of the plastic tray of food
makes my throat convulse in a barely suppressed spasm of sickness.
Eyes closed, disobedient tongue relentlessly probing a new ulcer down
there between lower lip and raw gum, I hear a voice coming through
the whispering drone of the engines. A man's voice, monotonous yet
gentle ...

The jet has come south from the end of the frontier and the dusk has
come west, from the cold Atlantic, over the milling dross of West
42nd Street, over the hammering mills of Cleveland and the rivers of
poison and the graveyard mountains of dead autos and the skin joints
and the chattering transmitters and the fire-consecrated ghettoes.

And the jet and the dusk arrive together over the dark breasts of the
hills and the evening tranquil rim of the blue pastel Pacific. We
cannot go farther than the frontier for beyond we will be consumed
in the pink explosion of the submerging sun.

—You'll see, you'll have yourself a wonderful time in San Francisco.

That was Weber's voice. She is definitely being nice to me.

I feel like crying, not out of sadness but at the stupidity of it all. Nobody told me that failure was the alternative to success. She waits for me by the door of the cab, her face expectant, almost eager. She is an American child, playground-wise. I am a fool but I have been given a look over the edge of the grave. We are driven towards hills adorned by glowlight chains of swaying firefly lights. The dusk air is soft and warm. It is true that the city looks like no other. It has no gridiron rigidity. Men stroll softnight sidewalks in flower shirts. Two girls walk across the street at the walk don't walk lights, one white, one black, books on hips, laughing. We drive up a steep hill behind a rattling cable-car from innocent days when mothers and fathers kept us safe and funny policemen fell flat-flaced off tailboards.

—You feel the atmosphere getting to you already?

I can say nothing. There wasn't enough of me to stretch across America. She takes my hand. Where she touches me my skin feels warm and *clean*. Scales fall off. She is holy and before her the evil creatures cringe and die. Is it too late? I feel a warmth between my numbly crossed legs. It is not so much a sensation as a memory of a sensation. She is trying to warm me up. She starts a game we have been playing on planes. Or was it in cities? Was it one plane and one city?

"I got one for you," she says. "What's a title for the Pope's new best-seller?"

"I don't know."

It's my voice that sounds foreign in my ears now.

"Oh dear Vatican the matter be?"

"Very good."

"Or—how's about—The Pill's Grim Progress?"

"Americans don't make puns."

"You think of one."

"Me? My brain doesn't work any more. What about—oh dear—Red Sox beats Cardinals?"

"Mine were better."

"I know. I taught you puns and now you've left me far behind. How symbolic of the special relationship."

"Come on, let's hear from good old laff-a-minute Cameron. Drive-in lunatic asylums?"

"If I laugh I may fall apart."

242

"Jumbo Oriental Drive-in Synagogues?"

"Oh stop it, woman, for God's sake."

"Topless funeral parlors? How's about a drive-in topless restaurant serving finger-licken-chicken and dunkin donuts washed down with sippin whisky?"

"How about a motion discomfort bag for travel-sick elephants?"

"You can do a lot better, fella."

"I know. Let me kiss your exquisite fist."

"That's more like the old you. Okay, you can put the hand down now."

So—everybody's entitled to the odd moment of despair, I think, new cheer rising in me as I turn my face into her hair and nibble her ear. A new city, a new chance. She isn't too serious about pushing me away. Is it possible that she has come to respect and admire me? It strikes me as rather strange that she pointedly never asked what happened between me and Arlene, back there in Portland. Yes, there is a definite warmth spreading from between my clenched thighs, down there where I used to live.

We come to the Mark Hopkins Hotel on Nob Hill. Weber checks us in. I see the beckoning bar but instead buy a newspaper. I'm rehearsing little lines—of course I was drinking heavily, I was eating my heart out for love of you, Sally—when my eye happens upon a black notice-board, there in the glamor-packed foyer. It has little plastic letters slotted along horizontal grooves. It lists the suite locations of the seventeen conventions currently taking place in the hotel. I smile wryly, thinking of some little guy saying he hadn't hadda night like that since he left the ammy. We go up to the fifteenth floor. In my room there is a basket of fruit under Cellophane, with a note, welcome to San Francisco. I eat a brilliantly red apple, frowning at the possibility that it is the first piece of fresh fruit I have eaten since landing at John Kennedy, at the beginning. The texture of the apple is mushy, the taste non-existent. I peel an orange. It has some juice. My tongue is not to be trusted with sarcasm against American produce, it is whisky-pickled and nicotine-charred. I take the basket to Weber's room. She is on the phone. I hold up an orange and mime its peeling. She shakes in the negative. I eat everything in the basket before she comes off the phone, cramming and munching and listening for vitamin news from my body. Is it too late?

"I have a dear friend here, she's picking us up for dinner," says Weber.

"Nice gesture, the fruit."

"You appreciated that, didn't you?"

Something about her voice. Suspicions.

"So what did I do to rate *fruit*? Don't tell me they've heard of me or my stupid book in San Francisco?"

"Well maybe the office did refresh their memories a little when they made our reservations. Don't be so goddam cynical all the time, Graham. Honestly, you just won't accept things at their face value, will you?"

I stand rebuked by her window, looking down over the roofs of apartment blocks. She goes to wash-up. She comes in and out of the bathroom in a nylon slip, bare legs, touch of powder at the mirror, new pair of nylons from a packet, sits on stool and pulls them on carefully, pushing back slip to get hold of suspender straps. I no longer rate as voyeur? I am eunuch, to see lower rim of bare buttock, to ogle at delicate woman's hands smoothing thigh, knee, calf, ankle? I no longer rate? There is enough new sap rising in me for this to rankle.

We meet Mirella. Divorced. Fortyish. Elegant. Brisk, with charm. Lived for some years in Madrid and Paris, sophisticated. Takes us across road to hotel where glass elevator takes us up outside of building to roof-top bar-restaurant. Two women chat about old times. Mirella laughs huskily. Weber laughs like young girl. Eunuch enjoys privileged proximity. See Oakland Bridge, with carnival lights. Soft golds, electric blues. Jack London ended up rummy in Oakland bars. Martin Eden practically castrated himself becoming genteel for brainless girl who wanted him as parlor pet. Not me, I think. I was only dabbling in self-destruction.

"That's the rock down there," says Mirella. We are at a window table. The lights of Alcatraz, no longer the living death fortress, just a heap of unused rock in a bay under the windows of a top-class restaurant.

We go to authentic Chinese restaurant ("It's where the Chinese eat themselves") in Chinatown. Celebration crowds in narrow streets, fireworks, dancers on stage in street, paper lanterns, yellow faces, warm air. Chew a little Chinese food, consciously drink very little. Listen to American ladies chatter. I saw this fashion magazine, probably *Vogue*, the back section had pages of ads for military colleges in southern states. Made me quite sick, to think of well-groomed women having such power over little men. Buy this new creation and here's where to deposit that awkward-age boy of yours, we'll end him as a man. Now, listening to them, thinking of how Weber let me watch inner secrets of thigh-strapping suspenders, watching Mirella's strong jaw, it doesn't seem so awful. American men merely living out masochistic streak that's in all men. Why not just accept it, be relieved of masculine strivings, become maid to dominant ladies? Men pay good money for that sort of thing, in London. Boy, I'm getting quite horny! This Mirella, she's desperately keen on creative writing and the arts, she's well impressed by my insouciant displays of insights into the creative process.

"Well, Graham, it's been a sincere pleasure making your acquaintance," Mirella is saying. She has small but firm breasts under wide shoulders. A very big mouth.

"Graham," says Weber, touching my shoulder, "I'm spending tonight and tomorrow at Mirella's place. I've arranged with Kyle Franklin—the local Tannenbaum Inc. agent?—to pick you up tomorrow afternoon, he'll show you the spots. And I'll see you back at the Mark Hopkins, tomorrow evening? Say about seven, we can have dinner?"

We are on a sidewalk, a very steep slope. Weber is carrying her overnight hatbox, first time I noticed it.

You mean?

YES!

Oh no!

YES.

They go off together in a cab.

Alone? No, tell me it isn't true. Oh no, it can't be. I can't believe she would, not now, please say it isn't true.

I go into a bar to take a breath. I look at faces but they are smiling over their shoulders at dates, beaux, escorts, husbands, steadies, studs, lovers, squires.

I am too numb to sob.

I am alone in a crowded yet lifeless city bar. I see morose men of older generation leaning heavily on zinc counter. They are silently watching Raymond Burr in first episode of 'Ironside'. It's set in San Francisco. Burr is crippled in wheelchair, pushed about by token black. I have the feeling that all of us men sitting at the bar have been abandoned by women. The one who leaves takes the life force.

I get out of there and take a taxi to Haight-Ashbury. Flower capital of the world. Walk in crowds. Girls with golden hair and soiled feet. Go into dark bar, folk-rock music so loud it can clean dirt off suits with sound-waves. Get to stool, order double bourbon. Young man's face smiles close to shoulder.

"Howdy-doody, man," he is saying. "These side-burns, they're real sharp. Buy you a drink?"

"Jack Daniel's on the rocks, water on the side. Are you a faggot?"

"You're very forceful, honey."

I take his drink and buy him one back. I don't even bridle when his hand touches my knee. I stare at him and find him boring. I get up and walk out. At the next corner a big youth in an all-black outfit, shiny shirt and toreador pants, is smashing the face of a twisting, crying man in a square suit. People walk by. The guy in black keeps on ramming punches into the crying face. I walk by. I go in other bars. A woman throws a fit and jerks about on the floor. Nobody bothers. She loses interest, gets up, tidies her matted hair, asks a solid man in a Hawaii shirt to buy her a drink, he says nothing but sweeps her away with a backwards arm jab into her face. She sits heavily on floor. He exchanges laughs with barman.

So I see this Topless Gogo Lounge.

At the far end of the bar, half way up on the wall on a little jutting platform the size of a barrel-lid, a blonde girl with Ayrshire udders is shaking her body about in approximate time to the rock record. She has a look of frenzied concentration on her surprisingly small face. Her pubic hair is covered by a triangle of satin.

On the wall running parallel to the bar another girl, on a similar platform but with cage-bars, is performing roughly the same movements. Her breasts are also very large and full, although her ribs can be seen and her legs are thin. She is close enough for me to see sticking plaster on her reddened heels.

The fat girl finishes her stint and climbs down a spiral staircase to be succeeded by a tall, thin, dark girl with very small breasts—at least by comparison. However, attached to her nipples are fluorescent green tassels that she twirls in opposite directions. The fat girl puts on a kimono and comes up the bar asking various sports if they will buy her a drink. Some gent does the gallant thing. I swivel back to face the mirror and ask the young bartender for another drink. Another dollar. I sink this one a mite faster. I look round when the girls change over, but when each comes up the bar in her dressing-gown some greedy bastard is always in first with hospitality.

The young barman says:

"You have this one on the house—we don't get many customers buy more'n one."

246

"A free drink, eh? You won't last long at this job, friend. Your very good health."

All along the bar these middle-aged sex-nonentities are desperately thinking of clever things to say to kimono-clad girls who, having smiled so eagerly at touting time, are now nodding disinterestedly and scratching rough spots on half-curtained thighs. I buy another drink.

"I hope your boss doesn't find out about the free drinks," I say companionably to the barman.

"Screw him. I'm only working here nights to pay my way through college."

"Any of these chicks worth investing a dollar in?"

"They're all pretty much on the level. Say this for the bastard who owns the joint, he don't hire hustlers."

So this dark-haired girl with the rib-cage comes up the line and I'm politely pleased to lay out a dollar for a drink. I am not the kind of creep who asks whores how a nice girl came to this. She can see I am not in the same bracket as these old guys who can't score any other way. I have long ago lost any notion that American women are impressed by my co-national status with Sir Cedric Hardwicke and Commander Whitehead. I have learned to speak from the back of my mouth with my nasal passage sealed off. She chats easily. Her kimono-draped thigh is not too far from my hand. She has green eyes and wears false fingernails. I decide it's time to clinch it. If I get pox I'll say it was Weber. All over New York I'll say it.

"Hard work, here, huh? What time you finish? We'll have a drink somewhere else."

"I'd like to but I don't knock off till one and I have a thesis to finish for Monday."

"A thesis?"

"I'm only working here to pay my way thru college. You think I bump and grind on a career basis? You're from England, aren't you? Jenny—the fair girl at the end—she's from England."

The next who gets up the gauntlet is, I'm happy to see, an obvious hustler or hooker or two-bit Annie or whatever the correct term is. She has a very low-class face, snubbed nose, mouth too wide, a lot of white eyeball between her pupils and her lower lids, always a sure sign. She shows a lot of podgy white thigh.

"I'll bet these old creeps give you the shivers, eh?"

"You bet they do. Jeez, some of them jerk off under their macs, you know, like *masturbate*?"

"Yeah, I can imagine. What time do you finish, we can have a

247

drink somewhere with less flesh on display."

"I'd like to but I have this Saturday morning tutorial?"

"You're not—paying your way through college?"

"You think I'd do this for a hunnerd dollars a week on a career basis?"

The English girl comes up the line, pointedly ignoring the old sex-creeps. She has a nice fat white neck and a chubby chin. I can tell she's got a touch of English class because when she hoicks her heavy behind up on the stool she pulls the kimono over her broad knee. She has a thick Somerset accent. She comes from Pensford, near Bristol? The West Country English put the same rising inflexion on the end of sentences as Americans, why not, that's where the first Americans sailed from.

"The pay's very good, a hundred dollars a week and it's only from ten till one, like."

"So how come a little Somerset charmer like you is working in a topless gogo joint in San Francisco. Don't tell me—ha ha—you're *not* paying your way through college?"

"I married this American boy in Bristol—he's at Oakland, the university like? I'm working here to pay his way through college."

I don't remember getting back to the hotel.

As mornings-after go, it isn't outstanding. As long as I walk doubled-up the blood doesn't get its full force behind the battering ram it is using to give me a topless head. I get into the bath with the *Examiner*. It is a very short bath, meant only to stand in while you're showering. I get my back under the water by simple means of splaying my legs up the wall. The paper shakes a lot and there doesn't seem to be any feeling in my fingers. Each heart beat is a kick in the chest.

> GADSDEN (Ala)—U.P.I.—*Franklin Beggs, 27, a warrior who got to Vietnam only by divorcing his wife, has returned home on leave his chest full of medals ... He was unable to get into the army in 1965 because he had one too many dependents—a 4-year-old boy—and no previous military experience. At the time Beggs said, "The only thing I could do to get in was divorce Linda, join up and then remarry.*
>
> *"My wife had enough faith in me to respect my desires and wishes."*

248

A pilot, Beggs said he was in combat flying almost every day ...
"It's one thing to be afraid and another to know that you don't
have to wonder about what you would do in the face of fear."

My arms are so lacking in strength that the paper keeps slipping
into the water. Where did I begin to go wrong?

SANTA CLARA—A 41-year-old man last night escaped with only
minor injuries from a wild, mile-and-a-half ride on the hood of a
woman's car. She subsequently was arrested for assault with a
deadly weapon (the car) and hit and run.
Alexander VanLeemtut, 41, told police here this story: his car
was involved in a minor collision with another driven by a woman
about 10 o'clock last night at De La Cruz Boulevard and Kifer
Road. Both stopped and an argument ensued. When he demanded
to see her driver's license the woman jammed her car into gear
and drove at him. He leaped into the air and came down clinging
to the hood of the speeding car.
He said the wild ride continued on to the northbound lane of Bay-
shore Freeway to the turnoff for the San Thomas Expressway.
There the woman suddenly stopped, threw Vanleemtut off the hood
and drove off.

The water is getting cold. I turn on the hot tap and let it trickle.
The effort leaves me without the strength to keep my eyelids open. I
drift into a doze, the paper sliding inexorably into the water. It will
be peaceful, the most pleasant form of escape. My whole body is
wracked by a monumental shudder. A vast jolt of grid-electricity pul-
verises my joints. I scrabble to sit up. The paper is a barely submerged
raft that sinks mockingly beneath the weight of my clutching hands.
Black waves pound through my head. I am on my feet and then I
lose my hold and fall, slowly it seems, striking the rim of the bath at
various points but feeling no pain. I am on my side in the water. My
arms are dead, one pinned under me, the other making a last feeble
wave to the shore as I go under. My breathing is shallow, the water
deep. Death is a crazy dream. I am to waken up from the gas and
see my mother and the dentist talking together. I am not. I waken up
aged 33 lying on my side in a cold bath in a ninth floor bathroom of
the most expensive hotel on the top of Nob Hill, San Francisco. My
mouth is half-full of bilge-water. I splutter and get the crook of my
elbow over the rim of the bath and drag my body an inch or so off
the bottom, just enough to free my other arm. I still do not have the

strength to get up. My twisted legs begin to push against the wall. Slowly my inert body is propelled up the sloping end of the bath, until I am sitting upright. I then manage to swing one leg over the rim and drag the other after it and more or less let gravity carry me over the edge on to the floor, where I flop on the rough mat like a limbo dancer who didn't make it. I lie there for minutes, breathing rapidly and hoping some of it is getting down to my lungs. Then I get to my knees and hang my head over the lavatory seat. There is nothing to throw up but my stomach insists on dry runs. My eyes are blinking back tears of exhaustion, I manage, moving slowly and with great concentration, to turn on the cold tap of the shower. Something solid rattles on the bath. It is my dental plate. I kneel beside the bath and fish for it in the shower-spattered bathwater. It has not been soaked in cleaning powder for many weeks. The translucent pink bridge is stained black and brown. The stain is heavily scratched. I get it into my mouth and let my head hang over the water. The paper is still floating just under the surface. I don't—can't—turn my head to look up but my hand feels blindly for the shower tap. The water stops. The bath becomes calm. I am breathing more slowly now. My chest takes my full weight on the rim of the bath but I learn to live with the painful ridge biting into my rib-cage. My eyes catch a headline. My hands weakly paw water until the paper floats round to a reading position. The water magnifies the printed letters.

The identity of a man who first failed to commit suicide in wet cement and then succeeded by leaping into a vat of molten iron was still being sought by police today ...

The man, described as a 'refined type' about 28 years old, yesterday climbed into a Bodie Cement Co. flat-bed truck filled with wet cement about a foot deep ...

Bill Nicolina, a P.T.&T. supervisor, looked out of the window to see the man stretched out face down in the cement. He told police he ran out of the building and pulled the man out.

The man pushed Nicolina away and said, "Leave me alone, I'm trying to make an impression." He then ran. A few minutes later workers at the Pacific Foundry looked up to see the cement-covered man leap into a three-foot-deep vat containing the molten iron. The temperature was 2500 degrees.

The man was described about 5-11, 150 pounds, dark brown hair. He was wearing a greenish jacket and a sports shirt.

*   *   *

So you took the easy way out, huh?

I collapse back on to the cold floor. I think I'm going to die laughing. I want to make an impression! Me, too, baby, that's why I'm
lying here giggling with my ear pressing down on the tiled floor.
Doctor doctor, you don't mean to tell me I've got athlete's ear? That's
nothing unusual, yesterday I had an Irishman in here pretending to
have deaf legs. I said, Shin Feign, huh?

The phone goes. I think—it's Friendly God wanting to book me
for the Great Talkshow above the clouds. It goes on ringing. I get
up, thinking—so *this* is why celebrities never appear until after midday!
It's a man who says his name is Kyle Franklin. He says he is
downstairs and will wait for me. I can't remember him but he seems
to take it for granted we want to meet. I probably ran into him last
night. He is either that Haight-Ashbury queer or some girl's black-
mail partner. I dress methodically, dark shirt and Texas Levis and
disintegrating empire shoes. I comb my hair in the mirror and say to
my cement-dry face, Yewall havin' a good time?
Kyle Franklin is, of course, the west coast rep for Tannenbaum
Inc. He is fiftyish, balding, flannel-shirted. I could imagine him
teaching for the Workers' Educational Association in East Anglia. He
has this fairly old car, without air-conditioning?
"If you would like, I can take you to see some of the local spots of
note? I spoke with Sally Weber on the phone. Unless you have other
plans?"
"No, I've just been lying about my hotel room. Nice of you to take
the time, Kyle."
So he says he'll show me the Golden Gate and off we go, windows
down, breeze in our faces, two strangers brought together for reasons
I don't care to analyse, merely grateful for somebody to speak to.
The last author he entertained was Kromidas, they had a dinner party
down at Sausalito, isn't Fred one of the gutsiest, ballsiest but nicest
guys you could meet? The Golden Gate is a long way up from the
water. The cables are very thick. A few remarks of apparent enthusiasm
show Kyle I'm not unappreciative of this scenic wonder. His wife and
daughters really liked Kromidas, he was surprisingly warm and human
for such a celebrity. Kyle sounds like an understanding type so it's no
wonder I suddenly tell him what a nightmare this trip has been,
especially with this inhuman bitch Weber who just pissed off and left

251

me on my own, I mean, I want sympathy. Kyle doesn't react too much either way. He asks if I've ever seen any redwoods and although I've always found trees more boring than cathedrals I want him to regard me as warm and human, so we go to see redwoods. He did say daughters, didn't he? Kyle is very interested in redwoods. They are in a dark glade, up which we stroll, to the very end, stopping to look up at all the redwoods except the smaller ones. They are very tall. They are the oldest organic things on earth. There is only so much one can remark about redwoods, after the first twenty. They are very big and they make you feel kind of small, don't they? I can tell I'm recovering because (a) I'm wondering when we get to meet the daughters and (b) I'm beginning to make sarcastic remarks about redwoods. Kyle isn't tuned to the sarcasm channel. He is the kind of man they describe as patently sincere. Eventually he says it's a pity but we can't spend much longer here with the redwoods as we have to go to dinner, down in Sausalito? Great, I say, leaving the fucking redwoods with the silent hope that the highway department and the real-estate sharks blow the lot of them to pieces. So we get to Sausalito, which is a kind of Mediterranean seaside village, and we go into this waterside restaurant and it's when we're sitting down that Kyle says pity his wife and daughters couldn't come along, they all have this dinner date tonight, that's why he'll just watch me eat? If that's okay? I say I'll have a little chicken. He says to have a drink by all means, he personally never touches liquor nor smokes nor eats flesh. I chew on a sliver of white breast and eventually palm it during a yawn and flick it away under the table. Kyle says he understands my digestion problem, all that hotel food? I find the beer goes down well. It's about six thirty. We drive along the waterfront. There are droves of young people in hippy attire squatting on sidewalks. We go back to San Francisco over a bridge, it might be the Golden Gate, I really don't pay a lot of attention. So Kyle drops me off at the hotel and I tell him how much I appreciated his showing me the sights and he says it's a pity he has this big dinner date but maybe he can fix up something for tomorrow?

Yeah, maybe we missed a fucking redwood, I think, watching him backfire out of the hotel forecourt. There are no messages for me. I go upstairs and get my money, seventy dollars which I've carefully hidden by leaving it lying on top of the writing-table. So I take off into the loving city night and this time I mean business and when I say business I mean cunt.

*   *   *

After only two drinks I am what I used to call drunk. Only now it seems like normal. I am happy, confident, and without detectable pain. I am also invisible and speak a little-known dialect from the high mountain country of Kurdistan. This is why such women as I accost in bars look right through me and don't laugh at my jocular introductions. So who needs them? I sit at bars thinking wry, ironic thoughts, a ghost unto myself. Not all the men in Frisco bars are queers. The other half of them are repressed queers and nervous with it. This is why they refuse to join me in conversational pleasantries.

I note that although two drinks is now enough to anaesthetise bodily sensation, twenty drinks is not enough to get me raving drunk. I hum a Bo Diddley rock number and float from bar to bar. Does this mean I'm walking on Bo Diddley air? I used to model my hairstyle on Zachary Scott. A couple of bartenders have never heard of Zachary Scott. They are not even interested in my James Stewart impersonation. I see a sad loon face in a mirror and telepathetically tell it I always knew I was a loser, anyway. I go back to the hotel, vaguely recalling Weber saying she is to see me on Saturday night. She is not there but they have a message. She will be back at ten in the morning and has arranged to drive to see a friend who lives next door to Henry Miller. Hopes I'm okay. It is about ten o'clock.

I see myself giving this cabbie five bucks to take me to a joint where I can find a genuine whore. I see myself in this bar-restaurant, sure enough I'm on arguing terms with this blonde broad, she is German or something, not young, I'm accusing her of working her way through college but she is insisting she is a whore. I see myself going outside with her and asking where the hell is her apartment and her telling me we have to go by car and it's parked in a side street and there's a guy at the wheel, and I'm saying, oh no, sister, you can fucking stick that up your jumper, and the guy is getting out the car and coming for me and I'm laughing at him and saying, you animal, you gutter-rat, I know he's going to bop me over the head for my money, I keep laughing at him and then I pull money out of my pocket and throw it in the air and I laugh as they chase the bills around and I lurch off, bumping into people.

Did this happen?

All I know is I'm down to five dollars in change when I check my pockets in the morning. It's nine o'clock when I come round. I'm in the hotel, right room. Not so much a hangover this time, more an urgent thirst. When I say thirst I mean all the fish in the oceans are leaping their last on the cracking mud at the bottom of the Cobalt Sea. But I have my body under control now. I shave and get into my suit and jacket, using a wad of wet shitpaper to wash a couple of yellow crusty patches off the front of my shirt. I head for the elevator and the jockey says the Top of the Mark bar is open at ten. I walk into the glass-walled, top-floor, sun-drenched bar at three minutes past the magic hour. There's a man already at the bar. He is wearing a crumpled lightweight suit. He is handing out his glass for a refill. He twists his neck to look at me. With the bartender there are three of us men present. I crawl on to a stool.

"Ah jist bin askin' Pally here, yuh reckon the east side or the west side for jumpin' outuh? Ah says the preevailent wind'll pin yuh agin the side of the buildin' if yuh jumps east-side."

"Just let me get a glass in my hand," I say, ordering a double-shot, with a beer chaser. I take a drag on the beer, a gargle on the J.D., light a fag and then look at the man. He has a thin dark face and straight black hair that flops, Hitler-style, over his forehead. He pulls his arm away from his jacket where a twisted brown claw covered with black hairs has been nestling, Napoleon-style. He shoves it towards me.

"Phial Tolluvuh, eh-en biee cee outuh nawlins?"

Phil Tolliver, N.B.C., out of New Orleans, I need no interpreter. After one drink we are close buddies in the grim carnivals we call our lives. Phil is a radio announcer on a four-day bat in Frisco to celebrate his fourth divorce, just been feeling so shook-up after yesterday's drunk he's been thinking of suicide, hence the question about the wind. He has a voice like a crashing gearbox. Apart from the twisted hand he has a scaly skin condition. Like any self-respecting radio announcer on a spree he wallows in the untrammelled luxury of free speech, cos sure as assholes they're a bunchuv motherfucking, cock-sucking, Bible-hypocrites in Nawlins.

"With a voice like that he broadcasts to the whole south and doesn't need a mike," I say to the wryly-amused bartender. "He just sits in the studio in Nawlins and hollers."

"Yuh write boo-uks, yuh say? Yuh ivuh thought a writin' 'em in Anglish, buddy boy?"

"How would a see-my-literate like you know the difference? Same
254

again, bartender, and give my cotton-picking Ku Klux Klan friend another snifter of vodka."

Around eleven other people start drifting in. They enjoy the unscheduled free bonus of the floorshow. The bartender answers a phone and asks if there's a Mr. Cameron in the bar and I tell him to say no, he just jumped out of the window in a westerly direction and I tell the good folks that was my lesbian tour manager and I tell them a few of the sexual irregularities she's been committing throughout the length and breadth of the U.S.A. and they seem to enjoy all this so I tell them a few of the choicer incidents of the tour and they laugh a lot, even the shy honeymoon couple trying to hide at the table beside the glass wall overlooking Alcatraz, and when Weber comes into the bar around midday she doesn't understand why, when I take her arm and introduce her as Angela Dundee, gutsiest pound-for-pound tour manager on the plugola circuit, they all seem to regard her as a whing-ding personality and burst out laughing when she tries to take me to one side and whisper urgent things and I keep repeating what she's saying and asking them if that ain't just the funniest dang thing they ever did hear—maybe I'm in an Irish accent by now, in response to some remark about Brendan Behan, and I keep grinning vacantly into Weber's tight face and shaking my head like a village idiot and then bawling some new witticism to my great friend Phial Tolluvuh and finally Weber gets it across to me that she has a hired car downstairs waiting to go visit the man who lives next door to Henry Miller, "Hey, Phial, me manager here wants to drag me away to visit wit' Henry Miller." Phial says:

"Ah'd nivuh desert a buddy."

"Look, you want to come now?" says Weber.

"Sure, darlin', I'll come if me pal Phial comes wit' us? I'd never desert a buddy, bejasus."

"That freak!"

"Why, don't yese like me friends?" I grin at her again. "Sure now, youse just go on Sally darlin', and give our love to Henry."

So she says Phial can come and then Phial and me say we never travel more'n ten yards from a bar without a bottle, so the bartender puts a quart of vodka on somebody's room bill and I stick it down the inside of my trousers before I realise we're big grown men and don't need to hide it. We give the Top of the Mark crowd a farewell duet and bow out. In the elevator Weber keeps giving me these narrowed, sidelong glances but all I do is wink back at her and burst into song with Clawhand Phial, root-tootingnest newsjock west of the Alleghenies, and there's me old mucker Kyle at the wheel of the car, he wouldn't even come into the bar to pick us up, this amuses Phial and me a lot and we get in the back and pass the bottle to and fro and Kyle doesn't say a lot but Weber actually takes a swig, her elbow over the back of the seat, and we drive in the sun on to some endless motorway lined by filling stations with bunting and I'm singing terrible sad songs from the Ould Country, whichever one that might be, and farting, though God knows what I have to fart with unless it was some fruit I seem vaguely to recall, and we drive about two hundred miles past gas stations and then I think I may have dozed off for the car is stopped and Weber is coming back from phoning and she speaks in a low voice to Kyle and he rolls the big auto back on to the highway and turns back to San Francisco and I get another pull at the bottle and note that Phial is a gonner and laugh to myself all the two hundred miles back and we're in the hotel and this bitch is telling me in a hard voice I sure exceeded myself this time and all I feel like doing is laughing and singing and farting and then I stretch out on my bed and the next thing I know there's a red-hot poker in me back and the bedcover is on fire so help me, just a little black hole from where me fag dropped out of me lifeless digits and the bitch is back again making more argy-bargy and I have the natural-born dignity not to tell her to fuck off but merely smile enigmatically and go back to sleep. When I come round it's almost dark and the lice are digging into me, shoals and nations of them, and the room is full of clutching fingers threatening me with Hell in American accents so I get the hell out of it up to the Top of the Mark to find my buddy only there's no sign of Phial and the friendly bartender isn't there and the morning crowd who laughed so much have changed for a pack of hard-faced snobs who edge away when I beam down on them and

How many of these mornings can one man take?

Zombie-fashion, I let the shower batter over me. I shave. My hands have stopped shaking but there is a dull, choked feeling in the veins and sinews of my arms. I know what that's the sign of. I see a black hole on the brocade bedcover.

Which city is this?

It's the same room they've been shipping round the nation.

I take the elevator to the ground floor. I find the coffee shop. I sit at the counter and take the automatically poured cup of black

256

coffee. I'm seriously thinking about going out to find a bar when these two men next to me start talking in very plummy English accents. I hear them with American ears now, a right couple of mincing faggots they sound. Yet the Briton in me says, don't sneer, it's these public school poofs who turn out to have the Military Cross. I'm on the point of saying something when I realise how their faces will react when they take a close look at me. I'm ashamed! Just then the waitress comes over. I was going to tell her the coffee was all, just shake my head and drop a quarter and shudder off to the nearest saloon. But I don't live here. I live with these dandyfied twits. I have an actual wife called Sheina who's living in London right now, as of this moment in time. I am not an American, to be coming apart at the seams because of a couple of light ales.

"Two boiled eggs and toast and another coffee," I say, softly, so my compatriots can't hear, not that they're listening to any of the crude vulgarities one hears in America.

"Shall I remove the shells, sir?"

"I've enough strength to take the top off an egg, thank you."

"It's nice to hear that, Scottie," she says loudly. "Most people they want the shell removed and if we leave a little-bitty they're squawking to the management and talking about how they'll sue."

"Get away," I say. My co-nationals look at me with faces poised for questions. I stare at them blankly. I mean, I'm suddenly proud to be British and all that but you don't actually have to like the English. Whatever they were about to say gets no chance to be said, for just then Weber comes into the coffee shop. I signal to the waitress to bring the eggs over to a table. I nod curtly at my fine-suited English masters and leave them wondering, for the rest of their lives, I trust. Weber has a face like fizz. I share a joke with the waitress, wink cheerily at Weber and knock the top off an egg.

"How's Sally then?"

"You're asking *me*?" She looks at me in some manner or other.

"Polite as always."

"You remember burning the bedcover?"

"I have a blanket memory."

"That's thirty-five dollars on the bill."

"I always was hot stuff in bed. So where's the schedule?"

She thought I'd be something the sewage department didn't care to handle. She wants to drag it all up, I mean, too drunk to visit with Henry Miller!

"So you say. Maybe if you'd ever read any Henry Miller you'd know he might not have been such an old maid about it. Now then, are we going to spend all day whining about yesterday or are we going to earn our corn?" I say briskly.

She has a schedule, which she's been secretly hoping I will be in no condition to fulfil and I make her eat up fast and we get a cab to a radio station and then a newspaper office and then another radio station and then a teevee studio and all the time I'm laughing at the absurdity of my own act—snap fingers, let's get this show on the road, baby—I can't explain it even to myself. Maybe I'm just the hero-type. I tell one mike that marijuana is growing in every British backyard and I tell a camera that four out of five British brides are pregnant at the altar and make a lightning quip here and a crack there, Weber just stares at me and fetches the cabs and I feel health-giving cigarette smoke getting down among my pipes and when she says do I want to hit the sack early I say hell no, kid, let's see a bit of nightlife, so there's Ike and Tina Turner on at the Hungry I and natch Weber has never heard of Ike and Tina so I watch her watching America's hottest woman lash her black hair across her Indian face and crack her jaguar body river-deep mountain-high and all the white Americans who've paid four dollars admission sit like half-assed zombies but you expect that from these middle-class white twits, so then I insist we drop into the friendly neighborhood sex-show, *Naked Hippy Love*, and you should see Weber's face when this hairy couple come on in the altogether and do an obscene wedding and simulate scaramouche and whatnot and fellatio, I never did catch up on the technical terms, and then I say I'll have another shot in the hotel, and she's waiting on me to give with some explanation, which I can't, so I relax with my double-shot and smile cheerily and say:

"I'm tired of convention hotels, when we get to L.A. let's find a motel, eh? A real live American motel full of dubious itinerants. These places are so stuffy and respectable, you know what I mean?"

And in the morning we get a cab through the hills and catch the early flight to Los Angeles and I'm the Good Humor Man with a vengeance and I don't mean ice-cream, I mean sickening jollity.

"By rights you should be hospitalised," she says, bitterly, shaking her head. We strap ourselves in.

"How's that?" I say, catching hold of the stewardess's arm and asking her for a quick shot soon as we're up there.

"God sakes, you still drinking? After Sunday?"

"Sunday?" I muse. "Oh, Sunday—too pissed to meet Henry Miller?

It's quite funny, really. Saturday was a bit livelier, I hit a few bars, met some interesting people. If you can't live it up a little what's the point, that's what I always say. Coupla drinks, coupla laffs."

Of course I know it's a sick joke of an act. I can't remember when I last ate a solid meal and the ulcers are all around my mouth now and the clogged feeling in my veins is a definite sign I'm now in a perpetual orbit of onrushing alcoholism—but what the hell, better to get it finished with here than let Sheina see me in this condition. I'm a fatalist, I tell myself with ghoulish mirth, everything I do is fatal.

Chapter Twenty-two

MALE SADIST, WHITE 28, ATTRACTIVE SINGLE AND SINCERE, DESIRES MASOCHISTIC FEMALE, 21 TO 30, CAUCASIAN OR ORIENTAL AND SINGLE FOR SEX AND COMPANIONSHIP. WRITE PAUL DUNCAN, 5819, GREGORY AVE, APT. 7, HOLLY-WOOD.

ATT: DRAG QUEENS, GENEROUS SEMI-STRAIGHT MALE STUD DIGS QUEENS PREFER EARLY MATINEE BUT ANY TIME YOU PREFER IS O.K. PHOTO IN DRAG AND PHONE BEST WAY. WRITE TO P.O.B. 1412, L.A. 90028.

ATTRACTIVE COUPLE SEEKS AC/DC GIRLS. HE 36, SHE 27. AFTERNOON OR EVE DATES. SEND PHONE AND PHOTO TO P.O.B. 5331, MISSION HILLS 91340.

Our motel has a pink, Moorish-pattern wall facing on to a dreary section of Hollywood Boulevard. Across the road are a filling station and a hamburger joint. Our place has a white and orange neon sign, twenty feet high with MOTEL in blue letters and topped by a four-pointed yellow star. The effect is curiously colourless, because I feel like death. It took Weber several phone calls and a taxi journey to cancel our hotel reservations and find this place. I wondered why she was going to such trouble, until she reminded me that I had insisted on a motel. I just sat in the cab and let her get on with it. I could see that she was not very happy about the change but she does not let personal emotions interfere with business. I have just realised that on all previous occasions of tentative intimacy she was merely humouring me. I am merely postponing my disappearance into the nearest bar until a moment that will cause her maximum embarrassment. The way I am now it's odds on I'll never get out of that next bar. I don't think my body can stand much more and I certainly can't stand much more of it. This curtained motel bedroom in Hollywood is an appropriate last address for the impotent, shabby, alcoholic ghost that she has turned me into. She deserves a lot of embarrassment. I hope the guilt nags at her guts for the rest of her life. The room has a single bed, a little locker with no Gideon Bible, a chintz-covered bedside lamp, a dressing-table with a mirror, a built-in wardrobe, a glass and steel shower recess, a washbasin, a rattling air-conditioning unit, an elderly television set. There is no phone or I might be tempted to call

Sheina. Sheina has never really taken me seriously, so a ration of vicarious guilt is in order for her as well. In twenty years the children will turn on her bitterly and accuse her of dire neglect in allowing me to suffer this lonely nightmare. The permanently-drawn curtains give the room the correct atmosphere of shadowy furtiveness. Presumably they are drawn to stop people from the rooms across the small back court gazing in on the sleazy goings-on associated with motel bedrooms. I leave them drawn. I have no sleazy immoralities to boast about. I am no longer virile enough for masturbation. My suitcase and cowhide bag are unopened on the bed. By now they should have been plastered with colourful labels, as in the movies of boyhood, but on the battered suitcase there is only the gummed address label I stuck on in London, just before I left on that excitable morning when we had only three British pounds in the house. At this moment I have, in warm, roughly-creased notes, four twenties, a ten, three fives, seven singles and a palmful of quarters, nickels and dimes. This should be enough. The straw man wanted a brain, the tin man wanted a heart, the lion wanted courage, Dorothy wanted someone to talk to late at night in St. Louis. There is no nice wizard at the end of the yellow road. When Dorothy and I are dead, blame Weber.

The door opens. Weber stands there in the shabby electric light, eyes hidden behind the reflections on her lenses. My only regret is that I shall be missing when she discovers I am missing.

"The cab's here, you have a top teevee in fifteen minutes if we can make it through the downtown L.A. traffic, these Two-World hotshots almost loused it up." She stares at my dreary face. She laughs. "Come on, Graham baby, let's get this show on the road."

"Screw the fucking show!"

"Think of your public, maestro. Let's hustle."

I follow her down the corridor. It occurs to me this is the first ground-floor room I have occupied in the U.S.A. My eyes start watering as we get into the cab. The driver says there's a city-wide smog alert going out on the radio, is it okay if we don't smoke, it fouls up the air-conditioning? I stare at the low, square, neon-tattered buildings. There are, of course, no Lana Turners in sweaters. As soon as she leaves me alone I will slip away and find the lost chance saloon.

I am sitting next to this college football star type guy on canvas chairs at the edge of a large studio floor. He has a box-cut and an open-neck sports shirt. He looks like the young Lloyd Bridges, a dim ox puzzled by his own masculinity. I offer him a cigarette. He nods up at a large no smoking sign. I see Weber by the escape door talking to a programme aide. I tear a match off the book. Muscle Head taps my elbow and points at the no smoking notice.

"Fuck the signs," I say, sepulchrally, chucking the match on the floor and taking a convulsive drag. He stares at me and finds me unhygenically subversive. A girl comes across the floor to take him out to the interview desk, where the light is like the solitary shaft of sun through a hole in a thundery sky. I see them fitting a neck-mike to Muscle Head. The interviewer is a burly young guy with shiny black hair and a raucous voice to go with his bouncy personality. I look towards the door. Weber has gone.

I'm off.

She taps me on the shoulder from behind. She smiles down at me.

"Father O'Flynn, you are widely-famed as the underwater priest," the interviewer is saying. To Muscle Head? I frown. "How many marriages have you conducted to date on the ocean bed?"

"Ten or eleven," says Father Muscle Head.

"Is this a gimmick God would approve of?"

"I can't go along with the description that it's a gimmick. My faith tells me God is omni-present. Some people wish to be joined together in holy matrimony in a ceremony that takes place under water. I have no reason to believe God is less likely to be with us on the ocean bed as in a great cathedral."

By the sacred suspenders of old Red Socks, follow *that*!

I hear the host, Ferocious Fred, introducing me in a voice that this close sounds like a line of advancing tanks. I think of *her* sitting out there in the dark beyond the lights and I feel savagely exultant at the panic that will seize her cold heart when she hears how I'm going to blast these bastards. I don't smile. He picks up the book. I'm ready for the crap.

"I read the first two chapters aready," he says. "It's great, man, I've bin to crummy swinging London, you really sock it to 'em, huh? Same old thing here, fascist finks exploiting kids and corrupting their minds. You think our crap's any better or worse than your British crap?"

Nobody told me about these new radical shows! This guy was pro-marijuana, anti-Vietnam, anti-Reagan, anti-Shirley Temple, anti-police—I got a real shock when he suddenly gave the two-fingered

262

salute to camera! This is when a noted Los Angeles columnist phones in to complain about a sneering reference to his white supremacy leanings. The phone call goes out live, no four-second bleepers. Then I realise the two-fingered salute means peace, not up yours. You could have fooled me. The way Ferocious Fred signals peace let's rush for the bomb shelter!

So I knock 'em dead. I mean, it's the kind of thing Graham Cameron, the actual person, would have been saying all along, if he hadn't been compromised into performing for the plugola circuit. I punctuate my brilliant flow of controlled spleen with aseptic throw-aways (e.g. a Chicago judge was found to be letting auto offenders off for a two hundred dollar bribe. I'm told this proves Chicago is the most honest city in the U.S. There's nowhere else in the U.S. a judge would keep his word for a lousy two hundred bucks).

Suddenly I feel good.

I know I'm knocking 'em dead because my original five-minute spot is stretched to thirty and then forty minutes, the director doing quick re-jigs, dropping film, ruthlessly disappointing other scheduled guests. Keep that Cameron guy talking!
It's the greatest feeling in the world. Outasight!

"You got a real hot teevee personality there, Graham," says the director when it's finally all over and the whole studio is saying sensation sensation. "You got a visa that let's you work in the U.S. of A? I can visualise a great show built round you."
"I'm not sure about the visa."
"We do the format right we could hit the networks. Leave a number where I can reach you in L.A. I know I can do real things with that teevee personality of yours. That broad over there, she handle you?"
"She used to."
"Like it! Whad I tell you, Fred, this year it's think British!"

The tour has been hell but I can see now why Fate ordained it.
I've done my apprenticeship in the boondocks.
I'm going to *be* a star.

I'm with Weber in a chauffeur-driven car sent by the head of studio publicity to take us to the Two-World lot. Imagine—I'm going through these gates as a celebrity! Only a little while ago I was sending away for Gene Autry's signed photo. You'd think I'd be in seventh heaven, wouldn't you? Am I hell. Just when things are really popping we have to waste time rubbernecking like wide-eyed rubes from some Kansas City coach party? Head of publicity is English-orientated, *love* that Rolls-Royce! God, does he want to talk about his fucking Rolls-Royce. So then we have to get this veep tour of the lot, led by this dim broad who thinks her fanny is the finest. We walk round corner from old New York street of brownstone nineties to cowtown street where they are shooting teevee horse-opera. See big global teevee star fluff line four times, watched by a hundred or so technicians and coach-party gawkers. Line he fluffs is, "Anythin' the matter, Miss Julie?"

I mean, he forgets it three times!

Fourth time he gets it right. Soundman lets them finish, casually removes earphones, reveals that soundtrack picked up hum of high-flying jet. Global teevee star twirls Colt .45, looks round rubes and says:

"Ah often wonder, who in hell ever watches this crap anyhow?"

The girl with the fanny wants to show us two-tiered row of dressing-rooms still bearing nameplates of immortal stars from dayswhen.

"This must give you a real bang, you being the big movie buff," says Weber.

"Yeah, great," I say. "Let's not waste any more time with this historical bunk, eh? When's this newspaper interview? What else have we got on the schedule? I need a haircut and I want to buy some clothes."

"You've a radio tonight and some more shows and things tomorrow —there's another but ..."

"But what?"

"It's a Dial a Dollar show—"

"So?"

"I didn't think we'd want to do anything so icky as a Dial a Dollar."

"I'm not here to indulge in good taste. It's got a good audience, hasn't it?"

"Okay, I'll fix it up."

"Yeah, and let me decide what I'm going on, okay?"

We're introduced to this studio press guy. He's young, dark, chunky, Richard Egan-type, if anybody else remembers Richard Egan. While Weber is phoning the Dial a Dollar show he says:

"If you want your ashes hauled I know this broad, she's happy to screw anybody the studio recommends, she isn't a pig, you know, you just give her a present, tell her it's a present, she isn't a hustler, I'll tell her to call you tonight, you'll dig her, man, she *knows*, I mean, she'll suck you or a blowjob, whatever you dig."

Weber gets back into Tad's car. I say to Tad:

"Yeah, tell her to ring me before seven thirty, I have a radio interview at eight thirty."

"Check."

Weber looks at me enquiringly but all she gets is a quick smile from the nose down.

We get back to the motel. It's six thirty. I shower quickly and nip out without knocking on her door. You get a lot of hangers-on in show biz. You can't afford to give every one of them a piece of yourself because you only have so much, know what I mean? I go into the little motel office by the forecourt. The manager is a friendly sort of guy in a flower-shirt, shorts and open-toed leather sandals.

"I'm just going to the hamburger joint," I tell him. "A girl may call for me, will you take her number and tell her I'll call back in twenty minutes?"

I have a giantburger, not feeling hungry enough for a big one, and a coffee. I smoke a leisurely cigarette and decide there's still a lot of movie-struck yokels hanging round Hollywood, even if the big studio lots are down to one teevee horse-opera. Locusts still coming West, Nat, should've stayed home, Horace. Books schmooks, who needs it? Some of these big talkshow celebrities do a regular circuit year in year out, thousand bucks a time if you really make it. Get my own show? Easy—hey, what happened to Gypsy Rose Lee? Must get back to motel and light a fire under that bitch. Stop in the office. Manager looking funny.

"Since you've bin out two guys bin in here and stuck up the joint," he says, holding out his wrists. "They tied me up so tight I'm bleeding. One of them, the colored, sits on my chest with his pistol in my mouth and tells me to give them the safe key. They're both junkies, I mean, wild-eyed, so I'm not about to argue. They got away with about three hundred dollars."

"Are the police coming?"

"They've bin and gone. Nothing they can do." He shrugs. "For three hundred dollars they should break sweat?"

"That's the name of the game," I say. There was no call for me. I go into the motel and knock on her door. She is resting.

"What about Gypsy Rose Lee?" I say, standing by the dressing-table, fingering my chin in the mirror, noting with professional detachment that I've become a lot tighter about the cheekbones, good for camera.

"I didn't hear from Howard."

"Better ring him then, or ring the producer. Get Tad from Two-World to fix it up. You think there's a shoe shop near here? I must dump these tomorrow. Imagine—shoes like that?"

I turn. She is lying on her bed, knees together, blowing smoke at the ceiling, eyeing me blankly through smoke. No wonder Americans don't remember old movies, they *live* old movies, they act out the stuff old movies are made of. Old movies, who needs it?

"I'll have a quick nap before we go to this radio show," I say, walking quickly out of her room. Dayswhen I'd have been on my knees slobbering all over her nylons. Who needs it?

The radio show is in a café. Smalltime stuff but it hits the book-reading minority. We are met by this dumpy blonde woman, quite a pleasant face, maybe 35. She takes us to the table where this barrel of lard is sitting behind pebble lenses. To do a good show, even on a crummy radio tape, you need something to latch on to. This fat guy, Laird Cregar without the style, is interested in sex in novels. Maybe it's sex'n'novels, who listens to crummy radio interviewers? I latch on to the blonde broad and direct my wit'n'wisdom at her and although it's meant for public broadcasting, or perhaps it's because it's meant for public broadcasting, I give her a line of *Ladies' Man* chat that has her squirming. Weber is full of frost. Maybe she *is* a virgin, poor clunk. After 30 it's probably too late to conquer your fears of that great big steam-driven piston. So we finish this interview and Fat Man tries his hand up the blonde's skirt, right there at a table in a café—so, you get all sorts in show biz, you'll find we're pretty tolerant of those of our number who are in work. The blonde tells him he's a furtive groper and he beams all over his blubber and says yeah sure we all got our own bag. He even tries his hand with Weber. It amuses me to see her coping with a five-fingered hunk of pork up her goose-pimpled gams. She goes to the girls' powder room and Fat Man packs up his tape-box and pisses off.

"I could screw you tonight," says the blonde.

"Really?"

"Here's my number, call me later, after twelve, I have to attend this premeer. I think you're a guy who could really ball me. I like balling guys."

266

"Okay, I'll see how it goes."

So we split up.

"You want to go for a drink somewhere, down the Strip?" says Weber.

"I suppose so, if there's no more on the schedule for tonight."

"Great stars must take some time out for relaxation."

"My wife often uses that mocking tone. She's more subtle with it, of course, not being American."

"I guess I don't understand how come you could stay away this long from that goddess among women."

I let that ride. When I looked at her now all I could see were legs that only a dutiful husband could pretend to adore, and a face that was quickly drying into arid stridency, like Rosalind Russell in *Picnic*. Any Hollywood hack would have polished off that little scene with me slowly lifting those stupid spectacles off whatever area of skull they were currently adorning and grinding them slowly underheel while saying, You can't fight this thing, Sally, you are a very beautiful woman. I worked a piece of peanut out of my molars with a plastic toothpick and yawned. We're in this dancing lounge on Sunset Strip —which is a bit like Blackpool without the Tower or the glamour. It's a pretty smooth joint, Guy Lombardo stuff, waiters in red jackets, olives and chips and nuts on glass lilies. Weber chose it. At least there are no topless psychology majors doing thesis up Mother Brown with silicone-boosted tits.

"You care to dance?"

"No."

"Love that old-world European gallantry."

"What time is this Dial a Dollar show?"

"Jesus. Dial a Dollar? I remember you telling me Carson was low-level crap. Course, that was before you bombed on your pre-interview."

"I wasn't adequately briefed. It won't happen again. And I don't know why you're sneering at Dial a Dollar. It's not as bad as some of the imbecilic crap you people call television, that consumer quiz show, for instance, where the housewives have to guess the prices of a row of canned groceries. That's entertainment? At least on a Dial a Dollar show the guest spot gives you a chance to project a little, know what I mean?"

"God sakes!" She stared at me for a long moment. "You'll miss your baseball game on television."

"That director guy this afternoon, Frank whatsit, he thinks he could

267

get his station to build a show round me. About three other people have said the same. You think I couldn't do better than all these failed actors and danceband vocalists who host the network talk-shows?"

"But you're a writer, Graham, you're a very promising novelist. You told me yourself."

"You got any idea what angle Gypsy Rose Lee is likely to take? British women compared to American women is a good line, I'll think up some more ad lib throwaways—"

"You wouldn't like to dance?"

"No. You want to finish that drink now?"

"Suddenly *I'm* the barfly? Christ, you may give me a terminal case of the upchucks, Cameron."

When we get back to the motel—motel? I must have been mad. What kind of slobs stay in *motels?*—the girl who screwed guys on a studio recommendation had not phoned. I am glad about that. She sounded like nonentity fodder. There is a message for Weber. I get on the phone in the office and give the little blonde a call, a nice anonymous screw for tonight. She says to come straight over and I write down the address. Weber meets me in the corridor.

"It's a guy from one of the hippy underground papers, he wants to interview you—I mean, tonight."

"Great. Where's it at?"

"Oh well being one of the radical underground he only condescends to drink in the Brown Derby. I wasn't sure if you'd want to this late."

"Why not. You go to bed if you want, I'll manage on my own."

Smartened up a bit I find this guy in the bar *next* to the Brown Derby. He is a naïve clunk who can't do shorthand and doesn't have enough money to pay for any drinks himself, but he's a pipeline to the young audience, isn't he? He's also working on the free press to pay his way through youknowwhat. I feed him a lot of good stuff and buy him a number of double shots. He is about as radical and sub-versive as Sir Hartley Shawcross but when he's pissed he says he will take me to meet some of the local activists. It's too late now to go calling on the little blonde so I throw away the piece of paper with her address. If she wanted it that bad she could have come to the motel. We take a cab to this house, it's a wooden beach chalet in back of a machine-shop close by a hamburger joint under an open-air awning. So inside there's about forty of these new generation cats sitting against the wall or on beds—anything but chairs—most of

268

them cross-legged, long-haired, beaded up like perambulating cheap-jewellery stands, the light too dim to tell which is guy or doll, not a sign of a drink in the place, a hi-fi playing that endless, tuneless, guitar-wanking stuff they call soul-rock. Nobody speaks to anybody and even when I flop down against the wall beside this blonde party with the black bikini-top and burlap maxi-skirt and ask her civilly if she caught me on the show this afternoon I can get no reaction so I get out of there and catch a cab back to the motel, not before I stop at an all-night druggist and buy some dental powder, into which I pop my plate before catching a good night's sleep. I used to dissipate, now I have to preserve, know what I mean?

So it's morning and we get a cab to Dial a Dollar and there I have to stand beside a big drum into which they've shredded the L.A. phone directory. I get the usual introductory plug from Jack the host and I get a little more time by taking the clipboard out of his hands and asking, simple country boy style, if I can read the official stuff, it's always been my ambition? So I get to announce the show as well and then pick the six lucky numbers out of the big drum and we start phoning.

"Hullo there, this is Mrs. Denny Oxnard?"

"Yes, this is she speaking. Who is this?"

"Well hi, Denny, you watching teevee right now?"

"Yes—who is this please?"

"Which channel are you watching, Denny? Cross your fingers for Denny folks! Whew! The suspense is *killing*."

"I'm watching the World Series."

"Ah! Denny, I hate to tell you, but this is Jack Silvestri of Dial a Dollar, channel twenty-one. Now if you'd been watching us we'd have called a cab and sent you right round a little envelope—with *three hundred dollars*? Sorry, Denny."

"I'm Josie, actually, Denny is my husband."

"A Josie by any other name," I say, winking broadly. The fifty or so middle-aged ladies in the live audience half-get it and then Jack repeats it and claps my back and says, "I told you gals this Graham Cameron is witty for real, dint I?"

Applause.

Jack dials Mrs. Joan W. Wagner on Gregory Avenue. Same routine. She is watching the World Series.

"Well, ain't that a pity, Graham. Joan's watching the baseball."

"Poor Joan," I say, "she just missed getting a little-bitty envelope

269

with four *hundred dollars* right to her door! Well, what can you expect from a woman whose grandfather wrote all those numbers that didn't hit the charts?"

"Didn't hit the charts? Oh—Wagner! All those numbers? I guess we weren't too familiar with Graham's name before this morning—but we sure heard of him now, right, gals?"

"Right Jack," they chorus.

"And just wait till you read my book, *The New Ladies' Man*," I say leeringly. "If it isn't too sexy for all you clean-minded ladies."

Ooooh they gasp at the naughtiness of it all. I note that the plug comes in too artificially. Things will be better when I get this book tour over and start appearing as straight guest celebrity. I'm sure it was the artificiality of the plugola game that had me drinking so much back there.

We phone Howie Muntwyler on North San Vicente Boulevard, West Hollywood. The jackpot is now *five hundred dollars*. To win it you have only to be watching the show. Paying the viewers seems eminently logical. Your so-called intellectuals deride this kind of stuff but it's only people talking to people, isn't it?

Jack and I exchange a little light patter as the phone bleeps.

"Wowrrllyagh," says our party.

"Is this Howie Muntwyler?"

"Waghrrll."

"Howie, are you watching teevee right now?"

"Gagrrlllshach."

"I didn't catch that too well, Howie, tell me, would you be watching Channel twenty-one at this time?"

"Gurlgh."

"I don't know, Graham, you on Howie's wavelength?"

"Hi, Howie," I say, "could you leave off scratching your armpit a moment and tell us what channel you're watching?"

"NYAGGHHURR!"

He rings off.

"I *heard* Dick van Dyke was living here incognito," I say.

"My sides are sore I mean *sore*—you can come back any time, Graham Cameron, ain't that right, gals?"

"Yes!"

We go to a newspaper interview.

"I'm going off newspapers," I say to Weber. "Teevee is the best.

You can speak direct to the audience. Still, I suppose it keeps your name in with the educated minority groups."

"Tad from Two-World says Gypsy Rose Lee is being taped here in L.A. tomorrow? The actual location will be communicated to us later, the execs are manning the studios and they don't want the pickets to find out in advance."

"Good thinking. Lousy technicians—they're dragging down about six hundred bucks a week, I mean, I'm all for unions but not when high-paid guys like them hold a pistol to your head."

"I've heard it all now. What happened to Joe Hill?"

"Organise your own career first, he should've said."

"Oh my God!"

Do another teevee, with singer Al Martino and some young broad called The Topless Twiggy. Martino is plugging new album, Topless Twiggy is plugging career ambition to dance legit. Martino is old hand, when cameraman says shiny L.P. cover is reflecting light into lens he flips his record across the studio floor and says, good-humoredly.

"If it's causing you guys problems screw it."

I admire his style but take care to hold my book across my chest with the title showing. On this show I expand a gambit I've touched on previously, that Britain should forget Europe and become one of the States. After all, with the U.S. tax the Beatles and Michael Caine and myself are paying we ought to have representation. They think I'm joking, especially when I say Our Mr. Wilson is no more than another beagle for President Johnson to yoick about by the ears. I steal the show easily, proving I'm versatile enough to register with all age-groups.

Another cab, another newspaper office. I walk through the open-plan room with all the shirt-sleeved guys batting away on typewriters and phoning and scratching their heads and showing sticks of copy to deskmen and complaining about the coffee and I remember my own days in this racket. It's as good a stepping stone as any. No future, though. Contracting industry. Low wages. No charisma. *Wages* —who needs it?

"I'll have a coffee while you perform for the lady," says Weber.

I've got her trained that much.

So I go into this cubicle-office and there is the deputy woman's page editor.

"Hi, I'm Portia Lands—you're too young!"

"Am I?" I say, quizzically. "Well, you know the old saw, Portia, if they're big enough they're old enough."

"I read your book, friend. Nobody your young could know so much about a woman's mind."

"I never knew she had one," I say, sitting down. It's like the old drummer with his magic-cureall, you make a lot of noise and gather the crowd and spiel all the promises and when you've got them jumping you quickly boil it down to hardselling and grabbing the dollars and vamoosing. All the magic in America is in advance. But it's how they do things and I'm as good at it as any native.

Portia Lands is what you'd expect in a newspaper office. A dark brown dress formal but inelegant. Dark brown hair wisping out of bobby-pins, just a mite greasy. A gold neckerchief round a wide throat with give-away lines. She has brown arms, solid, like the rest of her, hands that are by no means exquisite. She has nervous eyes and open pores on the lower slopes of her nose and she laughs far too easily and much too loudly. She's never going to make it on to the cover of *Vogue* but she might pass with a clean-up and regular screwing, know what I mean?

She is also a bum journalist. I mean, she writes it all down in long-hand and has never heard of Tina Turner, who I'm currently plugging as the most if not the only exciting female woman in the States. No angle, just giving Tina a deserved break is all. So I'm practically dictating this interview, the usual stuff, British women are giving it away, American women know the value of it, why promiscuity is on the up and marriage on the rocks and all the other topics relevant to our troubled but exciting times, as touched on in my most stimulating novel. When Portia does get the point of a joke give her credit, she doesn't just laugh, she has orgasms.

And something peculiar happens that I'm not planning.

I get an erection.

Not just the temporary tingle of a mild upsurge. No, a genuine zip stretcher. I mean, an erection over Portia Lands! She's slow-witted and fast-aging and she's got a mole with hairs instead of a black beauty spot and her upper lip is *fuzzy*, I hate that, normally, so why am I suddenly one great big re-militarised erogenous zone? She's got it as well, we're practically straining to get at each other across her desk, and by the time she's finished the interview we're panting to get into a grapple! It's all this talking about sex. It should be banned.

We stare heavily at each other.

"We'll have a drink when you quit work," I say.

"I'll pick you up at your hotel, seven thirty?"

272

"So long?"

"I have to cancel a long-standing dinner date. You don't know what lengths I'm going to."

"Oh yes I do."

"Jesus, get out here before I wet my panties."

"I'll write the address for you."

"Don't write so provocatively, you bastard, I may have to grab at you."

"Later, doll."

So we get back to the motel and I'm still telling myself—*Portia Lands?*—but there's no denying it, if I lay on my back my cock would form one half of the searchlight criss-cross over a big premeer!

I am lying on my back, when Weber pushes into the room. She has a busy look on her face. She sits on the edge of the bed. I examine her scientifically. I mean, she's got class, a bit long in storage, maybe, but she's neat and clean and well-dressed and intelligent, comparatively speaking, about the eyes, and her legs are slim and delicately feminine and her nails are immaculate. But I'm not shoving my dick into Graumann's wet cement for her, know what I mean?

"How does dinner at the Brown Derby grab you?" she says, after a while. "Tad said he would take us."

"Not tonight, thanks. I'm pooped. You and Tad will make a handsome couple."

"Yuks. He's a pimp and he looks it."

"I hope there is a Mr. Right for you, kid."

She looks at me but finds me a blank-faced enigma. Her voice is quiet and strained.

"What's with you, Graham, huh? This some new fantasy you're projecting? I mean, I preferred you the way you were before."

"How was I before, Sally?"

"I had you down as just a big healthy lush."

"Tell me, what good did it do me when I was a lovable big lush, eh?"

"I wasn't even an individual human being to you, I was just part of a fantasy you had about America. You just wanted to bed any available woman. I didn't even have a face, for you."

"Take it while it's going, that's how us grimy slobs behave."

We're both hypnotically aware of how close we are, on the bed, but she's too scared to make the first move and I don't want it. I hate her. In any case, it's twenty-five after seven.

"Somebody's calling for me," I say, getting off the bed and going to the washbasin. I hear nothing behind me. I splash my face with cold water and rub my shoes with the towel and pat at my hair and reach for my jacket on the peg at the door. Her voice is *small*:

"Do you have to go?"

"Why? You got plans to take care of my libido problem?"

"Couldn't we ..."

"Yes?"

"Maybe I see now how uptight I was—"

"Your next author will be grateful to me," I say, quickly leaving on the punch-line.

Portia draws into the forecourt in her little English sports car. She is in a very sporty mood. She drives down to the Strip. We go to various joints. I keep thinking each drink will wash stupid Weber out of my mind. We dance. She is a lot of flesh. I drink some more. At last I think I'm ready for it.

"Okay, Portia baby," I announce, "let's quit the stalling, your place or mine?"

"Yours," she says, breathing hotly into my ear. "I share with a friend, she's home right now."

So we turn into the forecourt and get out of the little sports car and go along the corridor and into my little room and grab each other and start feeling and groping and all that stuff and we get on the bed and she's crazy to get her hands on it and I kneel up and she gets it into her mouth and then I pull it away and start taking off her clothes and ramming my face into the slack fat of her breasts and feeling her fuzz rasping on my lips and we're both naked and kneading each other and sweating where our skins jam together and we twist and thresh until we are sucking each other off and her big thighs are clamped on my ears and I'm buried alive and suffocating and being chewed and her slit tastes of salt and her teeth are remorseless and we both come to our independent releases and we don't smile or grin or blush as we come face to face but lie there, side by side, fingers moving absent-mindedly over each other as we try to find the excitement again, and I can't stop thinking of Weber in the next room, neat and firm and ladylike, and her fingers are gouging into my flaccid dick and I freeze up and she says:

"Come ann, honey, Portia's a hungry girl," and I can see us both pounding each other like slabs of meat in a dark little motel room and I pull away from her and sit on the edge of the bed and she becomes impatient and then angry when I won't speak to her and she isn't going to hang around here with a guy who doesn't appreciate

274

her and she covers her big, dumpy body and I just sit there clutching my shoulders and saying nothing and she slams the door behind her and I get on my trousers and shirt and go out into the corridor and tap nervously on Weber's door and there is no answer and I tap more urgently and then the door swings away from me and the room is bare and empty and the manager in the forecourt office tells me she has booked out and left me this and it's an envelope and in it is a letter written in big strokes, I read it standing barefoot in the doorway of the office of the motel on Hollywood Boulevard,

Dear Graham, I have gone back to New York. Your ticket and the balance of your money I'll leave at the T.W.A. desk at the airport. You can arrange with the office about your Atlanta schedule. I hope you make it the way you think you want it. Don't call me in New York. Sally.

It is a very emotional moment for me. I go back to my room and pick up the phone. I ask for information and not being the British telephone system they do not treat numbers as state secrets.

"Hullo," I say when my party answers, "Graham here, you lovely person. Listen, I had a migraine attack back there, I get them so bad it paralyses me. I just want to tell you it wasn't anything to do with you."

"I get them myself, honey, I know exactly. You better now?"

"Better? I'm filling out a job application with Rent a Cock."

"I'll be round there in twenty minutes, you animal."

In twenty minutes Portia Lands is coming through the door, grabbing for it before she speaks. This innings I don't have time to develop any maidenly revulsions.

"I'll give you head," she says ferociously and I let her chew the fat some and then I take a twist of her hair and drag her up to my level and turn her over sunnyside up, tits falling sideways into her armpits, and thump it into her, and she calls me a runaway horse and hardly have I won the Grand National than she's giving me more head, and the amount of sweat around would drown bedbugs and she suggests a shower and Gadamitee she's on her knees under Niagara, all night it's *head* she wants and I get to know the top of her skull better than any other part of her and I have to laugh, looking down at her, thinking —parting is such sweet sorrel, me big oat-chomping mare. Between courses I manage it twice the straightway ... thinking of Weber the whole time.

Dawn over Hollywood finds us lying clamped together, two big defrozen carcases. I'm awake first and I lie there thinking, I'm *cured*. That's exactly how it feels, although I couldn't name the illness. Far from being disgusted by her fleshiness I am safely encircled by her big arms, face against the flat bone between her breasts, eyelashes flicking her skin. She moves and smiles with her eyes shut and her hand is wandering south again and she murmurs:

"I'm going to bite it off and keep it in a bottle by my bed."

"You're pretty fundamental—for an American."

"Quit yapping you verbal fetishist. You know what Portia likes."

"I'm the Boston Cuddler, a much gentler kind of sex maniac altogether."

"Still talking up a storm? Come on, lad, you gonna ball me or preach a sermon? Fish or cut bait, piss or get off the potty. You got me strapped on my back with my legs wide open, what you waiting for? Get to it, lad."

"Gee whizz, Portia, you really mean that, don't you?"

I am a man again and can prance like a loon without guilt.

We sit in the hamburger joint across the street. She says reflectively:

"You're the second British guy I've balled with, I like you people, I mean the men I know they're all screwed up, drinking problems, angina problems, stomach problems, virility problems—problems, problems, I get tired of guys blubbering into my shoulder. You people seem very uncomplicated, I mean you just get on and do the damn thing."

"We're not paying our way through college you mean?"

I tingle all over. I am *proud*. My eyes are pleasantly weary—the usual old post-coital stuff except I had forgotten what it felt like and never thought I'd experience it again. Our ankles rub together warmly.

So then she has to split for the office, can she drop me somewheres? I say I have to find out where the Gypsy show is being taped. She says she knows that already, she'll drop me at the studio door. So we beetle along the super freeway and come to the big studio building and we park across the road and sit thigh to thigh and blink cornily at each other. Across the road I see this line of men carrying placards.

"I'm going to be a big star with my own talkshow the man said."

"That's nice for you, honey. You can see me Tuesday nights or I'll take every dollar you make on a paternity suit."

"Pregnant are you?"

"For that kind of dough I'll provide the pregnancy."

276

We laugh a lot, heads touching.

"Imagine me going over that road and crossing a picket line to brandish my ego on a blacklisted television programme. You only talk rubbish on these things anyway. Sick, isn't it, what people will do in the name of success."

"I don't see any gun at your head."

"I'm booked to appear, they're expecting me—"

"You don't think anybody's ever bombed out of a teevee show before? They have replacement guests in every closet."

"What about my publisher? He'll go mad."

"They ordered Hemingway to go on lousy shows?"

"You're saying all the things I should be saying if I was man enough."

"You're man enough, honey, you better believe it. I don't screw all that often so I'm not picking all-American hall of fame squads but you're a man all right."

"All right, was it?"

"Fantastic."

"Pleased to be of service, ma'am."

"So you going in there to do some more boosting?"

"Am I fuck! Cross a picket line? A scab and a blackleg, that's what I'd have been without you, Portia."

"So where you going now?"

"Home! Yeah, to hell with Atlanta, Georgia. I can go home!"

"They won't miss me at the office, I'll take you back to the motel, you can grab your bags and I'll drive you out to the airport. How's that?"

"No, no, I'll get a cab."

"You do me a favor, I'm going to do you a favor. I think I'll quit this job and try for a London assignment. I'm sick of this place, problems, problems, everything's fouled up, the people are all screwed up—I could have myself a ball in London, right?"

"You could have mine, on Tuesday nights."

"Tannenbaum Incorporated, publishers," says the switchboard girl in New York. I swallow a lot. This American phone system is too bloody fast for ordinary mortals.

"Hullo Graham," he says, deep and clear and chilling. "How do you fare out there in sun-drenched California?"

"I'm going home, Milton," I say. Silence.

"Is there some problem, Graham?"

"Yeah, there's a picket-line in front of the Gypsy Rose Lee show and I'm not going to cross it, Milton, I don't care what it's going to cost me, I've had this tour, Milton, I'm sorry, I know how much you spent bringing me over here and giving me this chance, but I'm not going through that line, Milton, frankly I'm glad I'm not going on the show anyway, I mean I realise you've been doing all this for me but you haven't been doing the tour, Milton, I'm sorry—"

I break off. I think of that globe-headed puppet-master sitting there in the skyscraper in New York manipulating me long distance across a whole continent and all the hundreds of thousands of dollars at stake and the movie deal and the paperback escalators and all that important stuff and I feel like a bug that's going to be squashed flat.

"I had a call from Weber, she said she thought you were finding the tour heavy-going."

"She went back to New York last night."

"I guess you two just never were compatible. I thought maybe that wild Dylan Thomas act of yours would break her down, she'd either jump off a bridge or come back as your next wife."

"What a funny idea. I have a wife and two children at home. It's all been a mistake, hasn't it? We never hit the best-selling lists."

"Don't knock it, Graham, we've sold about twenty thousand hard-backs, maybe sell another ten, that's good going for a with all due respect unknown British author. No, I wouldn't say it's been unreward-ing."

"Well, I'm sorry about all these other shows—Gypsy Rose Lee would have been the first networked programme I was on."

"I shouldn't worry, Graham. I'm not too sold on the proposition that television appearances can sell a book of your type."

"You're not? Well what was I doing flogging my guts out from city to bloody city?"

"None of us has reached that stage where we can't learn a new lesson, Graham. You give me a call when you reach New York. Bye, Graham."

Jesus H. Gentleman!

So she puts back on her big shades and we quit the motel and drive through the smog that keeps your eyes watering, past the ghost sand-mountains where the movie stars live and the would-be movie stars and the boosters and plugsters and promoters and realtors and wheels and AC/DC gals and the Swinging Couples and the Bi Guys and we have a coffee together at the airport and she says why even

278

pretend we'll ever write and she kisses me goodbye at the end of the boarding tunnel and I choose a rear-of-the-wing window seat in the half-empty plane and see the great beaches and the valley of yellow smog-haze and the Pacific and the town streets forty-five miles long and I sprawl my legs out and light a revolting American cigarette and begin to hum that fine old ditty the like of which they don't write 'em like any more:

California, here I came ...

So I'm a very childish person. I should grow up and become a mattoor mortician?

The jet climbs into the sunshine over the Colorado Plateau and America begins to recede, backwards.

Yeah, he went across the nation like a latterday Johnny Appleseed, he gave everyone the pip.

Maybe I should start out again from New York and visit all the same places in the same order, remembering to buy a camera, dammit. Take Portia Lands as girl guide, man could get a lot of ideas off the top of her head.

Is it really a laughing matter, as that first electric chair incumbent whined when they ran out of nickels for the meter?

"... no, man, I ain't takin' you up to Harlem on no sight-seein' trip, sure I'm black myself, lissen, it ain't so much you bein' white, Harlem is jus' plain dangerous. Man, when I take this cab home nights I keep headin' on round an' round my block till there's a parkin' space then I swing in fast and lock that door and hightail it across the sidewalk and up them steps and *wham* that door behind me and *then*'s the only time I feel safe from my soul brothers ..."

Oh boy, I feel good. Tired and warm with a droopy-eyed smirk. The small of my back is stiff from all that unfamiliar interpersonalised sex. You'd think I'd been felling redwoods single-handed, judging by my lumbar cramp.

My lumbar cramp! I like it!

... so there's this pack of hard-faced, handbag-swinging broads in the bar, some city or another, you belt down a few bourbons and make your play and they aren't whores, goshgolly no, they're Tuesday night ladies' league bowlers relaxing pent-in ten-pin nerves. And Mormons to boot, which is what you get, the boot ...

I look down at desert and mountains, red sand and rock, a lone car on a white-ribbon road. It's all slipping away.

... it's high noon in Central Park and you see this lone rider loping tall in the saddle across the grass, horse just moseying along, the guy's got a gun on his hip and he sits at a slight angle, jes' squinting around for danger—from behind his dark glasses and under his shiny peaked cap, for that's where all the cowboys went, into the police force ...

Did I pass some significant milestone down there on that once-coveted agony trail? The evocative taste of a teacake changed Proust's life. Van Gogh handed in his ear at the back door of the local brothel. Louis Armstrong was given a cornet in the waifs home.

Did Picasso work nites in a topless bistro to pay his way through collage?

Well, what did you think of America, they're going to ask, back home.

They asked Clement Attlee the same question and all he had to say was, It's a very big country. But he was probably upset at having to listen to all those eulogies about Churchill.

I bombed in America, that's what I did in America.

... the cab stops at the traffic lights in the Bowery and it isn't only old bums who lurch out into the lanes to beg quarters from closed windows but big young white guys in torn white shirts and negro teenagers and former executives in torn-kneed Brooks Bros. suits and they're all dancing like puppets with half the strings broken ...

Funny. That expression. In America it means to flop badly whereas to go like a bomb in Britain means a smash-hit. Is this because we knew bombs from the delivery end whereas the cousins over here know bombs only from air-shots of bomb-bay doors opening thirty thousand feet over little brown men?

Cousins. Yes, that's what it felt like and not only in Texas. They left home a long time ago and I often had this impulse to say, so *this* is what you've been getting up to all these years.

... it's Friday afternoon in the cut-price liquor store in Washington D.C. and down the long counter the line of heads is jabbing, squawking, pecking. Ten male clerks in white aprons swing bottles and cases down from the shelves and the battery hens keep jostling for more ...

Back home, in the Disunited Kingdom, a man can go through a whole day in which almost everything he eats, wears, drives and just plain touches is a product of American capital. Is that enough taxation to justify a little misrepresentation?

... the pint-sized garment manufacturer tells us about this wonderful arrangement he and some pals have with these air hostess girls who have this house up on Riverside Drive? Us men go up there Friday afternoons and we sit around and chew the fat and have a drink or two and enjoy really being relaxed, you know—and the greatest thing about it? *We don't have to screw these girls, I mean there's no pressure or obligation, it's the good relationships we value. I guess sex would just foul the whole deal up ...*

... something strange happens to the faces of many elderly American women. The whites get darker and the blacks get lighter, until they are almost indistinguishable. It's possibly due to the common gene bank. It may be the reason for all those blue rinses—I mean, you ever see a colored lady with a blue rinse? It isn't a frequent or welcome topic of conversation at white dinner tables. Snigger, nigger, snigger, the next white American bastard you meet may be your Grandpa's.

Let's go, they say. Where? It don't matter—let's up and *go*! There's still a chance we can find a place other folks haven't got to first, if only we get up and go, fast enough and often enough. There may be no second acts in American lives but plenty of first acts. Remember me, they call me Al, buddy can you spare a thought for Jimmy Yancey and Paul Robeson and Horace McCoy? I guess I'm not too familiar with those names. Some nations ignore their geniuses, some persecute their geniuses. America has never heard of her geniuses. Who needs a lot of dead men? What are they grossing down there at the wooden box-office?

We are flying over flat Kansas farmlands. They stretch for a thousand miles on either side of the plane. There seem to be no towns. Patches of grey obliteration may be dustbowls, who knows, at this height?

... on Saturday mornings the teevee cartoons start at dawn, early enough to trap the little consumers before they drift off into the unprofitable outdoors ... the preteen dating problem? Is that worse than the teenybopper pregnancy problem? What do they learn at all these colleges anyway?

A distinguished studio executive leaves his air-conditioned apartment, goes down in his air-conditioned elevator to the air-conditioned basement garage, gets into his air-conditioned limousine, is driven to another air-conditioned basement garage, goes up in another air-conditioned elevator to his air-conditioned office suite, and tells you a lot of this exaggerated pollution propaganda is coming from known agitators. Who might be the old negro lady toiling up the steep Los Angeles sidewalk with her heavy bags of groceries, eyes wet from the poison in the air, or perhaps just wet from age. She never learned to hustle. Throw her a foodstamp and tell her not to impede the dynamic of progress ...

282

And while you were bombing miserably, big mouth, did you learn anything about fame?

Don't laugh, I was famous once, for about five minutes, in Dial a Dollar circles.

All I can say is that it smelt, from the distance, like a beautiful woman. Fame is to a man as beauty is to a woman. A famous man *is* a beautiful woman.

Yeah, but even as a nobody you didn't do so good, did you?

Happenstance I got hooked on the wrong woman.

On the other hand, she looked ripe for it back there in the motel. Why don't you give her a ring when this kite hits New York? Maybe you only landed in America when you met Portia Lands. British acts have second lives.

We meet dusk over the northern industrial belt and we are told we are landing at Newark instead of J.F.K. Marilyn Monroe should have had her name on the bloody airport, the stacking would have been a lot better.

So we land at Newark and I get the bus into New York sitting behind a lot of hilarious negro G.I.s bound for Vietnam and New York looks like home, a haven as cosy as toast, cool as an ice-box and safe as skyscrapers.

I can phone Milt or Howard and start making plans to exploit my new whing-ding teevee personality. I can phone Chuck and sit around the Oak Room comparing virility problems. I can phone Weber and rush over by cab for a cuppa Sanka and the latest news from the bedhopping front.

Nobody is going to believe it but the decision is made for me, in the west side airlines terminal, by my shoes. If I stay here another day I'm either going to have to buy a new pair or else get them polished and I'm not too sure I'll have the energy to resist doing it the easy way, sitting with a paper and a cigar while the black boy bends his aged back to do me homage. I get a cab to the east side airlines terminal and haul my cases to the J.F.K. bus and it's all over and in the B.O.A.C. bar I meet this bloke from Wolverhampton and we down a few jars and keep the stewardess busy with miniature whiskies till half way over the Atlantic some sleep-fetishist requests us to shut up and the next I know I'm a one-eyed wreck in front of a British Customs officer.

"Anything to declare, sir?"

"Two geodes and this hangover."

"Been over there long, sir?"

"Since Prohibition ended by the feel of it."

"Here, old man, try a couple of my Aspirins, had a heavy night myself."

And then I'm coming down the basement steps with my cowhide travelling bag from Fifth Avenue and my disintegrating suitcase that's only held together by a length of thin white rope provided by a kindly thin white porter in the Portland airport and there is my own dear wife.

"You're back! My darling! I missed you so much—oooh, you smell *awful*."

"I had a few on the plane. God, am I glad to be back? There were times I never thought I'd make it, honestly it was—"

"You can tell me all about it and how many flashy starlets you had but I was just taking Gavin to the doctor's, he's got a funny rash, you can look after Amanda till I get back, I won't be long, I didn't know when you were coming so I haven't done any shopping so if you're hungry you'd better put her in the pram and get some fish and chips. Did you bring us lots of nice presents? I must go now or we'll have to wait for hours in the queue—I did miss you, did you miss me?"

"It was so bad I nearly killed myself."

"Don't be silly. You had a wonderful time. I suppose it's all we're going to hear about for years. I'll only be about an hour. Oh, and Amanda's probably done poo-poo in her nappies. Bye bye."

So here's yesterday's star changing the most revolting nappy in history and wiping her bum with cottonwool and thinking:

It's in all the show biz movies, the hero always fails *the first time round*.